On the wharfs, line after line of warriors and slaves crossed gangways onto ships or descended ladders into canoes. It looked as if Gasam intended to take his whole kingdom in this armada. All on the platform were Shasinn.

"Gasam!" Hael's voice cut through the bustle of the harbor. "As a senior warrior of the Shasinn, I challenge you to the thorn circle!"

Gasam laughed loudly. "You are sadly out of date! There are no more spirit speakers to hallow such rituals. I have overthrown all custom and only my word is law."

"A warrior stands before you, Gasam. Fight like a warrior, if you know how."

Gasam turned to the nearest warriors. "Kill this fool for me."

JOHN MADDOX ROBERTS
THE
BLACK SHIELDS

BOOK TWO OF STORMLANDS

TOR
fantasy

A TOM DOHERTY ASSOCIATES BOOK
NEW YORK

THE BLACK SHIELDS

Copyright © 1991 by John Maddox Roberts

A Tor Book
Published by Tom Doherty Associates, Inc.
49 West 24th Street
New York, N.Y. 10010

ISBN: 0-812-50629-4

Printed in the United States of America

0 9 8 7 6 5 4 3 2 1

ONE

The king came riding from the hills astride the fiery cabo that the awed breeders had named Earthshaker. The animal's four small, curved horns had been tipped with balls of gold, not for vanity but because Earthshaker had gored some of the handlers.

Propped before him on his saddle the king held a beautiful, glittering spear. It was not the long, horseman's spear such as the Amsi favored, but the man-tall warrior spear of the king's native islands. A full third of its length was graceful, tapering head with inset steel edges in a body of bronze. Another third was a spirally fluted butt-spike. A haft of flamewood connected head and spike. It was a famous weapon, known from the snows of the far north to the jungle kingdoms of the south. It had become the symbol of his lordship, for it was little suited to mounted warfare and the warriors of his elite guard seldom let him risk himself in close combat any more.

Hael had spent the past night by a pool in the low foothills to the north of the town, meditating as was his frequent custom. His people assumed that he was communing with the spirits or performing magical rites at such times, but more often he simply wanted to get away from people, to be alone for a while. Sometimes he felt that this business of being king was a mask he assumed, that, inside, he was still a herdsman-warrior whose greatest pleasure was in standing solitary guard over the tribe's livestock.

His guard cheered and mounted when he rode into sight. Most of them were Matwa or Amsi, but there were representatives of a dozen other peoples. The guard was becoming unwieldy, but every time a new people joined his alliance, he had to take a few young men into his personal bodyguard, lest the newcomers should feel slighted.

The guard fell in behind him and he set off for the town at a trot. An hour's ride brought them to a low rise overlooking the town, now swollen to twice its usual size by the semiannual fair. Twice each year, the fairs of the western and southern merchant trains turned the once-tiny Byalla village of Hard Wind into a minor metropolis where a dozen languages could be heard on any street.

The king had encouraged the merchants to maintain permanent factors in this town and others within his domain, guaranteeing the safety of their caravans. His matchless mounted

warriors kept the grasslands free of outlaws as
well as foreign enemies. The king had a large
residence in the town, with barracks for his
guard. He spent a month or two of each year
there. There were other such residences in his
most important villages and towns. They had
been Deena's idea, for the queen detested living
in tents.

At thought of her he felt a tug of loneliness.
She loved the great fairs, but she was not with
him this year. She was in her mother's house in
the hills, soon to give birth to their third child,
if the babe was not born already. He hoped that
this would be a girl, for they already had two
sons, Ansa and Kairn. Since he was wed to a
Matwa, he had diplomatically given the boys
Amsi names over much in-law protest. At ages
eight and six, respectively, it was not clear
which of the two would succeed him. Perhaps
neither would. He was all too aware that these
things were governed by many factors, including chance.

King Hael's own power was as much spiritual as political or military. His diplomatic
skills had welded together peoples with centuries of enmity between them, and his feats of
invention and organization made them the masters of the hills and plains. Even so, it had been
the support of the spirit-speakers that gave him
the prestige to accomplish these things. The
Amsi hailed him as the Prophesied One, and the
Matwa believed him to be an inspired madman,
like many of their legendary heroes. It was
known to everyone that King Hael enjoyed a
unique and intimate relationship with the spirits of the land. He could mount a wild cabo and

it would behave like the best-trained domestic beast.

Just outside the town, near the encampments of the caravans, a wing of his cavalry practiced their complex evolutions. They rode at a gallop, loosing arrows as they went, riddling man-sized targets at a range Hael would not have credited just a few years earlier. Their bows were short, composed of layers of wood, sinew and split horn, bound together with a powerful glue. Hael had not invented these bows, but had asked his bowyers to improve on a crude design from a mountainous area where there was no proper wood for the traditional long, stiff wooden bow of the hill people. Now everyone thought of them as King Hael's bows. Hael himself was an indifferent archer compared to these young men, who had been boys when the new bows and the new king revolutionized the lives of the plains people.

The king cocked an eyebrow to see whether the others were getting the full benefit of this display. The trade delegation from the west watched the exercises of the mounted men with interest. Among them, Hael was sure, were a number of military spies. This suited him well. He wanted the western kings to know how powerful the plains people had grown under his guiding hand. These spies would be able to render expert testimony.

Beyond the training ground, the fair was in full uproar. The colorful tents of the traders were full of sophisticated goods and metals to exchange for the products of the land. Matwa, Amsi, Byalla and others brought loads of pelts, feathers, rare earths and medicinal herbs. Each year, Hael sent out small expeditions to comb the hills and mountains for new sources of trade goods. Most especially, he wished to find a source of metal, to reduce his people's dependency on the outlanders. Thus far, he had failed in this.

The king and his escort rode within the village walls to the loud cheers of inhabitants and visitors. The once-squalid town of despised and exploited farmers was now a colorful and prosperous community. Many of the Byalla had taken readily to the role of innkeeper, shopkeeper or company middleman. They were no longer treated as slaves by the Amsi and their loyalty to Hael knew no bounds.

The royal residence was a handsome structure of rammed earth and thatch, with skylights and windows of colorful glass, imported at great cost. This last was an extravagance Hael deemed justified for the impression it made on visiting chiefs. A southern or western king would have considered the building modest even for a royal hunting lodge, but Hael governed an outdoor people who were far more impressed by the number and ferocity of the men who followed him, and by his vast herds.

He dismounted and strode up to the broad verandah that encircled the residence. Envoys and messengers bowed him inside and he greeted each one courteously. A man wearing the livery of a Nevan messenger came forward, presenting a scroll-box.

"Letters from His Majesty and your other friends in Neva, King Hael," the man said. "Royal gifts will arrive later, by caravan."

"My thanks to your royal master," Hael said.

"I think he will be pleased with the gifts I have selected for him. Merchant Shong will bear them this year, as usual."

The messenger bowed his way out and the king handed the box to a Byalla steward, to be perused later, at leisure. He braced himself for a long day of giving audience, deciding which merchants should have which trading privileges, which breeding stock should be sent as gifts to the neighboring kings. The southern kings, as usual, pestered him to send some of his warriors to serve in their armies as irregulars. They offered handsome pay, but Hael put them off. He did not wish his young men to get in the habit of serving other kings.

Among the visitors were priests and wandering wise men of various religions. Some of these were spies as well, but most merely wanted a close look at this remarkable king who was also said to be a sort of priest or shaman. As with the merchants, Hael guaranteed the safety of all such travelers within his territory, although he usually found their preachings to be a mere nuisance. Long before, however, he had learned that these men often had traveled widely and liked nothing better than to talk about it. They could be veritable mines of information about foreign lands. Unlike merchants, the holy men rarely expected to be paid for any morsels of information they delivered. In consequence, Hael treated them with unfailing courtesy.

This group paid him elaborate formalities, using the ritualistic forms to hide their astonishment. Hael was used to that look. Priest or chief, merchant or warrior, none of them could quite believe that King Hael, who had come out of nowhere to create a vast kingdom from primitive tribes, who had established sophisticated diplomatic and trade relations with half the world, who had built a mobile army such as the world had never seen, was a young man still in his twenties.

Hael saw a dusty Matwa subchief enter the doorway and beckoned him to approach. "Any word from Broadleaf?" This was the queen's home village.

"Not when I left two days ago," the man reported. "The old woman guards the house like a longneck."

"My mother-in-law is intractable at these times," Hael said. His mind was set at rest. Had there been any difficulty, his wife's mother would have sent a hundred men to drag him back by force.

When the day's formalities were over, Hael called for the box of messages. Most were official or semi-official communications. A few were personal. Hael took one of the latter, a scroll closed with a seal he knew well. It was from the royal scribe Choula. Choula had penned several of the other scrolls in his official capacity, but this one was a personal letter to a friend. Choula had taught Hael to read.

Hael sat back and broke the seal. The letter was long and chatty, full of court and city gossip. He included descriptions of recent expeditions of exploration, complete with sketchy maps. Choula was also a topographer, and had drilled into Hael the importance of accurate maps. It gave Hael a warm feeling, to communicate thus with a friend he had not seen in the flesh for a number of years. Near the end of the

letter was a bit of information that transformed the warmth to heart-freezing cold.

> ... and our beloved king, Pashir, sends
> you assurances of his eternal friendship, al-
> though he considers it rather rude of you to
> go and make yourself a king when you were
> supposed to be working for him. In token of
> his esteem, he has recently named your old
> friend, the sea-captain Malk, as one of the
> masters of the newly reorganized Sea Mer-
> chants' Guild. Malk has become quite pros-
> perous, owning six vessels. He has asked me
> to pass along this odd bit of information: It
> seems that travel to the islands you once
> called home has become hazardous. A new
> king has arisen there, whose name I do not
> recall, and he has unified many of the is-
> lands into a sort of island kingdom. His war-
> riors sail and paddle their vessels from one
> island to another, conquering as they go and
> pressing the defeated warriors into the con-
> queror's service. It is said that they have had
> a few successful raids on the more remote
> areas of the mainland. He says that it is a
> peculiarity of these warriors that they all
> bear black shields. ...

Hael brooded long on this letter, and a great
sense of dread overtook him. He had thought
himself free of his former life. Here he had
made a life for himself that was unique, unlike
any other man's. He had thought that he had
made his people safe from the dangers he had
known would one day threaten them. But now
a greater danger loomed. Gasam was alive.

He had thought that Gasam was too mad to live, but, then, did many not believe Hael himself was mad? Gasam, his foster-brother, who hated Hael with a twisted, inexplicable hate. Gasam was not only alive but he, too, had become a king and a conqueror.

Hael turned and looked through the window toward the mountains to the west. He knew, as surely as he knew the face of the black-scarred moon, that Gasam was a tyrant as evil as any from legend. In his ears, unheard by anyone else, the voices of the spirits spoke to him. He knew now that someday, on the great coastal plain beyond those mountains, he would once again meet with his foster-brother Gasam, and that the meeting would be terrible.

TWO

The smoke of the burning dead was sweet in his nostrils. King Gasam stood on the steps of the temple and gazed into the plaza below. Upon one side, the new slaves continued to throw the corpses of the enemy slain onto a pyre of blazing timber. On the other, his warriors gathered the loot of the town, both animate and inanimate. Above the crackling of the flames he could heard the wailing of the women and the shrill sobbing of the children. He found these pleasing as well.

King Gasam was a tall, handsome man in his middle thirties. His long, bronze-colored hair flowed free down his back in the fashion of a Shasinn senior warrior. He eschewed the paint, feathers and furs favored by most Shasinn. His waist was girded with a belt which supported a shortsword and a loincloth of plain red leather. Among the color-loving Shasinn warriors, this set him apart as clearly as any royal finery.

"My lord."

He turned to see his woman emerge from the temple. Queen Larissa was acknowledged as the most beautiful woman among the Shasinn, whom all considered to be the comeliest people in the world. She was aware of the fact and wanted all to know it. She wore a great deal of fine jewelry and little else. It pleased the king that his woman could flaunt herself thus and no man dared respond. Today she had added something new. Her nipples were covered by delicately worked caps of gold, connected by a thin golden chain. She pressed herself to her husband and he gave the chain a tug, causing her to wince.

"What holds them on?" he said, grinning.

"That is my secret. Rest assured it is painful."

"Good," he said. His tastes and hers were not those of ordinary people. "Shall we inspect my new conquest?"

At the bottom of the steps his shield-bearer handed him his spear. The beautiful, slender weapon was made entirely of steel except for a short, wooden grip. He had had the steel edges stripped from the weapons of slain chiefs and smithed into this extravagant spear to symbolize his kingship and his difference from other men. The bearer fell in behind them, carrying the king's long, black shield. The warriors cheered in an ecstasy of hero-worship as their king and queen walked among them. The true Shasinn retained their proud bearing, but warriors of lesser peoples fell to their knees, some chanting hymns in a dozen languages. Bronze weapons glittered in the bright sunlight.

First the king and queen examined the heaps of precious metals, jewels and cloth, beautifully crafted vessels and plate. There were bulk goods: ingots of metal, stacks of glass in wooden crates packed in sawdust, bales of fiber to be woven and dyed.

"The mainlanders are rich," Larissa said. "There is too much here to send back to the Islands until you capture some larger ships."

"Nothing goes back to the Islands," the king said.

She looked at him sharply. "What do you mean?"

"It is time I had a mainland base. This town has a decent harbor and its look pleases me. How would you like to have a palace here, my queen? No more arduous voyages back to the Islands at the end of each raiding season, no more picking through the loot for small items that will pack well?"

She smiled and threw her arms around him. "At last! When can we start building?"

"At once," he said. "Since we won't be sailing home, I can raid to the south for another two months. Find craftsmen and laborers and put them to work. They are all your slaves now. What was the name of this place?"

"Floria," she said. "It is something to do with their flower goddess."

He smiled contemptuously. "Gods and goddesses! Only a race of slaves could believe in such things. Being conquered and enslaved by us is an improvement in their lot." The Shasinn had no gods, only spirits that might be helpful or harmful. Gasam did not even believe in these.

"We will give this place a name fit for the capital of a warrior king. We will start our palace there." She pointed toward a sprawling complex of structures capping a hill near the plaza. "That was the house of the local governor. I am told he fled as soon as your ships came into sight."

"Excellent," Gasam said. "Choose some personal slaves from these"—he gestured to the cowering flock of people who stood to one side of the plaza. "I am going to examine the captured soldiers and see if any are worthy to enroll in my army."

"Don't be too strict in your judging," she cautioned. "In the Islands there were thousands of splendid warriors ready to serve you, once they had been subdued. Here it is different. The kings have great mobs of soldiers who fight more from fear of their leaders than from love of fighting or loyalty to a chief. If you would conquer the mainland, you must use these war slaves."

He put his hand to the back of her neck, twining his fingers in her hair, which was so pale that it shone nearly white in the bright sunlight. "I know that, little queen. They are all tools to serve me, and I will reject nothing that is useful."

He turned to his next task and she began to examine the new slaves, satisfied that he would heed her words. He was shrewd and calculating, but sometimes his natural savagery overcame him and led him to acts of wasteful brutality.

The prisoners had been stripped to reveal any deformity or physical flaw. She studied their attitudes with interest. Some trembled and wept, some were stunned beyond any ability to react. Others were calm or resigned. These, she knew, had been slaves when the city was taken. They faced only a change of masters. She had no sympathy for them. Shasinn were never taken alive by slavers. If these had wished to avoid this fate, they could have chosen death easily enough. If they allowed themselves to be enslaved, then they were born to be slaves.

"Listen to me," she said. The sobbing became stifled as they waited to hear their fate. She knew that these mainlanders could understand her Island dialect. "You are now the slaves of King Gasam of the Islands. Your status may change later, according to how you behave. For now, resign yourselves to slavery. You live only at the king's pleasure. Those who obey will be well treated. Those who disobey will be beaten. Those who rebel will be killed. I am Larissa, the queen. My authority is second only to the king's."

The prisoners calmed a little. She knew that people needed strong rules at the outset. They were more easily resigned to their fate if they knew exactly where they stood. "You will obey instantly the orders of any Shasinn, unless it is counter to an order from the king or from me. By now, you all know how to recognize the Shasinn." She swept an arm toward a group of Gasam's elite guard, who leaned on their black shields, watching the gathering of loot with interest. They were tall men with long hair that ranged in color from dark gold to almost white.

Their naturally ruddy skins were deepened almost to copper by the sun and all of them had blue eyes.

"You will obey any order from a warrior of the lesser peoples, unless it conflicts with an order from a Shasinn. You have no rights that a free man or woman is bound to respect. Forget pride, forget the status you used to have, forget the past. From now on, you have only one virtue: obedience. See that you do not neglect that virtue. Now, I am going to choose my personal attendants from among you. Stand up and stop sniveling. You have already escaped death, and that is what you feared most."

She had specific aims when she wandered among her human property. She ignored the males. Raised among a proud warrior people, she could not abide the presence of able-bodied men who would not fight. She passed up women with children, as she did not want her servants to be distracted by lesser obligations. It was too soon to take on the demoralized women who had, just days before, been free, well-born, even slave owners themselves. Training them would be too much bother. She stopped before a tall, beautiful woman with black hair and very white skin. The woman stood serenely, embarrassed by neither her condition nor her nakedness.

"You are a born slave?" Larissa demanded.

"Captured as a child, Mistress." The woman kept her head and eyes lowered, but her voice was clear and steady.

"Where was your home?"

"The far south, Mistress. Near the border with Chiwa."

"Where did you serve before we came?"

"The house of Hanas, the high priest of Aq, Mistress."

"Good. You are familiar with the work of a great house, then."

"Yes, Mistress."

"Go stand by that young warrior." She indicated one of her personal guard, a smooth-muscled youth who wore his long hair in hundreds of tiny plaits, the mark of a Shasinn junior warrior.

Quickly the queen chose another score of slaves. She chose mainly for beauty and the habit of obedience. She chose a few free-born girls who were young enough to adjust quickly to their new status. Accustomed to the austere life of her native island, she had little use for the specialized skills boasted by some of the great-house slaves. She needed no seam-stresses, since she rarely wore more than a loincloth. Hairdressers and cosmeticians were an utter frivolity. She had no taste for the main-land music and her preferences in food and drink were simple so she ignored the musicians and cooks. She was about to go when a quietly bold voice stopped her.

"Mistress."

Larissa saw that it was a small woman who spoke, one she had passed by because she held herself a little aloof from the others, indicating a spirit that would take much beating to sub-due. At another time she might have found that a fascinating project, but with her new palace to build and her new city to put in order, she would be too busy. She could ignore the woman, or, better, have her beaten for the impertinence of addressing the queen without permission.

But she found that her curiosity was piqued, and so she paused.

"Yes?"

"Take me, Mistress?"

Larissa cupped the small chin and tilted the girl's head back. She saw that this was no girl, but a woman her own age. Her body was lush but compact, and her belly showed no sign of childbearing. Her hair was black and her skin tan, with huge, green eyes.

"What were you?"

"A noblewoman, of one of the greatest houses," she said, then, belatedly, added, "Mistress."

"In other words, you are useless. You have no skills or experience becoming to a slave."

"On the contrary, Mistress. I have every skill useful to a queen's companion."

This was quite unexpected and the queen found it amusing. "Explain."

The woman's full lips formed a slight smile. Her confidence swelled now that she had a hearing. "You are Queen of the Islands, my lady, but the ways of the mainland kingdoms are new to you. You will need advice on how to live like a queen."

"I live like a queen now. Except for my husband, there is none who does not obey me."

"Your pardon, my lady, but that is true only where the king's spear holds sway. The world is greater than you imagine. There are many kingdoms, and many queens."

Larissa bristled. "And what of that? All will bow down to King Gasam in time."

"Assuredly, Mistress. In the meantime, though, you will have to deal with them. There

will be embassies and royal visits. Even such
an all-conquering warrior as your lord must
deal with them as equals until he subdues them.
Their queens will seek out your every weakness
and lack of experience. They can be very subtle,
Mistress."

"So can I," the queen said. "You speak boldly,
to throw my ignorance in my face. Why do you
court my displeasure?"

The woman continued to smile. "I courted
your attention. I can help you."

"Why do you wish to help me? You would
still be a slave. Mine to reward, or to beat or
bind or kill, as I see fit."

"It seems I must be someone's slave, Mistress. I think I could enjoy being your slave."

Larissa looked at the woman for a long moment, thinking. "What is your name?"

"Dunyaz, my lady."

"Come with me." The queen and her new
slaves, escorted by her guard, began to walk toward her new palace on the hilltop.

Outside the city wall, King Gasam surveyed
the disarmed mass of surrendered troops.
Around him stood his captains, hard-bitten
warrior chiefs of a dozen Island races. He favored his fellow Shasinn, but he knew that most
warriors would be quicker to obey officers of
their own race, so he rewarded loyalty and ability with high rank, regardless of race or tribe.

"I've never seen such spiritless kagga," said
a hard-faced Asasa chief.

A few paces away stood about three-score disarmed men, some of them truculent but all vis-
ibly frightened. They had been stripped of their
armor and stood in tunics or loincloths. Stocky,

brown-haired men for the most part, they were typical of this region. The battle had been brief. The town's garrison had been taken by surprise when the Islander ships came ashore at dawn, discharging waves of spear-bearing warriors, all of them carrying black shields. The soldiers had scrambled to arms and had tried to repel the invaders but the sea wall was in ruinous condition and the tall, fearless invaders had swarmed through. Swept from the wall, the soldiers tried to fight through the streets, but soon saw that most of their officers had deserted. Those who had stood to their arms as far as the city's plaza laid down their weapons when an invader chief had offered quarter.

"The king will address you!" shouted a warrior. "Pay attention if you would live!"

Gasam came forward, his spear glittering in the sun. "You men have fought bravely," the king began, ignoring the grins on his men's faces. "I always welcome brave men into my service. I have come to the mainland to stay, and I will conquer it as I did the Islands. Look at the men who took this city. They stand all around you. You see men from many tribes, many islands. Some of them have risen high in my service. Any of you may rise as high. Even for the lowest, there will be loot in abundance, for I shall place all the cities of this land beneath my feet." He saw the soldiers' faces brighten at the prospect of loot.

"I want only willing soldiers. Those who wish to join my army, assemble over there." With his spear, he pointed to a field to his right. By ones and twos, then by squad-sized groups, the prisoners began to make their way to the indicated field, sullen and fearful; but relishing the prospect of campaigning for a victorious and rapacious king. Perhaps a hundred remained. Gasam beckoned a shaven-headed man to his side.

"Yes, my king?"

Gasam pointed at the men who did not want to fight for him. "Those men are not to be killed," he ordered, amused at the look of relief that filled their faces. "Geld them and cut off their right hands, then let them go." He walked into his city, cries of horror rising behind him.

Larissa approved when he told her what he had done. He found her sprawled face-down on a couch heaped with fine cloth and pillows, her chin resting on crossed forearms. Her slave women were putting her chamber in order. Its former inhabitants had left it in some disorder in their haste to snatch up valuables and flee.

"Excellent," she said. "This will work in your favor in a number of ways. First, the people who fled this city will spread the terror of your name. Then the handless geldings will show enemy soldiers what happens to those who refuse to join your army. Having seen that, they will then see the mainlanders serving with your forces even though they had taken arms against you. This will make them even more willing to capitulate and come over to your side."

"That is how I see it," Gasam said. "Thus, the enemy will be half defeated before he even sees us." Idly he fondled one of the slave women. Uncertain of her new status, the woman looked back and forth between the king and queen, but their faces told her nothing.

Larissa was pleased with Gasam's action with the Florian soldiers. Gasam's forces were fierce and powerful, but numerically they were few compared with the forces mustered by the mainland kings. Terror was an enhancement of their power. Subversion of the enemy soldiers was another. She knew already that most of the soldiers maintained by the mainland kings were conscripts levied from subject peoples, condemned for the most part to boring garrison duty. They had only the sketchiest loyalty to their sovereigns and would be quick to join a glorious conqueror who could give them victories and great plunder.

She was amused by her women's reactions to the king. Most of them showed the sort of uncertainty and apprehension natural to women who were both beautiful and enslaved. Their lives depended upon the good favor of the master, but it could be deadly to arouse the jealousy of the mistress. Larissa smiled to herself. They had nothing to fear on that account, not that she was about to reassure them. Fear was good for slaves. It made them more dutiful.

The king had only the most casual interest in women as such. Larissa attended to his peculiar personal needs quite satisfactorily. Close since childhood, they shared a bond that no mere slave woman could ever hope to alter. If, on a whim, he sought another woman, it was only as an object for his amusement. Larissa was the queen and the only queen. The customs of the Shasinn allowed men to take multiple wives, but Gasam had never shown any interest in marrying again.

What King Gasam craved was power. He felt that it was his destiny to conquer the world, and all other considerations were trivial com-

pared to that. He enjoyed wealth and ownership of slaves primarily as manifestations of
that power. In the same way he loved to see his
massed warriors and his armada of raiding
ships, knowing that these things were the instruments of his will.

And herself? She was forced to admit that
she did not really know what part she played in
Gasam's mind. She was the partner of his conquests, but was she one of them herself? It did
not matter. What mattered was that she was
beside him on his path to ultimate power.

"How long, do you think, will it be before the
king of Neva moves against you, my lord?"

"I will not wait for him," Gasam asserted. "I
will move against him first."

"It would be wise to know something of his
capabilities first," she cautioned.

"There is no rush. These kingdoms need much
time to mobilize their forces. In the time before
the end of the sailing season, I shall bring the
rest of my warriors across from the Islands. We
will use the stormy season to get them used to
operating on the mainland and maneuvering together as a great army."

This was something she most admired in
Gasam: he never took offense at her words of
caution. A lesser man might have thought them
an insult to his warrior pride, but not Gasam.
He preferred winning through trickery or in-
timidation or careful planning. He knew well
the attrition of warfare, and the difficulty of replacing good warriors. Long campaigning was
entirely different from the infrequent, exciting
clashes of their tribal days. Gasam believed in
boldness and caution equally.

"In the meantime," she suggested, "it would be wise to send spies to keep you informed of the king's preparations. Small merchants would be best. They travel everywhere and see everything."

"A fine idea." Gasam pondered for a while. "I will be busy with my army for much of the time. You may organize the spies. Use many and reward them well. Keep their identities secret from each other. A number of spies sent to the same location will be a hedge against deception, should their accounts vary too greatly."

"I think I'll enjoy this," Larissa said. Why should warriors have all the excitement of conquest? This could be as important to the king's destiny as battles and armies.

Gasam surveyed the new slave women idly, his gaze returning to Dunyaz. He beckoned and she came to his side, her skin quivering slightly under his caress.

"You are free-born, little one?" he asked gently.

"Noble-born, Master," she said, losing all the self-assured arrogance she had shown with the queen.

"There were very few slaves among my own people," he said, his voice absent, as if speaking of some long-ago memory. "We are not like the mainlanders, who often act and speak as if their slaves were not present. We do not forget that slaves are people with ears, and minds." Then sharply: "Do you understand me?"

"I will never speak outside the palace of what I hear, Master. I swear it." There was desperation in her voice.

"That would be very wise. Think of the very

worst thing that could happen to you. Then consider the fact that what you are thinking is as nothing compared to what will happen to you if you should ever betray us." His eyes were full of death.

When he was gone the queen set her women to their tasks and bade Dunyaz attend her.

"You understand that the king did not speak idly." It was not a question.

"I know that is true," Dunyaz said, her composure restored.

"Good. Now tell me about the king of Neva. What is he like and how did he come to be king?"

The queen was still sprawled on the couch, so Dunyaz sat on a cushion at its head, folding her legs demurely beneath her.

"The king is named Pashir. He is of the great royal family, the Halazid, but most of the great nobles are. He was cousin to the former king, a high general and head of the Council. The former king had no living male children by his queen. One day, word came from the palace that the king had died suddenly, after a brief illness. The Council had met in secret and had chosen Councilor Pashir to assume the throne after the prescribed period of mourning."

"Did everyone accept that story?" Larissa asked.

Dunyaz shrugged. "There were the usual rumors that Pashir had murdered the old king. It came to nothing. The common people are content as long as there is a king in charge. Royal succession concerns only the highest nobility."

"And you were of that nobility. How did they

regard these events, and what is their attitude towards Pashir *now*?"

"You understand, Mistress, that even noble daughters count for little. They are not included in the councils of the family chiefs."

"But you are not stupid, and I know that you take a lively interest in your own future and welfare. What did you hear?"

"Much depends upon which of the noble groups a family belongs to. The rural families, most of them from the southern part of Neva, regard Pashir as a usurper, but they have no pretender to put in his place. The families of the capital, Kasin, and its surrounding districts, are mostly supporters of Pashir. They considered the old king to be incompetent. Neva lost territory under his reign. Pashir is a soldier and they believe that he will restore the kingdom."

Larissa rested her chin on the back of her folded hands, her eyes level with those of Dunyaz. "And to which faction did your family belong?" Nothing in her look was threatening, but Dunyaz knew that she dared not lie.

"They are supporters of Pashir," she said.

"What is your family name?"

"Halazid, Mistress." The words came out almost in a whisper.

"Is the relationship distant or close?" the queen asked.

"He is my father's eldest brother, Mistress." She was trembling now, and Larissa found this pleasing. "I am useless as a hostage, Mistress. I was sent to this city in disgrace. I might as well be dead as far as my family is concerned."

The queen drew her fingertips down Dunyaz's

petal-soft cheek. "Hostage? What use would we have for a hostage? Why should I trade a perfectly good slave for anything when all the mainlanders have will be ours, in time? No, I want you just as you are. I am glad that I know this about you, though. Never try to conceal anything from me, Dunyaz."

"Yes, Mistress," she answered.

"Now, who are the king's enemies??"

"He is not presently at war with any of the neighbor kingdoms, Mistress." She gathered assurance, feeling herself to be on safer ground.

"Bring me some of that wine, girl," the queen ordered. "Pour some for yourself." Dunyaz rose and went to a table where a pitcher stood amid goblets of fine glass. She poured two and returned to the couch, handing one to the queen and resuming her place.

Larissa sipped the wine idly as she stroked the girl's glossy black hair. It was best, she knew, to keep slaves off balance, alternating threat with affection, familiarity with distance. This high-strung, overbred creature would require special care, but she would be worth it. Larissa knew how valuable she could be. The wine was delicious. Wine had been rare in the Islands, and only men had been allowed to drink it.

"The lack of open warfare means little, Dunyaz, you know that as well as I. All kings are rivals by nature. Who are Pashir's rivals?"

Dunyaz sketched for her what she knew of her world: To the south of Neva lay Chiwa, westernmost of the southern kingdoms. These lands were hot, colorful and exotic by Nevan standards, with jungle-clad hills aswarm with strange birds and reptiles. Its king was called the Caudo, as much high priest as ruler. They were said to practice human sacrifice to their gods. The kingdoms to the east of Chiwa were not well known, but were rumored to be rich and fierce.

Northwest of Neva was Omia, a disorganized kingdom of warring nobles. The current king was fairly competent and had the nobles in hand. Otherwise Neva would have annexed Omia by now. To the Southeast was a great wasteland under no definite ruler. It was mostly arid desert with a large area named, ominously, the Poisoned Lands. Only misshapen animals and humans dwelled there. Also in this wasteland was the Canyon, a fantastic place where the people were said to practice powerful sorcery.

Beyond Omia, on the other side of the great mountain chain, lay an area of grassy plain, the home of primitive peoples, nomads who lived their lives mounted on cabos and migrating from one pasture to another. Only in recent years had Nevan trade caravans penetrated to this area.

All of this sounded promising to Larissa. There was little chance that the mainland kingdoms would unite against the Islanders, whom they would perceive as a mere nuisance until it was too late. The noble classes of these lands were self-absorbed and decadent, unable to use the wealth and manpower of their kingdoms effectively. She thought that the land of mounted people sounded interesting. Since arriving on the mainland, she had seen a few cabo-riders, a sight unknown in the Islands. She asked if Dunyaz knew anything more of the grasslands.

"In the last few years, King Pashir has received letters from a man who claims to have united some of the tribes there into a sort of kingdom, although I do not understand how a primitive land without cities can be a kingdom."

"Who is this man?"

"He calls himself Hael, Mistress."

Larissa's scalp and spine prickled, and she almost spilled wine. Hael! Then she relaxed. It was a simple name, and the Nevan slave girl's pronunciation was strange. Surely it had to be someone else.

"Is he a tribal chief who has subdued the others, as my lord Gasam did in the Islands?"

"No, Mistress. He is an adventurer, not from the grasslands at all. I know this because my cousin, the Lady Shazad, told me about him. She met him several years ago." Dunyaz frowned. "Actually, she is Princess Shazad now. Pashir's daughter."

Larissa tried to sound casual. "What did this Shazad tell you of him?"

"He arrived in Kasin on a merchant ship, just a penniless wanderer. He came to her attention through a silly, embarrassing incident at a temple ritual, something about a sacrificial kagga that broke loose and gored some people. This man Hael subdued it easily. Since it might have injured her, Shazad felt some gratitude and invited him to stay at her father's palace." Dunyaz smiled. "It was not entirely gratitude. My cousin Shazad has a taste for handsome men."

"Go on," said the queen. Something in her

tone told Dunyaz that her mistress was not interested in mere gossip.

"Well, one day she allowed him to ride one of her half-tamed cabos. It was a vicious beast, and he had never even seen such a creature, but she let him ride it anyway, even though it might easily have killed him. Shazad is known for her many strange tastes in amusement."

Larissa was quite well acquainted with such tastes. She shared some of them. "It seems that he did not die, though."

"On the contrary. He controlled the animal and rode it almost as well as any expert, a thing unheard of. This brought him to Lord Pashir's notice. He gave the man a position on one of the caravans opening up the grasslands to trade, and there he disappeared. Two or three years later, these letters began arriving, written as to an equal. Is it not strange?"

"Very strange, indeed," the queen said, her eyes hooded. "Did your cousin say where this wanderer came from?"

The girl thought. "I believe he came from the Islands, like you and the king. I do not know which one."

Larissa buried her face in her arms. Hael. He was alive. It could be no other. The name could be a coincidence, but not that near-mystical affinity with animals. And now he had made himself a king, just like Gasam. Were they more than just foster-brothers? Did they share something more than just mutual hate? Hael had loved her, and she had betrayed him to become Gasam's woman. Gasam had been the older; a violent, treacherous man she had known would one day be great. Hael had been a mere boy with warrior ideals. He was an orphan in a society that despised orphans, a strange boy to whom spirits spoke, but unable to be a tribal spirit-speaker because of his orphan status. As a child, his only friends had been the old spirit-speaker, Tata Mal, and Larissa herself. She had been almost as strange as Hael. Her looks had been odd and, to Shasinn eyes, ugly. She had been protected from mistreatment by her position as daughter of the tribal chief and the head midwife. With the onset of womanhood she had blossomed into incomparable beauty.

In those days all the young warriors had courted her, but young warriors could not marry. She had known that soon she would be married off to some senior warrior or elder, and there was nothing a nobody like Hael could do about it. Only Gasam had offered a better way. The fiercely ambitious, cunning young warrior had told her of his plans to become chief of the tribe, then lord of all the tribes of the Island. She could be his woman, to rule second only to him. But first she must help him rid himself of his hated foster-brother, Hael.

She had thought Hael gone from her life years ago. Now he was back. Distant, it was true, but the distance was already closing with Gasam permanently established on the mainland. He was king over nomadic tribes, but had Gasam himself not begun with a few bands of warrior-herdsmen?

"Mistress, is something wrong?" She felt the couch shift as the Nevan girl sat beside her, felt soft hands gently stroke her shoulders. It was a pleasant sensation, unknotting the tense muscles of her back.

"Yes, something is very wrong, but don't stop doing that."

"I am sorrowed to hear that you are unhappy, and it would give me great joy to practice this art as long as you like." Her hands moved down the queen's spine, banishing nodules of tension as they progressed.

"I am not unhappy. I merely see a complication in the far future. Art? Is this like the paintings and sculptures and mosaics I have seen? It gives me even more pleasure than they do. Unlike most of our warriors, I have a liking for these refinements of civilization."

"You mean your people do not practice massage?" Dunyaz unfastened several of the golden and silver chains that latticed the queen's body, so that they would not bruise the flesh beneath.

"Only the warriors, after wrestling. This is different. Are all young noblewomen trained in this?"

Dunyaz smiled. "No, Mistress. This is a specialty of slaves trained for the bath. But many of us seek the instruction of those slaves, so that we may practice it. Among friends. There are many variations and refinements, Mistress."

"Show me all of them," the queen said.

THREE

King Pashir paced his throne room. Nervous courtiers paced alongside him, at a respectful distance. The room was vast, richly decorated but unfurnished save for the throne itself, a chair of state which the king seldom occupied. His predecessor had spent far too much time on that throne, and had lost it thereby.

Pashir was an exceptionally tall man, still erect and robust in his sixties. He had been a great soldier for much of his life, but now he faced his first military crisis since assuming the kingship of Neva. If, indeed, this truly was a crisis. The Island raiders had been a nuisance in the past, but this new development promised to be far more serious.

A chamberlain entered. "My lord, the Council is assembled."

All stood as the king entered the council chamber. There were forty men assembled. Some of them wore military uniform, others wore sacerdotal garments. The rest were in civilian clothes. The chamber was one devoted to war councils, and its decor was severely plain. The walls and ceiling were draped with heavy cloth, so that the room resembled a tent. The king strode to a low dais and seated himself on a great, folding armchair. The councilors then sat upon folding stools. The royal scribe sat at a camp desk next to the king, ink, pens and paper at the ready.

The chamberlain began to intone an opening ritual, but the king silenced him with a raised hand. "We've a long day to fill. Military courtesies only. Summon the officers of the Floria garrison."

A dozen men filed in, pale and trembling. They had been stripped of armor and insignia. Another was carried in on a litter. He was heavily bandaged. The king faced the unwounded men.

"You may speak, although I can scarcely imagine an excuse for the cowardice you have shown."

"Sire," began a man in a tunic of rich material, "we were taken by surprise. The savages were within the walls before we knew their ships were anywhere near our shores."

"You were charged with keeping coast watch, were you not?" demanded the king. "There is a rather fine watchtower built upon the promontory north of Floria, erected at some expense by my grandfather. Was it not manned?"

The soldier began to stammer, then fell silent.

"I see. It was not. There were few soldiers upon the wall that night, and the wall itself was in disrepair."

"Sire," protested another soldier, "upkeep of the wall was the responsibility of the city Council."

"Such of them as have escaped death and slavery shall be held accountable," the king assured them all. "The garrison, however, is the concern of the army. You were at full strength, were you not?"

"No, Sire," began the one who had first spoken, "less than ha—that is to say, many men were not . . ." His speech trailed off lamely.

"Less than half?" said the king. "Why, I had the impression that you were fully manned. Could I have been mistaken? Choula!" The king called the scribe's name in a whipcrack voice that made all present start as if struck.

The scribe took up a scroll bearing the seal of the royal exchequer. "Sire, less than one month ago a full garrison payroll was dispatched to Floria. Each of the men who stands before you signed this document, accepting pay for himself and a full company of soldiers." He passed the scroll to the king and Pashir examined it, then held it out to the trembling men.

"Have you anything to say for yourselves? Do you deny that these are your signatures?" The men had nothing to say. The king addressed the commander of his guard.

"Take these men to the camp prison. Tomorrow, summon the army to witness punishment. Their bodies are to be carved with the symbols of cowardice and corruption and they are to be crucified."

In silence, the men were led away. Now the king addressed the wounded man on the litter. "You fought until you were too badly wounded to continue and your men bore you away. For this you are spared punishment. Now tell me what happened."

Slaves helped the man to a sitting position and heaped cushions behind him. "Sire, I am Necha, under-officer of the Fourth Northern Borderers." He was pale from blood loss, but his voice was firm. "On the night of the attack, I was off duty, having taken the day watch. The alarm was struck just before first light. I rose and buckled on my armor, then ran from my house to take charge of my squad. I had only six men, although my commander, whom you just condemned, pocketed the pay of another six.

"The Islanders were already over the wall when we arrived at our station. I could see at a glance that they were mere savages, but they were very fierce and seem to have learned something of disciplined fighting."

"How so?" queried the king.

"They were organized into units according to tribe or race, each dressed and armed somewhat differently from the others, except for the black shields. Once over the wall, they managed to keep a sort of line, and only a few lost their heads and attacked alone, in a frenzy. Those were easy to kill. Most formidable was a band of tall, bronze-colored savages in fur and paint and feathers. They were absolutely fearless and their attitude was very strange. They carried remarkable spears, beautiful things all of bronze with steel edges."

"I have seen such a spear," the king mused. "Those were the Shasinn. What was strange about their attitude?"

"It is difficult to explain. They were in the thick of the fighting, but I didn't see one of them wounded. Even when fighting hardest, they seemed . . . they seemed to be *amused*!"

"Did you see their leader?"

"No, Sire. I was wounded in the arm when we fought at the wall, and again in the side after we had been pushed back to the town square. At the landward gate I took a wound in the head and then my two surviving men carried me away."

"Excellent report. When you are recovered, you shall have another command, full strength this time. I need every fighting officer I can get." He summoned the slaves. "Take him to the military hospital."

When the wounded man was gone, the king faced the Council. "General Tacs!" Again the whipcrack voice.

A richly uniformed man stood, his mouth compressed to a thin, horizontal line. "Sire?"

"The Northern Coastal District is under your command. Why did your inspection reports not mention this unpreparedness?"

"Sire, the late king gave instructions that he was not to be bothered with such things. He said the only danger was from Omia and Chiwa."

Pashir slapped the arm of his chair. "Do you take me for a fool? Your duty is to *me*, not to a dead king. I will not have you publicly crucified. To spare your family dishonor, you may take your own life. Do it quickly. Now get from my sight!''

Waxen but erect, the general stalked from the chamber. The king glared at his councilors and there was sweat on every face. Not since seizing the throne had he condemned nobles to death. The ease of recent years had lulled them into a sense of safety and security.

"Sire, may I speak?" The request came from a fat man dressed in the robes of a priest of the imperial cult.

"Do so."

"Sire, perhaps this deplorable incident is in truth a blessing. A few boatloads of savage Islanders can constitute no more than a nuisance, surely." A smile creased his fat face and he placed the fingertips of his pudgy hands together. "Disgraceful as it was, this incident has exposed the extent of corruption among your officer corps." The priest cast his smile upon the uniformed man, who stared back stonily. "Imagine how much worse it would have been should you have learned the truth only at the outset of a full-strength invasion from Chiwa. Perhaps this is a gift from the gods in the chastening guise of a defeat. Still, it is a trifling defeat. The savages have occupied a small port city. They will go back to their Islands soon and you may improve the city's defenses."

"Thank you, priest Geb," the king said. "Let us hope you are right. Summon the spokesman for the Sea Merchants' Guild."

The man who entered was stocky and weather-beaten. The flesh around his eyes was deeply wrinkled from a lifetime of squinting against the glare of the sun. He bowed deeply. "How may I serve my king?"

"Guildmaster Malk, my latest reports say that the savages still hold Floria. How late could they stay before sailing back?"

The shipmaster straightened. "They are already long past the latest safe date for sailing, Sire. All our shipping has been in winter port for twenty days or more. The navy vessels have been dismasted and put in their sheds for longer than that."

"Then you think they plan to stay?"

"I cannot think otherwise. The first storms of fall are upon us already. To sail this late would be utmost folly."

"But, by the same token, Sire," said the priest, "they cannot bring reinforcements across from the Islands."

"Perhaps they already have," the king said. "Malk, what can you tell us of these Island people?"

"There are many tribes, Sire. Some are fishers, some farmers and some hunters, but the fiercest are the herdsmen. They raid one another incessantly, sometimes for livestock and sometimes for honor. Of the herdsmen, the most formidable are the Shasinn. Until a few years ago, they never took to the sea.

"Then, this Gasam, who calls himself a king, appeared. First he unified the tribes of his home island, Gale. Then he hired ships to transport his warriors from one island to another, conquering as he went. In the meantime, the fishers of his own island were learning to build and handle the larger craft, so that he would not be dependent upon the maritime nations for shipping."

"Then he thinks ahead," said Pashir. "He is no mere savage."

"Truly, Sire. All this time, he was careful not to molest commercial shipping. He indicated that his sole ambition was to unite the Islands under his rule. With promises of rich loot, many mariners were eager to help him with transportation and navigational expertise."

An elderly councilor signed for permission to speak. "Did this ambitious rogue seek intelligence concerning the mainland?"

"Indeed he did," Malk said. "Between campaigns to subdue other peoples, he kept court in port towns. He welcomed merchants and other travelers, feasting and flattering them. He questioned them closely about the maritime nations, their ports and commerce. . . ."

"Their defenses?" the king interrupted.

"Yes, Sire. All of this was by word of mouth. The Islanders have no writing and they do not understand maps. I might add that his queen is as intelligent as he and does much of the questioning. She is an . . . alarming woman, although very beautiful and charming when she wishes to be. She is rumored to be as cruel and savage as the king when it suits her."

"I have known queens like that," Pashir muttered.

The king dismissed the seaman and listened to the advice of his councilors. Most thought the barbarian incursion to be of little account. Neva was a large kingdom frequently at odds with its neighbors. Small border areas changed hands periodically without upsetting the security or equanimity of the kingdom. A few of the men present urged immediate action against the Islanders. These were noblemen with land-holdings in the threatened area. After careful consideration, the king came to a decision.

"General Krasha, summon all the units stationed within three days' march of the capital. Do not touch the border garrisons. Assemble them at the war camp outside the walls. We march north as soon as they are together."

The general slapped his knees in acknowledgement. "It shall be done, Sire. But surely Your Majesty does not intend to take personal command of so trifling an expedition?"

The king shook his head. "You shall be in command, but I want to see my army under field conditions. We have been too long without a war, as this sorry business in Floria proves. The fighting should not amount to much, but it will be a hard, wet, muddy march and it would be well to discover all our weaknesses. Priest Geb spoke wisely when he pointed out how much worse this might have been. This will be a fine chance to hold some maneuvers without alarming our esteemed fellow monarchs."

"It shall be as Your Majesty wishes," said the general.

"And General Krasha," the king said.

"Sire?"

"I shall be watching closely for incompetence and corruption. Officers who arrive without men who have been carried on their payrolls will suffer sorely. I know all the tricks. I want to see medical documentation or leave orders to account for every absent man."

"Yes, Sire," said the general grimly.

"Any commander who suddenly finds that he is too ill to answer the summons shall be visited by a royal physician who must confirm the officer's infirmity. Each physician shall be accompanied by a royal executioner."

"As you say, Sire," the general all but whispered.

Pashir dismissed his Council and his courtiers. Alone, he walked into his favorite garden. His mind was heavy and his thoughts were not pleasant. He feared that this incursion from the Islands was far more serious than his councilors believed. A young, vigorous conquerer backed by enthusiastic warriors should never be underestimated. He did not seriously entertain the idea that his forces might be defeated by this upstart, but he felt that it would not be an easy fight. Far more ominously, he feared what this campaign might expose to his rival kings of the weakness of his realm. The minor success of this pirate-king might embolden one of his rivals to try a long-contemplated grab for Nevan territory.

"Father?"

The king turned. It was his daughter, Shazad. She was his only child and he beamed with pleasure, knowing himself helpless in her presence.

"Come here, child." She came to his side and he clasped an arm around her shoulders. She was a "child" only in a fond father's mind. The princess Shazad was in her late twenties and a widow. Pashir had always been careful never to look too closely into the circumstances of her husband's death. It resembled all too closely the death of the king he had succeeded.

"You are upset, I can tell," Shazad said. "Don't try to deny it. What is it? The Islanders taking Floria?" She smiled up at him so infectiously that he had to smile back.

"Truly, Daughter, that is it. Mind you, I do not fear these savages, but the incident has forced me to confront some things which, to my shame, I have willfully overlooked."

She wound her arm around his still sinewy waist. "Tell me about it."

He found himself describing the Council in every detail. Unlike most fathers, he never confused his daughter's failings with her capabilities. Shazad was an untamed creature, utterly ungovernable in her pursuit of sensual pleasure. Still, she was always discreet and, like her mother, she had an incisive intelligence and a ruthlessly accurate judgment of men. She listened to his words, then thought upon them for a while.

"You are right, Father," the princess said at last. "This Island king is not to be trifled with. You remember the boy Hael, who now calls himself a king?"

"Quite well. I received a letter from him last week."

"They are from the same island. It has been several years, but I think I remember Hael saying that he had fallen afoul of someone named Gasam, and that he had been forced to flee as a result."

"Strange that two such men should arise from the same obscure tribe."

Shazad toyed with the gold-embroidered tassels of her sash. She was still dressed in a riding skirt and jacket, her usual afternoon attire. She noted ruefully that she had put on flesh of late. Something more strenuous than an afternoon ride was called for to counter the effects of her habitual debaucheries.

"Father, may I ride with you when you go to take back Floria? You have never taken me to a war before."

"A war is no place for a woman," he said sternly.

She laughed and swatted at his beard. "Don't be silly, Father. Wars come to women all the time. What about the women in Floria? If war was no place for them, why are they wearing chains and being raped by savages this very minute?"

Pashir grumbled, but he knew he would eventually give in to his daughter, as he always did. Perhaps it would do the girl some good, he thought. The rigors of a rainy season campaign might bring her down to earth, reacquaint her with the brute realities of life. That might not be such a bad thing. There could, after all, be no great danger in the midst of the royal army. The skirmishers would probably do most of the fighting, with the main body having little to do save the mopping-up. That was how it usually went, fighting savages.

"Will you be sure to obey me instantly, without question, should I be so foolish as to allow you to accompany me?"

She threw her arms around his neck. "Don't I always, Father?"

"No." He unwound her arms. "You could give me no less reassurance than that. I am serious,

Daughter. The moment I give you the word, you are to ride for the capital on your fastest mount."

"I promise," she said, hugging him once more.

Later, in her lavish quarters which occupied an entire wing of the palace, Shazad prepared certain rituals designed to guarantee her success and safety in the coming campaign. Her personal priests and attendants stood ready with their instruments in a room filled with the sound of low chanting and the light of flickering candles.

Still dripping from her herbal bath and dressed only in ritual ornaments, Shazad stood in the middle of a complex geometrical design inlaid in the floor in multicolored mosaic. The attendants who would assist her later in the rite were bound naked to stakes around the periphery of the room, in preparation for purification by scourging. Behind each stood a robed priest bearing a scourge of nine thongs. Tiny, pointed bones were tied at intervals along each thong.

This cult, of which Shazad was high priestess, was one of many known to her world. It was one of a handful forbidden by law in Neva. It went far beyond the acceptable boundaries in the practice of orgiastic ritual and sacrifice, but it was widely practiced for the extreme potency of its spells. Among those assembled in the room were nobles, commoners and slaves. Her high position protected them all from prosecution.

An acolyte gave her a censer of pierced ceramic and she chanted as she swung it in half-arcs on its copper chains. Narcotic smoke rose to her nostrils and the sound of scourges on flesh accompanied her incantation. The groans and whimpers of those under the lash did not distract her. As high priestess, she required even more vigorous flagellation to purify her ritually for the rite to come. A priest stepped behind her and the thongs came whistling down onto her back. As the jagged teeth of bone bit into her flesh, the cadence of her chant did not falter. The priest would not stop until blood ran down to her heels. Outside the consecrated circle, the rite's other participants, human and animal, were being prepared. The rest of the ceremony would be far more pleasant.

FOUR

Pashir surveyed his army with a critical eye and an air of wry amusement. The march was shaping up to be every bit as arduous as anticipated. The stormy season had arrived with a vengeance, lashing the marching men with chill rains, turning even the best roads into muddy tracks that sucked at sandaled feet and slowed progress to a strenuous, exhausting crawl.

Mounted on his cabo, the king took his ease beneath a canopy supported by twenty slaves as he watched his army struggle by beneath him. Beside him, Shazad sat her smaller mount, erect and apparently unaffected by the weather. For the first two days of the march, he had been upset to see blood seeping through the back of her garments, but he had said nothing. He knew well enough of her scandalous religious practices, but he kept silence about them. He did not approve, but in many ways it was better than having her under the thumb of one of the powerful, established priesthoods. Priests were the curse of any monarch, but should any of Shazad's coreligionists seek to manipulate him through her, he would happily have the wretch crucified and face no difficulty from the troublesome temples. To his astonishment, his daughter seemed to thrive on the hardship of the march. To be sure, neither of them was suffering like the soldiers on the road below.

The king and his little party viewed the march from a rocky promontory twenty feet above the road. For its first ten miles from the capital, the road had been handsomely paved. However, the upkeep of the royal highways was no longer what it had been in previous generations, and now the soldiers slogged through knee-deep muck, every scrap of cloth and leather soaked, the bronze tips of their spears turned a dull green by the near-constant rain. Their lacquered armor was of tightly laced splints of horn or bone. The officers wore helmets made of overlapping plates sawn from toonoo tusk, and their once-proud plumes of dyed hair or feathers were sadly draggled by the rain. Men gasped with exhaustion as they hauled themselves and their packs over the mire. Behind them, pack-bearing and cart-hauling nusks squealed and snorted at this indignity.

"They make a sorry sight, Father," Shazad said. "If the savages saw them now, they would laugh."

"As well they might. It is my fault, my daughter. I have been too busy consolidating my position of king, and I have neglected my military duties. The past years, I should have ordered maneuvers each storm season. Then they would not have fallen to this pass." The king shrugged inside the shell of his bronze armor. "Never fear, this march will harden them, as soldiers should be hard. By the time we reach Floria, this rabble will look like an army."

"It will take more than looks to overcome the savages," she teased.

"I agree. They may think it most unmilitary to see a woman among the royal host."

"Yet your spies assure us that this Gasam has brought his queen with him," she pointed out.

"All the more reason to think that he is here to stay, unless we push him out. A handful of warriors means a raid. An army means an invasion. But womenfolk with the army means settlement. Men who intend to hold land fight harder than those who merely wish to escape with loot."

The princess had to speak loudly to be heard above the drumming of the rain on the canopy overhead. The slaves stood stoically with the rain running down the support poles and onto them.

"Still, it is just a band of primitives. Even in this state of . . . what shall I say . . . unpreparedness? Surely even now, these soldiers should be able to annihilate such a mob."

"Oh, I am sure of it," Pashir said. "But my latest intelligence has it that shiploads of warriors were still coming across from the Islands as late as two weeks ago. It occurs to me that we have never really known how populous those islands are. We may be in for a stiffer fight than

I had anticipated. Ah, well, we shall destroy them nonetheless."

Shazad smiled and stroked his arm, but her thoughts spun ahead, calculating. With a pang, she knew that her father was growing old. Ten years before, no enemy on Earth could have dismayed him. The younger Pashir would never have allowed his army to sink to such a state. She believed in him still, but she was already plotting her course, should something go wrong in the coming battle. She would have to get a look at this Gasam. He was a man, and she knew how to handle men, however powerful or fearsome they might be. Hael had been a Shasinn warrior, and one she suspected to be touched by the gods, yet she had manipulated him as easily as she had other men. True, he had been little more than a boy in those days, but she, too, was older now, and far more experienced. A royal princess and priestess should have no difficulty bending an ignorant tribal chieftain to her will.

The march continued for twelve more days. By the end of the first week, the soldiers were over the worst of their sore-footed exhaustion and the metal was returning to their spines. Soon they were making crude jokes about the terrible weather, and were hooting derisively at those who had not yet hardened to field conditions. By the end of the march they were singing as they followed their standards, their military cloaks flapping behind them when they were not soaked.

Pashir felt a certain satisfaction when he saw this. These men were not the hardened veterans they thought themselves to be, but now, he knew, they would remember that they were soldiers, and would obey their officers. They would not run at first sight of an enemy.

A fine, sunny day dawned as they came within two days' march of the city of Floria. The mud had dried and the morning sun shone on an army marching in fine order. Its cloth and leather no longer smelled of mildew, for this promised to be the third straight day of sunshine. The green was gone from the bronze weapons of the soldiers and the armor of the officers. It was not parade ground glitter, but it made a brave show and Pashir was well pleased. As on every previous day, the march had commenced two hours before dawn, so the men were fully awake and alert at first light. Long before, Pashir had learned that the canniest foemen attacked at dawn, a time when most civilized armies were yawning and bleary-eyed, an easy prey for hard men who rose early to attack.

The king's attention was drawn by a small group of riders, making their way toward the army at high speed. These were the scouts who always preceded the army, and they were spurring like men with something of import to report. He restrained himself from shouting an order, remembering his promise not to interfere with the command of this expedition. It would, after all, be unseemly for the king himself to show any sort of alarm on this minor campaign, which was more in the nature of a police action than a true war.

Within moments, General Krasha gave the order to put the men on alert, in preparation for changing from marching order to battle order, affecting the casual, almost bored tone expected of a noble officer. Trumpets blared and flutes shrilled, drums beat and orders were shouted in hoarse voices. The momentum of the army shifted as the men ceased their forward motion and prepared to move into line at order. Packs were dropped and animals, except for the mounts of the officers, were led to the rear. The small force of cabo-mounted troops, most of them noble youths performing their compulsory military service, rode up from their station far to the rear. The horns of their cabos gleamed with fresh gilding and as they halted they begged leave of their officers to dismount and break out their finest trappings. Since the enemy was nowhere in sight, leave was given and soon each mount was colorful with dangling tassels and extravagant saddle-cloths.

The general rode up to Pashir and bowed deeply from his saddle. "All is ready, Your Majesty."

"Excellent. The men seem to be performing well. Now let us hear what the scouts have to say."

The leader of the scouts rode up and reined in before the king. In his excitement he almost began making his report, but Pashir's stern expression reminded him that the king was here only as an observer, and he wheeled his mount gracefully to cover his gaffe. He rendered his report to General Krasha, supressing his eagerness with the affected languor of the well-bred young rider.

"My commander, it seems the enemy come to meet us, in some numbers. The gleam of sunlight on their spears is a most stirring spectacle."

"A spectacle we shall all enjoy soon," said the general. "When you say 'numbers,' my boy, precisely what sums should come to mind?"

"Why, sir, I could not call it a truly great multitude, but from the mass of spears I would have to estimate at least three or perhaps four thousand warriors."

"And do you think you saw the entirety of their host, my brave lad?"

"Indeed, sir, the mass of warriors did stretch rather far back, so that I could not descry their rear guard. It may be that I failed to make out, perhaps, another thousand."

The king bore this foolishness patiently. He was well aware that men needed these little rituals to control the natural fear of impending battle. As a young trooper, he had been just as nonchalant while his guts knotted with terror. To take away men's little poses and façades was to strip them of half their armor.

"And the speed at which these savages are marching?" the general queried.

"Why, sir, they are not marching at all," said the scout.

"Pardon me if I misheard you before, son of my heart, but nothing you have said thus far has intimated that the barbarian horde stands unmoving."

"Oh, far from it, Illustrious One. They are *running*!"

At this the whole knot of officers gathered around the king broke into laughter. "Running!" shouted an irrepressible junior commander. "They'll be so exhausted we shall be able to spare our weapons and simply trample them to death!"

"You did not ride out a great time ago," said the general, "and you rode back rather precipitately. How long, do you estimate, will it take them to reach this place?"

"At least two hours over this terrain, sir," said the scout, "if they do not pause. I can scarcely imagine that they could keep up such a pace without resting at some point."

"A most excellent report, my boy," the general said. Then, to his subordinate commanders: "We shall assume that they will not rest. Give the men a good meal, no fires. Then move them into line of battle. When we've had a look at these sea-bandits, I shall issue battle orders. Until then, keep in mind your standing orders and prepare yourselves for a brisk morning's work. Dismissed."

The officers hurried off to their units with the elation of men who faced an exciting, somewhat frightening, but not a truly terrifying prospect. As they spread their orders among their troops, a nervous, excited chatter could be heard coming from the men who now sat in place to eat.

"Choula," called the king. The royal scribe hurried up to him. "Map," said the king, tersely. Instantly, the scribe unrolled the map detailing the piece of ground they now occupied.

"Daughter."

Shazad knew this tone. The king wanted no pleasantries. "Father?"

"What cabo do you ride?"

"Beauty. She is my most most pleasant traveling cabo."

"Before the enemy are in sight, I want you on your swiftest mount. Should anything go wrong here, ride for the capital and do not stop until the city gates are shut behind you. Is that understood?"

"As you wish, Father." She tried to read the map.

"We are here, Sire," the scribe said, pointing with an ink-stained finger. "But this is an old map. It shows no elevations. I have always stressed the importance of elevations."

"I know you have, Choula, and I did not fail to notice the high ground to three sides of us. My eye for terrain, especially battlefield terrain, is probably better than yours."

"Father, is this a bad sign?"

"It would be if the enemy were strong in mounted or missile troops," the king answered. "However, our intelligence indicates that they have few missile troops and no mounted men at all. If they place their footmen on those heights, they will have some small advantage in a downhill rush, but not enough to offset the advantage of an army that knows how to hold its formation."

Shazad thought that her father's voice lacked its accustomed confidence. She signaled for her groom. "Transfer my saddle to Lightning. Put all the others on a single leader line." She wanted to be able to shift to fresh mounts quickly, should it come to that. The man saluted and went to find her swift mount.

For many days the army's line of march had paralleled a stream, and General Krasha chose to use this stream to anchor his left flank. His infantry he arrayed in three lines with shields almost touching. In the rear he kept a reserve of one fifth of his force, including all of his mounted troops. These he would commit when the savages began to waver. Primitives were always overawed by the sight of mounted men bearing down upon them, lance points lowered and gleaming with deadliness. The impact of those lances easily pierced the stoutest shield. Only disciplined infantry would stand up to a massed cabo charge. Savages, by definition, lacked discipline.

The ordering for battle was a leisurely process, since there was no need to rush. By midmorning each unit was in place and the commanders were dressing the lines to paradeground neatness. When all was in readiness the men were ordered to unhelm and sit in place, to keep them fresh for battle. An hour later, the savages arrived.

The king's eyes were still sharp and he spotted the barbarian on the ridge a minute or two before anybody else in the army pointed at him. The distance was too great to discern any details. All he could see was a little man bearing a long, oval, black shield. Within minutes others trotted up even with the forerunner. Soon there were hundreds. Many just stood, gazing down on the army below. Others capered and danced, giving voice to barbaric chants.

"None too formidable so far, my lord," said the scribe.

"They must be tired, after running so far," Shazad added.

"I see nothing to give me alarm," the king said. "Let us see what more this enterprising pirate has to show us."

The show commenced almost immediately. The savages massed on the ridge before the army, a scattering of long, black shields that quickly grew into a wall cresting the high ground. They held long, distinctive spears made almost entirely of bronze. Soon, in their center, there appeared a single figure, a man taller than the others, who strode out in front of the line. All the warriors began a deep, booming chant, stamping and beating their shields with their weapons. The lovingly polished metal of the spears flashed in the sun so that the warriors seemed to be standing amid flames. The spear in the hand of the lone figure shone silver.

"This, I take it, must be the illustrious Gasam," Pashir said. "Even the old kings of Neva were never so profligate with the metal." All metal was precious, but steel was the most valuable of all.

"I think he wants to parley, Father," Shazad said. The tall warrior was halfway down the slope, followed by five of the Shasinn. Before them strode a man of another tribe, dressed in a kilt of bright trade cloth, wearing the skull of a fanged reptile atop his head. He bore a long, stone-tipped spear from which fluttered a scrap of white cloth: the ancient sign for truce before battle.

"I will speak with him, Sire," said General Krasha. "I cannot imagine that he could have anything of interest to say, but one must observe the formalities."

"I will accompany you," said Pashir. "I want a close look at this fellow."

"Sire, I urge you not to do this," said the general. "First, it gives this pirate undue honor.

Second, these are savages and their primitive minds may not grasp the sacredness of the flag of truce. Third, he will be dead within the hour, so what is the point?"

"As to his honor," Pashir said, "he is a king, albeit an upstart. We kings like to pretend that we are all equal under the mantle of royalty. The danger is trifling. We are mounted and they are not, and it has been my experience that primitive people are far more fearful of violating taboos than civilized folk. As for his approaching demise, I must give him a chance to surrender, and a king will seldom surrender to any but another king."

"As you will, Sire," said Krasha.

"May I go with you, Father?"

Pashir studied his daughter. More pointedly, he studied her mount. It was the swiftest cabo in the royal stables and appeared to be in fine fettle.

"Very well. Stay behind me. Study this Gasam and his companions. Even if he is slain, the Islanders have had a taste of mainland blood and wealth, and we shall be seeing more of them, no doubt. Choula, come you also. Study them and give me a report when we return to the capital."

The little group ambled forward, a trooper in the lead with a white banner. The savages had grounded their shields except for their king, who bore none. He stood with an insolent smile, his long, steel spear slanted across one forearm. The Shasinn behind him leaned on their bronze spears in a curious stance: each stood on one leg, the sole of the other foot braced against the knee.

The savage who carried the flag of truce was a stocky man with bushy black hair showing beneath his bizarre helmet, and his skin was brown. The Shasinn were strikingly different. Their skin gleamed with fistnut oil and their long, bronze-colored hair was almost metallic in its gloss. Except for the king, they were fancifully adorned with paint and feathers, their arms and legs brilliant with bracelets and bangles, their necks draped with colorful beads. Their eyes were bluer than the clearest sky and their entire bearing was unbelievably arrogant. For all their gaudy decoration, Pashir had never seen such dangerous-looking men.

When the two parties were separated by a few feet, General Krasha spoke. "It is our custom to honor the flag of truce. Say what you have to say." Staring down his long nose from the height lent by his mount, the general tried to best the Shasinn in hauteur, without success.

Gasam glanced at the general, then ignored him. Casually, he faced the king. "You are King Pashir, aren't you?"

"I am. And you would be King Gasam. I greet you, but all matters concerning battle are to be addressed to the illustrious General Krasha."

"I have nothing to say to your slave. I wish to speak to you as one king to another."

"Very well," said Pashir. "You have caused us some small trouble, but we are ready to forgive. Vacate our city of Floria, release our subjects whom you hold captive, restore the wealth you have seized, and sail back to your islands. We agree to take no further military action against you and will not hold you accountable for the damage you have done. If you refrain from all raiding against Neva for the space of two years, you may send an embassy and we shall commence trade relations."

During this recitation, Gasam walked past the king and stopped before Shazad's cabo. With the back of his hand, he stroked its brow from the base of its gilded horns to the muzzle. The creature lowered its head with a contented groan. "This is a pretty beast." He stroked the animal, but his eyes were on Shazad. His voice was deep and melodious. It sent shivers from her scalp to her saddle.

"That is scarcely relevant to our discussion," Pashir said.

Gasam turned back to him. "We discuss nothing." Now his voice rang like the steel of his spear. "You may surrender your kingdom to me now. I will leave you your throne and your honors, but you will rule as vassal to me, first of the mainland kings to do so. You will not get another offer."

"Sire!" barked Krasha. "We waste time here with this madman." He leaned forward and snarled at Gasam. "I want to see these insufferable fools piss with fear when the lances come down and the cabos charge."

To their astonishment, the Shasinn roared with laughter, holding their sides and slapping one another's shoulders like boys who have heard something truly ridiculous.

"I regret that I must annihilate you all," Pashir said. "We might have been friends, as kings should be. However, since you have chosen this costly method of suicide, so be it." He wheeled his mount and the truce party trotted leisurely back toward the Nevan lines. Pashir, Shazad and Choula went to the royal canopy, now established on a piece of higher ground for a good view of the battle. General Krasha rode off to address his troops.

Attendants handed them goblets of watered wine. "Well, Daughter, what do you make of him?"

"He is startling, a man of great personal force. As for his Shasinn . . ." She smiled. "I have always been a connoisseur of comeliness in men, but the only word to describe them is beautiful."

Pashir snorted. "Beauty, let us be thankful, is not among the military virtues. Choula?"

"They are so similar they might all be siblings," the scribe said. "It is a sure sign of excessive inbreeding, although it seems to have worked well enough for them." He hesitated, then went on. "Sire, I think General Krasha made a mistake in seeking to overawe them with the threat of our mounted troops."

Pashir's gaze sharpened. "How so?"

"I spoke often with the youth Hael, some years ago. I do not know about those other savages, but the Shasinn are warriors and herdsmen from early youth. As mere children, they care for kagga, a fractious and often dangerous animal, and they must protect these herds from all manner of predatory beasts, in which their islands abound. They fear no animal, Sire."

Pashir frowned. "There is much in what you say. Still, I'll wager these barbarians have never encountered beasts ridden by skilled, disciplined warriors."

Shazad kept her own counsel. Already she was assessing her chances with the invaders.

Her father had judged the Shasinn as a warrior and Choula as a scholar. She had looked at them with a woman's eye, and she had liked what she saw. They were tall and slender, yet even in repose they had an aura of immense physical power, with long, smooth muscles that rippled like liquid beneath their glossy skins. In movement, they displayed the fluid grace of perfectly conditioned athletes.

She found their manner as engaging as their bodies. They had the unthinking arrogance and spontaneous gaiety of men for whom neither past nor future had meaning. They lived in the moment as only true barbarians could. They made the men she was accustomed to seem like pale imitations of manhood. She had known their like only once before: the Shasinn junior warrior Hael. But he had been too deep-thinking and sensitive to resemble these men save in appearance.

Gasam was a different proposition entirely. Even now, in the security of the royal enclosure, with the royal bodyguard between her and the savages, the memory of him still made her spine prickle. The man had an elemental savagery such as she had never before encountered. He was more like a force of nature than a human being. Yet he was intelligent and calculating. He had looked at her as no man had. She was accustomed to being looked upon with fear and with lust. Gasam had looked upon her like a man assessing a purchase in a slave pen. Most disturbing of all, she had enjoyed the sensation.

In the distance, they could hear General Krasha addressing his troops.

"Well, men, you've seen them now and they don't amount to much. Think of this as an opportunity to work up an appetite." The men laughed uproariously. "There is little loot in a fight like this," Krasha went on, "because most of what they have was stolen from Floria and must be returned. However, they have some weapons of good quality, especially those bronze spears carried by the people called Shasinn. I will pay a bonus for each of those weapons you capture. When the savages are broken, most will surrender or else be captured easily. They will be sold at auction and the proceeds divided among you all." This was greeted with loud cheers. "They will attack shouting and screaming, and they look fierce, but that is all sham and show. Noise, paint and feathers never killed a soldier. Just keep your formations, listen for signals and orders, and slaughter the savages methodically. We should be in Floria in time for supper tonight." The men cheered and waved their weapons.

"That was the wrong note to strike," Pashir said. "Belittling the enemy like that leaves the men vulnerable to a rude shock, from which they may not recover. Only victory in many battles gives soldiers a right to contempt for their foe."

"Perhaps," Shazad said, "you should have taken personal command of this battle after all."

Pashir said nothing. Then their attention was drawn by a shout from the ridgeline before them. The barbarians held their weapons high and shook their shields. From the Nevan ranks came the shrilling of pipes, the snarling of trumpets and the measured beat of drums. As one man, the infantry stepped forward and advanced behind the wall of their shields. With their spears upright, they resembled a forest on the move.

The chanting from the savages changed tempo and they too came forward, not to the sound of martial music but to the thunder of their own voices. They came downhill not with the machinelike paces of the Nevans, but in a series of perfectly timed bounds. It was an amazing spectacle to watch: a vision of barbaric fury combined with a rude discipline. The center of the enemy line was composed of a solid block of Shasinn, resplendent in their finery. The right and left flanks were formed by other peoples armed with a variety of weapons, unified only by their black shields. These wings were curved forward at their tips, giving the army the semblance of a great beast's head, with the Shasinn forming the brow and the allied peoples the curving horns.

When they were within range, the master of archers raised his trumpet and gave a long, piercing blast. A cloud of arrows ascended from the Nevan ranks and arched toward the barbarians, who merely raised their shields, not missing a beat in their loping advance. A very few of them went down. Within seconds, they were too close to the Nevans for the archers to loft their shafts over the heads of the front ranks.

From the rear ranks of the Shasinn came a storm of javelins—short, bronze-tipped spears which they hurled with great power and accuracy. There were screams from the Nevan formations as the heavy bronze points pierced bare flesh or crunched through light armor. Then the front lines collided and there began the familiar sounds of battle: the clatter of metal weapons against shields of hide and wood, the ringing clash of spear and sword, the snapping of spearshafts, the shouts, grunts, oaths, groans and screams of men locked in mortal combat.

"They are flanking us on the left," Pashir said. Even as he spoke, Shazad saw one of the enemy "horns" loop itself around the left end of the Nevan line. Even her inexpert eye could discern that the barbarian formation was too attenuated at this point to take full advantage of their position. She scanned the field for bodies, of which there were amazingly few, for all the noise.

"Not many of our men have fallen, Father," she observed.

He shook his head. "The real killing hasn't begun yet. Both sides are holding formation. The slaughter starts when one side or the other breaks and loses coherence. As long as formation is kept, the danger is all in front and each soldier can concentrate on what is coming at him. In the rout, death comes from all sides and no man can defend his own back when he flees."

There was another trumpet call and the cabo-mounted force, heretofore waiting impatiently in the rear, began to move. They made a wide circle around the right flank and trotted toward a position well to the rear of the barbarians.

"Too soon," Pashir growled. "Krasha should have waited longer, until those savages began to tire." His fisted hand beat the pommel of his saddle.

"Father," Shazad said, "I mean no disloyalty,

but I think those men could fight all day without tiring."

Somberly, he nodded. "You may be right. Still, we'll have them running soon. They haven't even noticed the mounted men behind them."

Shazad wasn't so sure of that. On the ridge where the barbarians had massed, she saw a lone figure leaning on a silver spear. As she looked, he raised the spear and shook it. Below, the mounted men were breaking into a trot. They lowered their lances and with terrible speed they bore down upon the rear of the barbarian formation. In moments, those lances would skewer bare backs and crush the Shasinn against the Nevan front lines.

She expected to see the Shasinn erupt in chaos with the arrival of the lancers, but the situation was transformed in an instant. There was no signal she could hear, but with dazzling celerity, the three rear ranks of the Shasinn whirled and knelt behind their shields, their long spears slanting outward. The cabos checked stride, slowed and stopped before reaching the enemy, deaf and unfeeling to their riders' curses and kicks. Instead of being carried by the unstoppable momentum of a mounted charge, the riders were reduced to poking futilely with their lances as the young warriors grinned at them. Then, from the midst of the Shasinn formation, there came another storm of javelins. These found flesh where the riders' heavy armor failed to protect them. More men were thrown by wounded and panicked animals, although Shazad could see that the Shasinn were taking some care not to harm the animals. After a few minutes of bloody, destructive milling, the riders drew back. Perhaps half their number lay upon the field.

A new smell came to Shazad's nostrils, one reminiscent of temple sacrifices. It was the smell of fresh-spilled blood, and she found it deeply stirring. In the temples, the blood of sacrifice was caught in basins of marble and gold, and it was diluted by the fragrance of incense. Here was the smell of blood spilled on the earth, raw and elemental. Perilous as their situation now was, she would not have exchanged this experience for anything. A flash of silver on the ridge above caught her eye. Gasam was signaling again.

As Pashir watched, his face frozen into a marble mask, the rear half of the Shasinn formation broke away from the main body. These split into two parts and began to trot, one detachment to the right and the other to the left. With less precision, the rear ranks of other units did likewise and soon the "horns" were heavily reinforced. With appalling speed, they circled the flanks of the Nevan war-host.

The Nevan right flank began to crumple quickly, as the long spears of the Shasinn lanced into their unshielded sides. Then the savages were past the flanks and in the Nevan rear. Now the shouts of the Nevans turned to screams of terror and panic. Some of the savages, stirred to a killing frenzy, broke formation and dived into the massed men, laying about them with spear and shortsword and stone-headed mace, killing until they were cut down in turn.

It was not a complete encirclement. There

was still a wide gap to the Nevan rear, and soon men were dropping shield and weapon in a crazed effort to get through the gap before it closed. Within minutes, the panic had spread through the entire force and the Nevan army lost all cohesiveness, breaking into knots of struggling or fleeing men.

The change was stunning. Where minutes before she had seen a brave, disciplined army, she now beheld a terrorized rabble. She saw the Shasinn spears rise and fall with terrible deliberation, spilling life's blood with each thrust. It was some time before she realized that the strange, strangled sound she was hearing was her father calling her name.

"Daughter!"

She turned, her eyes wide. "What happened, Father? Why do they run? There is no need for panic. We still outnumber them better than two to one!"

"In battle there is only killing fury and terror. Their fury died when they saw that the savages did not run as they had expected. The terror began when they knew they were outflanked, then surrounded. It has nothing to do with reason. Enough, we have no time for lessons. Ride now for the city."

"You must ride with me, Father," she said.

"How can I enter my capital with this shame upon my shoulders?"

"Don't be a fool!" she cried, furious. "They have won a small battle against a contemptible army. You have five times this number of soldiers in the outposts. You have allies. Summon them all, then come back and crush these barbarians."

Slowly, reluctantly, the king favored her with a frosty smile. "My daughter has more steel in her spine than the savage king has in his spear. I will come, but I must not be seen to run while I still have an army in the field."

"Most of them will be lying *on* the field, soon," she said. "Ride quickly, Father."

She rode to the chief of his bodyguard, who was staring ashen-faced at the spectacle below. When her knee touched his, she slapped him across the face, as hard as she could, numbing her own palm. Then she backhanded the other side of his face, her rings opening his cheek almost to the bone.

"Listen to me, fool! I now ride for the capital at my father's order. Take him from this place and follow me. If you are through the city gates more than an hour behind me, I will have the hide off every man of this guard. I will have them tanned and sewn into a royal canopy to remind the next guard of their duty! Do you understand?"

The man bowed deeply in his saddle. "It shall be done, Princess!"

She rode away satisfied. The men knew that she made no idle threat and in any case they wanted nothing so much as to ride from that place. Among the remounts she found her string of cabos and took the leader. Before riding away, she gazed for the last time toward the fateful ridge. With the clarity that comes of great emotional turmoil, she could see that a smaller figure now stood by the Shasinn king, his arm draped over its shoulders. This had to be his queen. If he was so formidable, what must she be like? With a shock that was like receiving one of the great Shasinn spears in her belly, she realized how terribly she envied the woman.

With a sobbing curse, she rode away.

From his point of vantage, King Gasam watched as his warriors slaughtered his enemies. One hand holding his spear, the other arm around Larissa's shoulders, nothing in his stance betrayed the throbbing excitement he felt. Only the queen understood this, and she knew that this would be a memorable night, for her and perhaps for some of the captive women as well. Gasam after a battle was a creature of awe and terror. She began to stroke him through his red loincloth, but his painful grip on her shoulder told her to desist.

"Later, little queen. For now, let me savor my victory."

"It is a great victory, my lord." Below them, she could see the allies pursuing those who fled on foot. The mounted survivors had already reached the limit of vision and the riderless beasts were being rounded up.

"Only the first of many," he promised.

"Did too many escape?" She had arrived in time to see the final stage of the battle. "Could you not have surrounded them entirely?"

"Of course we could have," he said, laughing. "Even the least of my warriors is swifter by far than these lumbering, armored turtles. But, surrounded, they would have fought with the fury of despair. If you would win battles, you must always leave your enemy a means of escape. Thus he is undone."

"You are wise, my love. Are your Shasinn taking well to the new way of battle?"

"It is just our old way of fighting in the tribal days, but with tighter battle lines and no warrior fighting on his own in a hot-headed frenzy. Let the men of the lesser tribes jump into the midst of the enemy in a berserk fury. They kill many that way but they are killed in turn. Those who hold their formation suffer fewer casualties. Let others die killing. The Shasinn will simply kill. I must conserve my Shasinn. They are the precious steel in the bronze of my army."

The sounds from below were dying out and the Islanders began an ancient victory chant. The king and queen descended from the ridge to view the carnage. As they walked toward the battle site, Larissa could see droplets of blood gleaming like gems on the stems of blowing weeds. Soon her thighs were spattered with it. By the time they reached the main body of the army, her feet were bloody to the ankles. The wounded enemy were still being killed, and a fine rain flew from the spears and shortswords and daggers as they were violently withdrawn from dying bodies.

"Kampo!" the king shouted. A heavy-shouldered Shasinn warrior trotted up and saluted with his spear.

"My king?"

"What are our casualties?"

"Less than one hundred of the lesser tribes, my king." To the pure Shasinn, all other peoples were lesser.

"And of the Shasinn?"

"Two killed. Two more who may die from their wounds."

Gasam smiled. "You see, little queen? My

warriors will quickly learn to like this way of making war, now that they have seen how cheaply a battle may be won."

Soon they were surrounded by a great circle of warriors, chanting and waving their trophies of battle. The ancient victory chant changed until it was a single name being chanted over and over again. "GASAM! GASAM! GASAM!"

In time the frenzy of hero-worship died down and the warriors returned to stripping the bodies of the slain and binding the captives. Gasam surveyed his queen. By now her face and hair and bare breasts were speckled with blood.

"Go back to the camp, little queen. I will join you in our tent soon. Keep your dark little slave woman with you and dismiss the others. Don't wash off the blood."

Smiling, she left him to savor his victory.

Riding her animals hard and changing mounts frequently, Shazad covered in a matter of hours the distance the marching army had required days to traverse. As she rode, she tried to plan what she would say when she reached the gates. How should she act? At all costs, panic and despair within the city must be avoided.

She wanted to summon the outlying garrisons at once, but she had no authority to do so. All such action would have to await her father's return. With a chill, she realized that there was real danger of a coup, should news of this defeat spread too soon. As a woman, she had been kept from the centers of political and military planning, but she knew priests very well. A plan began to take shape in her mind.

Dawn had not yet broken when she first saw the watchfires atop the city walls. A half mile from the city she paused to make repairs to her appearance. From her saddlebags she took a new traveling cloak and draped it around her travel-stained garments. With the hood up, she trotted toward the city gate.

She arrived just as the gates were opening. Outside, carts full of farm produce were lined up, waiting to enter. Shazad rode to the gate and presented herself to the gaping official. The man dropped to his knees.

"Princess! Is all well with the army?"

"Boring, actually. I decided to return early. There is far more amusement to be had in the city. Oh, my father has instructions for you."

"I live to obey, my lady."

"There were some deserters from the army. A few of them stole cabos and may try to pass themselves off as well-born troopers. If any of the cowardly knaves come here, they will probably be making for the docks to take ship away from here."

"At this time of year, Princess?"

"Oh. Well, to lose themselves amid the city crowds, anyway. Whichever, you are to arrest them the instant they arrive and hold them in the city dungeon. On no account are they to be allowed to speak with anyone. Is that understood?"

"I shall do my duty unfailingly, Princess!"

"Good. Get others to help you. Gag the prisoners if necessary."

"Yes, Princess!"

That taken care of, she rode into the city, cursing herself for forgetting that the sailing season was past. Luckily, the gate guard was too stupid to think her manner was suspicious. When she arrived at the palace, she sent slave messengers to summon the high priests of the five greatest temples. Then she ordered her bath prepared.

Stripped and soaking, she rejected all attempts by her women slaves to gossip. When the priests were announced, she ordered the slaves from the steamy room and bade the priests enter. Ordinarily, she did not receive male visitors in her bath, but these were not exactly men. Like all priests of the Nevan state cults, they were eunuchs.

The line of fat, self-important priests entered, their eyes widening at the sight of the naked, soapy princess. Their lusts were not inflamed, but their sense of propriety suffered a shock.

"My lady!" fluted the senior priest of the sea god. "What has transpired, that you call us thus from our morning devotions?"

She told herself not to laugh. None of these lazy old half-men had performed a morning service in at least twenty years. Anything strenuous or uncomfortable they always left to the junior priests and acolytes.

"I appreciate your promptness. Now I call upon your patriotism."

"Patriotism, my lady?" The priest sounded as if he had never heard the word.

"Listen to me. There is much to do and little time." Sponging herself vigorously, she sketched the outline of the events outside Floria. At intervals, she ducked under the water to scrub at her hair. Coming up for air, she had to simulate getting water up her nose to cover the laughter she could no longer contain. Their expressions were just too comical to resist. They paled, wept and trembled at this news of a defeat far from their homes. Recovering her composure, Shazad went on.

"Attend me. I saw a larger army defeated by a smaller because the men *thought* they were hopelessly surrounded. We could lose this city and the kingdom because the citizens could *think* that this trifling defeat is something catastrophic. And make no mistake, it wasn't much of a defeat. A sloppy, lazy rabble that didn't deserve to be called an army was beaten by some very fierce and unexpectedly well-disciplined savages. The king is safe and will return soon. About half of the mounted force will straggle in, although I have made arrangements for them to be detained until all is under control. Soon the king will assemble a worthy army and obliterate the barbarians. *If*, that is, we can keep things here in order awaiting his arrival."

"What shall we do, my lady?" asked the high priest of the storm god. He seemed to have a bit more spine than the others.

"This: It seems that, last night, you all had a vision, sent by your respective gods. They told you that very soon the city will receive news that will appear terrible, but that the citizens are not to lose heart, for the gods have demanded this bloodletting as a great sacrifice, a national cleansing for a people grown forgetful of their duties to the gods and their priests."

"But, my lady!" said a priest in the scarlet robes of the fire god. "This is shocking! To pretend a false vision . . ."

"It will keep your fat backside polishing the

temple throne for as many years as you have left to you!" Her shout echoed from the mosaic-tiled walls. "You will have saved the nation and your prestige will stand higher than ever! Surely the gods cannot object to that."

"It shall be done, my lady," said the priest of the sea god.

"Then go and do it quickly." The priests bowed themselves from the room.

Shazad shouted for her slaves to bring towels, her mind now much at rest. She had not believed in the official gods since childhood, but all such religions had their uses in controlling and manipulating the populace. The people were superstitious and loved the colorful pageantry of the temple services, so the institution of a state religion was a useful tool for any ruler. It was handy in an emergency, too, as she had just proven. It occurred to her that she might have a true gift for statecraft. She would need it, for it appeared that the times were going to be perilous and uncertain. She knew that she would have to learn more about international affairs. She had devoted much of her adult life to luxury and pleasure, and now was in danger of losing everything thereby.

All her life, her father had been the overwhelming presence. He was powerful beyond all others. The greatest men of Neva had acknowledged him as the best among them, in war as well as in statecraft. The king had been a remote, ceremonial figure of no great consequence. When her father had become king in his own right, it had seemed like a proper fulfillment of destiny, that he should have the honor and title of monarch when he had

wielded the true power for so long. It had also
seemed right and proper that she should become royal princess, in the place of those pallid
creatures who had been the old king's daughters.

Her father Pashir had seemed like a god then.
Now she knew that he was failing. Age had
seized him as it did all men, high or low. He
was strong and vigorous yet, and had many
years left to him, but he was no longer the man
he had been when she was a child. Very well,
he simply needed someone to help, someone
younger on whose shoulders he might shift
some of the burdens of power. She was already
fulfilling that role.

This line of thought contained an upsetting
corollary: She, too, would age and weaken. Her
beauty would fade, then disappear entirely. She
had learned some sharp lessons of late, and this
was one of the sharpest: Beauty faded and
youth declined, but power endured. If the old
could not hold it, younger hands would seize it.
She would have to direct her every action
henceforth to grasping and keeping power. She
had no brothers, and was surrounded by powerful nobles who lusted for the throne, men
much like her father had once been.

She knew that she had some powerful weapons at her disposal. The state cults were empty,
ceremonial forms intended primarily to give
unity to the citizens while giving minimal trouble to the rulers. There were other cults,
though, more ancient and far stronger. They
were forbidden by law for good reason. She
thought of the arduous ritual she had performed before setting out with the expedition

to fight the barbarians. It had been intended to protect her and give her success. On her ride back from the shattering defeat, she had thought that her dark gods had failed her. Now she saw that they were rewarding her in a way she could never have foreseen. Had she not gone on the expedition, had she not witnessed the defeat of the army and the evidence of her father's declining powers, then she would have no future. Now the course of her life to come was clear to her. Perhaps most valuable of all, her gods had permitted her a close look at Gasam. The memory of the man still caused a quivering feeling in the pit of her stomach, and she knew that their destinies were entwined. Once, she had felt similarly about Hael, a man of the same race as Gasam.

Tired though she was, she did not want to sleep until her father was safe in the palace. From her drug cabinet she took a strong stimulant and mixed it with weakened wine. Sipping this, she went to another cabinet and unlocked it. From it she drew three ancient books and opened them. Using their formulae as guides, she began to design her next ritual. It would be the most powerful she had ever attempted, and it would intimately involve King Gasam.

It was dark and the moon was high when the king returned. He was followed by a dispirited band of guards and officers, all as muddy and travel-weary as he was. Nonetheless, he held himself erect and his stride was steady. Shazad could see the effort this cost him. Furiously, she pointed at the captain of the bodyguard. Before she could speak, her father silenced her with a wave of his hand.

"Peace, Daughter. I appreciate your concern for me, but I will decide who is to be executed here. We did not bother to kill our cabos riding back here because there was no need for haste. There was no pursuit. How could there be, when the enemy is on foot? I waited until full dark to enter the city because I did not want my people to see their king return in defeat."

Shazad embraced her father and whispered, "Dismiss them."

Puzzled, Pashir turned to his followers. "Go to your homes and rest. Attend me here at first light. There will be much to be done." When they were gone, he turned back to his daughter. "Now, what is this all about?"

She told him what she had done, interspersing her low-voiced recital with shouted orders to the slaves to prepare the king's bath, bring food and fresh clothes, all of which had been in readiness for hours anyway. As he listened, Pashir nodded. "You have done marvelously well, Daughter," he said when she was done. "I am too weary now for further planning, but I want you with me tomorrow. By your actions today you may well have gone a good way toward salvaging this disaster."

Shazad glowed with satisfaction as she went, weary at last, toward her own bed.

The next morning, King Pashir was fully recovered. With his daughter by his side, he heard his police officials' reports on the condition of the city: The people were depressed and bemused, but the proclaimed "vision" of all the high priests had forestalled any kind of panic. Rumors abounded, as usual.

"Excellent," Pashir said. He turned to the official who had the duty of maintaining the city's military readiness. "Yes, Lord Russek? You seem to wish to speak."

"Sire, I have here the inventory of the city's stockpiles of food and fodder, of which we have a great plenitude, but much will have to be done to put us in readiness for a siege. There is timber to be cut in the hills for hoardings, useless foreigners to be expelled, weapons to be . . ."

"No!" said Pashir, his voice raised only slightly but emphasized with a violent gesture. "There are to be no preparations for a siege. That would only spread needless terror. The savages were successful in the field, but now we have their measure. They are in no position to besiege a city, even if they know how to. They are on the northern coast and will stay there, at least until the spring. By that time, they will no longer be a danger."

Shazad held her tongue throughout the council, but she watched and listened, judging each man present as she never had before. In each, she looked for subtle signs of treachery. Most especially, she watched the high nobles who might use this crisis in a bid for the throne. She saw which men were clear-eyed and efficient and which were fussy and officious. There were sycophantic lackeys and smiling, smooth-voiced men whose eyes were sly. She noted them all and stored the information for future use.

"Master of the Armies," said the king.

"Sire?" said the official thus titled. He was a

courtier in charge of recruitment rather than a soldier.

"We must replace our losses. Recruitment within the major cities shall remain as usual, but double the quotas for the village recruiters and triple the quotas for the great landowners. I want their best peasant lads for next year's host. You may stress that this will be a short-term enlistment, until the barbarian threat is eliminated. Failure to meet this quota will be grounds for seizure of estates."

"Sire!" said the Master of the Exchequer, without awaiting permission to speak. "How is this army to be equipped and paid? The treasury is . . ." The king's frown stopped his words and paled his face.

"My good Lord Hamas, I lost an army up north. You may start by scratching those unfortunate men's names off the royal payrolls. See that the death-bounty is paid to their families. Then you may levy some special taxes. Start with the merchants' guilds. They have suffered from the barbarians' depradations and will gain from their defeat. The northern landholders should be willing to pay, since their lands are most at risk. We will think of other sources, I am sure."

After the Council was dismissed, the king sat with his daughter while the slaves brought them refreshment. "I think things are well under control now," the king said. "I see that you wish to speak, my girl."

"Father, things are far from settled," Shazad said, with some heat. "Immediate panic has been forestalled, that is all. You are making the same mistake that that fool, General Krasha, did. You are underestimating the barbarians and making light of them."

He smiled. "I am doing no such thing. And do not speak so ill of Krasha. The mistake was mine. He was a loyal man and died fighting bravely. The ultimate responsibility is always the king's."

She slammed down her wine cup, spilling purple liquid over her hand. "Then why are you recruiting farmboys for a campaign *next year*? We have border forts and garrisons. Why do you not strip them? You are at peace with our neighbors and there is no threat of invasion. You have allies, there are military treaties. Why do you not call upon them for help?"

The smile remained. "You have much to learn of statecraft, my daughter."

"And I wish to learn," she said sternly. "Teach me."

"Very well. First off, my allies are my friends only because they believe me to be stronger than they. While two of us might unite to attack a third nation, or to defend against a common enemy, it is an act of utmost peril to invite someone else's army into your country to fight an invader. First, I would be serving notice to them all that I think myself weak. Chiwa and Omia might both take the opportunity to invade from the northeast and the south. If they see my border forts stripped, they would most certainly do so. Remember this, Daughter: A king's army does not consist of its total manpower; it consists of the number of men he can actually put into the field for a particular campaign. Those tied down by necessary border defense are not to be considered. That is Gasam's power. His army is small, but he has no borders or cities to defend, so he can use *all* of it. My army is huge on paper, but with potentially hostile enemies all around, I can seldom march with as much as one-third of it."

"I had not thought of it thus," Shazad admitted. "Forgive me for speaking rashly in my ignorance."

"No, my child, your sort of spirit is just what I need right now. It merely needs to be tempered with informed judgment and patience.

"Now, what I said of Gasam's army at the council is true: He has no siege train with heavy equipment so we need not fear him here. He will not move against us until well into spring, because he will use the early spring to bring across more of his savage Islanders. By that time, those waters will be swarming with my ships and he will lose most of his transports. I will blockade the port of Floria."

"That sounds fine, Father, but if you cannot make use of your border garrison troops for fear of your neighbors, do you really think that an army of green farm boys, however large, will be a match for Gasam's warriors?"

"Shrewdly put. It is true that I need allies, but there are options other than Chiwa and Omia. The king of Chiwa would send troops gladly enough, and I know he would not try a real invasion, but before those troops went home they would occupy our southern province and refuse to leave. They have claimed that territory as Chiwan for centuries and would demand it as the price of their support. Omia might well mount a full-scale invasion. When they get news of this defeat, I will actually have to strengthen the garrisons on that border.

"What is left, then?" she asked.

"Something I have been pondering since I left the battlefield." He raised his voice. "Choula."

The scribe entered from an adjoining room. "Sire?"

"Bring your tools. I have a letter for you to draft."

The scribe left and reentered with his writing case, which he opened on the table at which the king and his daughter sat. He removed pens, pots of ink and scraps of smudged, first-draft paper. "I am ready, Sire. How is this to be addressed?"

"It is to King Hael of the Plains." The king began to dictate.

FIVE

There was a heavy snowfall blanketing the ground outside the longhouse. Inside, though, all was warmth. King Hael, as was his custom, was spending the winter with his wife's people, the Matwa. The hall was thronged with family members and friends and a few domestic animals. A fire burned cheerily upon the hearth. Near the fire sat King Hael, his infant daughter balanced upon one knee.

Of all the habits of his subject peoples, Hael most disliked the Matwa custom of crowding into their longhouses until there was scarcely room to breathe. In the island of his birth, his people's custom had been for every individual past childhood to have a tiny shelter to himself. The Shasinn lived outdoors and only took shelter to sleep, escape bad weather or, sometimes, make love. The Matwa lived in a cold land and sought collective shelter for mutual warmth and companionship. He could never get used to it, but the life had its compensations. He bounced his daughter on his knee and made crooning, foolish sounds. He was convinced that she understood him and that her gurgles were sounds of affection.

His two sons were tussling on the floor somewhere amid the forest of adult legs. His wife's mother was fussing over dinner and Afram, his father-in-law, was making repairs to his old longbow. He would never reconcile himself to Hael's newfangled composite bows.

"Give me the child before she starves." At the peremptory order, the king of the plains handed the baby over to his queen, who unfastened the shoulder-clasp of her gown and put the tiny head to her breast. Noisily, the new princess began to feed. Hael put his feet up on the hearth and gazed at Queen Deena with adoration. After the years of turmoil and fighting, it was good to have time with his family, even if it meant enduring crowded Matwa longhouses.

There was a commotion at the door beneath the gable farthest from Hael. "Make way! Make way!" A small knot of men shoved their way through the Matwa. Soon three men in Amsi clothing of decorated leather stood before him. With them was a man in the livery of a Nevan royal messenger.

"We found him at the base of the mountain chain, near the great pass, half-frozen." The speaker was not an Amsi, but one of the Matwa from this village, spending the winter on the grasslands with the allied people.

"I have a message from King Pashir for King

Hael." The man scanned the hall. "Where is he?"

"I am Hael. Give me the message." The messenger gaped at the striking young man in colorful woven garments, at the woman nursing an infant beside him in most unqueenly fashion. He placed the copper cylinder into the outstretched hand.

"I thank you. You have had an arduous journey. Rest and have some wine. We shall be eating soon."

"I thank Your Majesty," said the messenger, unused to such royal informality. "I am instructed to bear your answer back with me."

"Cross those mountains again so soon?" Hael said.

The man shrugged. "What is that to a royal messenger?"

Hael grinned. "A good reply. You shall have one of my best cabos. Leave yours here to recover. Cabos are not as hardy as royal messengers."

The messenger went to seek a bench and Hael's relatives by marriage made a circle round him, holding their silence. He realized that they wanted to hear him read. None of them had the skill, and they considered it to be another of his magical accomplishments. He broke the leaden seal and twisted the cap from the tube. He shook out a scroll, laid the cylinder aside, and pulled a cord, breaking the waxen seal of the scroll. His watchers observed all this with great interest, as if he were performing some arcane spell. He cleared his throat and began to read.

"From Pashir, the King of Neva and lord of all its hosts, to King Hael of the Plains:

"I greet my esteemed and dearest brother king, Hael."

"He's in trouble," said Afram. "He never flattered you like that before." Now that he had a king for a son-in-law, the old chief fancied himself to be a master of international politics.

"Hush," his wife admonished. "Let the boy read."

"May all the gods grant that this missive find you prosperous in your reign, your lands wide, your people numerous, your coffers overflowing and your hosts great and powerful. I trust that your sons are well and your queen radiant. May the gods shower your kingdom with blessings, as they have mine.

"I have taken the extraordinary step of sending this message at such a season because of a new threat which has appeared upon our shores. Our Chief of Scribes, Choula, who even now pens this letter, says that he has written to you of the raiders from the Islands of the sea. Until this year they were raiders only, a mere nuisance which we dismissed as no threat to our sovereignty. All this has changed. It seems that all the Islands and their peoples have united under an upstart named Gasam who now styles himself a king."

At this Hael stopped reading. A look of mutual dismay passed between him and Deena. Of those assembled, only she knew the significance of that name.

"Give the boy some wine," said Afram. "Reading is hard work."

Hael continued.

"In the early fall of this year, the pirates had the audacity to take one of my cities, Floria, a town with ruinous walls and a garrison made soft by the long years of peace. Having put the city to the sack, they did not sail home as has been their practice in recent years, but rather they stayed in Floria, defying our royal will and insolently raiding the outlying hamlets.

"Receiving word of this, we summoned a small host and marched toward the northern coast to chasten these insolent rogues and their overweening leader. The barbarians, more numerous and better organized than expected, were able to repel our forces, necessitating our return to the capital, where we now prepare for the next season's campaign.

"For that campaign, we would esteem it a great favor if our beloved friend, King Hael, were to accompany us, leading a force of his famous mounted archers, that band of warriors who have become the terror and wonder of the world. Besides helping to rid the world of these pestilential Islanders, it would be a fine opportunity for our two nations to cooperate in that spirit of brotherly harmony which, we hope, shall prevail forever between us.

"We await your reply which, we are con-

fident, will be a pledge of substantial support in this campaign.''

Hael rerolled the scroll, a frown creasing the
skin between his eyes.

"Is that all?" asked Afram. "Did he truly send
a man across the mountains in winter to deliver
such a message?"

"I have learned," said Hael, "the language
kings use in official correspondence. Nothing is
quite what it seems. If he says that his forces
were repelled, that means he was soundly defeated. Is that not so, messenger?"

The man looked up from his wine cup in some
confusion. "Why . . . I am sure that my king has
told you what he wishes, Lord. It is not my place
to . . ."

"Were you at this battle?" Hael demanded.

Slowly, the man answered. "Well . . . yes,
Lord. The royal messenger corps always ac-
companies the king on campaign."

"You can speak freely," Hael assured him.
"King Pashir would wish it. He wants my aid,
but he cannot state some things baldly, lest his
letter fall into the wrong hands. Tell me what
happened. I must know before I can order my
forces on such a journey."

With more assurance, the messenger spoke.
"It was as you have surmised, my lord. The
king's army was not a great one, but it should
have been more than sufficient to expel a few
boatloads of savage pirates. But it did not fall
out as we had expected."

"Describe what happened," Hael said, signaling for a boy to refill the messenger's cup.
"Start at the beginning."

The longhouse fell silent as the messenger described the arduous, muddy march, the dramatic first sight of the barbarians, the parley which he had witnessed from a distance, and the catastrophic battle and wild rout which had followed.

"I was with the royal party, and saw everything from the king's vantage point," the messenger concluded. The Matwa applauded his recitation.

"You heard nothing of what was said at the parley?" Hael asked.

"Only what the king and some others said later, that the barbarian chief bore himself arrogantly and was so bold as to demand that the king should surrender not only his army but his very kingdom!"

"Sounds as if he might have been well advised to do so," Afram commented.

"He goes so far as to request 'substantial' support. That means that he wishes me to bring a large force. As this brave man has told us, King Pashir's own riders were of little use in this battle, and small wonder. No Shasinn, or Asasa, or any of the other herdsmen-warriors would be awed by charging animals. There are no cabos in the Islands, but they all know that animals will turn aside at a hedge of spears. The youngest herdboys know that the way to save themselves in a stampede is to stand together with spears or even pointed sticks slanted outward."

"No wonder he wants our help," said one of the Amsi who had escorted the messenger, "if that is the best he can do."

"He wants to surprise them with our new tactics," Hael said. "Pashir will have a stronger army in the spring, but so will Gasam. I know that the mainlanders underestimate the number of people in the Islands, and more than half of the population are warrior tribes. But they are all foot fighters, spearmen for the most part. Gasam has taught them to fight in a disciplined fashion; it sounds like he is using our old tactic of massing veteran warriors in the center with junior warriors forming the horns. Against this the riders were futile, but Gasam did not have to face strong archery. The Nevans use small, weak bows, more suited for hunting than for war. And they do not use many, because they think it the weapon of low-born hirelings."

"Would you play the 'low-born hireling' to this king?" said Deena sharply.

The Matwa warrior in Amsi garb snorted. "We should teach them who the true aristocrats of the battlefield are!" This was greeted with cheers.

"How do you intend to answer this?" Afram asked.

"I shall summon a council of all the chiefs," Hael said, "the war chiefs and the village chiefs and the tribal chiefs. The spirit-speakers as well."

"Surely you do not propose to take your warriors all the way to Neva to fight people who do not threaten us?" Deena said, aghast. The Amsi warriors were shocked. Not at her words, but because she spoke them. Among the plains people, women did not thus interrupt the councils of men.

"I must take them someplace," Hael said. "We cleared out the outlaw bands and settled our border disputes years ago. Warriors lose purpose without a fight once in a while. They are already clamoring for me to let them hire out to the southern kings. I have restrained them thus far, but I cannot for much longer. If I don't take them to war soon, then they will fall to fighting among themselves, tribe against tribe, as they used to before I united them."

"But so far!" the queen protested, shifting the baby to her other breast.

"We are an entirely mounted force," Hael said. "We can march in early spring, fight a campaign, and be home before late summer. We have no footmen or supply train to slow us. And it will cement relations with a great power. I will extract high pay for the men and important trading concessions for the nation. We will be established as a power to reckon with among all nations." There were murmurs of approval at this.

"It is not a bad idea," Afram said. "Young warriors are all troublemakers, as a rule. This would be putting them to good use. They do no work at any rate, so who will miss them for a season? Besides, a council of chiefs will be a good excuse for a feast in this dull time of year." There was agreement from the listeners.

Later, alone with his wife, Hael spoke more fully of his reasons for accepting Pashir's request for an alliance. They lay in a great bed in a room that opened off a side of Afram's longhouse. Hael had insisted on this private room, and the Matwa had humored him. They considered Hael mad as well as blessed by the spirits, and madness was esteemed among them. A small fire crackled on the room's tiny hearth and the baby slept in a cradle at the foot of the bed. Their sons slept in the great hall along with the rest of their grandparents' family.

"You do not do this solely for reasons of state," Deena said bitterly. "It is that man Gasam, the foster-brother you hate so. He is why you wish to go, admit it."

Hael was unused to such passionate disapproval from his wife, although she was by no means compliant at the best of times. "The reasons I gave tonight are true, and they are good ones. I would almost certainly do this even if it were not Gasam leading the raiders. I would certainly never take my young warriors on a lengthy campaign, one from which some of them will not return, solely to avenge myself upon him."

"Why, then?" she demanded, eyes bright with half-shed tears.

Fingers laced behind his head, he stared into the darkness of the overhead rafters, as if looking backward down a lengthy tunnel of years.

"I cannot hate Gasam for what he did to me. If I had remained a Shasinn, what would I be now? I could never be what I truly wanted, which was to be a spirit-speaker. By now I would be a senior warrior, like thousands of others. I would have a few kagga of my own, and probably a woman."

"But not the woman you wanted," Deena said.

"No," Hael admitted, "Gasam took her, too. I would not have had her anyway, though. As she herself told me, I was a junior warrior and could not marry. By the time I was a senior, she would long have been married to some elder. That was the way with the Shasinn. There was no variety to our lives. It was wonderful to be a young warrior, but that was the best part of life."

Deena sighed and rested her cheek against his chest as his arm encircled her shoulders. "I am glad that Gasam did what he did," she said.

"As am I. Because of him, I left the tribe. I have sailed upon the great sea. I have known great cities and a hundred villages. I have befriended the most interesting, the wisest and most powerful of men. Because of what he did to me, I found you when you were at the point of death, and made you mine. I created a nation and became its king, with the love of my people, my wife, and later fine sons and, now, a daughter. I cannot hate Gasam for this."

"Why, then?" Deena asked once more, a trace of resignation now tingeing her voice. "He is so far away. He is no threat to you or to us."

"Because Gasam is truly evil, in a way I have never encountered since. All men call their enemies evil, but this simply means that they want different things, or are competing for the same things. But Gasam is different. From childhood he has been one who used other people to advance himself, to their destruction. He sought out the influential and the powerful, and subverted them. The older warriors, the elders and chiefs, all regarded him with suspicion at first, but in time they fell under his spell and he made them his own. Only the spirit-speaker was immune to him, because Gasam had no spirit-force whatever.

"This may sound to you like the wailing of a thwarted boy, but I assure you that it is far more. You say that he is far from us, but he is not. Consider what he has done so far. A friend-less son of a humble family, he became the leader of our fraternity of junior warriors. At that early age, he was ingratiating himself with the elders, learning persuasive speech from a man famous for his eloquence, bearing and ges-ture from a noted dancer, and so forth. He ap-proached people of influence, flattered them, learned from them and used them. By the end of our first year as junior warriors, he was al-ready being treated as if he were a senior war-rior and minor chief."

"He is still far away," Deena insisted.

"He is not. Consider: Somehow, he made him-self master of our island. Then, he must have seemed far away from the other islands. But he came to each one, conquered and united them all. Even as King of the Islands, he was far from the mainland. Now he has established himself on the mainland and humiliated the greatest of the western kings. You see? Everywhere he subverts and conquers. If he is not stopped, soon he will rule Neva. Then Omia and Chiwa and after that the southern kingdoms. He will be on our borders then, so powerful that we would never be able to defeat him. He does not merely defeat his enemies. He overcomes them and makes them want to follow him."

"Gasam is you," Deena said, distantly, "re-flected in a dark mirror."

He was silent for a while. "There is truth in what you say," he said at last. "But of this I am certain: I must face Gasam, and which of us is victorious in that meeting will decide whether the world we know is to be the one we love or a nightmare place where Gasam owns men's souls."

The next day, Hael sat by a window, basking in the rare warmth of a winter sun. Spread before him on a folding table were his writing instruments and a roll of fine southern paper. His messengers had already been sent out to summon the chiefs and he was about to write his answer to Pashir's request. Dipping a split-reed pen into lampblack ink, he began.

My Esteemed Fellow-King and Friend Pashir:

Since I am my own scribe and lack Choula's wonderful skill with the elegant flourishes expected of kingly correspondence, I will dispense with them. Do not think the esteem in which I hold you any the less for the baldness of my prose.

I have read with great alarm your account of this invasion by Gasam, for invasion it is, let me assure you. I know the man well, and he is no mere raider, but a madman whose ambition will not be sated until the world lies beneath his heel. He must be stopped before he becomes firmly entrenched on the mainland.

It is good that you have sent to me for aid. Brave, skilled and disciplined as your armies are, I do not think they will have any great chance against the Island warriors on the open field. I believe you have discerned that by now. Against disciplined, civilized armies, an undisciplined rabble are helpless, however great their warrior zeal. But combine those warrior qualities with a disciplined order of battle, as Gasam has done, and you have a force of a power far in excess of its relative numbers. Until I come to join you, keep your armies in their forts. The Islanders have no siege-craft.

I have summoned a council of chiefs to make this campaign known to them. There will be discussion, but none will dispute my will in this. The young warriors are eager for adventure and our land is secure. The terms of service may await my arrival in your capital, but you will understand that they must return wealthier than when they left if my subordinate chiefs are to be agreeable to another such alliance in the future.

I can promise at least five thousand of my mounted archers. This may not sound like a great force, but I can promise you that their effectiveness on the battlefield is entirely out of proportion to their numbers.

We will assemble and march as soon as possible. From you I will require the following: Please have maps and letters prepared for me and sent by royal messengers. I will need two routes planned: A northern path through Omia along the customary trade route, and a southern one should the mountain passes be blocked with snow. I will need letters for rulers of those lands I must pass through, assuring safe conduct for my forces. I know that Choula has most meticulous records of the lands that will *lie in our path, and these would be of greatest value to me.*

I send this now by the same messenger who brought your letter to me. Be assured of my support and that I will arrive with my archers as soon as possible. Again I urge you: Take no open field action against Gasam until I am with you. My forces may mean the difference between smashing victory and utter defeat.

I remain your most devoted friend, King Hael of the Grasslands.

He rolled the paper and applied his seal. Perhaps, he thought, he had been too *blunt*. He had certainly done little to spare Pashir's royal pride. Well, the diplomatic ways of the old, civilized kingdoms were foreign to him. They sounded insincere at the best of times. Coming from a man like Hael, they would sound like mockery. He put the letter in the copper cylinder and called for the messenger.

"How long does it take you to deliver messages from here to the Nevan capital?" he asked, handing the tube to the man.

"Depending on the condition of the passes, I can be there in as little as two weeks."

"So swiftly! When I came hither years ago with a caravan, the journey took months."

"Once I am across the mountains I will be in Omia. Our kings maintain reciprocal use of each other's relay stations. Once in Omia, I will be able to change cabos every league. The country flies beneath your feet, traveling like that."

Hael nodded. "I will establish such stations

along the major routes of my kingdom. I like this idea of quick communication between kings. Perhaps your next trip in this direction will not be so arduous in its final stages." He took the messenger's hand. "The spirits speed your journey, and may you find the passes clear."

The council of the chiefs was held in a permanent camp at the foot of the hills, at the northern edge of the steppe. Since it was neither hill nor grass country, the chiefs of both Amsi and Matwa could meet there without feeling ill at ease. This was one of Hael's many breeding stations where his herdsmen increased the land's holdings of the valuable cabos, as well as experimenting with new patterns of breeding the animals, always seeking larger, swifter, stronger and more enduring beasts. There were numerous huts for the Matwa and the Amsi visitors brought their own tents. The council was to be held outdoors, although a long shed had been swept clean should they have to take shelter.

The chiefs began arriving within five days of Hael's summons being sent, and they continued to arrive over the next week. The king held feasts every day, and there were games and races for the entourages, along with music and dances. During the day also, men of both peoples went into the hills to hunt. For those days, the air was more one of festival than of serious business. Besides the two majority tribes, there were representatives of other, less numerous peoples who dwelled on the edges of the great grassland. On the evening of the day when the last chiefs arrived, Hael called the council to order.

Sitting on the ground around a long fire, the chiefs and their warriors were in an excellent humor from the days of feasting and recreation in this otherwise dull season. The late arrivals had missed out on it, but Hael had made up for it with lavish gifts: gaudy ornaments, fine weapons and blooded cabos. The spirit-speakers were more solemn than the chiefs or the warriors, but they seemed as pleased as the rest. Hael had overcome the last resistance to his authority years ago. Of them all, only he was chief, spirit-speaker and warrior combined.

Hael was not a king as such things were known in the older, more settled lands. These people had no dynastic tradition and no concept of royalty. Among the Matwa, village headmanship was hereditary, but no pedigrees were kept and any headman could be deposed for incompetence and another installed by a village vote. Among the Amsi, a man proved himself in youth as a warrior. The wisest and most capable warriors became chiefs. Spirit-speakers were chosen as children and raised in that craft, never to practice any other.

Hael had come from a far land and made himself a leader of these people, who took him to be a prophesied hero who would make them great. Although his power was kingly, he was always careful to defer to his assembled chiefs on any important decision. They seldom contested his decisions except to keep up appearances, but he knew they might rebel en masse if they felt slighted.

After a traditional speech of welcome, Hael

told them of the reason for this summoning, a garbled version of which they already had from the messengers. They were noncommittal for most of the recitation, although Hael saw their eyes brighten when he mentioned the wealth the young warriors would bring home.

Then each chief had his say. And each of them did, even though he might not have anything of importance to say. Fortunately, none spoke out in opposition to the expedition. They were warlike people, and the peace that had reigned since Hael's uniting of the tribes was unnatural to them. They feared that their men would grow soft. They rejoiced truly at this opportunity, especially since it promised to be profitable. None suggested that Hael might be undertaking this as a personal vendetta against Gasam. Indeed, to the extent that they knew about it, that seemed to them to be a perfectly good reason for going to war. Nor did any think it was a bad thing to be cementing relations with Neva. While they would have laughed to think that they might ever *need* Nevan help, they had all developed a voracious appetite for the goods brought by the foreign traders.

When the formal council was over and the men were talking excitedly among themselves about the upcoming expedition, the old spirit-speaker, Naraya, came to Hael.

"I knew something was coming," he said. "For many turns of the moon, the spirits have been acting strangely. The land itself knows that you are leaving."

"I will return soon," Hael assured him. Naraya had been his first supporter in this land, the first to see that Hael was marked by the spirits, was the Prophesied One.

"I know that this must be done. The Prophesied One is to make us great, but that means more than just unifying these tribes. If you did no more than that, they would drift apart after your death and become as they were before your time. No, your destiny is far greater than that, and this expedition is part of it."

Hael stared, brooding, into the fire. "I am not the only man of destiny on the mainland now."

"Is this Gasam another such?" Naraya asked.

"It is what he thinks. Our old spirit-speaker, Tata Mal, said that he could find no positive spiritual nature in Gasam whatever, but that he had a bottomless capacity for evil. Gasam was only an untried youth then. Think what he must be like now."

SIX

King Gasam walked beside the foreign sailor, an escort of his long-speared Shasinn walking proudly behind them. The neatly paved street, flanked with drains and stone flower-boxes, slanted down the long hill between the palace and the sea. The night before, a storm had lashed the city and the water still dripped from the eave-tiles of the white-washed houses. The air was cool, although it never grew truly cold in these lands.

"The ship is not in good repair, Master," the sailor said, "but you will understand its capabilities."

"That is what I need now," Gasam said. "Knowledge. Always I have been victorious on land, but I have no experience of these floating armies."

The sailor was a Nevan merchant seaman,

one who had spent years in the navy. The walk to the shore was a short one, and they turned to walk along the broad esplanade that paralleled the shoreline on the city end of the bay. A few ships still floated at dock, the same ones that had been there the day of the invasion, along with the transports that had ferried Gasam's warriors across from the Islands. Just before the pavement gave out where the rocky shoreline began, they went into a long shed. Within, a lean ship stood upright, resting on its keel. Slanting timbers propped its sides, keeping it from rolling over. At its bow was a bronze-sheathed ram. The remains of its splintered rudder lay on the ground below its stern.

"This is an old two-banker," the sailor said. "It must have been left here when the fleet sailed south. The city authorities must have been charged with its repair. As you found when you came over the wall, they took such duties lightly."

Gasam climbed a slanting plank to the ship's deck. "How does it fight?"

The sailor joined him. "The sails are for travel with favorable winds. It fights only under oars. Before battle, the masts are unstepped for stability. In narrow waters, the ships try to ram each other. Do that once successfully, and no more is required. But ramming takes perfect timing and conditions, and it's seldom successful. On the deck are mounted catapults, machines for hurling rocks or heavy bolts. Sometimes they will throw pots of oil mixed with other incendiaries to set the enemy ship afire. Usually they use the oil pots only from desperation, since you're about as likely to set your own ship on fire."

"Do they never fight hand-to-hand?" the king asked.

"More often than not, eventually," the sailor answered. "The rest of the missile fire is to soften the enemy up. This ship's catapults have been taken off but they . . ."

"I have seen the ones on the walls," Gasam interrupted.

"Well, as they draw closer, the archers and slingers shower the enemy. Those slots you see along the bulwarks can hold shields to protect the rowers. On the larger ships, the rowers are below decks. When they draw close enough, they cast grapples and draw the ships together to board. You always try to board at the stern. That's where a ship is weakest. And that way, if you're forced off, you can wreck the steering gear so the enemy can't come after you."

Gasam nodded, fascinated as always with new ways to fight. "How many fighting men do they carry?"

"It varies. Usually, a ship this size will carry twenty heavy marines, with armor and helmets and shortswords or axes. When the ships grapple, these board first. At need, the rowers can fight as light troops, with shields and hatchets or daggers. This is a small ship, mind you. The really big ones can carry two hundred marines and three or four hundred rowers. If they're sailing out from a base, or if a land army has been keeping pace with them up the coast, then just before battle they'll crowd on as many men as the ship will hold."

"That is very clear. Now, tell me: You see that

I have no true navy, just ships to ferry my men from the Islands. How do you think the king of Neva will use his ships against me?"

The sailor thought for a while. "He has a number of options, my lord. He could bring an invasion force right into this harbor. To do that, I think he would have to borrow ships from the king of Chiwa."

"Why from Chiwa?" Gasam asked quickly.

"The Chiwan navy has a few truly enormous ships, sir, great double-hulled monsters you can crowd a thousand soldiers into. Those would be the ones to take this port. They would send the big ones in first, let them pull up alongside the wharfs and drop big gangplanks. As the first marines went ashore, the Nevan vessels would pull up alongside them and send their own men ashore across the others' decks. I've seen amphibious operations carried out that way."

"If men fight this way," Gasam said, "then they must have ways to defend a port like this. How is it done?"

"There are ways to block access to the harbor mouth, my lord. Chains can be used, or spiked logs. It varies from one port to another. Some official will have had charge of the harbor defenses. If he is still here, he can be made to explain it. Otherwise, the warehouses will have to be searched for the devices."

"You have rendered excellent service," Gasam said. "I will give you some men and you shall search the harbor area for these items. Report to me when you find them."

The man saluted. "As my king commands!"

Gasam smiled. This was by no means the only Nevan who had chosen to follow the new conqueror. "Continue to serve me well. Soon I shall be building my own navy. I shall need experienced men and those of proven loyalty shall have high command." He saw satisfaction and ambition wash over the Nevan's face like the incoming tide. There were some things he could always count on in men of any nation.

"Now, you spoke of other options. Describe them."

"One, he could use his ships to land men on the coast and get them by short marches to the city. By now he knows better than to meet you in the field, but he may try a siege. He has engineers and sappers."

"Sappers?" the king said.

"Men who work underground. They tunnel under walls and bring them down or open ways beneath the city so that soldiers can steal in during the night."

All the Shasinn laughed. "Men burrowing like little nosehorns!" Gasam said, marveling. "It would be worth letting him come ashore just to see that. But, no, I would never let him get close to my city. I have observers stationed many days' travel in all directions. I would annihilate his army before he got near enough to do any damage."

"Now that he has seen how invincible you are on land, I doubt that he would try," said the seaman. "I only mentioned it as a possibility. No, what is most likely is that he will try a blockade. To do this, he will station a strong fleet off the harbor mouth. Nothing can go out or come in. Any supply or troop transports he will sink or capture. Using cargo vessels to keep the warships supplied, he can keep up a block-ade for months."

"What is the speed of these warships like?" the king asked unexpectedly.

"Well, sir, it is difficult to describe. Under oars, in calm waters, they move with terrible speed in short spurts. Under sail, they are slow."

"I need to have a better idea." The king thought for a while, then: "I have another task for you, seaman. I want this ship repaired, fit-ted out, armed and floating out there in the har-bor within a week. I give you full authority to draft all the men and supplies you need. Find oarsmen among the sailors who lie idle here in the port. Can you do that?"

"Why, yes, my lord. But I must warn you . . ."

"Warn me of what?"

"Well—this one ship, and a small, old one at that, will not constitute much of a navy."

Gasam laughed, a sound with a menacing edge although he slapped the man's shoulder in comradely fashion. "Have no fear. I do not in-tend to take on the whole Nevan navy with this little ship. Just get it sailing in the harbor, and I shall give you further orders. And find out about those harbor defenses."

"As my king commands!" said the seaman, saluting.

Later, in the palace, Gasam described his ideas to Larissa. The queen lounged on a couch, her women hovering about her. The house had been fully restored and the sounds of new con-struction drifted in from outside. A tame bird paraded through the room, pausing once to spread it spectacular cape of neck feathers, scarlet and emerald. It fluted a high, trilling cry and refolded the cape, then stalked away with brainless dignity. The queen smiled after it.

"The houses here are full of these tame animals: birds and beasts and tiny man-of-the-trees. The people here keep them for their beauty or their amusing antics."

He stroked her back. "They are rich and decadent. Such people are drawn to trivial amusements." Once, to him, great herds of kagga and other livestock had seemed the epitome of wealth and power. Now he knew that ownership of humans was even more important.

"I think you are right about the ships," she said. "We will know in a few days. And I believe your mariner spoke truthfully. My spies tell me that there has been lively coming and going between Pashir's palace and the Chiwan embassy and that messengers are passing back and forth between the two capitals at an unusual rate." The queen reveled in her new role as spymaster. For the first time she was able to take an active part in her husband's conquests.

"And with the other kingdom, Omia?" Gasam asked.

"No more than the usual. It is believed that relations are strained between the two kings. King Oland of Omia would like to snatch some Nevan territory for himself. He can always claim that Pashir is a usurper and Omia's treaties with the old king are abrogated."

Gasam tried to visualize how these kingdoms lay. "Do any but Chiwa and Omia share borders with Neva?" Maps were still new to him and he had difficulty in committing their subtleties to memory.

The queen looked at her diminutive serving woman. "Dunyaz?"

As always when the king was present, Dunyaz knelt with her hands atop her thighs, her eyes downcast. A band of riveted copper encircled her neck. Such bands now identified all slaves.

"Omia lies to the northeast," she said, "and Chiwa to the south and southeast. Between those nations lies an ill-defined area called the Zone. No nation truly claims this land. The people are strange and live in isolated villages. There is a place called the Canyon where the people are said to be great sorcerers. The land is barren desert for the most part, although there is one large river, the Kol."

"Sorcerers," the king muttered. "This might bear looking into. And to the north along this coast?"

"North of Floria ... excuse me, my lord, north of the City of Victory"—for thus had Gasam renamed the city—"the settlements become fewer and there is no clear boundary where Nevan power ends. The people of the north are primitive hunters and herders and have never been a threat, so there is not even a border fort in that direction. I could show you maps. . . ." It was a delicate and awkward thing, reminding the king that he could not read nor understand maps.

"I do not trust pictures drawn on skin or paper," he snapped. "Those can be made to mean anything. Land I know."

"Tell us about this desert," Larissa said, turning aside the king's annoyance.

"I have never seen it, just heard of it," the slave said. "It is a dry country, where there is little rainfall. People live along the river, or at oases where springs come to the surface. The people are hostile and resent intruders. There is a man there who some say is a king, but others say he is a sort of wizard. Nobody knows whether he is part of a dynasty, or whether it is the same man, reigning for centuries. Whichever, it is a poor land he rules, a place of sand and rock. It is a brutal place full of dangerous animals, things that live nowhere else. In the king's menagerie at Kasin there was a desert snake twenty paces long and as big around as a man. It was a torpid thing, and once a month the keepers fed it a whole kagga which it swallowed live."

"An uninviting place," said the king. "But I shall be lord of it as well, once I have conquered the more desirable places. This talk of magic, though ..." He brooded for a while. "I would hear more of it. My queen, have your spies bring me word of that land, and its ruler, and of this magic, if it truly exists."

"I shall do so without fail," she promised. "Do you detect some sort of threat from this?"

He shrugged. "Threat or promise, I wish to know about it. Even if it does not exist, it can be useful. Before I crushed them, the spirit-speakers of our islands had the people cowed, thinking that those mumbling chanters had magical powers."

"And yet," the queen said, "we know that real magic exists."

The king nodded. "Yes, but small magics. The hunters of the hills had the magic of the wild animals, and they had good fire magic. I never saw any that could give one people power over another, though."

"Do you believe such magic exists?" she asked.

Gasam smiled. "I will believe in anything that will increase my power."

Gasam watched admiringly as the warship went through its maneuvers in the little harbor of the City of Victory. With his queen beside him, he sat on a folding stool at the end of one of the long piers. In their honor, the pier had been draped with precious cloths and strewn with flowers from the greenhouse that had once belonged to the temple of the flower goddess. Unlike the rulers of other nations, however, they would never have dreamed of placing a canopy between themselves and the sun. The sunlight was bright and the day was a rare cloudless one, although there was sure to be a storm before sunset. There always was at this time of year.

A great crowd had assembled, on the pier behind them and on the other low, stone wharfs, which displayed how the city was changing under its new rulers. There were a number of Shasinn and other Island women, come across to join their warrior husbands; and the local population had changed its look. Upon proof of their usefulness, many skilled locals had been freed from their temporary bondage to serve the new rulers, and these had taken to imitating the newcomers. The men were growing their hair long in imitation of the Shasinn; and where before women of this land had worn close-fitting garments of complex tailoring, they had now assumed the simple drapes and wraps of the Island women. Few sought to imitate the near-nudity of the queen and her highest Sha-sinn ladies. For one thing, few of the local women had looks commensurate with the fashion; for another, few of them dared.

In the harbor, the mariner, Halba, had his rowers going through their paces. They would bring the galley up to high speed, raise and feather their oars, then slip them into the water and hold them motionless as the ship slowed in response; then plunge them downward and bring the ship to a quick stop. One side then kept its oars submerged while those on the other side whirled, raising spray and causing the vessel to rotate on its axis.

At a signal from Gasam, four large boats left the piers and rowed into the harbor. Each was perhaps one-sixth the bulk of the galley, propelled by five oars to each side. The galley began to chase them. With its greater oarpower, the galley was swifter, but each time it threatened to overtake one, that boat would swerve aside and change direction. The galley always lost way in slowing to change direction.

"It is as I thought," Gasam said. "The warship is faster, but it is less maneuverable."

"Those boats would be able to outrun it if they did not carry so many men," the queen said.

"The men are there to simulate the warriors these boats will be ferrying across from the Islands next season," the king said. "I must be sure that they will be able to pass through the blockade. The larger warships will be slower than these."

"Won't they begin to use smaller boats once they see what is happening?" she asked.

"By that time, most of my remaining warriors will be on the mainland. By the next year, I will have a navy at least strong enough to prevent a blockade of this port. Now watch." He gestured, and a tall warrior waved a long red banner back and forth.

At that signal, the boats turned and attacked the galley. Each tried to gain a favorable position at the larger ship's stern, but they tended to get in each other's way in doing so. The crowd ashore cheered as the warriors on both sides thrust with blunt-tipped spears and swung dummy war-clubs. These bore, instead of the usual stone ball head, a great ball of cloth rolled in colorful powder. Blunt-tipped arrows flew from the ship. Each weapon had been treated with a different color of powder or paint. When the sham fight was over, the participants would be examined to determine which weapons had made the most marks; the senior warriors on the ship and in the boats were supposed to be observing which weapons appeared to be most effective.

"This is going to take some practice," said the king, grinning. "The boats are effective, but they must learn to coordinate their attacks better." Like the rest, he burst into laughter as a tall warrior toppled into the water, arms pinwheeling in a futile grasp for balance.

"They need smaller shields, my king," said an Asasa chief who stood behind Gasam. "They are tripping over the tall shields."

"No," said another officer. "They need the tall shields to protect the boats from arrows and stones. Let some stay with the boats carrying tall shields and give the boarding parties small shields for the close-in work."

"Excellent, both of you," said the king. "And I think we need more shortswords. See, the men in the boats can use their spears well against the men lining the enemy ship's rails. Once they are on board, though, the spears are awkward."

Larissa let her mind wander. Men loved to discuss the minutiae of slaughter. There was much whooping and shouting from out in the harbor. Now they were playing like boys, but the practice was in earnest. The real fighting, when it came, would be bloody and awful. In this, too, she thought, men were like boys. It was all an extension of the games of dominance they played under the fond eyes of their elders. They had no craft or subtlety.

For months now, she had heard her slave Dunyaz's tales of the great courts. There, the high-born lived lives devoted to pleasure and intrigue. Her husband considered them decadent, but she found the prospect enthralling. What was the point of conquering the world, after all, if one merely went on living the austere life of a warrior village?

Gasam loved power for its own sake. Larissa loved power for the pleasures it brought her. Granted, domination over other people was a pleasure in itself, but it was severely limited to her taste. People groveling at her feet got to be a bore. But the ladies of the great courts had endless diversions. Dunyaz had introduced her to some of them: mild drugs that heightened the perceptions of pleasure, lovemaking practices never dreamed of in the Islands. Most of all, though, she enjoyed the idea of intrigue. No woman of her people had ever had such prestige as she enjoyed, but that was only because Gasam had chosen her to be his partner in conquest. When the Islanders honored her, they were simply honoring Gasam by extension. In reality, they only respected strength and the warrior virtues. Through intrigue, she could wield actual power.

"Perhaps, Mistress," Dunyaz had said a few weeks before, "you should correspond with some of the great ladies of Pashir's court, and of Chiwa and Omia."

Larissa considered this. "But my husband is at war with Pashir. This might be considered disloyal."

Dunyaz laughed, as she was permitted to do when she and the queen were alone. "Oh, Mistress, nobody cares about that. War is men's business and scarcely impinges upon the relations between royal ladies. Often as not, when wars are settled, victor and vanquished seal their new treaties by marrying off their daughters to each other's sons."

Larissa stroked the girl's hair. "And who should I send letters to in Pashir's court?"

"First of all, my cousin, the princess Shazad. She is the only lady anywhere near you in rank. And she is clever. She knows her father is old, and that he has already lost an important battle with our king. I should not be surprised if she were to prove anxious to establish good relations with you."

Larissa knew better than to deceive her husband, so she asked his permission.

"If you wish," he had said. "Soon I shall make

her your slave, so you might as well get to know her. What do you think you can learn from her?"

"As highly placed as she is, she could pass along as gossip things I could never get through my spies."

"If she is not stupid, she will pass along only what she wants you to hear," he said. "She might falsify things to her advantage."

"I think I will be able to tell the difference," she assured him.

"Then by all means go ahead. As with your spies, use double checks to make sure your words go out as you wish them to be, and have each letter you receive read to you by different scribes."

"I intend to. Perhaps I shall learn to read. The craft cannot be all that difficult."

"If it amuses you," he said.

So far, she was not making much headway in learning to read. The scribes she had engaged told her that it was a skill best learned in childhood. Even so, she persevered and found that she enjoyed employing her mind in this fashion. She was even learning to understand maps a little. She was learning that the world was a far more complicated place than she had ever imagined. Cities were not just villages grown large, but complex structures of commerce and politics, in which priests and merchants were as important as warriors. There was a continuity to them that was more than just that of custom. The nations were larger outgrowths of the cities, maintaining their existence through changes of rulership, changes of dynasty, century after century. Sometimes, she woke in the dark hours and wondered whether Gasam's conquest would be a mere incident in the long history of these lands.

My dear sister-queen Larissa, began the letter, I cannot express the pleasure with which I received your missive. Until now, you have been a figure of mystery, cloaked in the shadow of that formidable man, King Gasam.

The king smiled at this, as Dunyaz read it to them.

"It is difficult to imagine you in anyone's shadow, little queen," he said, lightly pinching the flesh of Dunyaz's arm, as if testing the flesh of a slaughter beast. Shuddering, she read on.

I have, by the way, met your royal husband, upon the occasion of his astonishing ultimatum to my father, just before that unfortunate battle.

"Unfortunate because her father lost," said the king. "So she was the woman at that parley. She looked much like little Dunyaz here."

"They are close kin," said the queen. "Read on."

It is unfortunate that this war comes between us, for it prevents our meeting, and I long for a chance to spend time in the company of an equal who is also a woman. This is a court of men, as I suppose all courts must be. Their endless war councils have made life terribly dull here.

There are innumerable comings and goings between the palace and the embassies of Chiwa and Omia . . .

"She is lying," said Gasam. "Your own spies have reported that relations between Pashir and Oland of Omia have been cold."

"Of course she is lying, my dear," said the queen. "I lied in my letter as well. We shall exchange many lies, I am sure. The trick will be to detect the occasional important bits of truth."

The king laughed richly. It was a sound she seldom heard from him. "It is good that at last you have found a game you truly enjoy. And already you are proving to be very good at it." He took her hand. "Of course, you would be. You and I are not as ordinary people, are we?"

She smiled and squeezed his hand. At moments like this she could feel her love for him almost overpowering her.

. . . and all of the attractive young men spend their days in riding and drilling and other glorious martial exercise. It is all deeply tedious. I suppose your beautiful warriors are behaving in much the same way.

"Surely this woman is not as empty-headed as she pretends?" Gasam said.

"I know she is not, but she feigns it well," said Larissa.

"Good. I saw her only briefly, but then she struck me as strong, willful and intelligent. I

would hate to think I could so misread anyone."

Your letter to me is written in a suspiciously familiar hand. Could it be that my
disreputable cousin, Dunyaz, has taken
service with you? She was in exile in Floria when your husband took the city, and
she was not among the refugees who
flocked here. There are only a very few
things which a lady of her station can do
to merit exile, and she did one of them.

Dunyaz stopped reading and her face turned
red while the king and queen convulsed with
laughter. She forged ahead.

I am glad that we have this link. She is
my favorite kinswoman even if her tastes
are, shall we say, unbefitting one of her
high birth.

Forgetting the King's presence in her embar-
rassment, Dunyaz slapped the letter down.
"That slut! Just because she is now a *royal* slut
she thinks that her own iniquities are permis-
sible. If you knew the rites she practices . . ."
"Rites?" asked the queen.
"There are cults which are not approved by
the Nevan state. They are forbidden supposedly
even to the high-born. But she has used her
father's protection to hide her evil ways."
The queen leaned forward, her face alight.
"Tell me more."

SEVEN

Hael studied the maps and scrolls before him. The maps were not finely detailed, and the scrolls held little information.

"The southwestern route," Hael said, musing. "Through the Zone."

"What does this mean?" asked Jochim, one of his Matwa officers.

"It means that all is not well between Neva and Omia. This is not entirely unexpected. When I asked safe passage from King Oland, he sent back a dozen lame excuses why it could not be. I suspect that Pashir did not even ask."

"Do you intend to go through with it?" asked Naraya.

Hael nodded. "Too many preparations have been made already. I have been thinking for years of sending an expedition to explore the Zone. This will accomplish some of that. It has annoyed me that a great district lies adjacent to our own land, yet we know less about it than we know of the jungles far to the south of the southern kingdoms."

"We know that it is dry," Jochim said.

"According to these maps, there are streams we can follow for almost the whole distance."

"What about the Zone dwellers?" Naraya asked. "Might they be hostile?"

"Nobody knows," Hael said. "Dwellers in a dry land are apt to be jealous of their water, but I intend to take along gifts to ease our way."

"They are said"—Jochim's voice was hushed—"to employ powerful sorcery."

"If so, I want to see it," Hael said. "It will not be a bad thing, to establish relations with the Zoners. Perhaps soon we can begin trade."

Jochim snorted. "What can these desert-dwellers have that we might want?"

"It will be interesting to find out," Hael said.

The expedition began on a dim, chilly morning. Hael and a thousand Matwa riders assembled at the foot of the hill country. The rest of the force would join them as they progressed through the grasslands, until they would be six thousand strong.

His parting from Deena had been tearful but it was not the first nor, he knew, would it be the last. His sons had clamored to be allowed to go along and he had said, as fathers usually do, perhaps next time.

Before the sun was high, they were out upon the gently rolling plain. Sun-warmed and stimulated by the steady gait of his cabo, Hael felt he was breathing free for the first time in years. The everyday concerns of his life were behind him and new land lay ahead. For a while at least he was free of crowded long-houses and settling disputes for his subjects. The Zone beckoned, a land so mysterious that it lacked even a true name. Beyond lay Neva and the sea and, at the end of that . . . Gasam.

From time to time throughout the day they were joined by bands of riders who whooped and waved their weapons as they joined the main body amid a jingling of harness, pennons streaming from upraised lances, and their bronze points gleaming in the sunlight. It was good to be leading warriors again.

The great plain abounded in game: wild kagga, fat, hairy toonoo, leaping packs of curl-horn and branchhorn, dozens of other grazing and browsing species that shared the veldt with men and their tame herds. Each day of the journey, hunters rode from the main body to harvest meat. Hael had ordered that all pre-served food was to be hoarded for the lean times that lay ahead in the desert. What meat they did not consume was cut into thin strips that dangled from lances and saddles, drying in the rushing wind of their passage.

At night, there were songs and stories around the small fires. Despite the multiplicity of tribes, there was little friction. The king's presence forbade it, and, in any case, they were all in a good frame of mind. They were follow-ing the warrior's path once more.

Around their camps lurked the innumerable predators and scavengers of the plain, drawn by the smells of meat and blood: stripers with terrible, bone-crunching jaws, the smaller varieties of longneck, carrion bats, the rare great cats and the killer birds: flightless creatures with heads as big as a cabo's and powerful legs terminating in claws like hooked daggers.

Each night, as the Moon rose, Hael gazed upon her blackened, scarred face and muttered his tribe's prayer of apology, asking forgiveness of the Moon for having wounded her so. Although he had severed all other ties with the Shasinn, rejecting their beliefs and taboos, he still felt he owed this duty. Far in the past, in an age of great sorcery, men had launched the fiery spears to mutilate the Moon. The true nature of that ancient war was forgotten, and every people had a different version of the tale.

Although they were in their own land, Hael insisted on the same marching order they would use in doubtful or hostile territory. Scouts rode far ahead, to the flanks and to the rear. A strong advance guard rode ahead of the main body, but staying within sight. While on the march, there was to be no riding back and forth between units save upon orders, so that each officer knew exactly where all his men were. In past years, his followers had chafed at these strictures, considering them to be unwarriorlike. This had eased when they understood how formidable the new order made them in battle.

The army carried no heavy baggage. Some pack animals bore spare weapons or small campaigning tents, but no more than that. The riders were expected to live hard while on the march, for their mobility was their greatest strength. Relying on their bows, they had no need to come to close grips with an enemy. By avoiding close combat, they had little need of armor. Some tribes favored protective jerkins made of several layers of hide, and some wore headgear of hardened sinew. Most men carried small, round shields of hide. Hael forbade anything heavier, and in any case the majority wore no protection at all, deeming their shields to be adequate defense against enemy arrows and lances.

Hael was confident that he had created the most powerful land force in his world, a flexible instrument combining warrior bravery and enthusiasm with civilized discipline. Thus far, it had never been tested against an organized army. It was ironic, he thought, that its first test would be against a similar force, unmounted, raised by his foster-brother.

His feelings were mixed when he thought of leading his army against his former people. Shasinn society had not been kind to him, but he had good memories of the life of a young warrior in the Islands. He remembered friendships forged in the closeness of the warrior fraternity. He remembered the woman he had loved and who had betrayed him.

On the tenth day of the march they halted at the base of a low mountain range. They were now at full strength, but the boisterous confidence of previous days had turned somber. What lay before them now was unknown territory. The tribesmen ranged freely over the grassy plain, but none of them had ever ridden beyond these mountains. None had so much as ridden up their lower slopes. What lay beyond was the stuff of legends, of dark sorceries and evil spirits.

Just now, Hael was more concerned with climate than with sorcery. He studied the green grass all around him and the great clouds piled high overhead.

"Here there is grass, mostly green the year around," he observed. "Yet the desert is supposed to begin just beyond these mountains. They are not high, you will notice. Why should it be dry on the other side?"

"Because the land lies under a curse," said Bamian, one of his Amsi chiefs. "The spirit-man of my tribe says that the Moon cursed that place because it was from that land that the giants of old launched the fiery spears."

"As good an explanation as any, until we see the place," Hael said. "We camp here today. See that the cabos are well watered. Then I want every man to range over the nearby plain and cut as much grass as he can load onto his mounts. We have no idea what sort of forage we may find on the other side, and I want to be prepared."

These orders were relayed and the warriors set to work. Most of them had a great dislike of anything that resembled manual labor, but they were willing to do anything that involved the care of cabos, however menial the task might seem. Each warrior carried among his gear a sickle made of wood, the inner curve of its edge inlaid with razor-edged chips of flint. Soon the men were scattered over the plain, gathering armloads of the long grass, stooping to shear it close to the ground, and binding each armload with a few strands of the grass twisted into a cord. At home, such work was carried out by women, but men expected to endure hardships while on campaign.

Jochim rode up to Hael, who was surveying the unusual scene. The Matwa was almost invisible behind the bundles of grass fastened to the front of his saddle.

"It was worth riding all this way just to see Amsi doing work," he said. "It is a good thing their womenfolk can't see them. Consider it a tribute to their loyalty to you."

Hael smiled. "It is a tribute to their horror of walking. They know that starving cabos carry no warriors, and it is bad enough being set afoot in their own land. Where we are going, these animals are all that will keep us alive."

When the forage was gathered, Hael deemed that there was enough daylight left to make a start into the mountains. The scouts had located a path that ascended toward a notch in the mountain wall. It was small and ancient, but it had seen use in the past. Whether human travelers or migrating game had used it was unclear. It paralleled a narrow stream that ran along a rocky bottom, its music the only sound to be heard in the steep, craggy land.

Darkness overtook them while they were still well below the crest, and Hael ordered a halt. They would camp as best they might where they were, making fires from the wood of stunted bushes and trees that grew sparsely in the thin soil, letting the cabos graze on whatever grass was to be found.

It was a strange land, and Hael could feel no welcome from its crabbed spirits. In the fading light of dusk he could see a strange phenomenon. Here on the northern side of the mountains, the clouds piled into huge, cottony towers, but there they stopped as if at a wall. To the south, the sky was clear. This was a mystery, and it made him apprehensive.

All around the men bedded down for an uneasy sleep, each man with his best cabo picketed near. They did not like this place, and wanted to be able to leave it at short notice. There was no singing at the low fires this night.

Despite the general air of foreboding, the night passed without incident. All the men were up and mounted well before daylight, anxious to be away as soon as possible. As daylight grew, the long column picked up speed, although the terrain never permitted more than a careful trot, and more often a walk only. At a shout and clamor from the advance scouts, Hael rode ahead to see what they had found.

The small knot of warriors milled in the notch of the mountain crest, pointing at things surrounding them. Hael rode up to them and stared in wonderment. The notch may have begun as a natural feature of the land, but it had been greatly improved by the hand of man.

For a short distance, the path became a genuine road, its surface of cut stone as even as that of any city street. Carved in high relief from the stone of one wall of the cut stood a colossal figure of a man. It stood three times the height of a tall man, but its proportions were broad and squat, with treetrunk legs and a barrel-like body clad in a short-kilted robe. One arm hung straight at the side, the other

bent at the elbow, its hand fisted around something that had long since broken away. The
face wore a long, square beard arranged in
stylized curls, its hawk nose and lowering
brows fierce. It was topped with a high, cylin-
drical headdress circled by bands of leaves.

The wall that faced the statue was covered
with writing. It consisted of row upon row of
figures each made up of a single, vertical line
from which branched varying numbers of
straight or curved lines. There were at least a
hundred rows of this writing, the uppermost
parts perished from the crumbling of the
stone. The warriors stared upon these things
in astonishment.

"Have you ever seen the like?" asked Jochim
who, along with some other officers, had
caught up with their king.

Hael shook his head. "I saw many statues in
Neva and Omia, but none like this. I think it
must be very ancient." This statue, although
beautifully carved, was crude and brutal, while
the Nevan sculpture was, if anything, over-
refined. This had a vital forcefulness unlike
anything he had seen before.

"What does this writing say?" asked an Amsi
chief.

"I don't know."

"I thought you could read," said Jochim.

"There are many ways of writing, but I don't
know this one. I would not be surprised if no
one living can read this. Look at the weathering of that stone at top. Come on, let's see what
lies beyond." They rode through the pass, the
hoofs of the cabos clattering hollowly on the
cut stone, echoing from the high walls to ei-

ther side. What must once have been a forbidding area of crags had been reduced to a fairly easy roadway, although it was sometimes necessary to ride around or over rockfalls.

"It must have taken tremendous labor to carve this," Hael said.

"Easy for giants," Jochim answered. "That's who must have made this. Was that a giant carved in stone back there?"

"Giant, god, king, who can tell?" Hael said. "If we could read that writing, we might know."

"Perhaps it was a real giant turned to stone," said an Amsi sub-chief. "He might have been set there by magic to guard the pass."

"He let us pass without any trouble," Hael noted. "That's poor guarding, if you ask me."

"Probably knew we come in peace," said Jochim. "Or perhaps he could tell you're a king." Hael glanced aside to see if the man was mocking him. It was hard to tell with the Matwa. They considered a joke twice as funny if it was delivered with a straight face. In any case, they had little concern for supernatural things and were apt to take them lightly.

Soon they came to the mouth of the pass and looked out over the far side. The sight of the arid wasteland stretching to the horizon stunned them. It was a sere, wrinkled, brown landscape, striped here and there with niggardly bands of green, some of these widening at intervals into ragged splotches.

"This explains much," said Hael, surveying the mountainscape before them. The mountain range had appeared low from the northern side. Here it sloped away in a tremendous escarpment that descended thousands of feet to the desert floor below. Hael knew that the great differential in elevation had something to do with the way the clouds halted at the mountains as at a barrier. From below came a constant, dry wind. Broad-winged birds soared upon the upcurrent, and these were the only signs of life.

"The green means water," said Bamian. "So it is not completely dry."

"Nor completely barren," observed Jochim, "although hardly inviting."

"We're not here to settle," Hael said. "We just need to get across this land as quickly as possible."

"I'm glad we brought our own grass," said Bamian, looking out over the grim vastness.

The descent proved to be easier than it looked from the mountain crest. The paved road continued down the south side, winding across the easiest slopes and switching back frequently to keep the angle of descent tolerable. Parts of it were collapsed, but never quite impassable.

"The path on the other side must have been paved as well," Hael said as they descended. "But over the centuries the rain has destroyed it. Here the dry climate has preserved it." The listeners nodded as if they knew what he was talking about. They had no comprehension of the gulfs of time he spoke about, and none of them really believed that these were works of ordinary men.

It was not immediately apparent when they were finally off the mountain and onto the desert floor, for the ground was rolling and rocky, studded with thorny bushes. It was not quite as bare as it had looked from above, bearing frequent if sparse vegetation, but the plants were many shades of brown with only a little green showing and, here and there, occasional small but startlingly bright flowers.

Nor were fauna entirely absent. They merely lacked the size and the tremendous numbers common to the grasslands. Wherever the cabos trod, small creatures scurried from hiding and looked for new cover. Hael, fascinated as always by new animals, studied them. They were reptiles and mammals and a few flightless birds, variously patterned but always in dull, neutral colors. Most were built close to the ground and had a habit of darting a few feet, then flattening and hugging the soil, motionless. From this Hael deduced that most of the predators in these parts were the flying type, for such tactics would be little use against a predator that hunted by smell, or lurked in ambush.

"Where are the big killers?" said Bamian, looking about as if disappointed.

"Big killers need big prey," Jochim opined. "But that doesn't mean all is safe. Small creatures can be venomous."

"Nightfall will bring a different breed," Hael cautioned. "There are larger animals here, and some are killers. I can feel them. I want a heavy guard on the cabos tonight."

None questioned his assertion. They had long since learned that their king had a sense of communication with wildlife that was more than natural. Soon some of the scouts were leaning from their saddles and pointing at marks on the ground. They were tracks, but such tracks as none of them had ever seen. The creatures that had made them had thin toes that splayed at odd angles, each toe tipped with what had to be a long, hooked claw.

"What kind of animal could make such a track?" wondered an Amsi.

Even Hael found it hard to picture such a beast. It went on two feet most of the time. At intervals it would descend to a four-footed gait, but the marks made by the other feet were even stranger: double-hooked scratch marks greatly smudged, perhaps by dangling fur or fleshy appendages.

"Enough of this," Hael said. "We'll find out what it is soon enough. I want to camp by water tonight. Scouts, I want you to spread out but do not separate. Watch the game tracks and see where they travel in a straight line. Where many paths converge, there we will find a waterhole. Locate one big enough to water all our animals and ride back."

Happy to have an important task and break the routine of the march, the scouts rode off, whooping. The rest of the army paused while the last units made their slow, single-file way off the mountain so that Hael could reassemble his forces. When he was satisfied with their order, the march resumed. Strange as their surroundings were, everyone was much relieved to be off the mountain.

Before they had gone many miles, the road disappeared. It might have been built specifically to provide a mountain crossing, but Hael suspected that it had crossed the desert as well, but was long since buried beneath the sand, dirt and brush of the arid land.

Late in the afternoon the scouts returned. They had found suitable water. This turned out to be a shallow, scummy pond choked with weeds, its banks churned to mud by the feet of what probably constituted every animal for many miles around. It was determined that, by bringing the cabos to the bank in small groups, all of them could be watered without stirring the pond to undrinkable muck.

"It's nothing to make poems about," Hael said, "but water can be hard to come by on the plains, too."

Just after moonrise, a high-pitched shriek brought every man to his feet, weapons at the ready. It was a blood-curdling sound so bizarre that it froze the heart of the bravest, beginning as an ululating warble and ascending to a screech painful to the ears. Men shouted questions and gripped their spears and short-swords.

Hael shouted for silence, but it was no use. The first shriek was answered by another from a different direction. Then the screams came from, seemingly, every direction at once. Hael tried to locate the creatures, but to no avail. The panic of the men thwarted his best efforts and it was difficult to concentrate on anything with the nerve-jangling screams filling the air. With most animals, especially the larger ones, Hael could quickly pinpoint the location of an individual in the blackest night. This time it was different. Besides the tumult surrounding him, the creatures had some way of cloaking their spirits, or else their spirits glimmered but dimly, eluding him. And there were many of them, moving rapidly. That much he could detect. How did they move so swiftly at night?

"Secure the cabos!" he shouted. He could feel the panic growing among the beasts. At least that got the men to forget their own fear and run to control their mounts. Cabos in an extremity of fear tended to attack each other, so soon the warriors were fully occupied with dodging flailing hoofs and snapping teeth, all the while making crooning, soothing sounds to quiet the animals. The scene was so ridiculous that, had Hael not been distracted by his efforts to locate the marauders, he would have collapsed into laughter.

With a snap of hide rope, a cabo broke away from its picket pin and ran into the night in a blind frenzy. Instantly, the sounds changed. The shrieking halted and became a low chuckling pierced with occasional, excited whoops. Direction changed as well. Hael could tell that the creatures were no longer all around, but were massing in pursuit of the fleeing cabo. He slapped at a group of warriors nearby.

"Get your weapons and come with me! They are like stripers! They cut out one animal and chase it in a mass. Let's go!"

Amid great shouting, they set off. This was a great relief to the warriors. At least these terrifying things were now acting like a common pack-predator of their familiar plains.

"They're just some kind of scavenger," Hael shouted hopefully. "They hunt at night but they're all noise! Let's go kill them and save that cabo!" Some seized torches as they chased across the desert beneath the pale moonlight, the men after the cabo and, in between, what?

Hael heard the cabo squealing in fear, and by the sound he knew that it had stopped to turn at bay. Dimly, silvered by the pale moonlight, he could see it far ahead of him. It was surrounded by dark shapes that chuckled and whooped. He put on a burst of speed and then thought to look behind him. Abruptly, he realized that he was alone. Raised as a Shasinn warrior, he was a superb runner. The Matwa hillmen were plodding joggers, far behind him. The Amsi, raised in the saddle, could barely walk. Nothing to be done about it. He could not leave one of his beloved cabos to be killed by these night-horrors.

Another burst of long strides brought him close to the cabo. The things around it were roughly man-sized, their shape irregular and impossible to determine in the uncertain light. One whirled at his approach and he thrust his Shasinn spear. It connected with something solid but not terribly substantial. The thing emitted a trilling whistle and collapsed. Others turned. Hael could make out no details, but moonlight glistened on what looked like needle teeth. Something seemed strange, even amidst the general strangeness. Then Hael realized that he should be seeing eyes as well as teeth, but he saw none.

He could see the dark forms leaping upon the embattled cabo. The beast caught one with a horn and pitched it high. The thing whistled and made a strange, fluttering sound as it flew through the air. Hael waded in among the massed predators. With his spear in one hand, he drew his longsword with the other. Using both weapons to slash and stab, he cut down a number of them. It did not seem to make a dent in the population. They were everywhere.

Hael was ready to give up and retreat when the first of the Matwa arrived. Some had torches that illuminated the scene with a nightmare light. The creatures they were fighting resembled, if anything, dwarfs in black cloaks. Their heads were little more than bumps bristling with teeth and they had huge, pointed ears. No more could be discerned amid the chaotic action as men stabbed with spears and shortswords, swung stone-headed clubs and even laid about them with riding whips.

Minutes later, the tardy Amsi came upon the scene. One of them had the presence of mind to mount the beleaguered cabo. Beating the attackers away with a long-handled stone hammer, he rode the animal out of the mob and back toward the army's encampment.

With their prey gone and many of their number dead, the strange creatures drew back, fleeing into the outer darkness, away from the fires and the milling men. For the first time since moonrise, there was quiet.

"What were they?" said someone.

"I cannot say," Hael answered, "but let's return to the camp. Bring some of them so that we can get a look at them in daylight."

None of the men wanted to touch the horrid creatures, but they fastened ropes around a few and dragged them back. Behind them came new sounds: low, gobbling cries followed by ripping, tearing noises. There was a dense rustling. A man came up to Hael, bearing a torch. It was Jochim.

"They are eating their dead," said the Matwa disgustedly. "If they are night-haunting spirits, they're of a low order."

"Just scavengers," Hael said. "They are too weak to make clean kills. They must chase an animal to exhaustion and bring it down by sheer numbers. It is the dark and their frightful cries that make them seen terrible."

The light of the small fires was inadequate to make out any details of the attackers, so Hael ordered a heavy guard posted. All others were to sleep. The exhausted men needed no urging. The scavengers gave them no further trouble that night.

With the light of morning, they examined their trophies of the night before. Even in good light, they were so strange as to defy comprehension. They were just under man height and covered with short, gray-black fur. The small, round heads were hunched between narrow shoulders. The long, curved teeth protruded from wide mouths below flat, triangular noses made up of convoluted membranes spreading over half the face. Their eyes were mere dots flanking the nose and their ears flared around and above the head, extending into tall points.

Strange as these features were, the limbs were stranger. The lower legs were short and crooked, terminating in splayed feet with hook-clawed toes. The upper limbs were jointed almost like human arms, but were so long that, standing upright, their elbows almost touched the ground. The forearms were almost as long and ended in five-fingered hands. Three of these fingers were long and claw-tipped. The others were vestigial. Great flaps of hairy skin hung below the arms, giving the cloaked effect they had seen the night before.

They puzzled about these repellent creatures for some time. It was an Amsi, a young warrior on his first campaign, who supplied the answer.

"They are bats," he said, "just big bats without wings." This was argued amid much exclamation.

"He is right," said Hael. "See, these flaps of skin must once have been wings. They are blind, so they hunt at night."

"Who ever heard of a walking bat?" someone asked.

"Why not?' Hael asked in return. "There are flightless birds, and flying lizards. There are warm-blooded fur-bearers that swim as well as fish. Why not ground-dwelling bats?"

Jochim shrugged. "The sort that fly are strange enough. I think we'll see even odder things as we go farther into this accursed land."

They mounted and began the day's march. Hael planned to travel south before swinging west toward Neva. The central and western parts of the Zone were much better covered in the maps Choula had sent him. Not that they were going to be all that helpful even so. The information in them was mostly over two hundred years old, so much might have changed in the interim. What he needed more than anything else was information about water and grazing, and there was very little of that in the maps he was sent. A native guide would be helpful.

He looked around. In land as low as this, a

mounted man could see for a great distance. Unlike his men, he did not find the desert oppressive. Land was land, and each place had its own spirits. He would learn this place and master it, as he had his island, the sea, the coastal plain and the grasslands and the hill country. Unlike other men, he felt that he had no limits.

EIGHT

"It is still too early, my king," said the admiral. He stood beside King Pashir on the great naval wharf of Kasin. A driving, wind-blown rain made visibility limited. The hills sloped up from the huge harbor, but among them the king could not see his palace, which was easily visible on a clear day.

They were at the northern end of the harbor, where the wharf jutted from a circular, man-made pool surrounded by roofed docks where the fleet of Neva waited out the stormy season. When time came to sail, the ships would be rowed to this wharf to take on stores.

The two men were sheltered from the rain by a canopy borne by slaves. The king gazed seaward. Past the mouth of the harbor he could see the craggy headland called Point Shipwreck. Just off the point, on a small island, stood the great lighthouse of Perwin, the tallest structure in the world. During the sailing season, slaves toiled up a stairway on the sheer, polished-stone exterior carrying baskets of oil-rich fistnuts to burn in the huge fire basket at the tower's apex. That basket had been cold since the end of the sailing season.

"The pirate Gasam does not think the season too early," Pashir said. "My spies report that he is already bringing across boatloads of warriors from the Islands."

"Then he will lose many, Sire," the admiral assured him. The admiral's name was Hanu, a squat, weather-beaten man who looked much like the stanchions to which ships were roped when at dock. Like most of Neva's senior naval officers, he had spent much of his life as a merchant skipper, learning every island and every stretch of coastland known to his nation. Unlike army positions, naval commands could not be handed out on a basis of birth or court influence. Seamanship had to be learned from early youth and honed by years at sea, both as sailor and as commander.

"That is not what I hear. He has stopped using merchant ships to transport his men. They are coming in great canoes with out-riggers. They have light masts and sails so they aren't top-heavy. At sign of a storm, they take down the mast and half the warriors paddle while the other half bail."

The admiral rubbed his bearded jaw. "It is a rough way to travel, but such boats would be unlikely to sink."

"We have already learned that the barbarians do not shrink from bold enterprises." The king thought a while, tapping his leg with a riding crop. "Admiral, summon the harbormaster. Order him to kindle the fire in the lighthouse." This was the signal that the sailing season had officially commenced.

The phlegmatic seaman all but gasped. "Sire, it is more than a month early!"

"No skipper will be forced to put to sea any earlier than he desires," the king said. "But all other preparations must begin now. All sailors and officers of the fleet are to assemble at the naval barracks. The ships are to be outfitted and victualed and ready to sail within fifteen days. In the first clear weather, we sail north to blockade Floria."

"As my king commands," said the admiral. He left the shelter of the canopy and began to bellow orders. Soon the sound of drums and gongs reverberated throughout the naval harbor.

In the afternoon the rains stopped and the skies cleared, as happened almost every day at this time of year. Anything else would have been a startling break in routine. Princess Shazad and her ladies and slave women took advantage of the clearing to move from the musty interior of the palace onto one of the broad terraces overlooking the city. Young girls went out first to towel the stone furniture dry and spread cushions, while gardeners meticulously combed the flower-boxes, pruning away dead or wilted plants that might offend the eyes of the highborn. The slave women came out bearing trays of refreshments, armed with shades, fans and flywhisks. Last of all came Shazad and her ladies.

The princess was dressed in clothes deemed suitable for afternoon in the season of storms. Her billowy pantaloons were pearl-gray, the color of the storm god. Her close-fitting bodice was pale blue shot with streaks of white, the colors prescribed by ancient law. The pearls sewn upon her slippers and strung through her black hair were likewise required as semi-formal wear by ladies of her station. Her high-born attendants were similarly dressed, with minor variations proper to rank and precedence.

The ladies seated themselves at the marble benches and chairs and musicians on a balcony above began an afternoon melody on harp and flute. The women made court gossip, speaking of affairs and intrigues, marriages and appointments. Always they kept an eye and an ear ready for any signal from the princess, but she seemed little inclined to participate. She had been greatly abstracted of late.

Shazad toyed with a platter of sweetmeats but she had little appetite. Indeed, now that she considered it, all her appetites seemed to be in abeyance. Ordinarily her tastes were varied. In the past she had loved these frivolous sessions in which the court women plotted and intrigued as if for the spoils of empire. She had spent her mornings with her cabos and her evenings with whatever man had most recently taken her fancy. She had presided as priestess over great state ceremonies in the sanctioned temples, and the darker side of her personality had been sated by her indulgences in the forbidden rites of the black cults. Very little was forbidden to a woman of her rank, and she had pursued her pleasures almost without thought.

The greater part of this now seemed tedious to her. She had had a taste of real power, and everything else seemed insipid. She had seen men struggle and die in a battle that might have destroyed a kingdom, and such a spectacle made all others meaningless. Especially she had the knowledge that it had been her own actions that had prevented the disaster in the field from becoming a catastrophe in the capital. Since then, though, her father had taken little advantage of her growing skills, a thing she resented.

He was immersed in his preparations for the coming war with Gasam. At first he had allowed her to attend some of the planning and strategy councils he had held with his nobles and military commanders. Immediately she had seen that these men resented a mere woman at their deliberations; especially, although none had voiced it, a princess who was rumored to be a devotee of forbidden practices. Her father seemed to need the support of these men rather than hers, and he had ceased bringing her to councils. She had not even seen him in several days.

Her correspondence with Queen Larissa had become a fascinating game. The woman was untaught and naive, but what she lacked in education and polish she more than made up in sheer barbaric vigor. Like her husband. In truth, it was Gasam who fascinated Shazad. She had not gotten over the effect the man had had on her when she had seen him, briefly, at the parley before the battle. Sometimes she felt that he had placed a spell upon her, that she lay under some kind of enchantment.

Her father had seemed to her all that a king should be. He was strong, wise, ruthless when necessary. He had always been loving and affectionate toward her, and was deeply suspicious and distrustful of all others. This, too, seemed kingly. He had unsurped the throne, but she knew that what he had done was correct. The old king had been unfit and only her father had the strength and the ability to seize the throne and to reign as a true monarch. She had always thought of him as a king, even when she was a little girl and he was only a duke among many others.

Gasam was different. He was a barbarian, a force of nature as mindlessly powerful as an earthquake. He was out to conquer the world because it seemed unnatural to him that any land or people should exist save beneath his spear. Compared with his youthful power even the father she worshiped seemed dim and frail.

And Gasam was beautiful. She now knew that she had never understood human beauty until she had seen the Shasinn. They were the most beautiful people on earth. Who would have dreamed that they were also the fiercest warriors? When Gasam had looked at her, she had felt a shock that had begun at her loins and radiated to her scalp and toes and fingertips. She had begun experimenting with men as soon as she was physically capable, and they had never been more than an amusement for her. She made use of them and dismissed them as soon as they began to bore her. She had never thought she might surrender to one, until she had seen Gasam. And if he was so beautiful, what must his queen be like?

One of the court ladies gasped, rose from her seat and rushed to the parapet surrounding the terrace.

"What is it?" asked Shazad, startled from her reverie.

"Look!" the woman said, pointing to something far away. "The lighthouse!"

Now all were on their feet, high-born and low, free and slave, crowding the rail. "It can't be," someone said. "A reflection. Perhaps the bronze fire basket is being polished."

"The sun is too far west for that," said Shazad. Then, unmistakably, a thin column of smoke rose above the glimmer. "By all the gods!" Shazad said. "The sailing season has begun!"

"Impossible!" said a court lady who was also a priestess of the sea god. "The temple priests have not yet determined . . . it . . . . it is still far too early! How can this happen?"

"Only my father the king has that authority," Shazad said grimly. She was furious that he had said nothing to her about this.

One of the women wailed, "Now we will all have to go home and change clothes, and all of my spring garments are packed away!"

"I've put on weight," said another, "as I do each stormy season. None of my spring clothes will fit! I'll have my seamstresses working day and night. It will be days before I can appear at court or in public!"

Shazad felt as if all her blood vessels would burst and she would drop dead of apoplexy. Something momentous and unprecedented had taken place, and all these women could think of was their clothes. She longed to go back to her chamber, get one of her whips, and begin flailing away at them. She knew she had to calm herself. These were important ladies who could do her great harm. To control herself, she concentrated on the musicians, who had paused in their playing. Now they started again, using a different tune. She recognized it as spring afternoon music. When she knew she could speak without screaming, she addressed her little court.

"Yes, I think you should all retire home and see to your attire. This is undoubtedly a part of my father's military preparations. He wants to take the fleet north against the pirates at the earliest possible date. Lighting the fire in the tower of Perwin is the ancient signal to summon the fleet, that is all. The boatswains will be dragging drunken sailors from their taverns now, and the officers will be summoned from their country estates. In time of war the king has no need to consult with the priests to order this."

There was relieved chatter at this announcement, as if the very foundations of their world had been shaken by the change of routine, and her words had soothed them. For the first time an upsetting thought occurred to Shazad: *Perhaps, if we have grown so decadent, we deserve to be conquered by barbarians.*

When her ladies were gone, Shazad dismissed most of her other attendants and went to her chambers accompanied only by a few body slaves. She called for her riding clothes and sent a runner to the stables with orders to have one of her mounts saddled and brought to the palace. She was in no mood to amble through the city streets at the pace of a quartet of matched litter slaves, pushing their way through thronged paths and slipping on garbage.

The slaves undressed her and blotted the elaborate cosmetics from her face. Carefully they untwined the strings of pearls that bound her hair and brushed it out into a flowing mane while she stepped into her undergarments. Next came her tunic with billowing sleeves, her short leather vest and brief trousers. Last of all she sat as slaves drew on her thigh-length boots of soft leather with the elaborate laces that fastened at the sides.

"I'll wager Queen Larissa doesn't have to go through all this," she muttered to Tiwala, the closest of her body slaves. "She rises in the morning, puts on a scrap of cloth, and is ready for the day. By all accounts, there are some days when she doesn't bother with the scrap of cloth."

"Any slave or peasant woman can say the same, Mistress," the woman reminded her.

"Yes, but Larissa is a true queen. She needs no material sign of her rank. She can go clothed only in her beauty because all the world goes in terror of her. Any slight to her merits results in death and her every wish is instantly obeyed. That is true queenship."

"Those people are savages, Mistress," maintained the slave woman, "just usurping pirates. They are not true royalty."

Shazad knew better. All royal houses began with bandits, pirates, savages who were strong enough to conquer and hold. Only in later years, when their descendants became civilized and yearned for respectability, did the priests make up genealogies for them, tracing their ancestry to the gods. The founders of the great royal house of Neva had no doubt been barbarians as primitive and vital as these Shasinn. She hoped so.

When her mount arrived she stormed out of the palace and down the front steps, leaping into the saddle and clearing the mob of servitors out of her way with her whip. She was in no mood to trifle this afternoon. People leaped from her path as she clattered through some of the narrower thoroughfares of the city. Riding and draft animals were forbidden in the city after the early morning hours, when the farm carts made their deliveries to the markets. Shazad ignored this law as she did most others.

She rode through the main plaza of the city, where the rain from the day's earlier storm still dripped from the temple eaves and smoke from the noon sacrifices still rose in oily skeins laden with the smell of burning flesh. Priests and commoners gaped to see the king's daughter galloping through the market, scattering livestock and citizens from her path.

When she reached the harbor, she turned north toward the great naval pool. At one pier, she could see a barge being hurriedly loaded with fistnuts to be rowed out to the lighthouse, which burned several tons of them every day during the sailing season. Other than that, the docks were idle except for the small landings where the fishing boats unloaded their catch. These small boats were taken out every day in good weather, and could usually make it back to the protected harbor at first sign of a dangerous storm. If caught by a sudden storm, the small boats had waterproof covers that could be laced in place, allowing them to ride out most blows in tolerable safety—and acute misery for those on board.

At the naval harbor, all was frenzied activity. She rode past a row of great warehouses where self-important officials supervised the unsealing of the doors. Clerks stood by with scrolls of paper, brushes and ink, preparing to take inventory. From some of the buildings which had been opened and inventoried that morning, slaves carried great coils of rope, tubs of paint and tar, bolts of heavy cloth to be sewn into sails. Everywhere there was confusion and ill-temper. Most work teams were short-handed, as if it had been impossible to summon a full complement of laborers at such short notice.

Shazad stopped and surveyed the scene. The officials had started at the south end of the row of warehouses. Six were already open. The seventh still had its seal intact. The eighth was being opened. A thin, balding official squinted at the pottery disk that sealed the doors. It bore the mark of the royal house and completely covered the latch that held the doors together.

"Warehouse Eight," the official called, as a scribe made swift marks on a parchment. "The royal seal has been examined by the public accounting office and found to be intact."

A fat, oily man who reminded Shazad of a high priest stepped forward. "Break the seal!" he intoned. His voice and beard stubble, at least, proclaimed that he still had his masculine equipment. A public slave stepped to the door and smashed the seal with a single blow of a mallet. The doors swung wide and a group of scribes and slaves went in for the inventory. Shazad walked her cabo over to the fat man's side. He started, saw who she was, and bowed deeply.

"Princess! You do us too much honor." He straightened, wiping sweat from his brow with a kerchief. "I am Supervisor Quama, of the Naval Harbor Supply and Victualing Office." He made it sound like a viceregal appointment.

"What do you do here, Supervisor?" she asked.

"Things we did not expect to do for nearly another two months, my lady. Is this not a strange and busy day? Here we are taking inventory. It was quite a task, rounding up the proper officials, the marine guard required by law, the . . ."

"I can see what you are doing," she said, cutting him off, "but why do you take inventory *after* the doors have been sealed? Surely this was done before."

"Of course, Princess," he said, as if speaking to a child. "By law the seal must be examined and proclaimed to be intact by the proper official, then a second inventory is taken, and this is compared with the first one at the Admiralty Records Office."

"Compared for discrepancies, I take it? To guard against malfeasance?"

"Exactly, Princess. Of course, such a thing scarcely ever . . ."

"Why has that warehouse not been opened?"

she asked, pointing with the handle of her whip at the sealed doors of the seventh building.

Quama turned to look, as if he didn't know what she meant. He shrugged. "Oh, that is a storehouse for wine. It will not be needed until the crews are assembled and the fleet almost ready to sail."

"Open it," she ordered.

"I beg your pardon, my lady?" The supervisor looked around. The nearby officials and dockside idlers were watching with interest. "I can do no such irregular thing. These matters are subject to immutable rules of procedure."

She pointed to the lighthouse, where a tower of flame ascended toward the clouds. "Ordinary procedure has been suspended, in case you had not noticed, Supervisor! Open it!"

The man crossed his arms. "I refuse. Only my superiors . . ."

"Your superiors!" she screamed. "What do you think I am, you crawling reptile?" Her whip slashed out, drawing a line across his face. For an instant she had a glimpse of white cheekbone, then the deep channel filled with blood, which flowed like a curtain down his face and tunic. Blood flew from her lash and spattered the wall of the warehouse. A shocked silence followed. She turned to the bald official.

"Examine the seal on that warehouse!" she ordered. Followed by his scribe, the flustered bureaucrat scurried to the doors and looked over the seal. He paled a bit.

"Warehouse Seven," he called out. "The royal seal has been examined by the public accounting office. It has been tampered with."

An excited babble broke out. Shazad found a

marine officer and he popped to attention. "Arrest him," she said, pointing to the fat official. The marine officer snapped his fingers and two armored men seized Quama by the arms. She rode over to the doors. "Show me."

"See, Princess," said the bald man. "It has been broken, then repaired with wax."

She signaled to the slave with the mallet. "Break it, but save the pieces." Instead of using his mallet, the slave took the disk in both hands and twisted. It broke easily, in two pieces, which the slave put in a pouch at his side. The doors were opened, and she rode inside.

She was immediately assaulted by a stench of spilled wine. Generations of clumsy slaves had broken jars here, and the floorboards were soaked with a sticky, vinegar-smelling mess. The cabo reared at the scent, but she kept it under control. The interior was filled with row after row of tall wine jars standing in special racks. Each had two handles and a long, pointed base. They were awkward on land, but at sea the points would be thrust into the soil of the ship's ballast and would ride there securely in the roughest weather. Each was closed with a wooden plug and sealed with beeswax.

Shazad signaled for the marine officer to come to her. "Give me your sword."

He handed her the weapon and she walked her cabo to the nearest jar. It was made to hold twenty gallons. She leaned over and rapped it with the sword pommel. It rang hollowly. Taking a foot from a stirrup, she placed it against the jar and pushed. Jar and rack leaned, paused, then toppled to the floor. The jar smashed, spilling perhaps a gallon of sour lees. She rode down the first row, rapping at each jar, kicking over those that sounded hollow.

Minutes later, Shazad came out into the clean air. She stopped beside the trembling Quama, now flanked by the marines. She tossed the sword back to the marine officer. She looked at the first six warehouses, where slaves still carried out ship's stores.

"There isn't much money to be had from rope and paint and tar and ship's canvas, is there, Supervisor Quama?" The man said nothing, his bloody head hanging, his mind full of his fate. "But there is plenty in wine, isn't there? His Majesty's purchasing agents must buy good quality drink for the navy, our guardians at sea. The tavern-keepers here must be anxious to buy it from you at a no doubt advantageous rate. Most years, you would have plenty of time to refill the jars with watered slop, wine condemned by the inspectors of the vintner's guild and bought cheap. Plenty of time to hire an artisan to craft a new seal and put it in place at night. After all, in other years the priests give notice several days ahead of time when they will begin the new sailing season and order the lighthouse fire to be kindled. But not this year!" The snap of her last words was as shocking as the blow of her whip.

She turned to the marines. "Bring him along, and see that he does himself no harm. The whole city must witness his execution. Watch him closely near the water. If he drowns himself, you will take his place upon the cross!" Wheeling her cabo, she set off toward the warship wharf.

A great warship was tied alongside the wharf,

glistening with new paint, its hull smelling richly of fresh tar. Lines of public slaves carried stores and arms aboard: oars and rope, sheaves of arrows and javelins, dismantled catapults to be assembled aboard, stacks of round shields for the marines. Dismasted, the ship looked bare and incomplete. When it was loaded and armed, it would be rowed to the timber yard for its masts and spars, and to the sail loft for its canvas and banners. A knot of officers stood amidships. In their midst, she could see the tall form of her father. Behind her, she could hear the marines catching up with their prisoner in tow. The men amidships looked up to see what the commotion was. The king looked from his daughter to the bloodied official and back, his face filled with consternation.

Shazad saw a gangplank slanting from the wharf to the decking over the stern of the ship. Her cabo shied, its eyes rolling, but she forced it down the gangplank, flogging its rump with her coiled whip. A catwalk extended from the aftercastle to the bows between the two rowing pits. She rode along this and, finally, dismounted. The men there pulled away from her as if she bore some awful contagion. Then only the king stood before her. The anger drained from her like water when she saw the rage on his face and knew that she had overstepped her bounds.

The king snatched the whip from her suddenly numb fingers. "What is the meaning of this, Daughter? Have you assaulted a royal official? What do you mean by riding your beast onto my ship, while I am in consultation with my officers? I could have you executed for this!"

Appalled, she dropped to her knees before her father, something she only did on ceremonial occasions. On both knees, palms flat against the deck, she abased herself, pressing her cheek against his foot.

"You may kill me, Father," she gasped, "but what I have done has been for you and for the nation." The foot jerked from beneath her face, then it pressed against the back of her neck, grinding her cheek into the deck. For a terrified moment, she was sure that he would lash her to shreds with her own whip.

"Speak quickly," he said.

Swiftly the words tumbled from her, muffled by the way her jaw was pressed against the deck. When she was finished, the king looked up to the wharf, where the marines and their officer stood with their prisoner.

"It is as the princess says, Sire," said the officer. "We have the tampered seal. The empty wine jars speak for themselves."

With infinite relief, Shazad felt the foot lift from her neck. Roughly, her father seized her hair and hauled her to her feet. He addressed the marines. "Take that carrion to the prison and have the carpenter measure him for a cross." To his officers: "Resume your duties." Then he took Shazad by the arm. "You come with me." Not too ungently, he led her to the bows of the ship where they were left studiously alone.

Gradually the king's face regained its color. "I have never experienced such insolence! I could still have you crucified."

As her fear lessened, some of her anger returned. "Insolence! You are surrounded by treason, and you talk of insolence? Once you have executed all the rogues that surround you, there may not be enough timber left in the kingdom to make a cross for me!"

The king glared at her for a minute, twisting the coiled whip in his fists. Slowly the corners of his mouth quirked upward. First, he loosed some short chuckles, then he gave up and laughed aloud. All over the ship, tension relaxed. He tossed the whip to her and she caught it.

"Here. You wield it better than the Shasinn use their spears."

Peaceful rapport reestablished, she took her father's arm gently. "Father, a few months ago, you found out how slack and corrupt your army had become. Did you think the navy would be different? At least this time you have a chance to root out corruption and inefficiency and repair things *before* the battle."

He nodded. "Aye, you are right. I should have kept you by me these months. My commanders think only men are fit for military office."

Now it was her turn to laugh. "Men! Father, the tackle between their legs does not make them men if they have the hearts of eunuchs and slaves. Sometimes I think I am the only *man* in your service." She leaned close and said seriously: "I am the only one you can trust and rely on, Father. There is no other."

He sighed sadly. "Aye, that is true. What is to become of the kingdom?" He walked to the edge of the forecastle and called out to the assembled officers: "Listen to me! Henceforth, the

Princess Shazad shall be Overseer of Naval Offices for this campaign. All the gods will be no help to you if she finds you failing in your duties." The king strode down the catwalk and up a gangplank onto the wharf.

Shazad's heart exulted within her, but she kept her face as rigid as stone. She walked down the catwalk and the officers looked at her with dismay and puzzlement. She was a small woman, and she did not like having to look up at her subordinates. One of the sailors had taken her cabo's reins and stood stroking its brow. Like any sensible animal, it did not like being on board a ship. She took the reins and mounted. That felt much better. Now they were looking up at her. The extra height gave her moral ascendancy as well.

"Hear me!" she called. By now, many of the dock personnel stood on the wharf, drawn by this unexpected display. "I will have a strict accounting of everything pertaining to naval stores, not just the presence of each required item, but its condition as well. I will inspect every foot of rope, every bit of timber, every arrow, shield-strap and bowstring. I will be everywhere and I will see everything. We have plenty of time before we must sail. If I have to order a ship unloaded so that I can inspect the keel, that I shall do. Anyone who is inefficient I will dismiss. Anyone who is corrupt, I will have executed. This is the king's will!"

The officers were startled and resentful. Now that they knew she was serious, she would use reason. Men were always ready to listen to reason when they knew death was the alternative.

"Today, without authority, I discovered gross malfeasance in the very first operation that I came upon. Think what this means! Bad wine means bellyaches and discontent among the crews. But what will it mean when a catapult cable snaps during battle because a munitions inspector was too lazy to carry out his duties and discard unfit equipment? What will it mean when a storm breaks over the fleet and half the masts are made of green or rotted timber? What I discovered today was a small corruption. The greater ones can lose us a battle. I do not think that the men of our navy are at fault in this. Truly, they are the ones most at risk because of it." On the wharf and in the holds below the rowing pit, she could see men nodding at this. "But there are far more people ashore outfitting these ships than will ever sail them into battle. There are suppliers and contractors and government officials whose performance has not been subjected to scrutiny in years."

She glared about her and was gratified to see men quail before her glance. "When this fleet sails, it will be the finest ever to leave the harbor of Kasin. I will be here at first light tomorrow morning. Be prepared to answer my every question. Who is commander of the marines?"

A man in civilian clothes stepped forward. "I am, Princess Shazad. Fleet Captain Harakh at your service."

"Put a heavy guard on the storehouses tonight. I want nobody to sneak in tonight and hide evidence of wrongdoing. And be in uniform tomorrow."

"As the princess wishes," he said, bowing. He

smiled, but she could tell that it was a smile of pleasure, not of insolence. At least she had one officer who was pleased with the change in authority.

"Be ready in the morning," she said. "It is the king's will!"

She rode up the gangplank and down the wharf toward land. From behind her, she heard a ragged cheer. That was good, but she tasted bitterness knowing that the cheers would have been louder for a prince.

As she rode back to the palace, this time in a more leisurely fashion, she pondered her new task. It felt good to be back at the center of affairs, but she had many things to think about. For one thing, she knew little about naval matters. The things she had said about rope and canvas and timber had very nearly exhausted her expertise. No matter. Her life at court had taught her that no one person ever knew everything there was to know. A superior merely had to choose knowledgeable subordinates. She needed knowledgeable subordinates; but she wanted nobody connected with the navy, the court or the government in any way.

Malk. That was it. He was one of the masters of the merchant seamen's guild. She no longer remembered where she had learned of him, but someone had spoken of the skipper as a great seaman and uncommonly honest. She would need such a man. As soon as she reached the palace, she would send a runner to summon him. She felt filled with boundless energy.

The thought of the thieves and profiteers occupying offices of trust infuriated her. She could understand great evil, but not this sort of petty corruption. Very well, she would root it out—and break the imperial service to her will. This was far better than worrying about having to switch to slippers decorated with topazes instead of pearls.

NINE

They saw the pillar of smoke two days before they came within sight of its source.

At Hael's orders, they had been traveling at an easy walk. He did not want to exhaust their cabos or risk injuring them in this unfamiliar terrain. They had already learned that the desert possessed an abundance of burrowing creatures. In a land where there was so little cover or shelter from the sun, animals had to make their own. The risk of stepping in holes and breaking legs was high. There was no need for haste, Hael assured the men. They would be in Neva well before the middle of spring. The younger ones were impatient for action, but they knew better than to provoke their king.

The ground-bats had been only the first of the strange creatures they encountered. Almost as unnerving were the great serpents. These creatures, some of them fifty paces long, with bodies as big around as a cabo's, made a sluggish progress along the surface of the desert, and only roused themselves at the approach of a large creature, such as a mounted man. Even then they showed little inclination to attack. Hael suspected that they hunted at night and were half-somnolent at this time of year, like common snakes. What, he wondered, did animals so huge eat?

There was great speculation when they saw the smoke. At first it lay along the horizon like a dirty haze. As they drew nearer, they could see that the haze was high in the air, and that a column of smoke ascended to it. At first they had thought that a dwelling was burning. Then it seemed that a whole town must be afire. But by the end of the day they seemed to be little closer to it.

"A grassfire, perhaps?" said Jochim.

"There isn't enough vegetation here to support such a fire," Hael said. "Maybe we shall see tomorrow."

The next morning, when they arose, they noticed that they, their tents and their gear were dusted with a fine, powdery ash. It coated the backs of the cabos and men had to snort it from their nostrils before they could breathe easily.

"What sort of fire is that?" Bamian asked, "that it can cast its ash so far?"

"And such ash," Hael said, sifting a handful of it through his fingers. "It is more like . . . a powder, or the finest sand."

"Even fire does not behave the same in this land," Bamian said. "Best we were away from here as soon as possible."

By the time the sun began to lower that day, they could see the source of the smoke. A whole mountaintop belched smoke with a low rumbling sound they could hear from miles away. With awe they watched flames and streams of liquid fire arch from the base of the smoke and what appeared to be great rocks flung skyward as if cast by the hands of giants.

"The Smoking Mountains!" Hael said. "My maps show them far to the south of here. Perhaps this is the northernmost. They have been known to spring up from the flat earth almost overnight and grow to great mountains in a matter of months."

"Mountains should not behave like that," Jochim maintained stolidly. "Mountains are meant to be permanent. They are not supposed to be like flowers, that spring up quickly and flourish."

That night, they watched in stunned amazement as the mountain flamed and roared like a giant's forge. Men cried out and pointed whenever an especially lurid stream of liquid fire shot up, to fall back like a spray of glowing water. The air had a strange smell, but the wind kept most of the ash from them. There was little sleep to be had that night.

The morning's march left the smoking mountain behind them. More than unusual mountains, Hael was now far more interested in water. The weed-choked water holes were becoming hard to find. The men attributed this to the smoking mountain, but Hael could not see any connection. He dreaded the thought of making a dry camp.

At least the weather remained mild. Had they

been making this crossing in the middle of summer, the heat would have been terrible. The land was cut with deep channels, indicating that rain, although rare, was torrential when it came.

The second day after leaving the smoking mountain, the scouts came riding back excitedly. The heads of the cabos were drooping. The water hole the night before had been little more than a mud pit, where men had had to scoop holes in the muck to let murky water seep into them. There had been insufficient water for the beasts, and none at all for the men.

"A water hole!" shouted an Amsi scout. "And a strange one!"

Wondering what this could mean, Hael rode ahead of the advance guard. A few miles farther on, he followed the scout into a sheltered hollow where he was greeted by an utterly unexpected sight. Spread before him in the bottom of the hollow was a field of greenery, hundreds of yards in extent. Grasses and trees with strange, bushy tops proliferated everywhere. Then his cabo scented the water and he had to restrain it from breaking into a gallop.

He rode beneath the shade of the trees and smelled fragrant flowers and other things, spicy and nose-tickling. Insects buzzed up from fallen fruit. He could hear water ahead of him. Not merely flowing water, but falling water. This seemed to be an odd place to find a waterfall, even a small one.

"Here, my king, look at this," said the guide, shouldering his own cabo between two clumps of high grass. Hael followed. On the other side of the grass was the water, and at its edge Hael stopped his cabo and stared. This desert was proving to be full of wonders. It was not a water hole, but a man-made pool. It was perfectly rectangular, perhaps a hundred paces long by fifty wide. The sides were of cut stone and slanted from the level of the ground to the water several feet below. Hael guessed that this was done to prevent animals from falling in and drowning, polluting the water. The water itself was beautifully clear and Hael allowed his cabo to walk down the short slope and drink.

Even stranger than the pool was a great statue at one end. It was carved from white stone, in the form of a kneeling nude woman. On one shoulder she held a jar and from this water gushed into the pool. Her beautiful, serene face gazed out over the pool enigmatically. When his mount had drunk enough, Hael rode to the statue and studied it.

It was carved from a hard, white stone that was unlike anything he had seen since entering the desert. If it was built up of a number of stones, the joints were too finely crafted to be seen. Seen from close up, it was not perfectly smooth, but showed some pitting and weathering. How many centuries had it stood, or rather knelt there? He ran his fingers along one thigh and felt great age. It was not as brutally forceful nor as crude as the statue they had seen in the pass. Had it been made by the same people? Hael felt somehow it had not. There was no writing connected with this one, so that evidence was lacking. Why had it been put here? Was it a goddess? A spirit of the spring that poured so abundantly from the jar? Or was it just a thing of beauty, put here by people who loved beauty? He knew he would never find out, and that saddened him. This desert was full of mysteries, and he would never even encounter most of them, much less solve them.

The main body of the army arrived, and they cheered and whooped happily when they saw the pool. Hael quickly distributed orders. The cabos were to be watered. Men were to fill their waterskins from the stream that flowed from the jar. The animals could be put out to graze and fallen wood gathered for fires, but nothing was to be damaged or molested in any way. When the necessities were taken care of, those who wished to could bathe.

There were still at least two hours of daylight so Hael sent out hunting parties. With all this water, he was sure that there would be abundant game nearby. He ordered them to be careful not to harm anything that looked like it might be domestic livestock. He was surprised that he had seen no evidence of human habitation in this beautiful spot. The water and good soil would support a sizable farming community, and he was certain that farmers had been here once. Most of the trees were fruit-bearing, and it was unlikely that this was by chance.

Before long the hunting parties returned. They had found toonoo and a sort of wild curlhorn that had only two horns. The smell of roasting flesh began to drift on the desert air. A fire was built for Hael and the chiefs near the statue. Soon they were gnawing the tough meat off the bones of wild game.

Jochim lowered the rib he had been gnawing

and looked up at the statue. The firelight glowed ruddy on the undersides of the stone breasts.

"This giant is prettier than the last," he observed.

"At least she doesn't look as if she means us any harm," said an Amsi underchief. "I wasn't so sure about that one in the pass. He was something to frighten children with."

"Did men make this, my king?" asked Bamian.

"Yes. When we get to Neva you will see works of men far larger than this, although I do not think you will see anything more beautiful. The wonder is in finding it here, so far from anything else. And it seems to be abandoned. That makes little sense, since there is water and the land is fertile."

"Perhaps," Jochim said, "there is something that keeps people away from this place."

"Or," Hael said, "it may be that this place is not abandoned. The people who use it may just be away. There could be nomads who travel from one pasture and water hole to another to avoid overgrazing and ruining the land. If so, they could be back any time and may resent our presence."

Bamian laughed. "With our strength, we can stand a lot of resentment." The others laughed as well.

"Truly they would need a very large army to threaten us," Hael said. "But I wish to stay on good terms with the people here. If we meet any who claim this place, we will be courteous and offer payment. Do nothing to provoke the natives and fight only if attacked. Those are my commands." After this had sunk in, he went on.

"Our men and, more importantly, our animals, are tired. We will stay here tomorrow. Everyone, man and beast, will eat, drink and rest. On the morning after tomorrow, we resume our march."

Later, when the fires had burned low and most of the men were snoring in their blankets, Hael stood beneath the stream of water pouring from the huge stone jar. It felt wonderful to wash the dirt and sweat of travel from his body. When he felt clean, he sat on the accommodating knee of the giantess and wrung the water from his long, bronze-colored hair. On an impulse, he put on only a loincloth, picked up his spear and walked out through the vegetation and into the desert beyond. A surprised guard saluted him, but knew better than to question any of the king's odd whims.

The night air was cool on his skin, but he was inured to the severe winter of the hill country. This felt much like standing night herd-watch as a boy back on his home island. He walked for half an hour, wanting to get well away from the great mass of men and cabos.

This was a pleasure he had seldom enjoyed in recent years. Just being alone to commune with his surroundings was a great pleasure to him. When he had gone far enough, he stopped and opened up his mind and spirit to the land. Unconsciously, he adopted the characteristic stance of his people: leaning on his spear, the sole of one bare foot braced against the knee of his standing leg. Shasinn could stand thus for hours and this had given them the name of "stork people."

Gradually he began to feel the creatures near him. On the plains and in the mountains or on his island this could be an overwhelming experience, but not here. Animals were fewer here, and they were somnolent at this time of year, with many sleeping in their burrows. The great number of men had frightened many away for the duration. To his great relief, he could feel no ground-bats. They had not been troubled by the creatures since the first, hectic night.

Something impinged on his consciousness and he turned his face to the southeast. He was sure he felt something there. Then it came again: a faint, troubling sensation that was not quite animal in origin. Was it human? He seldom felt any emanation from human beings, save sometimes from very primitive men who lived in the deep forests or the high mountains in close communion with nature—people compared with whom the Matwa and Amsi had scaled the heights of civilization. This was not quite the same.

He began to walk in that direction, the stones of the desert rough beneath his bare feet. With the spear swinging rhythmically at his side, he trotted for a while, then stopped. It was still there, keeping its distance, farther away than he had thought. He wanted to go look but he knew that would be foolish. With a sigh, he turned and walked back toward the camp. This was yet another mystery, but he felt wonderful, like a man who has just removed bandages from his eyes and ears.

He reentered the camp and strode toward his tent. Some of the chiefs woke at his approach. "Something to the southeast," he said "too far to go and see tonight. I think we'll see them tomorrow. Be prepared in the morning." With that, he crawled beneath the simple shelter of his tent and rolled into a blanket. His spear stood thrust into the earth like a sentinel before the low entrance. The chiefs did not question what he had said. They all knew that Hael was not as other men. He could detect things that other men could not see. If he said there were living things beyond sight and coming their way, then it was true. It was one reason why so many disparate, warring tribes had put their squabbles aside to follow him. King Hael possessed great mystical power. These people had no gods, but they believed in a multitude of spirits. The spirits were strong in Hael.

The next morning, Hael sent scouts to the southeast. They were instructed to locate what they could, return and report. For this task, he chose men who were exceptionally reliable. At noon, some of them came back in, reporting that they could find nothing. This troubled Hael. He knew that he had felt something. It had been within a mile or two. Perhaps, he thought, they had stolen away before dawn.

During the day, men rested, cleaned and repaired clothes and gear, and tended to their mounts. They brushed the animals' glossy coats, polished or repainted their horns and renewed designs drawn on the animals' heads, limbs and bodies to protect them from baleful spirits.

The evening meal was being prepared when there was a shout from the sentries. Men frolicking in the water dashed for their clothes and weapons. Hael looked up in consternation. Where were the scouts?

"Riders come!" a sentry shouted.

"Which way?" Hael called out.

"Southeast!" the sentry called back.

"Sub-chiefs," Hael cried in a voice that carried from one end of the oasis to the other, "gather your men. Stand by, ready to mount but stay here. Chiefs, mount and gather by me." There was an orderly bustle as his commands were carried out. A young warrior brought the king's own cabo and he mounted. His bow was already strung in its case with a quiver bristling with one hundred arrows. His longsword hung at the pommel. With his spear propped upright before him, Hael began to amble slowly toward the southeastern edge of the vegetation, followed by his chiefs.

"They are below that rise, my king," said the sentry as they reached the verge of the open land. "I saw them along that ridge, then they came down its face and into a gully."

"How many?" Hael asked.

"Forty or fifty, but, my king, their mounts . . ."

"What about them?"

"Look!" one of the chiefs shouted, pointing. The riders had come out of the gully and over the crest of the small rise, perhaps two hundred paces from the little band of chiefs. They wore billowing robes and carried long lances. These details were of minor interest to the watchers. Their mounts had two legs.

"What are they?" said Jochim. "Killer birds? Dusters?" The killer birds were terrible creatures, the most ferocious of the grassland predators. Dusters were relatives, just as large and likewise flightless, but herbivorous.

"They are a breed I've never seen," Hael said. "And I have never heard of men riding birds. Cabos, nusks and humpers I have seen used as mounts, but never birds." Fascinated, he watched the approaching men. At least, he assumed they were men. Their shape was not easy to determine beneath the robes, which were of the colors of the desert: gray, dun, tan and black. As they drew nearer he saw that the robes covered most of their faces as well. The birds were of the same colors, and they moved with a strange, loping gait, heads bobbing forward and back with every stride. If they were not killer birds, they were something very near, with narrower beaks and eyes set in flaring ridges of bone. The legs were neither as stout as a killer bird's, nor as slender as a duster's. They were tipped with vicious talons and looked capable of great bursts of speed.

They were in no particular formation, although a rider on a black bird rode several lengths in front and the others seemed to be following him. Abruptly, without any signal being passed that Hael could detect, all the birds halted at once. It was an eerie sight, as if all the birds possessed a single brain. The lead rider came a few paces forward and stopped. The others remained where they were.

"I will go out and speak with him," Hael said. "Come with me, and halt at my command. I will go on alone to confer with him."

They started out at an easy walk. The bird-riders had halted a hundred paces from the oasis. Behind Hael and his chiefs, warriors came to the edge of the vegetation, making no demonstration but with bows held casually at their sides, arrows nocked. Hael knew that, if the riders should treacherously attack him during a peaceful parley, not a man or bird of them would be alive within five seconds of the first hostile move. They might believe themselves safe, but they had undoubtedly never seen such bows as his men carried, nor such archers. One hundred paces was beginner's range for Hael's army.

"Stop here," Hael said, still thirty paces from the lead rider. His chiefs halted and he rode on. He stopped less than three paces from the rider. His cabo did not like the bird, but it made no attempt to fight Hael's control. The bird-rider sat as still as the statue at the pool, then he jammed his lance into the ground by its butt-spike and it stood swaying, its long, ribbonlike pennons fluttering in the light breeze. Hael did the same with his much shorter spear. The man spoke a few words, then repeated them. On the repetition, Hael recognized the language as a dialect of Southern, which was a language he understood fairly well.

"Who are you?" the man asked. His head-dress covered all but his eyes.

"I am King Hael."

"You come from the north. Men have never come from the north. Where is your home?"

Hael gestured behind him. "Beyond the mountain. The grasslands of the high plains, and the hill country beyond."

"You came through the pass? You passed by the Guardian? That is forbidden."

"No one forbade us," Hael said, "and the Guardian did nothing to stop us." He remembered, though, how uneasy they had all felt the night before on the mountain, before they had even seen the Guardian. If it had some ancient power to guard the pass against intrusion, perhaps some bit of it remained.

"Why do you come here?"

"We cross the desert on our way to Neva," Hael said patiently. "We mean you no harm and you have nothing to fear from us. Now, my friend, who are you?"

"I am Joz." The first sound of the name was a guttural not used in any dialect Hael knew. "We are the Webba, this is our country, and that is our oasis. You and your animals drink our water."

"For which we are most grateful, I assure you," Hael said. "We are a great-hearted and generous people. We wish to be friends with everyone. We did not know whose water this was. In the grasslands, water holes may be freely used by anyone, as long as they are left in good condition, and livestock do not overgraze the grass."

"This is no common water hole," Joz asserted. "This was made for us by a goddess, and given by her to our ancestors."

"And a generous deity she was. Did I not mention that we are generous as well? I have brought gifts for those who wish to be our friends. Your spring is abundant and we and our cabos have not lowered the level of the pool one inch. The land is fertile, and the grass eaten by our animals will grow back before another turning of the moon. This land is unknown to us. Guides would be very useful. Friends might provide such guides." Hael judged these odd people to be nomads, and such people sometimes were offended by talk of "payment," thinking that this reduced them to the status of lowly workers or merchants. On the other hand, they seldom had objection to "gifts."

"You speak like an honorable man," Joz said. "I will speak with the goddess to see if all is well. Let us ride to the pool." Joz retrieved his lance and Hael took his own spear, wheeling his mount so that the two rode stirrup to stirrup. At least Hael thought so until he glanced down and noticed that Joz rode without stirrups, his bare brown feet peeking out from beneath his dun-colored robe and pressing against his bird's black-feathered side, just behind the stubby, useless wings. Behind them, the other birds moved at the same time as Joz's, each one stepping off with its right foot at exactly the same instant. The sight made the hair at Hael's nape prickle.

"What will you ask the goddess, if I may inquire?"

"Whether you have mistreated her. Whether she approves of you partaking of her water and grass and the fruits of her trees."

"And if she doesn't like us?" Hael asked.

"Then we will have to kill you all."

Hael carefully refrained from laughing. How fifty riders armed with lances, however oddly mounted, were going to kill six thousand warriors armed with powerful bows implied tremendous confidence, if nothing else. And despite his amusement, the way those birds behaved made Hael reluctant to risk hostilities with these people.

As they passed into the trees, the Webba began a high-pitched, melodious chant. Hael tried to understand the words, but he could not. Either they were using a different language or they were chanting nonsense syllables. At the pool, the birds lined up at the edge of the water, standing at intervals as precise as if they had been placed by a drillmaster. As one bird, they lowered their heads and drank.

Hael's warriors gathered around, intrigued by the spectacle. Worried lest the great press of men should upset the Webba or their mounts, Hael ordered his officers to move their men back. Unlike the cabos, the birds could not swallow with their heads down. Instead, each drew in a beakful, then threw back its head and swallowed noisily.

When the birds had drunk, Joz dismounted and strode to the statue. Dismounted, he was a small man, Hael was surprised to note. Having noticed that, he saw that they were all small people. They looked so imposing on birdback that their stature was not immediately apparent.

Joz walked to the statue and chanted something, this time too low to hear, with palms upraised. Then he pressed his palms and face against the stone thigh, and remained in that posture for several minutes. At length, he straightened and called an order to his followers, too rapidly spoken for Hael to interpret. The riders all dismounted. Most took cups from inside their robes and dipped up water, drinking as thirstily as the birds.

The birds themselves ceased to behave with the machinelike unity they had displayed while ridden. They began to walk about the clearing, their heads bobbing, making gravelly squawks. One found a dusty patch of ground, lay down and rolled in it vigorously.

"The goddess approves," Joz reported. "She says you behaved respectfully, and did not abuse her hospitality. You are welcome to our spring."

"Then please do me the honor of joining me and my chiefs for a meal. We were about to eat when the sentries reported your arrival."

"I join you most gladly. Commanders!" Four of his followers strode to his side. "These are my leaders-of-ten. They will join us, if you will permit."

"They are most welcome. Your other men may make free of any of our fires. My men will share everything." They walked to the king's fire and sat. Joz and his chiefs carefully covered their crossed legs with their robes.

"You came from the southeast," Hael said. "I had scouts out in that quarter. How were you able to avoid detection?"

"When we do not wish to be seen, we ride in the gullies. Our birds can run crouched very low. I will show you. Do you have no riding-fowl in your land?"

"None. We have some birds, a few of them as large as yours, but no one has ever mastered riding them. The killer birds are too vicious and dusters are not strong enough. Do your people not ride cabos?"

"It would not be fitting," Joz said. "South of

here, people ride cabos and humpers, but they are lesser people."

"What do your birds eat?" Hael asked. "I notice they are not going for the fallen fruit and those beaks look more suited for a livelier diet."

"They are meat eaters. We hunt together and share the kill."

At that moment the roasted game was brought to the king's fire and serious talk was halted while the men ate. One of Joz's men brought a broad leaf piled with fruit from the trees of the oasis. The grasslanders had been reluctant to experiment with these, although many of the fruits looked luscious. It was always safe to eat game if it was properly cooked, but a man never knew what might happen if he ate an unfamiliar plant. With the example of the Webba, they tried the fruits and found that they liked most of them. This was a welcome variation in diet, especially for the hill-dwelling Matwa who, unlike the Amsi, grew much of their own food. The Webba fed their birds with raw, gamy meat from bags carried by each rider.

When appetite was satisfied, the serious discussion began.

"Why do you come across the mountains?" asked Joz, "and cross the desert, and fare to faraway Neva, where the folk live packed into little chambers confined by walls, as if they hate the sun and the sky and the free wind?"

"A brother king has asked my assistance. He is at war and, although he has a powerful army, he lacks fine mounted archers like my men. We ride to his aid."

"A war!" said Joz enthusiastically. "Will there be raiding and looting?"

"Undoubtedly," Hael assured him. "The civilized kingdoms like to pretend that they do not make war that way, but in truth they are just more organized about it. Would you and your men like to accompany us? I am sure that my brother king, Pashir of Neva, would esteem such ... such *unusual* allies. And I can absolutely guarantee that the people we are going to fight would be struck with terror to see men charging down upon them mounted on killer birds. That is what the birds would look like at first."

Joz sighed. "Alas, my friend, it is not to be. Our birds will not leave their desert home. Many times we have tried to take them raiding in the jungles of the south or the farmlands to the east, but they balk and become sulky before they are far from the desert, and we must bring them back. Their spirits dwell here. Many thanks, though, for your kind invitation." He gazed into the distance, as if at fondly remembered sights of murder and rapine.

"How unfortunate," Hael said. Now that he had established goodwill, he decided it was time to negotiate a little business. "In order to reach Neva in time to take part in the war, our way would be greatly facilitated by reliable guides. I have only written accounts of this country, long out of date and of doubtful worth."

Joz nodded. "That would be wise. Only those native to this desert know where the water is, and this great mass of men and beasts must have much water every day."

"Very true. Also it would be a great saving in time if we had someone to go ahead of us to speak to such towns and peoples as may be in our path, assuring them of our peaceful intentions and negotiating for such supplies as we may."

Joz nodded wisely and stroked his chin. He had lowered his veil slightly to eat, revealing a dark face with small, precise features. A diminutive beard formed a circular patch on his chin. The beard was startlingly red in color.

"That is sensible. With our company, you would meet with no resistance from the people in your path. All fear the Webba."

Hael forbore to point out that anyone who might be overawed by fifty bird-mounted warriors would surely be cautious about attacking six thousand on cabos.

"Then," Hael said, "we shall have nothing to fear. Will you accompany us, then?"

"Well, we must rejoin our people, who range far to the south of here, and it might be pleasant to wend our way thither in company. Still . . ." He paused elaborately. "We had wished to hunt this land for some time longer, while the game is abundant."

"There is no need to rush your decision," Hael said. "We still have all of this most pleasant evening, at this lovely pool given to your ancestors by your equally lovely goddess. And now, I have some gifts I think will please you." At his command, several saddlebags were brought. After sorting through them, Hael brought out some finely crafted ornaments of silver and several coils of copper wire. He had brought coined money but wished to save that for more civilized locales, and metal was prized by everyone. Joz accepted the gifts as if they were no more than a polite token of gratitude for the free use of his oasis, and he was only showing good manners by accepting them and praising the giver. But the next morning, the fifty bird-riders accompanied King Hael's army southward.

TEN

As Princess Shazad boarded the *Moonglow*, the sailing master, the crew and the marines bowed deeply. As was her practice when visiting the docks, she wore her riding outfit as most appropriate for her newly active life. There was no feminine equivalent for a military uniform, and she feared she would look ludicrous if she tried to wear one. Now that she had established the respect of these men, she could not afford to be laughed at.

The *Moonglow* had been her personal yacht, a pleasure boat suitable for fine-weather cruises and floating parties. She had ordered it completely renovated and rerigged as a light naval cutter. Most of its luxurious appointments had been torn out and replaced by warlike simplicity. Her elaborate bedchamber had been cut away to lower the little ship's profile and make it more seaworthy. In its place, she now had a tiny, spare cabin. Benches for rowers had been installed, and tholes now lined the bulwarks. The ship was painted green and yellow, the colors of the Nevan navy. Like her father's flagship, the *War Dragon*, *Moonglow*'s sails were striped red and white, the colors of the royal family.

She returned the salutes and acknowledged the cheers of the crowd gathered along the piers and in the great plaza just behind the merchant docks. For weeks now, on every day when the weather was good, people had been coming to the waterfront to see the new fleet taking shape. The navy had always been the pride of Kasin, and the citizenry took a proprietary interest in it. They knew that the amazing princess had overseen its restoration and she was now, after her father, the most popular person in the kingdom.

She had seen to it that the people knew who was responsible for this naval renaissance by sending her agents out into the city to spread the story. Everywhere, in taverns and markets, in gaming-houses and brothels, had been spread the story of the princess who was more capable than any nobleman, who had taken the decrepit navy in hand and restored it to its former glory. She had been the scourge of evil and corruption.

By glancing at the mole that formed a water-break for the merchant harbor all could see the results of that scourging: row upon row of crosses. Each bore the body of a man who had once held a position of trust. Her investigations had been ruthless and thorough, and they had uncovered incredible corruption, waste and inefficiency at every level in the military, the civil administration, and civilian contractors. Unlike the admirals and high noblemen who customarily oversaw these warlike matters, she did not consider this combination of clerical and police work beneath her; and corruption and inefficiency had been the least of it. She had uncovered espionage and treason. She had seized the private papers of high ministers and petty bureaucrats alike, and had found great and damning evidence.

Not all of it had been so unpleasant. On one memorable day, she had had every rower in the navy lined up at the docks, rank upon rank of them, all naked and shivering on an uncommonly cool day. She had worked her way down each rank, examining every one. She had poked and prodded, pinched and tested for firmness and muscle tone. She had rejected and dismissed any that showed sign of weakness or disability. She had checked for signs of rupture, piles and even more embarrassing afflictions. When she had examined them all, she chose the forty handsomest as rowers for *Moonglow.*

Now, the day before sailing, she was satisfied that the nation's navy was the best, in manpower and material, that it had ever been. About its leadership she was not so sure. That was one area that was not under her control.

She did not think that she had acted underhandedly in personally spreading word of her doings, in building her own reputation among the populace. In the first place, she felt she deserved it. She was spreading no falsehoods, and the time might come when she would need popular support. Mere high birth was not enough for a woman, as it was for a man. She also had her previous reputation to dispel. For years she had been known only for her numerous debaucheries and forbidden religious practices. A few years before, the nation had been swept by the titillating rumor that she had poisoned her husband. She had not, but she made no effort to prove her innocence. The suspicion kept noblemen seeking an alliance with her father from suing for her hand. Another marriage had been the last thing she had wanted. Now she found that her eligible widowhood could be a useful political tool.

"Your orders, Princess?" said the sailing master.

"A last turn around the harbor, Master Saan," she ordered.

To the music of a flute, the rowers went through their oar drill: an intricate and graceful ceremony that over the centuries had been refined into a dancelike exercise in which each man took his oar from its rack around one of the masts and took his place standing by his bench. Then, in unison, the rowers sat, slid their oars outboard along the tholes and feathered them with a single, precise turning of the wrist.

The fluting changed pitch and rhythm and the oars dipped and rose, dipped and rose, and *Moonglow* backed away from the pier. At an especially complex series of notes played on both pipes of the flute, the rowers on one side lowered their oars into the water and held them there unmoving while those on the other side stroked vigorously. *Moonglow* rotated on an axis defined by its mainmast, its small, decorative ram making a perfect half circle. The rhythm changed again and the ship sped across the harbor. The crowd ashore applauded to see the maneuver performed so expertly.

Shazad seated herself beneath the awning erected in the stern of the ship and had *Moonglow* rowed completely around the fleet, which now lay at anchor within the harbor. After her circuit, she rowed between the ships, examining each with a critical and, now, a knowledgeable eye. Guildmaster Malk had been an invaluable teacher and assistant. He had taught her how to judge a ship's trim, so that now she could tell, just by the way it sat in the water, whether a matter of just a few hundred pounds had been improperly stowed. He had taught her the telltale signs of poor caulking and improper stepping of the masts.

The two of them had examined all the stores to be taken on this voyage, and he had brought his years of experience to picking the best ropes, tackle, rations and all other things necessary to keeping the fleet at sea. He had personally supervised the refitting of *Moonglow* and had picked its crew (except for the rowers).

Moonglow and its mission had been the cause of stormy arguments between Shazad and her father.

"I must sail with the fleet, Father!" she had said. "I have saved it from the sink of ineptitude into which it had fallen. I have restored it. It is *my* fleet! And I must sail with it into battle."

Pashir had turned scarlet and she feared he might have a seizure, but she had remained stubborn. "*Your* fleet!" he had roared. "*I* am king of Neva. The land and all its people *and* its navy are mine. Just because I have allowed you to be a glorified clerk . . ."

"Clerk!" she had screamed. "What kind of clerk takes up crucifixion as a pastime? The sailors all love me now, and it will put spirit in them to know I am there."

Her father had calmed a little. "You are a woman, my daughter, and I do not want you to take the risks of battle."

She smiled and stroked his arm. "Father, I know you are concerned for me, but consider: In battle, *Moonglow* will stay well away from the fighting. I am not foolish enough to sail a converted yacht in among warships. You will be far more at risk in your flagship since you insist on leading personally. If you are lost, I dare not return to Kasin, with as many enemies as I have made these last weeks. I might as well have a head start on pursuit."

In the end, he had acquiesced. In spite of her elation, this, too, was evidence that her father was failing. Once he would have either said yes or else have thrashed her, but he would not have argued. It was just as well, she thought, that she was going to accompany the fleet. She might well be needed.

Now, as she gave the ships her final inspection, she felt a pride and an exhilaration such as she had never known before. Her former pleasures and interests now seemed to her puerile, childish. This mass of ships, men and armament represented real power, and she now knew that power was the only thing in the world worth having, worth scheming and fighting for. She now understood what drove Gasam.

It was a glorious morning for sailing. From every rooftop and tower in the city, great banners hung and flapped in the breeze. Columns of smoke rose from every temple, where special sacrifices had been decreed for the success and safety of the fleet. Gongs boomed and on the shore bands of musicians played horns and drums, and were echoed by the trumpeters and drummers on the ships.

The whole city and half the surrounding countryside had gathered along the quays to see off the fleet, which was going north to retrieve the honor of the kingdom. There were songs and loud, communal prayers invoking the sea god and the winds. An impromptu fair roared up and down the waterfront, with vendors, prostitutes and street entertainers doing a business unprecedented for a date so early in the year. The hundreds of prostitutes made assignations for the evening. Silence came over the crowd as a huge drum began to boom on the flagship.

Like the multitudinous legs of a centipede, the long oars slid out from the sides of the great ships on three levels: the topmost set in tholes and the two lower levels thrust through holes in the sides. The oars on the other ships appeared as well. Slowly and with ponderous dignity, *War Dragon* began to move. To the flashing of oars, the great galley headed for the harbor entrance. One by one, in single file, slow and stately as a parade of dowagers, the other ships followed. First came the three-banked ships, then those of two banks, and finally the smaller cutters that bore only a single bank of rowers at main deck level. Last of all came *Moonglow*.

The supply ships and tenders would sail later in the day without ceremony from the merchant harbor. These would be exceptionally numerous, because the Nevan fleet was bound for blockade duty, and might well spend weeks at sea before real battle commenced.

When all were gathered outside the harbor, *War Dragon* spread her two great, triangular sails, striped red and white. The following ships displayed their white or brown sails, and the watchers on the shore could see the diminutive red-and-white sails of *Moonglow* catch the morning wind that blew from the shore. Slowly, the majestic fleet began to pick up speed as the crowd ashore cheered themselves to exhaustion.

Shazad lounged in her chair beneath her gold-threaded awning and, for the first time in weeks, relaxed. She had done all she could do and now she would enjoy the cruise. She had brought only a single body slave, and the girl sat on the deck by her side, tending to her tray of delicacies and a pitcher of iced wine. Shazad had stowed several hundred pounds of ice from the royal icehouse in the ballast. She had no intention of leaving behind all civilized luxuries.

Idly she studied the rowers who lounged on the main deck now that the ship was under sail. They were an uncommonly handsome lot, members of every race and having a great variety of skin, hair and eye colors. As they rowed, she had admired the ripple of perfectly toned muscles beneath the glossy hides, the smell of sweat

mingling nicely with that of the fistnut oil with
which she insisted they be anointed every
morning. Idly, she thought of selecting one to
keep her company that night and was amazed
to realize how little the idea interested her.

She thought about it. Had it been weeks, no,
months since she had taken a man into her bed?
Not since before the battle with the barbarians,
anyway. And she had not felt the lack, either.
That was truly astonishing. In fact, for quite
some time only one man had interested her:
Gasam.

She held out a beringed and braceleted hand
and the slave girl placed a frosted goblet into
it. The girl made an excellent body slave. Mute
since birth, she was extremely quick to detect
the slightest signal from her mistress. She was
a good listener and never tired Shazad with the
sort of prattle even the best slaves plagued their
masters with. Best of all, she kept secrets extremely well. Shazad sipped the wine, which
was made on one of her own estates.

"Mina," she said to the girl, "this is a glorious fleet, and I am sure that we shall be handily
victorious at sea, but I have some small doubts
about Father's overall strategy." The girl nodded, her small, olive-complected face solemn
beneath a shag of brown hair. Her eyes were
large, green and beautiful. Shazad spoke to her
because she often found it easier to sort out her
thoughts when she spoke aloud, and there were
few people she dared trust with some of her
thoughts.

"Going up to fight this early, for instance.
King Hael must be well on his way by now, with
a fine mounted army of his steppe warriors. I

think Father should have waited until King Hael arrived, and then marched with the combined Nevan-Grasslands army to Floria, leaving the naval operation to one of the admirals, thus hitting Gasam from land and sea at once. He says he wants to stop Gasam bringing warriors from the Islands, but I think he is just too impatient to avenge his humiliation." She could never have spoken these words to someone who might have repeated them.

"Did I ever tell you that Hael was once my lover?" The girl shook her head. "That was long before you came into the household. He was splendid, the handsomest youth I ever saw. But, still, he was just a boy." She gazed into the cup regretfully. "He was of the same race as Gasam, but comparing the two would be like"—she looked about for a simile—"like comparing *Moonglow* to *War Dragon*. Of course, Gasam must have been little more than a boy then as well. Hael certainly seems to have made something of himself. When I last saw him, he owned one cabo and a spear and he was joining a caravan as a guard. Now he is a king. He must be a very interesting man, by now, perhaps as interesting as Gasam."

For two days the fleet sailed northward and westward along the coast in fine weather. The breezes held fair and little rowing was required, just enough to keep the rowers in good practice. Storms came every evening, but they did not bring dangerous winds. The rains meant that the water barrels were always full and there was plenty left over for bathing and washing down the ships. This was taken as a good sign for the voyage, as a lengthy cruise with rationed water could turn heavily manned warships into foul-smelling, pestilential, floating slums. On the third day they reached Point Despair, a frowning crag of rock thrust into the sea like the fist of an angry god. There, at a signal from the flagship, the fleet dropped anchor.

It was not yet late, and the day was fair. Puzzled at this development, Shazad had *Moonglow* rowed alongside *War Dragon*. King Pashir came to the rail of the huge galley and smiled down at his daughter.

"What do we do here, Father?" she asked, looking upward and shading her eyes with one hand.

"We wait," he said. He would say no more.

For the rest of that day and all of the next, the fleet lay at anchor. Bored, Shazad wanted to swim in the clear, blue water, but she was uncharacteristically reluctant to do so under so many ogling male eyes. Somehow, she felt that it would not be in keeping with her new dignity. So, she waited like everyone else and conversed one-sidedly with her slave.

"Isn't it just like a man?" she asked rhetorically. "He wants to show me that he still has his secrets, that there is much in which I have no say and no power." She sipped iced wine and fretted at her inactivity. She had become accustomed to being busy.

On the morning of the next day, Shazad lay in her narrow bed, lulled as always by the gentle rocking of the ship. She woke and heard the gentle breathing of the slave girl who slept on a pallet alongside her bed. She could not remember what had awakened her. She heard the familiar creaks and scrapes, the low voices of the watch out on deck. All the crew had strict orders not to speak loudly while the princess slept. Then she heard something out of place, almost below the threshold of hearing. It was a deep, rhythmic booming, repeated over and over. Could it be thunder? If so, it was like no thunder she had ever heard.

"Wake up," she said to the slave girl, gently shaking a brown shoulder. The girl sat up, rubbing her eyes.

"Something is wrong out there," Shazad said. "Hurry, get me ready." The girl rose and filled a basin from a pitcher and helped her mistress wash her sleep-puffy face and brush out her hair. She got Shazad hastily into her clothes and tidy. That done, the princess stepped out onto the deck.

It was a gray morning, the last of the night's stars fading from the sky and a band of pinkness beginning to show in the east. She shivered slightly, for the night's chill lingered well into the morning this early in springtime. The sound was clearer on deck, and she saw that the watch had gathered at the southward facing rail.

She crossed the deck to that side and tried to see the source of the sound. In the dimness she could make out shapes several hundred paces away. As the light rose, she thought she could see four ships, but something seemed wrong. She turned to a man who stood next to her. She saw that it was the flute-player who timed the rowers.

"What is it?" she asked.

He turned and saluted casually, smiling and

showing a gap between his front teeth. "Chiwan war galleys, Princess. Two of their biggest."

Now, as the ships drew nearer and the morning brightened, she began to see them clearly. Each had two hulls, and the hulls were each larger than *War Dragon*. Their oars seemed to be in four banks, on both sides of each hull. A common decking connected the two hulls, with massive wooden towers constructed fore and aft. Their tremendous, square sails hung slack in the windless morning, their yards hoisted on masts made of two trees leaning together for extra strength. Hulking shapes of war machines spiked the decks and the towers. The booming came from within the hulls; giant drums beating to time the hundreds of rowers.

Saan, the sailing master, came to her side. "Have you ever seen such monsters, my lady?"

"Never," she said, enthralled despite her anger at not having been told of this. "What are they like? Other than what I can see, of course."

"They are slow as time, but nothing more powerful floats on the sea. The Chiwans are wretched seamen, so they had to make ships that cannot overturn. They are floating fortresses. The rowers cannot double as light marines, as ours do, because the Chiwans use slaves chained to their benches."

The sun breached the horizon and the sails of the Chiwan galleys shone purple streaked with gold. The hulls were brilliant with scarlet and gilding, the oars polished white. The booming jarred through her in a strange, stimulating way. She wanted to see what it was like, aboard those ships. Around her, she could hear the sailors talking about the approaching galleys. For the most part, they spoke disparagingly; of their gross size and clumsiness, of their slowness and lack of maneuverability, of the fact that they were little more than floating prisons. But they said these things in low, hushed tones. Despite their contemptuous tone, the sailors were as impressed as she was with the image of brute power presented by the Chiwan galleys.

She had never been to Chiwa, and the only Chiwans she had met had been ambassadors and merchants. Rumor had it that the great power to the south was rich and luxurious even by Nevan standards, that their religious practices were lurid and bloody, that they had sacrificed entire enemy armies to their gods. They traded and made war mostly in the southern ocean, but in the last two generations they had been establishing closer ties with Neva.

Within minutes, a signal appeared at the masthead of the flagship: Princess Shazad was to join the king. Saan gave orders and *Moonglow* began to thread her way among the anchored fleet. Shazad retired to her tiny cabin with her slave girl.

"Quickly," she said, "make me presentable!"

The nearer of the Chiwan galleys lay alongside *War Dragon*. The main deck of the monstrous vessel was at least fifteen feet above the level of the flagship's. A long boom hinged to the double mast swung out over *War Dragon*. Beneath the boom was slung a broad gangway, not just a plank but a veritable staircase complete with side railings.

"Do you think that contraption is safe, Father? It could fall and crush us both."

"I do not think they will risk killing an allied king. Let us assume that they know what they are doing."

The king and his daughter carried out this conversation with practiced court faces, only their lips moving slightly. Pashir was resplendent in parade armor and scarlet cloak, his hair and beard newly dyed black. Shazad wore a court gown for outdoor summer occasions, and her face was heavily made up to give the proper masklike effect required when meeting foreign dignitaries.

Slowly, creaking loudly, the gangway was lowered until it touched *War Dragon*'s deck. Two sailors riding on the end of the gangway hopped off, unhooked the cable suspending it from the boom, and made it fast to the flagship's rail with heavy ropes. Then they prostrated themselves on the deck.

"Come, my dear," Pashir said.

Walking three paces behind her father on his left, Shazad stepped onto the stairway, noting that it was covered with beautiful green cloth. On the Chiwan ship, men blew long blasts on conch shells and low-toned double flutes. There was a rattling of tiny drums and a jingling of bells. At the top of the stair stood a man dressed in an enormously elaborate loincloth with a short cape of feathers thrown across his shoulders. He bowed and backed away as they came aboard. An elderly man knelt by the gangway and as they stepped aboard he raised his hands with palms out and cried in a high, quavering voice: "Welcome, a thousand times welcome, King Pashir, glorious leader of Neva, brother king of Diwaz the Ninth, king of Chiwa! Welcome, five hundred times welcome, Princess Shazad, daughter of King Pashir of Neva, daughter-of-the-heart of King Diwaz the Ninth of Chiwa! Welcome, fifteen hundred times welcome aboard the ever-victorious galley *Crusher-of-Barbarians-Beneath-the-Heel-of-Diwaz*!" The language was Classical Southern, which Shazad had learned in childhood.

"All honor to you, King Pashir, Princess Shazad," said the man in the feather cape. "I am Under-Admiral Prince Matchaz, one hundred twenty-fifth son of King Diwaz the Ninth."

Shazad blinked and was immediately angry at herself for registering shock. She was glad that her father could not see. It had always been his teaching that, on occasions when royal impassivity was called for, a princess of the blood should be able to let a fly land on her eyeball without blinking.

"In the name of the people of Neva, we greet you, Prince Matchaz, and we welcome you to our royal fleet," said Pashir. From behind him a herald called out the greeting, using the ritual formula.

Matchaz bowed again. "This"—he motioned to a similarly dressed man who stood just behind him—"is Nobleman of the Sea Prince Schtichili, eighty-ninth son of King Diwaz the Ninth, and commander of our sister ship, *King-Diwaz-the-Ninth-Is-Victorious-Forever*." More greetings were exchanged and the notables of the Chiwan ships were introduced, then Pashir did the same for the high-ranking officers who had come up the gangway behind the royal pair.

Finally, the formalities ended and Matchaz offered them a tour of his ship. At last Shazad could drop her rigid pose and look around. Everywhere incense burned in small pots and braziers, filling the air with sweet or spicy scents. Even so, these could not quite disguise an underlying stench. All those rowers, she thought, chained to their benches. Frequent bathing must be out of the question.

Officers and crew knelt in rows on the huge deck that spanned both hulls and the forty feet between them. Besides the two fighting towers at each end of the deck, there were several other structures, all of them elaborately decorated in the complex Chiwan style. Everywhere stood soldiers in bright loincloths and feathered headdresses, wearing lacquered armor of split bamboo stitched over with reptile hide, and bearing short spears and axes with stone or bronze heads. Most of the men, she noticed, wore plugs through their lower lips, rings through one or both nostrils, ornaments through piercings of the ears, including ornamented spools that stretched their earlobes so wide that she was sure she could put her fist through them. They wore more paint and had more tattoos than she had seen on the savages in the battle outside Floria.

There were women as well, dressed in short kilts and nothing else except feather headdresses and, if possible, even more ornaments and paint than the men. She took these at first for slaves but saw, to her astonishment, that some were armed warriors. These arms-bearing women, unlike the others, had elaborate patterns of scars carved on their bodies, arms and thighs, and they wore rings or dangling ornaments through their pierced nipples. As

Matchaz guided her father, Prince Schtichili fell in beside her.

"Please allow me to guide you, my lady," he said. With the formalities dropped, he had an engaging smile, marred only slightly by the jade plug through his lower lip.

"Please do, Prince Schtichili." She had an embarrassing time trying to pronounce the first sound in his name. It was a sound absent in the Classical Northern spoken in Neva.

"Please, address me as Li. Everyone does at home."

"Splendid. Call me Shazad." She had not expected such friendliness from a man who had a seven-pointed star tattooed across his face. "I am dazzled by this ship. We have nothing like this at home."

He laughed, exposing teeth filed to points. "We learned shipbuilding from you Nevans, centuries ago. At that time, all we had were rafts. We didn't trust ships at first, so we put big rafts on top of ships and the results you see."

"It can't be as simple as that!" she said as they went into a large structure with a frond-thatched roof. Inside, a banquet had been laid out.

"Perhaps not," Li admitted. "It makes a good story, anyway."

The company sat crosslegged at low tables and began to eat after a few healths drunk to the sovereigns and to victory in the coming campaign. Li offered Shazad a skewer strung with bits of meat and fruit, which she bit into delicately. It was delicious.

The banquet was long and leisurely. Musi-

cians played continually. Since the music was
completely strange, it sounded like mere noise
to Shazad, wailing and discordant. Some of
the women came in and danced. Prince Li explained that the dance represented an ancient
tale concerning a deposed king, a serpent goddess, a number of heroes and lovers and many
extremely bloody events. Considering the
subject matter, the dance was solemn and
stately.

After the banquet, Li took Shazad on a tour
of the great ship. They began in the rowing pit
of one of the hulls where she was shown the
rows upon rows of benches, each with a rower
chained to it by an ankle. For her amusement
they were put through their paces, tugging at
their oars, kept in time by the beating of the
huge kettle drum, disciplined by the whips of
the overseers. It was an enthralling sight. Never
had she seen so much human musclepower har-
nessed to a single purpose. The big, thickly
muscled men behaved like units in a great ma-
chine which, in a sense, they were. In time,
though, the stench grew insupportable, despite
the smoking censers constantly swung by attendants.

On deck, she was shown the massive engines of war, much larger than those on the
largest of the Nevan ships. They were almost
the size of the catapults atop Kasin's city
walls. The towers fore and aft were twenty
feet high and could be built even higher at
need with timbers stored aboard the ship. The
warriors were paraded for her in their dress
finery. Among them she saw archers whose
arrows were fletched with the feathers of col-

arrows were fletched with the feathers of colorful birds and tipped, exotically, with heads of volcanic flint that looked like black glass. She was intrigued by the female warriors and asked about them.

"They are taken as children in tribute from the subject peoples," Li explained. "They are raised in barracks and never know another life except the king's service. The scars on their bodies identify their units, those on the arms and thighs denote rank and battle honors."

"They cannot be as strong as male warriors," she said, pinching the thigh of a particularly ferocious-looking virago, one who bore many scars that were clearly made by enemies rather than an army cosmetician. She punched the woman's belly with her small fist. It was ridged with muscle and scar tissue and felt like hitting the reptile-hide shield at the woman's side.

"They make up for it with the pitiless savagery of their fighting," Li said. "They have no purpose in life except to fight. They have no lands, no husbands or children to distract them from their duties. The scarification rituals begin in childhood and prepare them to bear pain unflinchingly. As children, they help to interrogate prisoners and to kill the wounded after a battle. So they are well experienced in war even before joining the ranks as warriors."

"Fascinating," Shazad murmured, admiring a tear-shaped ruby dangling from the woman's nipple. These slaves were obviously highly valued. She noted that the women did not wear lip plugs. That pleased her, for she found the ornaments grotesque. "I don't suppose it would be possible for me to buy a few of them?" The woman had a face made up of flat planes and angles, her cheekbones high beneath gray eyes.

"I fear not," Li said. "They are the king's property. However, I will be most pleased to present you with a squad as your personal bodyguard for the duration of this campaign."

She smiled brilliantly. "That would be most kind. I would like to have this one among them." For the first time she addressed the woman. "What are you called?"

"Bloody Ax," the woman said.

"They do not have real names," Li told her, "only titles gained through deeds."

"They have no fondness for other people's titles, I noticed."

"Their arrogance is famous. They obey their officers and they worship the king. Beyond that, they will not acknowledge any lesser dignity."

Before leaving the ship, Shazad asked a question that had been bothering her since coming aboard. "Prince Li, since you are the eighty-ninth son of King Diwaz the Ninth, and Prince Matchaz is only one hundred twenty-fifth, why does he outrank you?"

"Among us, princely precedence is determined by the rank of our mothers, not the order of birth."

War Dragon drew alongside and the gangway was dropped back onto its deck. In stately procession, the king and his daughter returned to the flagship. Stepping onto its deck, Shazad was struck by how small it looked, compared to the great ship they had just toured. She longed to change from her court clothing and back into sailing garb, but first she needed to confer with her father.

In his luxurious cabin, he was divested of his armor and she sank to a well-cushioned settee. From a body slave he took a cup of wine. She knew that his physician had mixed it with a drug to forestall the aches and pains of age. She worried that it might also have some deleterious effect on his mind.

"Well, Daughter, what do you think of our allies?" He seemed inordinately pleased with himself.

"They are certainly colorful. Are they really cannibals? I thought it impolitic to ask."

"I have heard those rumors," he said, settling upon a couch. "But then, the Omians no doubt say the same thing about us. I admit, though, that I eyed some of that banquet rather closely. However, their dietary habits are not why they are here. What do you think of their ships?"

"They are extremely large and impressive, even terrifying. And they have no rams."

"Eh?"

"They have no rams, Father. I do not claim to be an expert on naval tactics, but even I can see that those monsters are not designed for fighting sea battles. I thought that we were going north to attack Gasam's transports and try to lure him out to fight us on the water."

"That is part of the plan, of course," the king said blandly.

"You intend to attack the city, don't you?" she said. "You intend to sail right into the harbor and storm the seaward walls."

"That is what I intend," he said. "If my preliminary reconnaissance indicates that the docks and harbor entrance are too heavily defended, the floating towers will be used. The seaward walls of Floria are low. The towers will overtop them easily."

She restrained her temper and forced herself to dull the edge of her tongue. It was remarkable that he was telling her this much.

"But, Father, why do you not wait until King Hael arrives? With a force on land and a force at sea, you could smash Gasam like a nut between millstones. Why try to storm the city now?"

Smiling, he spoke patiently. "Daughter, King Hael has written me, saying that he marches to my aid with a strong force. That may or may not be true. If true, political realities dictate that he must cross the Zone, a dangerous and largely uncharted wilderness. Who knows what may befall him there? Even should he come through with most of his men and cabos, he might well be too late to be of help. Should he arrive early and in full strength, he will be most welcome, but it is nothing I can count on."

"But Gasam may be in great strength by now. If he has risked bringing his warriors across all through the stormy season, he may be strong enough to hold the city."

Pashir waved a hand dismissively. "Gasam surprised me once. We expected a barbarian rabble and we found a half-disciplined army. But that was on land. Neva is supreme at sea, and in amphibious operations. You can train foot soldiers to fight in formation in a few weeks, but it takes a lifetime to make a seaman.

And it takes centuries of experience to use naval forces properly."

"That sort of thinking has already lost us one battle," she pointed out.

"Enough, Daughter." He glared. "The transports bring a strong force of foot soldiers for taking the docks and the walls. Gasam cannot withstand such an attack."

She seethed. He had been listening to his advisors again, instead of conferring with her.

"Father, Gasam and his people are savage nomads. They don't *need* that city! If you prove to be too strong for them, what is to stop them from simply walking out through the landward gate? With no army without the walls to contain them, they will take a leisurely stroll down the royal highway and take the first city that strikes their fancy. What will you do then? Pursue them across land in this fleet?"

"Silence!" he barked. "I have brooked enough insolence from you already. Return to your ship. You have earned the right to watch as we smash Gasam and his savages. Your work has been invaluable, I own that. But I will not have you resisting my will!"

She rose and bowed. There was nothing to be done and she wanted desperately to remain with the fleet. "Father, forgive me. I live only to serve you. It is just that I cannot stop myself from worrying for your welfare. I cannot abide the thought of your taking more risk than necessary. Forgive me if my concern makes me speak over-hastily."

"You are forgiven," he said, mollified. "Have no fears, this is most carefully planned. You shall see. I will crush Gasam in short order."

Back aboard *Moonglow*, Shazad cursed as her mute slave girl helped her out of her court clothes. "I have a terrible feeling about this. Father is going into battle on assumptions again. He *assumes* that Gasam will fight the way he wants him to. He *assumes* that Gasam has not been studying naval tactics, even though he is now in possession of his own port city and the gods alone know how many willing Nevan traitors."

Shazad splashed water in her face from a basin and held her peace while the girl scrubbed the makeup from her. No sooner was she in her sailing clothes than the sailing master knocked on her cabin door.

"Princess, there is a Chiwan launch approaching."

She went out on deck. A long boat was drawing alongside, its prow carved in the shape of a three-headed serpent. Besides the coxswain and the rowers, it contained ten barbarically clad warriors.

"This is my new bodyguard," she told the master. "A loan from our Chiwan allies."

"Where shall I put them?" the master asked, scratching his scalp.

"They can sleep on deck. They pride themselves on their ruggedness, I hear."

The sailors gaped as the women warriors climbed aboard, lithe and sure as cats. The last one in the boat tossed bundles up to her sisters, then pulled herself over the bulwark.

"Bloody Ax, come here," Shazad called in Southern. The woman, like her sisters, was staring haughtily and somewhat contemptuously about. At Shazad's voice, she turned and strolled to her. The warrior's body was pungent with smoke and sweat.

"Bloody Ax, you have the most scars, so I take it that you are the senior warrior?"

"I am."

"Excellent. You are in charge of them. Now, you may begin by addressing me as Princess, or Mistress, or my lady. Pass that order along."

"It is not our custom . . ."

"I know what your custom is. Now let me explain my custom. I am not physically strong compared to you, Bloody Ax. But I have a whole kingdom of strong men to do my bidding. It is my custom, when I have been offended, to have people nailed to crosses, where they often have four or five days to regret offending me. Do you understand? Your king will not upset relations between our nations just because I crucify a slave-warrior, or even ten of them. Is that understood?"

The woman stared at Shazad and saw something that frightened even her stony soul. "Yes . . . my lady."

"Very good. I do not like the way you smell. Every day, while you are aboard my ship, you are to bathe and rub your bodies with fistnut oil, like my rowers."

"As you wish, my lady."

"You probably think you have been cheated out of battle. If so, you will like what I have to say next. It is true that this little ship is not supposed to take part in the fighting and my father wants me to hang back out of range of the weapons, but I intend to do no such thing. I am sure that we are going to be in the thick of it, and I expect to see you live up to your name."

A broad smile broke across the woman's face, exposing teeth that had not only been filed but were equipped with bronze points. "We will not disappoint you, my lady!"

ELEVEN

The desert was almost flat. For ten days, they had crossed the monotonous landscape, broken here and there by ranges of low hills and strange, perfectly circular craters so ancient that their edges were eroded and indistinct.

Each day, Hael thanked the spirits of this terrible land for sending him the Webba. With uncanny precision, the bird-riders could find their watering holes amid the seemingly trackless waste where there were no landmarks Hael could see. More surprisingly, Joz told him that the Webba never used the same route twice, lest they wear a trail that could be followed by enemies.

Often the army had to be split into several parts, each to be guided by a different bird-rider, for there were few water holes large enough to accommodate so many men and animals.

"Tomorrow," Joz said on the evening of the tenth day, "after we pass the Forbidden Crater, we will be passing into cultivated land. This will mark the beginning of Canyon territory. They are miserable farming folk, but there are powerful sorcerers among them, so one must raid carefully."

"I have no intention of raiding anybody," Hael told him.

Joz shrugged. "As you will. You have such a powerful force, though. It seems a shame to waste it."

"Why do you call this place the Forbidden Crater? You have avoided all the craters we have seen so far."

"They are forbidden places," Joz said, "but the Forbidden Crater is even more forbidden. Evil spirits dwell there. It is deadly."

"How is it deadly?" Hael asked. "How do men die who enter it?"

"How should I know?" Joz said. "No one has entered it in a thousand years. Our gods and ancestors have forbidden it."

The next day they passed a raised lip of earth and stone that defined the edge of the crater. It was far larger than any they had seen so far. It was the only one with its rim not yet eroded level with the surrounding earth. Hael halted the column.

"I want to go look at it," he said. He felt drawn to the mysterious place, and he could feel no spirits there, evil or otherwise.

"No!" Joz called out. "You cannot do that! You will die!"

"I will not," Hael said. "I am a spirit-speaker, and I know that the spirits of this place will not harm me." He knew it would be worse than useless to try to tell the Webba that their gods and ancestors had given them a false warning.

"Shall we go with you?" Bamian asked.

"No, I will go alone. Wait here; I shall not be long." He turned his cabo and trotted toward the rim of earth, while behind him Joz and the other Webba began a wailing prayer. He hoped they were praying for his safety.

He could not have said with certainty why he was drawn to the place. Perhaps it was simply the curiosity that always took him to new and possibly dangerous places. If there was any mystery about a place, he had to look into it. He came of a profoundly conservative and custom-bound people, and he never let pass a chance to make up for the lack of adventuresomeness in his upbringing.

The cabo plodded up the rim of the crater with no hesitation. Whatever might haunt this place did not bother it. At the top of the rim, Hael halted the beast to examine something. A gray-white mass protruded from the rim, and something about it did not appear natural. He leaned from his saddle and touched it, feeling the coarseness of small stones buried in a hard matrix. It was concrete: not the soft, porous stuff used in some cities as a cheap building material, but the hard artificial stone of the ancients. On its surface were streaks of dirty red-brown.

Hael's heart beat a little faster as he looked down into the crater. It was not very deep, just a few yards, but it was incredibly wide, almost a half mile in diameter. An act of unthinkable destruction had occurred here a long, long time ago. Perhaps the site had been poisoned for generations, giving rise to the legend of its deadliness. Whatever malefic influence it had was departed now, or at least it was dormant.

The bottom of the crater was covered with outcroppings of the artificial stone, irregular lumps and huge, upended slabs jumbled about as if by an incredibly violent earthquake. As Hael guided his cabo carefully into the crater, he scanned the ground. He saw no small pieces of the concrete. Apparently these ruins had remained untouched since the event that had made the crater. His heart soared.

Stopping by an immense, irregular chunk of red-streaked concrete, he dismounted. Jagged masses, carbonized black or corroded into dirty red lumps, protruded from the whitish matrix. Copper and lead sometimes appeared in an odd, tubular form, but iron rarely occurred except in I-shaped masses buried in a porous but massive gray stone matrix. With a piece of stone, Hael pounded and scraped at one of the red lumps. Heavy flakes of corrosion fell away under the pounding, until a surface of gleaming silver was exposed.

Hael raised his face to the sky, wanting to thank the gods of this place, but not knowing their names. Steel! The most precious substance on Earth. Hurriedly he remounted and rode over the bottom of the crater. Everywhere there were great chunks of concrete, and from most of them protruded the rusted masses. The exposed steel had rusted away centuries before, but what remained buried in the concrete was pristine. There had never been mining operations in this place.

His mind raced. If he could bring a labor force here, with proper tools, he could take many tons of steel each year. His kingdom would be the richest in the world, and the best-armed. But how to bring men into this remote, waterless place? It would bear some thought. In the meantime, he was in possession of perhaps the greatest secret in the world.

The Webba cried out in wonder when Hael came riding back. They had not expected that he would ever emerge alive from the Forbidden Crater.

"You are truly a powerful sorcerer," Joz said, "to come forth unharmed."

"It is an uncanny place," Hael said. "I think that your gods wished me to see it." After that, the Webba treated him with the greatest respect. Three days later, they encountered the Canyon Dwellers.

The land was far from lush, but compared to what they had just passed through, it was beautiful. It was hill country, with sparse, brown vegetation on the rolling hillsides where dwarf branchhorns nibbled daintily at the thorny growth. In the valleys, narrow streams were tapped for irrigation by farmers who dipped the water up with leather buckets suspended from long poles. The poles were counterbalanced by great mudballs, so the effort required to bring up the water was minimal. The buckets of water were tipped into irrigation channels that meandered among the small, neatly kept fields that yielded grains and vegetables. The people were small, thin and dark, looking much like the Webba and speaking a nearly identical dialect, but the proud bird-riders would acknowledge no relationship except that of predator and prey. The farmers were mere scratchers of the earth, the rightful victims of bold nomads.

Hael could understand this attitude. It was much the same as his own people had held. His outlook had broadened enormously since his young warrior days, but farming still seemed to him to be a wretched existence, little better than slavery. Why people would endure it when they could roam freely over the seas or the grasslands or even the awful desert escaped him.

The villagers gaped to see the great mass of riders who seemed to appear from nowhere. Although Hael gave strict orders not to molest the locals, he made no great effort to befriend them. That would mean endless ceremonies and delays. Instead, his cabos drank from their streams and grazed their meadows, doing no lasting damage. If they had to open a field wall to pass through, Hael would always leave a bit of copper in compensation for the damage. Joz thought even this a great waste.

"These nosehorns can repair their walls without payment, great *bruyo*," he said, giving Hael the Webba title for spirit-speaker. "It is all they are good for anyway. You have no idea how happy they are just to be alive with their villages undestroyed."

"Nonetheless, I wish to leave some small goodwill behind me. I shall be back this way before very long and I don't want them running away at the sight of me. I may have some business to discuss with them."

"Business?" Joz said wonderingly. "With *farmers*? What possible business could a warrior have with them, save to take their belongings, wretched as they are?"

"*Bruyo* business," Hael said. He had made sure to record every landmark since leaving the Forbidden Crater, so that he would unfailingly be able to find it again. The dwellers here might well provide him with the labor force he would need. They were willing to do hard work, unlike his warriors, and they were near the source, unlike those people within his own kingdom who were accustomed to hard labor, such as the Byalla.

Secrecy might be a problem, and he turned over possible solutions in his head. He could pick up his workers at the edge of the desert and lead them by a circuitous route, possibly blindfolded, to the crater. There they could do a season's work and then be returned, without knowing where they had been. Food, water and other supplies could be brought in by caravan, and the season's takings would be transported back to the grasslands. He would need to acquire good, desert-hardened nusks for transport. Cabos were far too valuable to use as pack animals. It would be best to set up furnaces at the crater to melt the steel into easily transportable ingots, but he could not imagine how to get enough fuel for the task.

There was also the problem of getting the steel free of the artificial stone. It would take tremendous labor to break up the concrete. Then an answer occurred to him: Take a forge there and make tools out of the first of the steel they freed. That would not require such prohibitive stores of fuel. The concrete could be broken up quickly if the workers had hammers, picks and wedges of steel. This was a novel idea. Who would ever think of using precious steel for mere tools? Steel was for the weapons of important warriors. Only jewelers had tools made of steel, and theirs were tiny. When at last the steel mine was exhausted, the tools could be converted into weapons as well. He was lost in these pleasant thoughts when the Canyon Dwellers came into view.

"Humpers!" Joz said. He pointed to a hill in the distance where Hael could just see tiny dots that were men mounted on animals. They were not moving, but they were directly in the army's line of march.

"Who are they?" Hael asked.

"Canyon Dwellers," Joz said. He did not sound frightened, but neither was he pleased. "They will want to know who you are and what your business is."

"That is understandable," Hael said. "Anyone who comes into *my* land with six thousand armed men owes me an accounting. I think we will have no trouble reaching an understanding."

Joz shook his head. "They are great sorcerers, evil." Then he brightened. "But you have no fear of sorcery, do you? The man who dared the Forbidden Crater, and whom the gods smiled on for doing it? Yes, I think you can deal with these Canyon Dwellers. But I think it is time for us to part company here. The Canyon Dwellers and my people do not mix well together. We will resume our trek southeast. Our people will be pleased to see the presents you have given us, and they will be anxious to meet you when you pass this way again."

"May peace prevail always between your folk and mine, then," Hael said, clasping Joz's hand. Amid effusive farewells, the Webba rode off and soon were nothing more than a line of bird tracks in the dusty earth.

Hael resumed the march. Ahead of them, the humpers and their riders grew larger as the distance between them decreased. Humpers were grotesque animals, tall and gangly, with long, curving necks and wedge-shaped heads decorated with four stumpy horns. From their upper jaws protruded a pair of flat-tipped tusks seven or eight inches long. They took their name from the varying number of humps on their backs where they stored fat. Their hides were patchily covered with curly fur in the usual desert colors: tan, dun, gray, brown and black. They had bad tempers and smelled abominable. For all their bad qualities, though, they were prodigiously strong and their endurance was legendary. They could eat well where a cabo would starve and they could go for days without water. And they were among the very few animals useful for riding.

When the long column was almost at the base of the little hill, the humpers began to descend. The animals wore decorated trappings, with hanging fringes and many dangling tassels. The riders wore the loose, flowing clothes that seemed to be the preferred wear of the desert people, who required protection from the terrible sun of their environment. These people wore brightly colored garments in stripes of contrasting hues, their heads covered by deep cowls. They carried lances and bows and some of them wore longswords belted at their sides.

There were only ten of them, so none of Hael's men bothered making warlike preparations. The cabos did not like the look or the smell of the humpers, and they pranced sideways in agitation. The humpers drew rein a few paces from Hael and the riders lowered their veils. A murmur went through the riders around Hael.

Of all the many strange people Hael had encountered in his travels, these were by far the oddest. Their skins were blue. At first, Hael thought it was paint, but he quickly decided that it was their natural color. Just as strange were their eyes. No two of them seemed to have eyes of the same color. They were blue, brown, green, gray, yellow, purple and other, less assignable colors. Their hair was long, curly and almost silver-white.

"The Canyon greets you," said one man. He was tall and thin like the others, with bright yellow eyes. "We would know your name and whence you come, and on what business." He spoke yet another dialect of Southern, possibly quite archaic. His speech was musical and his words were quite formal.

"I am King Hael of the Grasslands. We come from far to the north, across the wide desert and the mountain wall. This is my war-host, but we come to your land in peace. It is our desire to make our way to Neva, where Pashir, my brother king, desires my assistance. We will do no harm to you or yours. Our only wish is to be across this land as soon as may be possible.

"Chimay," the man said, "judge this king, and see if his words are truthful."

A humper came forward and Hael's cabo shied, but he quickly controlled it. "I must touch you," said the rider. "Do not be alarmed." The voice was a woman's. It was difficult to discern sex among these people; this woman had slightly fuller lips than her male companions. All had fine-drawn features and the men were beardless. They wore their hair the same and the flowing robes covered all else.

Her humper was much taller than the cabo, so that she had to lean out from her saddle to lay her fingertips against Hael's forehead. Her hands were narrow and long-fingered, with delicate bones. Her touch was cool against his forehead. She carried no paraphernalia to differentiate her from the others, but Hael could detect in her the unmistakable signs of a spirit-speaker. Her eyes closed and her lips moved silently. This went on for two or three minutes, then her eyes opened very wide. They were the palest violet. She withdrew her hand and drew back bodily, almost recoiling.

"Does he lie?" the first speaker demanded. Hael was glad that few of his men spoke Southern. The more hot-headed ones might have struck the man down.

"No!" the woman said, shaking her head vigorously. "He speaks the truth. But he is . . . I cannot say. He has a power. The spirits . . . they flow through him like the waters of the Kol flow through the Canyon."

"I am a spirit-speaker," Hael said, "as well as a king and warrior. It is nothing to be alarmed at." In truth, he was the one who was truly alarmed. He had never encountered this kind of spirit-work. This woman could touch a man's brow and read thereby the truth or falsity of his words. He had known others who claimed this power, but this woman had it. The same touch had shown her the nature that had set Hael apart from others all his life. For the first time, he began to believe the stories of the Canyon people possessing strange powers.

"This should be studied," said the yellow-eyed man. "As long as you mean no mischief, you are truly welcome. Allow us to guide you. Not far from here you will reach the River Kol." At this name all of them made a sign of reverence, lifting fingertips first to their lips, then to their brows. "There you will find plenty of water for man and beast. We will follow it for several days, then you must turn northwest for the Nevan border. The way is plainly marked from there."

"I thank you most sincerely," Hael said. At last it seemed that the end of their journey might be nearing. From the Nevan border it would still be a long trek to the capital, but they would be in a civilized land with the king's welcome, and they would receive every assistance.

"Come, then. We can reach the river by nightfall." The speaker and the woman fell in beside Hael and he translated for his men what had just been said, leaving out the woman's truthreading.

"I am Manwa," the man said, "of Holy Well. That is our town. You already know Chimay, our spirit-wife." He gave the names of the others and Hael filed them away. Half were women. "Who is the King of Neva warring with? The old king sent an expedition here many years ago, to demand tribute from our king. We sent them home with no tribute and no desire to return."

"I once sailed with a man who was on that expedition," Hael told him. "He claimed that you struck his general dead with sorcery."

Chimay smiled. "We have our ways."

Hael smiled too, but inwardly. People never admitted that they did not possess powers others attributed to them, and a veiled innuendo was better than the loudest brag. He had made use of such tactics often.

"King Pashir has been plagued by raiders from the northwest islands. Now they have invaded to stay, and he wants the assistance of my riders."

"Then he will not be plaguing us for a long time," Chimay said.

"Just as well," Manwa said. "We have trouble enough from Sono and Gran." These were two of the southern kingdoms, jungle lands with which Hael traded.

"Please do not use your sorcery against Sono," Hael asked. "They make our finest saddles."

The man and woman laughed, as musically as they spoke. Their lyrical voices, graceful gestures and elegant appearance made the strongest possible contrast with the beasts they rode, Hael thought. With cabos it was the other way around. The cabo was such a beautiful creature that it made even an ungainly rider seem graceful.

As they rode, the Canyoners spoke in turn with Hael. All had the same fine gift of speech.

None would converse deeply on any serious subject. Always they would deflect such talk with a joke or an adroit change of subject, as if they wanted to feel him out before proffering anything of importance. It seemed odd to him that he should, by chance, encounter in this near-wilderness what seemed to be a group of polished courtiers.

The sun was still well above the horizon when they reached the Kol. Hael's riders cried out in wonder at sight of the great river. Their great plains home was a land of small, narrow rivers that only carried a great flow after the heaviest of rains. This river was a hundred paces across and the main current flowed swiftly. It was strange to see such a great body of water, for they were still in desert land, although the broad floodplain of the river was grassy.

"Water the cabos and put them out to graze," Hael ordered. "Then make camp." For once there was no shortage of wood. The banks were covered with dry driftwood left by the floods of past years. Hael noticed the rapt way that the Canyoners were looking at the river and remembered that it was sacred to them.

"Your pardon," he said, feeling that he had been ill-mannered, "perhaps I acted hastily. Are there ceremonies I should perform before we use your river's bounty?"

Chimay smiled again, this time with open friendliness. "No, this great river takes little note of what we humans do. It is presumptuous of us even to think that we can offend her. But I thank you for being so considerate of our customs."

"I try never to offend other people's gods or

spirits, and I try to abide by their customs when I can, especially when I am in their land." He dismounted stiffly. It had been a long day in the saddle. The Canyoners dismounted as well. Their humpers sat on their haunches and the riders slid off backwards, somehow performing this act without awkwardness.

"You had Webba riding with you when we first caught sight of you," Chimay said. "You must truly have great skill at making friends if you had their goodwill."

"You have had dealings with the Webba?" Hael asked.

Manwa chuckled. "Everyone has dealings with the Webba, whether he wants to or not. They are a difficult people, who manage to be both few in number and impossibly arrogant. They think riding those silly birds makes them invincible warriors, although they are just raiders and thieves. They are matchless in the deep desert, though, and you did well to acquire them as friends."

That evening, as they sat around a crackling driftwood fire, Hael spoke of the journey they had made, and of some of the strange sights they had seen: the Guardian with his enigmatic writing, and the pool with its beautiful goddess.

"We have legends of the Guardian, the stone giant who guards the pass," Chimay said, "but the wonderful oasis with its goddess, that is new to us. No wonder the Webba keep it a secret, though. It must be unique."

"And we have heard of you, King Hael," said Manwa. "We trade regularly with the southern kingdoms, even when we are at war with them.

The traders have spoken of the new king in the north, who has made a kingdom out of tribal peoples and holds sway over a vast land of grass and hills."

"What do they say of me?" Hael asked.

Manwa grinned. "They say you are not rich."

Hael laughed. "They are wrong. I am rich in people and cabos, in villages and land. I have the broadest horizons, the biggest sky and the most beautiful mountains of any monarch. I have a wife and family I love and trust above all others, and that is a claim I have never heard any other king make."

"You are the most fortunate of kings then," Chimay said. Outside the circle of firelight, the tethered humpers were making the most unmelodious of noises in great variety. "Now, tell me, why do you ride so far, braving the terrible desert, leaving your beloved queen and children behind, exposing your prized warriors to such hazard, to aid this king of Neva, who is just one of many kings, and far from you at that?"

This was a probing question, and ordinarily he would have given it a guarded answer, but something made him give it serious thought and answer fully. He seemed to be speaking only to Chimay, although the other Canyoners sat around the fire as well. He spoke of his boyhood on the island, and of how Gasam had persecuted him. Of how he had sailed to Neva and was befriended by Pashir. He spoke of the deep evil he detected in Gasam.

They all listened intently and when he was finished they were silent for a while. Then Manwa spoke.

"It is good to hear an account of the world's doings from one who is closer to the center of things. So much of the time, we have to depend on third-hand accounts, rumors, the stories brought to us by merchants, who often tailor their accounts to increase the demand for their wares. Now it may be that we can tell you something of importance." He turned to a young man who sat near him. "Hosway, bring me the long bundle." Then he turned back to Hael.

"King Hael, have you had any dealings with a nation to the east called Imisia?"

"I have heard the name. Traders from the far southeast speak of trade with a land of that name."

"Among us," Chimay said, "there is an ancient tradition that the east is an evil place, and that no good can come from there. For a long time it was thought that there were no people at all in the east. Other peoples have legends that their ancestors came from there, fleeing some terrible war or catastrophe."

"In the islands that were my home," Hael said, "we had no stories at all about the east. Our conception of the mainland was very unclear, for that matter. As a boy, I thought that the mainland was just a sort of large island, just beyond sight over the water. The peoples I rule now have no love for the east, although I know of no specific reason for that."

The boy returned with a bag nearly two yards long, in which a number of objects rattled. Manwa took the bundle and laid it by his side.

"About a year ago," Chimay said, "A trader from the southeast came through our land. He was stricken with illness, and he was left behind when his caravan had to return. Our healer was able to cure him, and in gratitude he gave us this. He said it is uniquely valuable, and it comes from Imisia, near the Great River." From the bag he took a flattened container, a sort of flask with a narrow spout at one end. From this he shook a little grayish-black powder into his palm, and he cast the powder into the fire. With an abrupt flash and a loud hiss, it disappeared amid a cloud of dense, foul-smelling smoke.

"You are not surprised," said Chimay, sounding disappointed. "You have seen this before?"

"From time to time, traders have brought this flashing powder. They give it as gifts, a novelty. None of us has been able to devise a use for it. They have said it comes from the Great River country."

"There is a use for it," Manwa said. "I shall demonstrate." From the bundle he took a pouch with a long shoulder-strap and an object unlike any Hael had ever seen. It consisted of an oddly shaped piece of wood to which was fixed a long tube of what appeared to be some sort of ceramic material. Standing, he poured some of the powder down the open end of the tube. Then he took a small ball from the pouch, wrapped it in a bit of fine cloth and placed it atop the tube's opening. He then withdrew a long stick from a hole drilled into the wooden part beneath the tube and with this he rammed the wrapped ball down until it rested atop the powder. He replaced the stick. Holding the thing horizontally, he showed Hael its back part. "Now watch carefully." At the very rear of the tube, there was a shallow indentation in the upper surface, and this was pierced by a tiny hole. Above the depression was a mechanism consisting of a curved piece of bronze with a flaring end that was somehow hinged within the wood part. Manwa drew back on the bronze piece with a thumb and there was a click from inside. The bronze piece stayed back and a smaller strut of bronze protruded from the under-surface of the wood. From the pouch he took a small reddish pellet and this he placed into the depression at the rear of the tube.

"This is a weapon," the man said, "and now it is fully armed. "Now, let me see. . . ." He looked around. It was still dim twilight, the stars not yet visible. Something moved fifty paces away, where the humpers were tethered. "Do you see that skulker?"

"A striper," Hael said with distaste. They were creatures of poor spirit and every herdsman hated them. They killed more newborns than any other predator.

"One of our humpers has a cut leg and it smells the blood. Watch." He raised the weapon and placed the wide end of the wooden part against his shoulder. Squinting along the tube, he seemed to be leveling the thing toward the striper. His finger stroked the little, protruding strut of metal and the larger bronze striker fell onto the red pill. There was a loud, startling *crack!*, like a miniature clap of thunder, and a tongue of flame shot several feet from the tube. Men jumped to their feet in alarm, then sat again when they knew it was only a noise, some sort of conjurer's trick. They did not notice what Hael saw immediately: that the striper was on its side, kicking.

One of the Canyoners rose and walked toward the beast, which stilled after a few seconds. He returned dragging it by its hind feet. In the firelight, Hael examined it. The striper had been pierced completely through, as if by a lance, with a small entry wound on one side and a gaping exit hole on the other in which he could see bits of shattered bone amid the torn flesh. The nose-stinging tang of the smoke still hung in the still air.

"How was this done?" Hael asked. He took the weapon from Manwa's hand and examined it. It was astonishingly light, its tube made of a ceramic far harder than any Hael had ever seen. It rang when he tapped it with the butt of his dagger. Manwa opened a small sliding panel on one side of the stock and revealed its mechanism, which consisted of a few small, bronze parts and a single curved spring of steel that powered the striker.

"These little pellets," Manwa said, showing him one, "flash instantly when the striker hits them. The flame leaps through this little hole and fires the main charge, in the base of the tube. That drives the ball out of the tube with tremendous force. It will kill any animal and will pierce any armor." He tossed one of the killing balls and Hael caught it. It was about the size of the tip of his thumb and heavy for its size.

"They use lead when they can get it," Manwa explained. "They make balls of clay as well, but these are lighter and less effective and are used mostly for hunting."

"It is impressive, and the noise and flash are frightening," Hael said, "but it is so slow. An archer can launch ten arrows in the time it took you to charge and fire this weapon."

"So it seems to me," Manwa said, "but the merchant told us that there are armies in the east armed with these, and they sweep all before them. The weapons are not supposed to be traded or taken to other lands, but the merchant had smuggled this one out, hoping to make a fortune selling it to a western king."

"These eastern armies you speak of," Hael said. "Have any of them marched this way?"

"We have only the accounts of the merchants who come in this direction. As I have said, their words are not always trustworthy. But they seem to have grown more populous than their lands can support and they are expanding."

Hael handed the weapon back. "I still cannot understand what makes this so terrible."

"The ball is so small and flies so fast that it is invisible," Chimay pointed out. "And it is deadly at a great distance, although it is difficult to hit a target beyond a hundred paces."

"This will bear thinking about," Hael said, "and I thank you for this demonstration. It may be worthwhile for me to take a long journey eastward someday, just to see how they use these in battle."

That night, he considered what he had seen. Like any warrior trained as he was, he had been contemptuous of the thing's many drawbacks: its awkwardness, its slowness, its short range compared to a bow. Unlike other weapons, it was not beautiful. These were warrior thoughts. He forced himself to think like a king, contemplating arming his troops with such a weapon. What were its good points?

The first that occurred to him was its durability. The compound bows his men used were complex and temperamental weapons, requiring constant care and protection from the weather. The fire-tube was simple and looked like it required little care. It used little metal, although he had no idea how the hard ceramic was made. It was possible that the weapons could be made cheaply. Once made, they might seldom have to be replaced. The compound bows came apart after a few years of hard use. Arrows were costly and difficult to make. Lead or clay balls would be cheap and were probably reusable.

So much for the weapon. What of the user? This was more promising. Manwa had demonstrated the weapon, but it might as well have been Chimay, or a child. The thing took no great physical strength to use. The bow and the hand weapons took a strong man to wield; and hand-to-hand fighting took raw courage and spirit. The fire-tube could be used by anyone. Its accuracy was not great beyond one hundred paces, but an army in the field presented a great mass of men and there would be no need to pick targets carefully.

Hael's eyes widened and he sat up straight when the full implication hit him. Good warriors were few in any kingdom. Even to find competent soldiers took careful selection and long, hard training. But these fire-tubes could be wielded efficiently by anyone with legs, two arms strong enough to lift them, and eyesight adequate to discern an army at two hundred paces. It meant that, *if* the weapons were cheap, there was no limit to the size of an army a king could raise. Virtually every remotely able-bodied man in the kingdom could be a soldier. He could even think about a special corps of women. . . .

He lay back down uneasy, and sleep was a long time in coming.

TWELVE

The shore was verdant, the matchless color of spring, with flowering vines draping an abundance of trees, all crowding their way down the hillsides almost to the beaches. Just offshore, the sea crashed and foamed over rocks, spilling into tidal pools where innumerable forms of shallow water marine life made great beauty while struggling for existence.

To the north, Shazad could see the estuary of the river with its breakwater, protecting the small harbor of Floria. The fleet was on station, blockading the city. The Chiwan ships, far slower than the Nevans, would not catch up for another day or two. Thus far, there had been no reaction from the city. She could just see the top of the seaward wall over a low spit of land to the south of the city, and behind that a hillside covered with white buildings. The city was not a large one, but it was lovely, or had been until the barbarians came.

"Princess!" a sailor called. "A signal!"

She crossed to the other rail and shaded her eyes with a hand. Colored flags were being draped from the yard of the nearest ship. Each ship, upon seeing a signal, repeated it to the next ship down the line.

"What does it mean?" she demanded.

The sailing master came up to her. "The northernmost vessel has sighted enemy ships coming from the northwest."

"Finally!" she said. "Saan, take us north. I want to see what happens."

"As you wish, Princess." He snapped commands and the sail was raised. By tacking, they could make their way northward. There was no need to tire the rowers until real speed was needed. Her blood began to race. In the waist of the little ship, her women guards, who had been profoundly bored, began to chatter animatedly. They began touching up each other's paint and rearranging the feathers in their headdresses.

"Do not get your hopes too high," Shazad warned. "I fear it is unlikely we will have a chance for action today." Nonetheless, her own hopes were high.

An hour later, they were gaining the northern end of the blockade line. Not far beyond the last ship, she could see a line of low shades nearing amid a rapid flashing. She called Saan to her side. "What are we looking at?" she asked.

"Canoes," Saan told her. "Very large canoes.

They were using merchant ships for transport last year. This is something new."

"Why do they flash like that?" she asked.

"The canoes are being paddled instead of rowed." Now she could see the paddles. Their blades were much broader than those of oars and they lifted and dipped at a furious rate.

"Why would that be?" she said.

"Paddling is faster in short spurts. You cannot keep it up for long." He thought about it for a while, analyzing the problem. "It is not easy to describe. When you are rowing, you sit or stand at a bench. The work is done mainly with the back and legs, and the stroke is very long. A small canoe is paddled while kneeling, a big one while standing. Either way, the work is done mostly with the arms and shoulders, which are not so strong. But the paddles can be raised and dipped much more swiftly."

"Meaning," Shazad said, "that they can outrun our oared galleys?"

"That is what we are about to find out," he said.

"Saan, place us inshore, near the harbor mouth," she ordered. "Stay out of range of the catapults on the walls."

"As you command, Princess." He gave the requisite orders.

She watched the incoming canoes as the ships to the south came north under oarpower. With their great numbers of rowers sitting in multiple banks, these were the swiftest ships in the world. But the Islanders were not in ships, they were in canoes. Now she could see that the canoes had stabilizing outriggers. There were at least thirty of them in sight now.

A two-banker was now moving to intercept the lead canoe. Arrows began to arch from the ship, but the canoe was still well out of range. It made straight for the harbor mouth but, swift as it was, there was no doubt that its path and that of the two-banker would cross before it got much farther. Like spectators at a sporting event, the crewmen and the women guards on *Moonglow* cheered, shouted encouragement and gesticulated wildly, as if their demonstrations could have some sort of influence on the outcome of the race.

By now, the nearer ships were bearing down upon the mass of canoes. A few catapult stones described parabolas in the air but, like the arrows, they were still out of range and ended as futile splashes. Within the big ships, the rowers were working at a heart-bursting rate, one they could not maintain for long. Sails and masts had been lowered to the decks to give the ships greater stability.

As the first arrows began to reach the lead canoe, it sheared aside, and now Shazad saw another advantage of using paddlers. The canoe had a steering-oar at its stern like the ships, but it could change direction much more quickly by alteration in the attitude of the paddles. The galley dipped its oars on one side in an attempt to change course, but the canoe slid past easily, its paddlers and rowers jeering. The few arrows from the ship that reached the canoe were easily intercepted by the tall shields of the warriors.

The fleet of ships and that of canoes were now intermixed, but none of the other ships were having any greater success in catching any of the canoes. They were like fat, old stripers amid a herd of leaping curlhorns. One by one, and then in groups, the canoes passed through the milling fleet and assembled inshore. They turned their bows toward the harbor mouth and began to make their way shoreward, with the fleet in ponderous pursuit.

"What shall we do, my lady?" Saan asked, his face apprehensive.

"For now, we keep out of their way. Stay near, though. They should not attack us. That would stall them long enough for the fleet to catch up. Stay near them, though."

He did as she ordered and the flotilla of canoes passed within easy bowshot, the warriors standing in its center pointing with wonder at the little ship, its women warriors and the regal lady standing in its stern. The first canoes passed the breakwater, where they were cheered by a crowd that had gathered to watch the show. The bulk of the flotilla passed *Moonglow*, and then there were only two stragglers in the rear. She pointed at them.

"There! Saan, make for those two!" The sailing master shouted at the oarmaster and that officer gave orders to the flute-player. *Moonglow* began to move, gaining speed quickly as the women warriors moved to the bow and began a savage battle-chant. Two sailors went to Shazad's side. They bore shields and had been given the sole task of protecting her.

Her stomach fluttered, but she put on her court face and her court bearing. She would not allow any of these low-bred people to see a princess show common fear. She wore the riding outfit that she customarily wore for sailing.

She had never used weapons so she bore none, only the whip coiled in one hand. That she knew how to use.

The steersman made for the nearest of the canoes. She saw that it was full of tall, lithe men with hair of copper and bronze and gold, and ruddy skins. They carried long spears made almost entirely of bronze and had long, black shields.

"Those are Shasinn!" she called out. "Leave them alone! Make for the other canoe!"

Saan repeated the order and the steersman complied. The last canoe tried to change course, but *Moonglow* was far smaller, swifter and more maneuverable than the great galleys. The men aboard the canoe, both paddlers and warriors, were stocky, swarthy savages, their long, black hair decorated with bones and shark's teeth. They carried spears with bronze points and some had daggers. A few whirled slings, but the cramped confines of the canoe were not suited to such weapons.

"Prepare to ram!" shouted Saan, then: "In oars!" The oarsmen slid their oars back through the tholes and braced themselves for the shock. The faces of the savages showed alarm, anger and fear at this unexpected turn of events.

Moonglow's diminutive ram caught the canoe just forward of the stern. The small ship was still far larger than the canoe, and the stern lifted and slewed sideways with a splintering of wood. Warriors and paddlers tumbled to the bottom of the vessel and some fell overboard. The sailors cast grapples onto the canoe and lashed it securely alongside. Then the real fighting began.

It was an interesting battle, and Shazad forced herself to watch it dispassionately, although she was as excited as she had ever been in her life. The men in the canoe outnumbered her ship's complement, but *Moonglow*'s sides were higher and made a better fighting platform. The rowers had left their oars and snatched up weapons and small shields, and she found that it was pleasant to watch such comely men fight.

Even more exciting were the Chiwan guards. The women fought with a maniac fury that clearly appalled the Islanders. Still it was no easy victory. The Islanders were desperate and furious. Also they seemed to be solid knots of muscle and lightning reflexes, despite the long sea-passage they had just endured. They sent little throwing-clubs whirring through the air, to strike with bone-snapping force, and their spears licked out from behind their black shields with great power and precision.

A few of the women warriors gained the stern of the canoe, cutting down the Island warriors and making way for more of their sisters. The Islanders ceased their futile efforts to board the ship and instead tried to win back their canoe, hacking frantically at the grappling lines. Rowers on the ship dropped their shields and picked up their oars again, this time to bring them crashing down upon the heads of the men in the canoe. The smaller vessel became a slaughterhouse.

When she saw Islanders jumping over the far side of the canoe and swimming for shore, Shazad strode to *Moonglow*'s rail, her two sailors still holding their shields alertly before her.

"Take some alive!" she shouted. "I want prisoners." Bloody Ax screamed something at her squad and they began working in small teams, one defending while another seized the weapon of an enemy and a third began to wrestle him into submission. They all carried short cords for the purpose of trussing prisoners.

Less than ten minutes after the fighting had begun, it was over. The bottom of the canoe was full of corpses and blood which was quickly growing diluted from the water coming in through the holed stern. A few survivors were swimming frantically for shore and a half-dozen groaning prisoners lay on *Moonglow*'s deck. The Chiwan women were festooning the stempost at *Moonglow*'s bows with severed heads.

The last of the canoes were disappearing behind the breakwater. As she had expected, none had turned to aid her victim. That would have put them back among the Nevan fleet, which was nearing fast now that all the big warships had managed to turn around.

"Saan," she ordered, proud that her voice did not tremble, "take us alongside the flagship."

"My lady, we have two rowers and a sailor killed and two of your guards . . ."

"Obey!" she snapped. "Tell me about the dead and wounded later." Why was the man bothering her with trivialities? Now she saw Bloody Ax approaching. The woman smiled her vicious, bronze-toothed smile.

"That was most enjoyable, my lady. But why did you not let us attack the Shasinn? We wanted some of them. They are very pretty."

"Yes, they are, Bloody Ax. And you shall find out all too soon why I did not want you to tangle with them just yet." She went into her cabin, where the mute slave awaited her. The girl knelt composedly, face down and hands atop thighs, trying to hide the fact that, minutes before, she had been curled into a terrified ball beneath Shazad's bed. As she looked up at her mistress, her eyes widened. With her hands she made a wringing motion.

Shazad looked down at her garments, then felt her hair. She was drenched with sweat. "That's curious," she said. "I've been standing in one place on a mild day and I'm soaked with sweat. Battle is a strange business. Come, girl, get me out of these clothes and sponge me off. I think I have some clean garments left."

She was not sure of her reception, but she was relieved to see her father beaming down at her from *War Dragon*'s rail an hour later. She had had Saan stall while she made herself presentable. Now she wore casual outdoor dress and her still-wet hair was covered by an intricate golden net. Beside the king, red-faced sea officers glared down at the princess and her toy-like little ship. Marines gazed with envy at the clusters of heads decorating *Moonglow*'s bows.

"Greetings to the only ship with trophies to show for this day's work!" Pashir called out. She could detect the false heartiness in his voice, but it was preferable to his wrath.

"I lay them at your feet," she called out in an ancient Nevan formula.

"Come aboard and receive your sovereign's praise," he said, completing the formula.

Lightly, she climbed the ladder and stepped over the rail, steadied by a marine officer. She stood before the king, who embraced her. Then, his arm around her shoulders, he turned her to face the men crowding the deck. They clapped and cheered; the high officers because they had to, the sailors and marines with sincerity. She saw that there was one officer who did not have to force his applause. She tried to put a name to his face, then she remembered: Fleet Captain Harakh, the marine officer she had spoken to her first day on the job. He had approved of her planned reforms, even though she had berated him for being out of uniform.

From the side of her mouth, she spoke in a court-whisper: "Do not use me as a whip to flog your captains, Father. It is not their fault that warships are too slow to catch canoes."

A long sigh escaped the king's lips. "Aye, that rascal Gasam has outthought me again. Does some demon speak in his ear?"

More likely one blocks yours, she thought, but said: "No, he used his native intelligence and he sought expert advice. There was no lack of Nevan turncoats in that city, and many ships were caught in port, with their officers and crews. He knew the exact capabilities of our ships months before we set sail."

"That savage!" the king muttered, still too quietly for the others to hear. Then, wearily but still with a note of anticipation in his voice, he added, "Well, so much for the blockade. It looks as if storming the city is all that is left."

She needed all her court training to keep from closing her eyes and groaning. He had learned nothing.

Sunset light was red on the sails of the monstrous Chiwan galleys as they worked their way carefully through the shallows of the channel. Where the Nevan ships could sail with confidence, the Chiwans had to sound every foot of the way, lest they run aground.

"Well," said Harakh, "if anything can force the harbor, those floating castles can." Shazad had invited him for an informal dinner aboard her ship, while she was transferring her prisoners and wounded to the flagship, and the two sat at a small table on *Moonglow*'s little quarterdeck. A sailor was clearing plates that bore the remains of fresh-caught fish and fruits carefully preserved in crates belowdecks.

"That is a major 'if,'" she pointed out. She had already spoken to him of her doubts, not, initially, as forcefully or as bluntly as she had voiced them to her father, but leaving no question in his mind of her feelings.

"Hazard and uncertainty are always a part of war," he said.

"They should be reduced to the minimum," she countered. "No sovereign should ever go to war with only an even chance of winning. I would never march forth unless I was in such overwhelming strength that victory was as near certain as possible. Even then, I would have more than one alternate plan in case of a reverse."

"But this time we did not simply go to war. The war came to us. The savages took a Nevan city and your royal father could not very well ignore it."

She held out her cup and the slave girl refilled it. "I do not speak disloyally, Harakh, but I do not think Father has handled this as well as he would have fifteen years ago. There was no need to move so hastily. There was plenty of time to put together a combined land and sea campaign."

"Well," he said uncomfortably, "there is the threat from Omia. He could not very well strip the capital of defenses while King Oland wants to snatch Nevan territory."

"It might have been wise to take care of the Omian threat first," she said.

"And leave the barbarians in possession of Floria?"

"Why not? Make peace with Gasam, leave him there for a while. He could always be dealt with later. He might even have made a useful ally."

"Ally?" he said, sounding shocked.

"Certainly. We could have dealt with him. He could help us in the field and then we could give him Omian territory to plunder. It would keep him happily occupied for years. Kings have always paid off mercenaries by giving them somebody else's land."

"But after they had seized a Nevan city, it would not be . . ."

"Captain Harakh, if you start prattling about 'honor' I shall be very disappointed in you." She rolled the goblet between her palms and admired the tricks the wine played with the light of the setting sun. Harakh did not speak for a while.

"Princess," he said at length, "what do you want of me?"

She leaned toward him. "When those Chiwan monsters are ready, assuming that they do not gash their hulls open on the rocks, we shall assault the city. It may be that we shall carry the city easily, or it may be that we will win only after a long, hard fight. Either one will suit me well. When all is over, we will go home and have a fine victory parade in the capital.

"But it may not work out that way. Gasam is exceedingly resourceful and he may yet have many surprises in store for us."

"And if that should happen?"

"Above all, the king must be protected. Many assault troops are being brought up on the transports. There will be no need to commit the marines early in the fight, especially the marines aboard *War Dragon*."

"Of which I am captain."

"Exactly. I want you to keep alert for whatever tricks Gasam might try. I want you to stay close to the king and watch his close officers. I do not trust any of them. They might try to kill him and take over the fleet, or hand him over to Gasam in exchange for favorable treatment, or any other sort of self-serving treachery. If you and your men are committed to the fight ashore, I want you to hang back and keep your men together."

"You are asking me to disobey orders?"

Her hand slapped down on the table. "I am *ordering* you to protect the king! If the battle seems irretrievably lost, my father may try to kill himself. If so, seize him and drag him by force if need be back here to *Moonglow*. Like all too many men, my father believes in honor. What is one battle? What are a few thousand men? We will go home and lick our wounds and make our plans. We still have the capital, we still have an army there and spread around the borders, we still have a kingdom! I am quite prepared to spend the next thirty years fighting Gasam, if that is what it takes. The idea of winning or losing a war in one glorious battle has caused many thrones to change hands."

He sat for a while, toying with his wine. "You think long and deeply, Princess."

"It seems I am the only one in the kingdom who does. Will you do as I tell you?"

"I will, Princess."

"Good. Since that is settled, I will tell you more. Harakh, more of the defense of the kingdom is falling to me. My father is served by fools. I will not allow such men around me. I want two things in my servants: loyalty and ability. I will not choose men to serve me because of birth or family influence. I would rather be served by a loyal and capable third son of a country squire than some degenerate duke. Those men shall grow great in my service."

She looked to the south. The Chiwan galleys were almost ready to join the fleet. "It grows late. You have my leave to rejoin your command, Captain Harakh."

He rose and bowed. When he was gone, she called for her box of writing instruments. A cutter would leave for the capital at first light, and she had messages she wanted to send on it.

Like some unstoppable force of nature, like an avalanche or a tidal wave, the Nevan fleet bore down upon the city. There was none of the breakneck speed and heavy rowing of the earlier action. Ahead of the fleet, wallowing boats laden with seasick assault troops headed for the breakwater and the nearby shore. They were to seize these points and keep the enemy from stationing catapults there to menace the ships coming behind them. So far, the shore was quiet.

Shazad stood at *Moonglow*'s masthead, above the long, slanting yard. Beside her stood Sailing Master Saan. She had ordered the ship's carpenter to build this vantage point from which she could view the battle. A small rack fastened to the railing held a fine telescope made by one of Neva's best lens craftsmen.

Abruptly a landing craft struck something in the water. Its bow rose as if pushed up by a giant hand and men tumbled into the water. Across the distance separating them, she could hear thin screams. Another boat did the same and the rest dug in their oars, coming to a stop.

"What happened?" she asked Saan, who had snatched up the telescope for a look.

"Underwater obstacles," he said, handing her the glass. "Could be slant-stakes buried in the sand, maybe spiked logs."

"What happens now?" She studied the scene. Whatever the obstacles were, some of the men had been impaled upon them. Blood stained the water and drowning men scrambled over one another while others clung to the wrecked boats. She took her eye from the glass and Saan pointed to the transport ships. More men were climbing from them into boats.

"Sappers," the master said. "Military engineers and naval divers. They'll clear out the obstacles. It's special work they're trained for. It's going to be a long day."

"It's still early," she said.

The sun was only a little above the shoreward horizon. As the day wore on, she watched with fascination as the sappers did their work. They cut through ropes lashing spiked logs together and fastened other ropes around slant-stakes. While divers dug at the bases of the stakes, rowers backed their boats away to tug them loose. Some of the most stubborn obstacles were embedded too deeply for the boats to pull out. Then long lines had to be passed back to one of the galleys, which would then pull the thing loose, provided the rope did not break. All this was done under a constant rain of arrows and yet more boats had to be brought up with mantlets: portable walls that protected the workers from missiles.

So this, too, was war. Somehow she had never pictured battle as a matter of labor rather than combat, but she was glad to see that these engineers, at least, knew their jobs well. She, for one, was not itching for a great, glorious battle. Perhaps the Nevans could beat the enemy this way. The barbarians were great warriors, but she had never heard of savages who relished hard work.

The breakwater and parts of the nearby shore had been occupied without resistance, but now objects began to leap over the breakwater. At the angle from which she was viewing them, they seemed to rise vertically. But then they came crashing down among the sappers' boats, raising large splashes and occasionally crushing men and watercraft.

"Where did those come from?" she asked.

"They must have brought up catapults on rafts," Saan said. "They're firing from right there inside the harbor." As he spoke a mantlet was smashed and arrows began to rain through again, fired from atop the seaward wall.

"Look there, my lady, just to the right of that tower."

She trained the telescope in the direction of his pointing finger. Two people lounged on couches atop the wall, watching the spectacle. They were tiny even as seen through the glass, but she knew it had to be Gasam and his queen. She stared at the woman until her eye ached, but she could make out no features, except that she seemed to be wearing very little if anything. The same light that caught the silver of her husband's steel spear struck brilliant highlights from the ornaments she wore, but Shazad could tell nothing otherwise of her appearance.

The long day wore on. Several times Shazad descended from her perch to eat or refresh herself. Knowing how ridiculous it was, she still lamented what all this exposure to sun and wind must be doing to her skin. But if that woman could lounge atop a city wall all but naked, she was not about to adopt a hat and veil to protect her complexion. During a late afternoon meal, Bloody Ax came to her.

"My lady, is this a war or a building project? I have never seen so many working men and slaves pretending to be warriors."

"Would you rather be out there digging up underwater stakes?" Shazad asked.

"No, but . . ."

"Do you not make war like this in the south?"

The woman grinned. "In the south, we fight! The kings and their warriors assemble on the battlefield and the battle takes place. Blood flows and honor is won. That is how warriors should fight."

"Then why does your king have those?" she

asked, pointing at the Chiwan galleys, now lying idle in the water.

"There are some island and peninsular strongholds," Bloody Ax said, "held by rival petty kings, pirates and savages. The big ships are useful in storming them."

Shazad wondered what on Earth someone like Bloody Ax might consider to be a savage.

"Patience, my pretty one," Shazad sighed. "Blood will flow in great abundance soon, as much blood as you could wish for."

The sun went down and the work went on, now illuminated by torchlight. Fire-baskets on long spikes were jammed into the shallows and filled with blazing fistnuts. The engineers continued to toil and the divers continued to dive. Shazad was entranced by the sight. It was unlike anything she had ever seen. The lighting made it difficult for the missile-casters ashore to judge distance, so they ceased their bombardment rather than waste ammunition. Shazad ordered Saan to take *Moonglow* closer.

Rowing quietly, the master brought the ship close to where the men were working. She could see their bodies gleaming with sweat and seawater and could smell their pungency above the sea odor that permeated everything. The divers wore goggles of sleen-skin set with round lenses of glass. Again and again these men dove, seemingly tireless, as they dug, chopped and roped. Bits of wood floated on the tide along with occasional corpses. The current carried them south; they would be out of sight by morning.

She could see no lights atop the city wall. If Gasam and his queen were still there, they watched from darkness. It was more likely that they had retired for the night. There would be no fighting until morning, if then. She gave orders to take the ship out of range and retired, exhausted, to her own cabin.

By the next morning, a wide passage had been cleared through the obstacles. As soon as the sun cleared the horizon, Shazad was back in her lofty perch, observing. Flags were raised and lowered on the flagship and the others. Drums rolled and trumpets blared and the fleet once again moved.

This time, not all moved at once. The two-bankers began to row toward the harbor mouth, forming an orderly line as they drew ahead. Then the three-bankers moved out. *War Dragon* stayed in position.

"Saan!" she called down to the deck. "Take us as near the breakwater as you can. I want to see what is happening inside the harbor."

"As you will, Princess," he said, "but if they shoot at us, I must retire out of range. Your father has ordered me."

"Just do as I say. We will discuss missiles later." She could see no archers on the breakwater today. It seemed to be in the hands of Nevan troops. And she doubted that the enemy would waste catapult ammunition on her yacht, when they had a whole battle fleet to shoot at.

They came alongside the breakwater just as the first ship entered the harbor mouth. From her platform, Shazad could see over the breakwater and into the harbor beyond. She was used to the great harbor of Kasin, and this one seemed small and cramped. She wondered whether her father really proposed to jam a whole fleet in there.

Enemy warriors crowded the wharfs, waving their weapons and chanting. The catapult rafts had been drawn back so that they could launch their missiles into the harbor. Atop the city wall she could see much larger engines, and their casting-arms were being drawn back.

Something whizzed overhead, startling Shazad. She looked up and saw a large, jagged object hurtling toward the city. It struck the top of the city wall and bounced on into the town. She looked back to see whence it had come. One of the Chiwan galleys had drawn near, and a catapult atop its forward tower had fired the stone.

"At last," said Saan, who had joined her at the masthead, "those hulks are beginning to earn their keep."

The first two-banker entered the harbor amid cheers from the Nevan soldiers atop the breakwater. The galley assigned this point duty had been armored with a heavy timber shield covering its bow. A roof of lighter timber had been erected over the rowing pits.

As soon as its ram came through the entrance, the catapults on the rafts began to shoot. They had already been sighted in on the entrance and their stones came down on the armoring with thunderous noise. The stones bounced away until one came down on some oars, smashing them to splinters. She could hear screams from inside the ship, as whipping oar-butts pulped the rowers.

Another ship came in behind the first. Another storm of missiles rose from the catapults.

This ship was not as heavily armored and it fared worse. Stones struck its deck, smashing assault troops and marines crowded on the narrow catwalk between the rowing pits. A number of rowers were killed, but the ship's momentum carried it through.

The next two ships ran the same gauntlet, suffering but forcing their way into the harbor. As the fifth ship entered, the great catapults atop the city wall came into play. These did not use twisted ropes for power, but rather had great weights on one end of their throwing-arms. These in turn terminated not in cups or baskets for missiles, but rather in huge slings half the length of the arms. A weight fell, the arm rose to a crossbar and stopped there, then the sling whipped around and released. The stone climbed impossibly, seeming to rise straight up, then it began to fall, so slowly that it seemed almost to be floating. But when it struck the two-banker just behind the stem of the ship, it went through the deck, through the ship and out through the bottom. The stone was ten times the size of those thrown by the raft catapults.

Amid screams of fear and dismay, the ship shuddered, its nose going down quickly as water gushed in. Within seconds its steering oar was lifted free of the water and was useless.

"Oh, no!" Saan all but croaked. "Look at that!"

Another ship was passing through the entrance, making full speed to get through the entrance and into the harbor where it would have room to maneuver and not be a sitting target for pre-sighted catapults. It was a three-banker, and its great bronze ram hit the wounded two-banker in its raised stern, raising the smaller ship until it was almost vertical, ripping a tremendous hole in its bottom. Now the screaming was truly ghastly as men were crushed or tumbled forward through the doomed ship. Large pieces of its stern crashed down onto the bow of the three-banker, crushing men there. The water was a chaos of drowning men and shattered wood. An enormous cheer rose from the shore.

More three-bankers came in. The stones continued to rain down, but the rate of fire slowed. The machines were very slow to rebrace and reload. Three more three-bankers came into the harbor and it began to be very crowded. Arrow-shooting engines on the ships concentrated their fire on the raft-borne catapults while those on the Chiwan ships concentrated on the city walls. A tremendous crash signaled a direct hit on one of the huge stone-casters atop the wall. Now it was the turn of the Nevans to cheer. The town was now under concentrated fire from both of the Chiwan warships.

Shazad scanned the carnage ashore with the telescope. Half the raft-borne catapults were now out of action. Some were being dismantled and carried into the city. She guessed that they would be reassembled atop the wall and continue their fire from there. Only one of the huge stone-throwers had been put out of action, but she could see that their accuracy was poor. The harbor mouth had been sighted in, but now no more ships were coming through. The big hurlers were being shifted to fire on the Chiwan ships, but even the huge vessels were difficult targets at that range. The stones made great splashes but they only seemed to have a rate of fire of perhaps ten shots each hour. She lowered the glass from her eye.

"The engines are not served by Shasinn," she said. "I do not think most of them are even Islanders."

"That makes sense," Saan commented. "It's a workman's job, not a warrior's. I doubt these savages ever saw a war engine before they came here. With a few turncoat soldiers to manage the things and prisoners to work them, he can save his warriors for better things."

"That is what I would do," she said. She wondered where Gasam and his queen were. Not out on the wall this morning. She looked up and corrected herself. The sun was already at zenith; they might be in one of the towers flanking the harbor gate. She did not think Gasam would be there, though. She trained the glass on the little plaza just beyond the wharfs. There was a great crowd of Islanders there, and among them she found the Shasinn, easy to spot because of the flashing from their extravagant spears. Truly, she thought, they were golden men. She thought she detected a silver streak among them, but she could not be sure.

There was a commotion at the far end of the harbor, an area lined with ship sheds, the covered docks where vessels were kept during winter or when being repaired. Lean shapes began to slide from them, half a dozen or more from each shed.

"The canoes," Saan said. "I've been wondering where they were."

"What can they do with canoes in that madhouse?" she wondered. The ships in the harbor were trying to sort themselves into some kind of order. They were backing, to get their sterns toward the northern side of the harbor so that all would be forming a line facing the city wall. The first three-banker through the entrance was still trying to clear itself of the wreckage of the ill-fated two-banker. The water was filled with struggling men and drowned corpses.

They did not manage to get into formation, because now the canoes were among them. The ships, without the speed and momentum that made them terrible at sea, became mere fighting platforms. Their stone-casters were no use against the canoes and the powerful, crossbow-like spear-launchers were not a great deal better. Some of the canoes stood away from the ships and showered them with missiles: arrows, javelins and sling-stones. Others paddled in and tried to board. The rowers fended them off with flailing oars, so they concentrated on the vulnerable bows and sterns. Warriors with tall shields fended off the missiles that rained from the ships. Others wielded long spears, thrusting at the ships' rails to clear a space for boarders. Shazad could see them casting grapples aboard.

"What do you think?" she asked Saan, lowering the telescope from her aching eye. Her muscles were stiff and she realized that she must have been watching far longer than she had thought.

"It's smart tactics," the seaman said, rubbing his stubbled chin. "They've figured out how to use boarding pikes. They're not taking many casualties. That bugger Gasam's being cautious, using crafty tactics. Most of all, he's denying our navy its greatest strengths. The ships are just wallowing tubs like this, it's not a real sea battle. We have a great many marines and soldiers, skilled fighters, but only so many can get to the rails to fight. If the savages get aboard in any numbers, all that order and discipline isn't much use. Believe me, my lady, in a deck fight, it's savagery that counts."

She thought of the carnage in the great battle outside this city, how the Islanders had surrounded the Nevan army and forced them together, pressing in until no man had room to use his weapons. Something else came to her.

"Saan, those catapults of theirs . . . why haven't they used them to try to set our ships afire?"

"I was thinking on that myself, Princess. It's not like a real sea battle, where they have to worry about setting their own ships aflame. As I figure it, King Gasam wants those ships."

She was stunned. "Wants them? But . . ." It took her only a moment; even before he spoke the words, the answer was clear to her.

"Gasam has an army, and a better one than ours, if you'll pardon my saying so, Princess. But he doesn't have a navy, except for some canoes. He'll have one if he wins this fight." His tone was nonchalant, but his face was pale and grim beneath his windburn.

"But won't our skippers scuttle their ships before they allow them to be taken? Are they not bound by oath to do so?" Already she knew how stupid that was.

"Princess, I don't think I need to tell *you* what our senior naval officers are like." He spat to leeward. "They won't scuttle their ships and they won't fall on their swords. They'll surrender and take service with Gasam if he gives them the chance. They'll kiss his backside in gratitude."

She gripped the railing and her knuckles turned white. "What kind of man is he?" She knew, though. Gasam was a king and a conqueror and, unlike so many other kings, so many other would-be conquerors, he was every bit as capable as he thought he was. A new sound came, beating in time with the throbbing in her temples and at first she thought the sound was inside her head.

"Now what?" she said, looking around.

"It's *Crusher*, my lady." This was the name the Nevans had adopted in place of its interminable Chiwan title. The other they called *Victorious*. Slowly, ponderously, the ship was maneuvering into the harbor entrance, which was barely wide enough to admit it. The pounding she heard was the thunder of the kettledrums beating time for the rowers in the twin hulls.

"Its rails are twenty feet from the waterline," she said, hopefully. "Surely the barbarians cannot force their way aboard from canoes!"

"Let us hope not, Princess," Saan said. He looked below to make sure all was in order on his ship. Shazad looked as well. The sailors below were keyed up and apprehensive, but at the same time happy to be out of the action. The Chiwan women were all but chewing their shields in frustration. All day they had been hearing the sounds of battle without being able to take part, and now their sisters were going into battle aboard *Crusher* without them.

Victorious waited outside the harbor entrance, its catapults keeping up a steady fire on the city wall. Its engines, though, were no more accurate than those in the city, and were firing from a mobile platform. Most of the stones were wasted. Behind *Crusher* came a flotilla of transport ships full of soldiers.

"What is this foolishness?" Shazad demanded, pointing at the troop ships. "What are those things coming in for? They have no armament!"

"I think, my lady," Saan said, "that the idea was for the warships to beat the harbor defenses into submission. Then the Chiwan monster craft were to come in, suppressing fire from the city wall and at the same time land assault forces to seize the dock area. The transports were to tie on behind the Chiwan ships and send in soldiers to pass over their decks to reinforce the assault on the harbor gate. The towers on those ships are high enough that they could drop gangways onto the city walls and assault across them. That was the plan, anyway, I think. Maybe it can still work."

"Why is only one Chiwan ship coming in? No, don't answer, I can see for myself. This harbor is too small for both of them and the whole Nevan fleet." She could see savages forcing their way onto the decks of some of the Nevan ships. The fighting was furious all over the harbor now.

"My lady," Saan said, "may I make a suggestion without fear of being crucified?"

She thought about it for a while. "Saan, you

have been a good and loyal man. You may make one treasonous suggestion and I agree in advance to forget it."

"No treason, Princess." He looked aloft, at the little pennant atop the mast. "The wind is fair from the north. Let me raise sail and take you back to Kasin. When things go bad on a day like this, they go bad without end. Let me take you home, Princess."

She took a deep breath, closed her eyes, and tried to think through the unceasing din. The temptation was great. There was nothing she could do to affect the outcome of the battle. She was no bone-headed hero to worry about charges of cowardice. She shook her head, the rich, black locks tumbling around her face.

"No, I will see this through to the end, Saan. But yours are the only sensible words besides my own I have heard since leaving Kasin."

Now the huge Chiwan ship was inside the harbor and there was a great exclamation from the shore. The warriors there stood waving their spears, shaking their shields, shouting defiance. Atop the wall, a line of shields appeared as the defenders took up their stations. The shouting ordered itself into a rhythmic chanting.

Shouldering smaller craft aside, *Crusher* rowed into the middle of the harbor and turned so that its double bows were facing the seaward gate. All over the harbor, the other ships were battling the canoes. One of the two-bankers seemed to have fallen into the hands of the savages. It was drifting away from the ragged line of the other Nevan ships. Soon a number of the canoes had it in tow and were taking it toward the sheds.

"When will the Chiwan attack?" Shazad demanded worriedly.

"I think they are waiting for the king to arrive, my lady," Saan said.

"What?" Saan pointed silently. "Oh, no!" she cried. *War Dragon* was cruising into the harbor at high speed. Once through the entrance, the ship dug in its oars and halted as perfectly as if it were on naval maneuvers. The oars on one side backwheeled vigorously and the ram swiveled to face the city gate. Then both sides backed water. The ship reversed, stopping only when its towering stern nudged the breakwater. The stern of *War Dragon* was now no more than thirty yards from *Moonglow*, just on the other side of the artificial mole. It anchored the southern end of the fleet's battle line. Immediately, a dozen canoes paddled to attack it.

"Father!" Shazad screamed. "Get out of there!" There was no chance of his hearing her over the thunder of battle, and no possibility that he might pay attention if he could hear her. Flags waved aboard *War Dragon* and the great Chiwan assault vessel began to move forward.

The multitude of oars dipped and rose, dipped and rose, moving the huge vessel at a slow walk. Anything faster would risk shattering both hulls when they made contact with the stone wharfs. Great pads of hemp had been hung from the bows to prevent just that, but the momentum built up by the great ship would be terrible.

With a shuddering impact, the great vessel came to a stop. A huge cheer went up from the

Nevan fleet as broad gangways crashed down from the wide deck that covered both hulls. Simultaneously, narrower gangways dropped from the forward tower upon the city wall. The troop transports pulled up astern of *Crusher* and assault troops swarmed up ladders onto the deck to reinforce the Chiwan soldiers who were already charging down the gangways. For the first time, Shazad noticed that the stern tower of the ship was built higher than the forward tower, so that its archers could shoot over the one forward, or directly down on it should enemy warriors force their way aboard.

Shazad began to feel elation. Perhaps they would win after all. The savages must be demoralized by this display of brute power. There was a commotion at the city gate and she trained the telescope on it to see what was happening. For some reason the image was not clear and she wiped the eyepiece with her scarf. Then she saw that the light was dim. Looking to the west, she was amazed to see that the sun was setting. Where had the day gone? It seemed like less than an hour since the first Nevan ship had entered the harbor mouth.

"They're opening the gate, Princess," Saan told her. She swung the telescope back toward the city and saw that the gate was swinging wide.

"Why aren't they barring it?" she asked. It looked as if the huge ram protruding from the forward tower would not be needed. Did the savages not know how to defend a city? Then she saw the horde of warriors pouring out through the gate. The barbarians were going on the attack. Rank upon rank of them were disgorged from the city, rank upon rank of tall, black shields and long, bronze spears.

"The Shasinn," she said, her voice hoarse. "This is what he has been saving them for."

On the wharfs, a brutal, hand-to-hand struggle raged. Arms clashed continuously with a rattling of metal and a splintering of wood. Missiles rained town on shields of hide or wood or wicker, adding to the din. And everywhere was the sound of human voices: cheering, chanting, screaming, groaning. Men were forced from the wharfs and fell into the water. Men staggered and tripped over the bodies of the fallen.

Above, assault troops tried to force their way onto the city walls, but with no success. Shazad could see why. Gasam had built a broad fighting platform at the place where he knew the gangways must be dropped, and it was crowded with Shasinn. Instead of a few warriors striving to hold a cramped, narrow wallwalk, the assault troops faced a small army concentrated in one spot. Soon the Shasinn forced their way onto the upper gangways and there was fierce fighting on the narrow front. Men toppled over the sides to crash down on those struggling for control of the wharfs. Those behind the ones fighting at the front raised their shields and formed a roof to shelter them from arrows coming from the stern tower.

Within minutes, the assault troops were cleared from the wharfs and the Shasinn were storming the gangways leading up to the deck. It was an uphill fight, but they were fierce and strong, killing with remorseless efficiency, their keen-edged spears seeming to draw blood each time they darted forward. From the wharfs,

Shasinn unable to reach the gangways hurled javelins onto the deck of the ship. Shazad would not have believed that the short, bronze-tipped spears could be hurled with such tremendous force and accuracy at such ranges. These were not the long, beautiful spears with which the Shasinn fought hand-to-hand, but they were just as deadly. The heavy points crunched through the lighter shields and impaled the vulnerable bodies behind them. They would pierce the lacquered armor of the Nevan troops and it soon became a major task just to keep the corpses cleared from the decks.

"Why don't they cut the gangways loose and back off?" Shazad cried.

"Because those javelin-throwers are killing anyone who goes near the moorings with an ax," Saan told her.

She saw that it was true. Officers were urging soldiers to cut the heavy ropes that secured the gangways. Even as she looked, a man rushed toward the twisted cords with ax upraised. Instantly, three javelins pierced him and he tumbled to the deck writhing. Some sailors came forward with a shield improvised from a hatch-cover and behind them came more soldiers with axes. Taking casualties but with the determination of desperate men, they hacked at the ropes. Already, though, it was too late. The Shasinn cleared the last defenders from the upper and lower gangways and were storming onto the deck and the forward tower.

Shazad lowered the telescope wearily. "Father might as well take the fleet out of the harbor while he still has some ships left," she said. "This is over."

"Not yet," Saan told her, pointing at the stern tower of *Crusher*. Flags were waving frantically, transmitting some sort of signal. Again she heard the great thunder of kettledrums. *Victorious* had taken up station just outside the harbor. Now it was coming in.

"It is almost dark," Shazad said numbly. "How do they expect to fight in the dark?" Already torches were being brought from the city to illuminate the wharfs. The ships, still under attack from the canoes, were hanging out firebaskets so that they could see to fight off the attackers. She could see that the savages had captured two more ships, one of them a three-banker, and were towing them toward the sheds. She could also see something coming from the largest of the sheds.

"What is that?" she asked. Saan took the glass from her and looked.

"As near as I can make out, it's a two-banker. Probably captured when they took the city."

"How is it moving? I see no oars working. It isn't yet so dark that I couldn't see them."

Saan studied the scene for a minute more. "They're pushing it. They have canoes behind it paddling for all they're worth."

The two-banker made a slow, careful path through the struggling craft in the harbor. The remaining Nevan ships were all backed against the mole and *Crusher* was fastened to the wharfs, leaving a relatively clear channel down the center of the harbor. The paddlers chanted as they pushed the ship through the wreckage and the bodies, living and dead. Its ram pushed aside overturned canoes and the ones still manned hastily got out of its way. The ship was headed straight for *Victorious*, which was making its own slow, careful way through the harbor entrance. A man emerged from belowdecks on the two-banker, ran to the side and dived overboard, cutting the water cleanly and stroking for shore. Shazad was mystified.

"Are they going to ram?" she asked. "Surely that ship is too small to . . ." A plume of smoke emerged from a hatch on the ship.

"I think, Princess, that we won't need to worry about the darkness much longer."

Now a small flame licked up through the hatch and the paddlers redoubled their already frantic stroking, churning the water to a froth beneath the broad blades of their paddles. The ship entered the space between the two hulls of *Victorious*. Oars snapped loudly and the drums fell silent. The two-banker ground to a shuddering halt and the canoes began to back away, cutting themselves free of the long pole with which they had pushed the ship. *Victorious* drifted a few more feet and stopped.

The deck of the fireship burst open and a tremendous gush of flame erupted beneath the deck of the Chiwan ship above. With the inrush of air, the rest of the smaller ship's cargo ignited: pitch-soaked bundles of hemp and barrels of fistnut oil erupted like a volcano. In an instant, the huge ship was a mass of flame. More than two hundred yards away, Shazad felt scorched by the heat.

The cheer of exultation from ashore was deafening. The Shasinn were in control of *Crusher* now, and she saw a group of warriors atop the ship's stern tower raise a shield over their heads, and on the shield stood a single figure. He raised his spear of steel and the entire harbor and city wall erupted in a barbaric chant of worship. Saan's voice brought her back to herself.

"It is over, Princess," he said for the third time. "The channel is blocked, the fleet cannot escape. They are trapped here. The defeat is total. Let's go!"

Desperately she searched the fantastic scene, looking for some shred of hope amid the chaos. "We still hold most of the ships!" she cried.

"Not for long. Look." At the mainland end of the mole, a strong force of Shasinn were attacking the Nevan troops who still held it. "They'll have control of the mole soon, and then they'll be aboard the ships by the stern. It'll be finished then. May I give orders to set sail?"

She turned on him, her eyes half-mad with fury. "You will stay where you are! You will not move until I bring the king out of there!" Wasting no time, she slid down a backstay, burning her palms for the sake of speed.

"Bloody Ax!" she screamed. "Get your women over the side and onto the mole! Follow me!" Shazad tore off her confining jacket and leapt over the side, into the shallow water. A few strokes later she found stone beneath her feet and she trudged up onto the mole. All the soldiers had rushed toward the mainland end to resist the Shasinn, so there was no one to help her. The weight of her soaked boots and trousers dragged at her and she wished she could tear them off, but there was no time. The breath burned and tore at her lungs as she ran the short distance to *War Dragon*'s stern. It towered above her, then two of her women warriors were beneath her, lifting her high enough to get a finger-purchase on the rail and pull herself aboard. After her, the women swarmed aboard.

A knot of men clustered at the forward rail of the sterncastle, and in their midst she could see what appeared to be her father's ghost. The course of the day had aged him twenty years. The men surrounding him were shouting, and in the babble she could hear the word "Surrender!" many times. Someone made a stealthy way behind the king, a dagger bare in his hand. Shazad pointed and one of the women buried an ax in the attacker's skull.

The king turned, startled. "Shazad? What are you doing? Why are you not . . ."

"Get aboard *Moonglow*, Father!" she screamed at him.

"No!" shouted an admiral. "We must surrender! He may give us good terms if . . ."

"If you turn the king of Neva over to him?" Shazad said. She pointed. "Kill him! Kill all of these fools!" Enthusiastically, her women obeyed. The deck grew slick with blood.

"But, Shazad . . ." the king said, his voice quavering. "I must . . ." She ignored him and leaned over the rail. Below, the marines were defending the ship, but Shasinn had gained the bows and were crowding onto the forecastle.

"Harakh!" she bellowed, so forcefully that she felt blood come into her throat. The man turned, his face covered with sweat beneath the helmet of sawn toonoo-tusk. His cuirass of layered sharkskin bore many gouges and his muscular arms bled from numerous small wounds.

He shouted something to his men and made his way aft.

"Princess?" he called, saluting.

"Get your men together and take the king off this ship. Look!" She pointed to where the Shasinn were advancing up the breakwater. "They will be standing here soon!"

Harakh whirled and raised a small whistle to his lips. He blew a complex series of trills, the piercing tones lancing easily through the clamor. In orderly fashion, the marines backed from the rails and fell in around Harakh. Shazad leaned on the railing, almost faint. It was so wonderful to have someone who obeyed instantly and forcefully. She shook off the faintness. There were things to be done before she could collapse. The canoe warriors were storming over the rails now. These were light-skinned men with shaven heads, a breed she had never seen.

Harakh raced up the stair, followed by his marines. A few faced the enemy and backed slowly toward the stair. "Princess?" he said again, not wasting words.

"Take my father. *Moonglow* is just on the other side of the breakwater. Whatever else happens, we must get him to the capital." Instantly, Harakh barked orders at his men. They bundled the king, protesting feebly, over the stern. Impulsively Shazad grabbed Harakh by the bloody shoulders and kissed him.

"I'll make you a general for this! Now, come, we have to get away from here! We must order the master of the supply flotilla to be away, too. At least we can deny Gasam that much."

They rushed to the rail and Harakh scooped

her up, dropping her into the arms of her female bodyguard and then jumping after. The savages swarmed over the ship, killing the last few marines Harakh had ordered to stand fast. Harakh led the way up the mole and onto its top. She could see Saan aboard *Moonglow*, frantically waving to them. The sounds of fighting grew very close.

Bloody Ax whirled to say something to her, but a javelin passed through her throat and cut off whatever she might have had to say. The last of the Nevan soldiers went down and suddenly there were Shasinn everywhere. The women clustered around her, fighting to protect her and to save their own lives. Through the confusion of struggling bodies, she saw Harakh and a few marines climbing aboard *Moonglow* as Saan raised the sail. Harakh made no foolish effort to come back and rescue her. A good man, she thought, wishing she had had more of them.

The women around her fell fighting, the Shasinn spears piercing them one after another. Shazad made no effort to resist and soon she stood alone, surrounded by exultant Shasinn. A hand on her shoulder forced her to her knees and something cold touched the soft skin of her neck. She glanced down and saw firelight gleaming along the blade of a Shasinn spear. Another bronze blade touched her neck on the other side and the two blades crossed just in front of her chin. *If they draw back on those things hard enough*, she thought, *my head will come right off*. The thought failed to upset her greatly. She wished they would kill her and get it over with. The spears were taken away and someone gripped her arm and hauled her to her feet. Then she understood that the business with the spears was some sort of prisoner-taking gesture, the way the desert peoples were said to grasp a defeated enemy by the hair in token of his captive status. Prodded by spear-butts, she began to walk toward the mainland end of the mole, toward the city. Her ordeal was not over yet, she thought with despair. But there was one thing they could not take from her: She had gotten the king safely away.

THIRTEEN

As dawn broke over the city, the hulk of *Victorious* and the fireship still flamed sporadically, sending up clouds of smoke. The wreckage of the two-banker that had been hulled by the catapult stone and then gutted by the Nevan ship behind it lay on its side in the shallows. The corpses and floating wrack had drifted with the tide toward the harbor mouth, but the wreckage blocking the channel would let little past.

Shazad leaned back against the city wall near the gate and let the rising sun warm her chilled body. At least she was not wearing soaked clothes any more. This was because the Shasinn had cut her wet clothes away, leaving her wearing nothing at all. Then she corrected herself: I am wearing this yoke.

A bar of heavy wood lay across her shoulders,

curved in the middle to fit around the back of her neck. The curve was padded, but it still forced her head forward. Her wrists were tied into u-shaped forks at the ends of the bar. She sat with a group of forty or fifty other prisoners, most of them laborers and slaves brought along on the expedition. The soldiers, sailors and marines had been taken somewhere else. Many wounded lay about untended. From time to time an Islander would examine one and, deciding the man would not live anyway, dispatched him with a quick thrust of spear or sword.

Her hair was snarled, tangled, matted. She was heavily bruised and she ached in every part. In past years, it had sometimes amused her to play slave, usually with other high-born men and women. They had worn tokens of slavery and it had been pleasant and exciting to submit to another's dominance, always with the knowledge that the game could be ended at will. She knew that the experience of the reality of slavery would not be as pleasant as those games.

A pair of scarred, straddling legs stood before her. "Up, girl," a voice ordered. Awkwardly, unable to use her hands, she complied. Under the yoke, she could barely raise her head enough to see his face. It was as scarred as his legs. His head was clean-shaven except for a topknot secured by a gold ring. His ears were pierced for several gold hoops and he wore a leather tunic girdled by a wide belt studded with coral. This was no Islander, but a Nevan slaver.

"What is your name?" he demanded. A curious crowd of Island warriors idled about, watching with interest. Shazad said nothing. The man nodded to someone behind her and abruptly, shockingly, her back flamed with agony. Someone had lashed her with a multi-thonged scourge. The man stepped closer.

"Why do you make no sound?"

"I have been whipped harder than that by junior priests," she snarled. Bracing her feet, she twisted her upper body as hard as she could. The end of her yoke slammed into the slaver's jaw and a ferocious joy coursed through her when she heard the bone snap. The man fell heavily to the flagstones, unconscious. Now, she thought, maybe they will kill me. Instead, the men roared with mirth, as if this were the funniest sight they had seen in years.

"Turn around." This was a woman's voice. Slowly she turned. Two women stood there, surrounded by Shasinn warriors. The taller wore only a tiny loincloth and a great many ornaments. She was the most beautiful creature Shazad had ever beheld, and Shazad had spent her life surrounded by beautiful men and women.

"Queen Larissa," she said, her voice hoarse from all the screaming she had done the day before, "at last we meet."

The queen held a scourge. It had been she who had lashed Shazad. Now she placed the handle beneath Shazad's chin and tilted her head back, the movement made painful by the yoke.

"Who are you, girl?" The queen's voice was melodious, her breath fragrant.

"Princess Shazad of Neva," she answered. An astonished babble broke out among the on-lookers. The queen turned to the smaller woman who stood beside her. She was dark-haired and honey-skinned with tilted eyes, and she wore a collar riveted around her neck. She stood close and examined Shazad's face.

"It is difficult to tell, Mistress," she said, "with her face looking so frightful and all these bruises and scrapes."

"The slave collar becomes you, Dunyaz," Shazad said. "You were always the most willing slave in those games we used to play, years ago."

"And the yoke looks good on you," Dunyaz replied. "I would ask my mistress to allow me to flog you for your insolence, but I know how much you would enjoy it." She turned back to the queen. "It is she."

"Come with me," the queen said, turning. Perforce, Shazad followed, her bare feet pain-ing her with every step on the rough cobbles. Even in her pain and humiliation, she could not help staring enviously at Larissa's long legs and incredibly shapely bottom. Never had the princess felt so unattractive as in the presence of this stunning woman.

"A warrior came to me this morning," the queen said, not bothering to turn around. "He told me that his squad had taken a woman prisoner last night. When it grew light he saw how rich were the clothes they had stripped from her and he remembered that she had been trying to escape from the Nevan flagship. He decided she was some high officer's mistress and he knew that I like to acquire comely women for my household. It seems we've caught a rare prize."

"Will you not release me from this yoke?" Shazad said.

"Why should I do that?" Larissa asked.

"I am a royal princess," Shazad said, "not a common prisoner. As a royal hostage I should be treated as my rank demands."

"Nonsense," said the queen. "You are a slave, nothing more."

"That is not how things are done among civilized people," Shazad said, beginning to breathe heavily as the road turned steep. Everywhere people bowed as they passed, except for the Shasinn warriors, who saluted instead.

"I am not civilized," Larissa said, "and the more I see of civilized people the happier I am of that fact. I have enjoyed your letters, though. Sorting through your lies and deceptions has been wonderfully amusing."

"You see?" Shazad all but panted. "You *are* growing civilized. Your own lies were rather polished, and I detected the hand of my cousin Dunyaz in that. I thought you and I had come to be friends, although we had never met."

"My possessions are not friends," Larissa said. "I own you. Do not forget that."

To Shazad's unutterable relief, they had reached the palace. It was a crude place by her standards, a fine mansion where the barbarian queen had accumulated whatever loot took her fancy without regard to good taste. Here she was turned over to a slave woman who wore a sheer gown, apparently in token of her status as overseer.

"Bathe her and dress her hair," the queen

ordered. "Then have her collared and bring her to me." The queen left and, with a last, malicious look, so did Dunyaz.

The woman took her to a bath in an annex. It was not the sort of luxurious bath she was used to at home. This one was obviously used by the household staff. It was, however, far better than the accommodations aboard *Moonglow*, which had consisted of a basin and a slave girl with sponges and towels. The bath attendants helped her to scrub at her body and hair until she felt clean for the first time in many days. She ignored the sting of her many small injuries. It was joy enough to be free of the yoke. She hoped that they would not make her resume it afterward.

After vigorous toweling, the woman in the gown had her sit on a low stool while a hairdresser carefully brushed the snarls from her luxuriant black tresses and a cosmetician did what she could to cover the bruises and scabs. Shazad knew that this was not the pampering reserved for a princess. It was more like one of her own cabos having ribbons braided into its tail and its horns gilded before she came down from the palace to ride. Like her, the queen was offended by the sight of things that were not beautiful.

The last illusion of pampering was dispelled when she was taken to a small blacksmith's shop and a metal ring was fastened around her neck. She was forced to kneel awkwardly by the anvil, which was equipped with a special stake on which slave-rings were riveted. The neck ring itself had a number of smaller rings attached to it for the attachment of tethers or leashes. When she had been suitably prepared, she was taken to the queen's chambers. The neck ring was her only garment.

"That is much better," Larissa said, looking up from her couch. The queen lay on her stomach, her head resting on her crossed forearms. Beside her, Dunyaz sat on the couch, massaging her mistress's shoulders and neck. "Put her over there." The queen indicated the wall she faced, where a short chain dangled from the wall to waist height. The slaves made Shazad sit and clipped the chain to her neck ring.

"Is this necessary?" Shazad asked.

"It is my will," the queen responded. She pushed herself to a sitting posture and she faced the princess. Her breasts and belly were covered with welts from the wrinkles in the cloth she had lain on, but these disappeared within seconds. Shazad had never seen such perfect skin tone.

"I have been collecting information on you, Shazad," Larissa continued. "I have many spies in Kasin. I have heard all about how you took the navy in hand."

"Much good did it do us," Shazad said bitterly.

"Speak when I ask you a question," Larissa said. "I do not need your other comments. As I was saying, I know that you are notoriously strong-willed and independent. This means that you might foolishly try to escape. For that reason I will keep you chained or confined until I am satisfied that you will be obedient. I have a great deal of time and it amuses me to tame rebellious creatures. Eventually I will find the punishment to break your will."

Someone came into the room and Dunyaz and the other slaves rose to their feet and bowed. The queen looked at him and smiled.

"What have we here, a new plaything?" Shazad felt her veins fill with ice. It was Gasam.

"Just my new slave," Larissa said. "Formerly Princess Shazad of Neva, Pashir's daughter."

The king came to her and dropped to one knee. He was so tall that she still had to look up to face him. "Why, so it is! I saw you yesterday, watching the battle from the mast of that little ship. I, too, have telescopes now. You Nevans make such marvelous, clever things. Soon you shall make them all for me." He smiled at her pleasantly, but behind his eyes she saw terrifying gulfs.

"Greetings, King Gasam," she said in her best court voice, "and congratulations on your great victory yesterday."

"Wasn't that a wonderful battle?" he said. "That was my finest victory thus far."

"It was truly overwhelming," she said.

"An excellent word for it," he agreed. "But it left behind a terrible mess. I have set the prisoners to work cleaning up my harbor. The smell is already getting bad. I like blood, but only while it is fresh. Battles in the field are cleaner. You just walk away from the dead and the scavengers come in to clean up."

"But this one made such a splendid spectacle, my love," said the queen. "None who beheld it will ever forget. The crashes in the harbor, that burning ship! The legend will live forever."

"So it will," Gasam said. "My queen, you

must write a letter to my brother-king Pashir. Tell him that we have his daughter and will keep her safe."

"My father will pay a rich ransom for me," she assured him, wondering whether this war had already bankrupted the kingdom.

Gasam chuckled. "Why do my well-born captives always think that their kinsmen have something that I cannot take by force? I do not wish to sell you back. It amuses me to own you, and your father's treasury already belongs to me; I merely have not yet taken it from him."

"How unfortunate that we did not capture him as well," said the queen.

Gasam shrugged. "It matters little. If I had taken him, someone else would seize the throne as soon as the news reached Kasin. Someone is going to be king of Neva until I have it in my grasp, so it might as well be Pashir." He touched Shazad, much as she had examined the rowers and tested her female bodyguard. She felt fear and revulsion coupled with a deep, terrible excitement. She saw the triumphant look on Dunyaz's face and tried to keep her face court-impassive. She could feel heat rising all the way from the pit of her stomach and hoped that her face was not flaming.

"How did it go with the warrior women?" Larissa asked her husband.

"They are splendid," he said, "but they refuse to take service with me. I think I shall work on them instead of killing them, or mutilating them and turning them loose. Such rare creatures are worth a little extra effort."

He turned back to Shazad. "You had some of them aboard your little ship. What makes them so difficult? Most surviving soldiers are anxious to take service with me."

"They worship the king of Chiwa," she said. "To them, he is a god. They are raised in barracks from the time they are infants."

Gasam sat back on his heels. "If they are going to have a god, it should be me." He turned to Larissa. "What should I do about this?"

She gave it some thought. "Work on their pride. First of all, they feel ashamed that they were taken alive. Let that humiliation sink in. Then tell them that they were duped, that their king is a fraud. *You* are the god-king and only you deserve to be served with the devotion they once gave to the unworthy . . . what is his name?"

"Diwaz the Ninth," Dunyaz said.

"Diwaz the Ninth. They will jump at the chance to submit to your oath. They have no concept of themselves except as loyal warriors of a god-king and their only choices are your service, death, or a nothingness that is worse than death."

"What would I do without you, little queen?" Gasam said happily. "My power is over the bodies and wills of men, but only you know their minds. I shall do as you say."

"These women warriors will make a pretty ornament to your army, my lord," said Larissa, "but you won more important prisoners yesterday. How did you fare with the naval prisoners? The skilled sailors and the rowers?"

"There we've been far more successful." The king stood and turned away from Shazad. He went to a table and poured a glass full from a pitcher. The liquid was amber with a thin foam on top. "Most of the surrendered sailors and marines have taken my oath. The losses among the rowers we can make up with slave rowers from the big Chiwan ship. I plan to start naval training for my men in the summer."

"What will you do with the big Chiwan ship?" Larissa asked.

"I think it will be useless to me. There are better ways of taking a city and it ties up too many soldiers and machines and, especially, rowers. I think I shall have it broken up and use the timber to build more ships. I have an idea I want to try: a new kind of ship, with only a single bank of oars but with a far wider deck, so that I can crowd on more men."

"Will it have enough speed with only a single level of oars?" Larissa asked.

"It will if there are two men to each oar, perhaps three. We forget about ramming. That takes complex rowing and steering, and the enemy ship is sunk instead of captured. We concentrate on boarding instead, where weight of men counts."

Shazad was stupefied. These people had a single-mindedness unknown in her own world. She began to think that they had no trivial pastimes or amusements, but were always thinking about war, about seizing and wielding power, about controlling people. What could stand against such people? They had a primitive vitality that was exhausting merely to look upon. Again, unbidden, the unwelcome thought occurred to her: *We are decadent, and we deserve to be conquered.*

* * *

Moonglow entered the harbor of Kasin on a bright afternoon. The king did not want to skulk into the city under cover of night again. There was no need to, since it was unlikely that word of the catastrophe had reached the city overland. The dockside idlers would see only the princess's yacht returning. Her covered litter was stored below and the king would be taken to the palace in it with the curtains tightly drawn. Before the ship reached the docks, Captain Harakh addressed the assembled crew and his little band of marines. Their battle-scarred harness was stored below so that nobody would see that a fight had taken place.

"None of you is to speak a word of the battle," Harakh said sternly. "The king wants nothing to be said until he has spoken with the important men of state. If any of you speaks, I shall know of it, and you shall have cause to envy men who are merely crucified. To anyone who asks, you shall only say that the princess was taken ill and had to return."

When they were lashed to the wharf, the king emerged from the cabin and climbed into the litter, screened by the marine guard. Then they went ashore and the guards prevented any curious onlookers from getting too close to the conveyance. Harakh walked alongside and Pashir talked to him nervously through the curtain.

"My daughter," the king groaned, "what of little Shazad?" It was as if he spoke of a child.

"I saw her taken," Harakh said yet another time. "She appeared unharmed when they led her away as we made our escape. No doubt you will receive a ransom demand soon."

"Anything. I will pay anything to get her back. My child!" Then his voice lost its querulousness. "She was the only good counselor I had, and I listened to fools instead! The gods curse *me* for a fool!"

That made Harakh feel better. Perhaps there was some of the old Pashir left.

"She saved your life, that's certain," the captain said. "She may have saved your kingdom. She could have escaped, but she went into the thick of the fighting with just those mad women guards to bring you out, then she ordered me to get you home at all costs." He knew it would not hurt to remind the king that he, for one, had appreciated the princess and that she had trusted him in turn. He had not forgotten her promise to make him a general.

"I must get her back," the king said yet again.

At the palace, he left the litter and bade Harakh wait for him. The servants looked stunned, but as always they jumped to do his bidding. The first order of business was to restore his regal appearance, then to summon the Council, at least such of the Council as were not dead or captured in Floria.

Soaking in his bath, sipping at watered wine laced with painkiller, he pondered. How to handle this? Would Shazad's trick with the priests work yet another time? It was worth a try. He would summon them. If it did not work, it would be the priests' credibility that would suffer, not his own.

There were a number of high nobles whom he was certain would attempt a coup if they knew he was seriously weakened. He would arrest them before they had the opportunity.

There was no need for executions just yet. He sorted through his memories for names of men to give emergency powers. They would have to be men whose fortunes were tied to his own, who would fall under another king. At least there was no shortage of those. He would keep Captain Harakh close; the man had proven his loyalty.

How long could he keep morale in the city from collapsing? Then he remembered Hael. How close was the boy? He still thought of him as the youth who had stayed for a while in his old, ducal palace, years ago. If young King Hael showed up unexpectedly, with a strong force of mounted savages to shore up the throne, it might do wonders for the spirits of the citizenry. He would sent out riders to the southeast. If they intercepted Hael, they could bid him make haste. If Hael was coming at all.

Four hours later, Pashir came from his chambers and Harakh fell in beside him. "To the council chamber," the king ordered. Bathed, groomed, his hair and beard freshly dyed, and dressed in fresh robes, a good meal in him, the king looked and sounded fifteen years younger than when he had arrived at the palace. Harakh had never beheld such a change, and he hoped it was not merely temporary. Harakh was now in the uniform of the royal guard, his dress armour gold-lacquered, but he retained his marine short sword.

The councilors bowed as the king entered. He had already spoken to the priests and, having no choice, they had agreed to his demands: they were all about to hear yet another startling revelation from their gods. The king took his seat and the councilors rose.

"I come to you with heavy news," he began. "I . . ." He saw a man who was not supposed to be there; a dusty officer in travel-stained garments. "Lord Ashgar, is that you? Why are you here instead of at your post on the Omian border?" It was a serious offense for a border lord to come to the capital without leave.

Lord Ashgar rose. "Your Majesty, I come with heavy news also. Even now, the Northeast Borderers fall back toward the capital. I rode here posthaste with warning. We have another enemy, Sire. King Oland of Omia has invaded and he marches hither this very hour."

Pashir fought to keep his face impassive. Was this the crowning disaster? Slowly the fingers of his right hand curled into a fist. Where was Hael?

FOURTEEN

They emerged from the desert with a sense of profound relief. The year was advancing, and the last few days had been blisteringly hot. The last of their native guides had left them at the base of a range of rugged hills that were not quite large enough to be deemed mountains: They were the southerly end of the tremendous mountain range that separated the high plains region from the low country to the west. Beyond these hills, all water would flow to the western sea.

The desert crossing had cost them only two men and not a single cabo. The men had died from the bites of unknown serpents, while carelessly gathering firewood. There had been no sickness, and this Hael attributed to their lack of close contact with the native peoples. The desert was largely empty and it had been easy to avoid the villages. Once they entered more settled land, he knew that he could look forward to having at least a few men incapacitated by illness, fit as his were.

Crossing the hills was an arduous, dry process. They found not a single spring, and the footing was treacherous. The hills seemed to be made up mostly of loose rock compacted by dirt, and progress had to be very slow and careful to avoid falls. As they came down the western slope, spirits soared. In the distance, they could see green land, patterned with the neat lines and squares of cultivation. Along the base of the hills ran a small, shallow river, and here the army watered its animals.

Jochim reined in beside Hael as the animals drank. "Shall I send out hunters, my king? There must be plenty of game hereabout."

"Not until we know who is in control here," Hael told him. "And you won't find as much wildlife in these cultivated lands as we are used to in the grasslands and the hills. And no raiding! The men are to be strictly cautioned about that. From here on, the people are King Pashir's subjects and I will not have them molested, even if they are mere farmers."

They rode through a beautiful morning, and scouts rode back to report sizable villages ahead, and a border fort. Soon the fort was in sight. It was a small, mud-brick building with cracked battlements and a royal banner flapping listlessly in the breeze. Danger seldom approached Neva from the southeast, so little of the annual military budget was expended in this province.

A man rode from the fort, mounted on a cabo.

Behind him came about a hundred footmen. The men formed two lines facing inward and Hael could see that a road began just a few hundred paces ahead of him. It was not paved, but the hard-packed earth was flanked by well-kept drainage ditches. The men stood at rigid attention and as Hael approached they brought up their spears in rigid salute. Their officer wore a faded cloak over fine armor and held a toonoo-tusk helmet beneath one arm. With his other arm, he saluted stiffly.

"King Hael, I take it?" He dropped the salute and took Hael's outstretched hand. "Of course, you must be. Who else would be riding out of the desert with several thousand mounted men? We were told to expect you at any time, and this was the most likely place for you to enter Nevan territory. What a crossing you must have had! Please, come join me in the fort. Your men can pitch camp here, if you wish. It's too late to push on today." Hael had the distinct impression that this man seldom had anyone to talk to in his remote outpost. "I am Superior Captain Twula, at your service."

"I thank you, Superior Captain. Have I your leave to send out hunting parties? I have already given my men orders not to raid."

"But of course! I am sorry that I cannot feed so many men, but from here on you will have full rights of requisition at every government storehouse. The best hunting is to be found due south of here. And don't worry about the local peasants. They are worth nothing, or they would have taken better land from someone else."

Hael put his officers in charge of the army

and followed Twula into the shabby fort. His quarters consisted of a comfortable house with a well-kept rooftop garden. Beneath a thatched awning in the roof garden, the captain's servants served Hael chilled wine and trays of delicacies. Twula seemed to do well, considering his undesirable posting. For servants, he preferred attractive young boys.

"I apologize for the poverty of my accommodations," he said as a boy helped him out of his armor. "One must put up with want in a province like this. The natives are desert savages little better than those on the other side of the hills, and they must have scoured every jail in the kingdom to find this garrison."

"What do you hear of the war?" Hael asked, little concerned with the man's woes.

"Not nearly enough. The last word we had, which was at least twenty days ago, had it that the king was preparing the fleet to sail north to eject the pirates. I have no idea if the fleet's sailed yet. They never bother to inform us of much down here. This outpost hasn't been important since the Moon was white."

Hael was amused to hear the old expression, which was used even in his home islands. The Moon had been white in the days before the fiery spears, unthinkable ages ago.

"Surely the king will not sail until I reach the capital," Hael said. "How long a march is it from here?"

"For a mounted force, about eight days, if there are no late storms to hold you up. I wish I was going with you. In war there is a chance for advancement, for coming to the notice of one's king, instead of serving in this tomb."

Eight days, Hael thought. They would pick up the pace and make it in six. That would help tone the cabos as well, restricted as they had been to a walk while crossing the desert. He would requisition plenty of the best fodder from the government storehouses to build up their health and endurance. When the time came, his army would be in prime condition for battle.

The next morning he bade Twula farewell. The man had been hospitable and helpful in his way. Hael had no idea what he had done to condemn him to this forsaken mud fort, but he assumed he deserved it.

The men were delighted with the acceleration of their pace. They were growing bored and this was refreshing. They roared with laughter to see the peasants run at first sight of them. Equally amusing were the townspeople who crowded the ruinous walls of their settlements, wailing in terror at this apparition from nowhere. Only government officials had been told to expect an army from the desert, and they had not bothered to inform anybody. The warriors found all these new sights enthralling.

Hael used his royal authority ruthlessly, requisitioning anything he thought fit, from baskets to blankets. Mostly, though, he requisitioned food. The royal officials cried out and tore their hair to see how much food and animal fodder this army could consume. Tons of flour, preserved meats and fruits left the warehouses. Multiple tons of fodder disappeared from the silos. Whole herds of domestic kagga and quil were slaughtered to feed the hungry warriors. Hael reasonably pointed out that these men had made an epic march to help King Pashir, and they were entitled to anything they desired. He further pointed out that they could easily take it by force if they had to. The officials saw his point.

As they rode, the land grew more settled and more heavily cultivated and far richer. The towns had fine walls and the army began to cross rivers by way of beautiful, stone bridges. The warriors found these bridges a great marvel and at first were reluctant to believe that they were man-made. They gaped at shrines erected to gods along the roads, thinking that the sheltered images within, made of colored ceramics, were tiny human beings.

Soon, though, they became jaded with new sights and could ride by a glowering colossus without sparing it a second glance. And once they were over their first shock, the townspeople crowded around, eager to see this unexpected and no longer menacing army at close range. The women, especially, were eager to see these handsome warriors.

"Their men are a poor lot," an officer commented to Hael. "No wonder they find real men such as we attractive."

"We have no time for dalliance," Hael said, "but when the fighting is over I have no doubt that the Nevan women will prove as hospitable as any hot-blooded young warrior could wish for."

"That is half the reason we came here," said the officer, an Amsi who was extraordinarily vain about his long, black hair, to which he had fastened innumerable tiny, silver bells and silver shell ornaments traded by the southern merchants.

"The other half was loot and fighting," Hael said. "You'll have plenty of all three before long."

Three days from the capital, a royal messenger stopped before Hael. Once he was assured that this was, indeed, the king of the plains, he handed over a letter bearing the royal seal.

"It arrived by fast cutter yesterday morning," the messenger reported. "It was in four copies, to be sent along all the routes where you were most likely to be encountered."

"By cutter?" Hael said. "Then the fleet has sailed already?"

"Many days ago," the man said.

"What does this mean?" Jochim asked, after Hael had dismissed the messenger.

"I do not know. Perhaps Pashir wants me to march directly to Floria, to hit it from the land side while he blockades it from the sea."

"Besiege a city?" Jochim said. "That is not our kind of warfare. Open battle in the field is what we came here for."

Hael broke open the message tube and unrolled the scroll.

King Hael, it began baldly, *greetings from your old friend, the Princess Shazad.*

"Who is this?" Jochim asked.

"Pashir's daughter. I knew her long ago." He read on.

My father has not waited for your arrival, but has taken the fleet north, trusting that there will be no late storms. We are now anchored outside the harbor of

Floria. Gasam's warriors have been coming across from the Islands by canoe, and it seems that this fleet is useless for blockading such vessels. Listening to the advice of his noblemen, instead of to mine, he proposes an amphibious assault against the city at first light tomorrow. I feel that this is a terrible error and urge you to make all haste to join us. I fear some awful catastrophe. Just as happened last year, my father and his advisers underestimate the number of men Gasam has at his command. I have seen with my own eyes what terrible warriors the Shasinn are. Since you were Shasinn, you know what I mean. Again I beg you to make haste, for I think we will need your aid very soon.

It was signed with minimal flourishes.

The knot of officers who surrounded Hael looked concerned. "What will you do about this, my king?" asked Bamian.

"Exactly what I have been doing," he answered, rolling the letter and replacing it in the tube. "If King Pashir has done something foolish, I do not propose that I and my men shall pay for it. We shall proceed to Kasin, and there I shall learn how matters stand. Let's continue."

As they rode, he thought about the letter. Shazad did not sound like the vain, lascivious young woman he had known. She had been little more than a girl then, and he had been a boy. According to the letter she had even accompanied the fleet when it sailed, and that sounded little like the Shazad he had known.

On the morning of the seventh day after leaving the desert, the scouts came back to report something that puzzled them. The army was climbing a spine of verdant hills terraced for the cultivation of vineyards and orchards. The scouts had ridden to the crest.

"There is something wrong with the sky," said an Amsi. "It is not easy to describe," he admitted.

"What now?" Jochim wanted to know.

They rode to the crest of the hills and Hael surveyed the scene, which the other scouts were still trying to puzzle out. Great clouds towered to the west, and below them was a great blue-green-gray stretch, a vista that the plainsmen could not interpret.

Hael laughed aloud. "That is the sea!" he told them. "The land just ends there, and there is nothing beyond but water and some islands." They did not understand. "You see, we stand on the land. Above us is the sky, and over there is a mass of water as great as the land we have come across."

"Like a big lake?" Bamian asked.

"Not exactly," Hael told him. "It is no use to describe it. You will have to see for yourselves. Come, we can be there before noon."

The great column wended its way down the hills and onto the coastal plain. Here the farming was quite intensive, and wildlife was rare. The royal road was now fully paved and well maintained. There were watering tanks for livestock every few miles, and stones recording the distance to the capital and to the major cities and forts. A stretch of the road ran along the beach and the plainsmen were stunned by the enormous size of the ocean, the sound of the surf and the unfamiliar smells. Some rode out toward the surf and forced their cabos a little way in. Man and animal both were surprised by the saltiness of the water.

Here and there, they saw young boys and girls practicing an ancient coastal sport; riding along the tops and the fronts of waves on narrow boards. The riders took this for magic. They thought, at first, that the sailboats they saw were sea creatures. When they came in sight of the capital, they thought its walls were natural cliffs. These walls ran from the water all the way to the hills to the east, completely blocking this narrow strip of coastal plain, where a great bay indented the shoreline. Hael's officers were appalled at the size of the place, which was like all the villages and towns they had seen thus far placed together.

"Is it possible for an army to take such a place?" one asked.

"It can be done," Hael assured him, "but only with great difficulty. You can see how it was built in a fine defensive position. It blocks this plain, with the hills to the east and the sea to the west. You cannot see it, but on the north side there is a great river which runs along the northern wall. Where the river empties into the bay is the harbor. A city like this can be starved if you have a powerful army and navy. Or it can be stormed, or, if you have confederates inside, it can be treacherously surrendered."

Atop the walls, banners unfurled and the music of trumpets came to their ears. They had been seen by the daywatch. Hael ordered the column to slow to a walk and to form up neatly in ranks, by units. Bannermen and standard-bearers rode to the front to ride behind Hael and the higher officers. Men straightened and dusted off their clothing, and donned ornaments carefully stowed away in saddlebags, and settled stern expressions on their faces. They did not want to disgrace their king by making a poor showing in front of the city-dwellers.

When they were only a few hundred yards from the city gate, a crowd of gaily dressed noblemen, mounted on splendid cabos, came out to greet them. Some were in court robes, others in military uniform and armor. All wore broad smiles. A herald rode forth and began a loud, formal greeting while the nobles applauded. Hael did not see the king among them.

At last the herald bade the glorious King Hael and his equally glorious warriors enter the capital of Neva and receive the welcome and praise of the citizenry. By the time the procession reached the gate, the top of the wall was lined with citizens, cheering frantically. Within, they pushed their way through narrow streets lined with men and women who cheered and waved banners. From balconies and rooftops, they showered the riders with flower petals. Householders and tavern-keepers held out cups and pitchers and skins of strong drink. Since Hael had not thought to forbid this, the riders accepted.

"These people are happy to see us," Jochim shouted above the crowd's din.

"They are more than glad," Hael said. *These people have been badly frightened*, he thought. *They welcome us not as allies but as rescuers.*

They passed through plazas and markets, through wide boulevards and past huge temples from which ascended great pillars of smoke as sacrifices of gratitude were offered to the gods. They stopped before the king's palace, where a broad stair ascended a man-made hill to the main building. Hael could see the king standing in lonely grandeur at the top of the stair. With his army massing in the plaza behind him, Hael dismounted.

"Await me," he told his officers, who remained mounted. A young officer in the glittering uniform of a royal guardsman walked down the last few steps. As he came close he paused, a startled look on his face. He tried to cover this by bowing quickly.

"Greetings ... ah ... King Hael. My royal master bids me escort you to him." Hael began to climb and the guardsman fell in beside him. "I beg your pardon, King Hael. I was unforgivably rude. It was just that ... your appearance ..."

"I look just like the Shasinn you have been fighting, eh?"

"Well, yes. It is a distinctive look, especially that spear, and your hair and eyes. Those of us who have survived these last two battles have nightmares about those spears."

Hael smiled. This was better than some fawning courtier. "Yes, I was Shasinn. Did Princess Shazad tell you that?"

"Yes. So did His Majesty. The sight is still startling. I am Captain Harakh, formerly of the marines, now of the royal guard."

"You sailed with the naval expedition?"

"Yes."

"And it ended in disaster."

"Exactly." The captain spoke hastily. "We must speak later, in private." They were almost at the top of the steps and Hael was shocked at the king's appearance. When he had seen him last, Pashir had been a powerful, commanding man in his vigorous middle years. This was an old man valiantly striving to hold at bay the debilitating effects of age. Cosmetics and hair dye could not completely cover the evidence of his decline. He embraced Hael, and the crowd below roared.

"Doubly welcome, Hael," Pashir said. "Come inside with me. I am having a banquet prepared in your honor, to which all your officers must come. Your troops will be led to the military assembly field. They may use the barracks there."

"Some will prefer to pitch tents in the open," Hael said. "Most of the Amsi have never slept beneath a roof in their lives."

"All will be taken care of. I wish I could entertain you properly, but you arrive at a dark hour."

"I noticed that the guard on the walls was heavier than last time I passed this way. Does Gasam march on the city?"

Pashir sighed. "Not Gasam. Gasam still sits in Floria, picking his teeth with the remaining splinters of my beautiful fleet. I have been a great fool, Hael. I did not wait for you, and in pride and vanity I tried to take Gasam from the sea. It was not to be. But meanwhile my relations with Omia have been precarious for years. King Oland heard of my defeat last year, and knowing that I would be preoccupied with Gasam, he invaded and seized all of Neva north of the River of Lizards."

"This is heavy news," Hael said, "But I have been to Omia. It is a pastoral land, not agricultural and mercantile, like Neva. The population is thin and widespread. Surely you can take care of the Omian problem once this matter of Gasam has been settled."

Pashir smiled. "You have learned to think like a king, my friend Hael. That is good. But my true fear now, and I admit to you that I feel fear, is that Oland and Gasam will unite against me. I do not know how Chiwa stands now. I know that I cannot count on any support from that direction, since I lost two of King Diwaz's prized castle-ships in Floria Harbor."

They had come to an intimate receiving chamber laid with refreshments. At Pashir's gracious gesture, Hael seated himself at a small table and Pashir, joints creaking, sat on the other side. One wall opened on a beautiful courtyard with a fountain playing in its center.

"You truly find yourself in an unenviable position, King Pashir," Hael said, "but I have come here to help you fight Gasam. My kingdom, too, borders upon Omia. My northwestern trade routes pass through that kingdom. You and I have no treaty of alliance concerning aggression from Omia. I came here upon your personal request, to help you repel this invasion from the Islands."

"And to settle an old score between you and Gasam," Pashir countered.

"He is our mutual enemy. I would not have come just to revenge myself on him."

"And if Oland allies himself with Gasam, your enemy and mine?" King Pashir pressed.

"Then," Hael admitted, "I shall have to rethink my relationship with King Oland of Omia."

A suite of rooms had been put at Hael's disposal, and he went there to rest for an hour or two before the banquet. As he entered the rooms, a staff of servants bowed to him. Then a seated man rose.

"Choula!" The two men embraced warmly.

"Hael, my friend." The scribe held him at arm's length. "Well, you don't dress like a king, but you look like one anyway. Come, sit and have something to drink. I would like to exchange pleasantries and talk over the last several years and all the things that have happened since we parted, but I have more recent events to catch you up on."

"Yes. Were you at this sea battle?"

"I was. It wasn't really a sea battle, as you shall hear. Luckily for me, the king had all the noncombatants stay with the transport ships when the warships went in to battle. I returned to the capital with the supply fleet and only arrived a few days ago. There is someone else you should speak with. Ah, here he is."

Hael looked to see who was coming in. "Yes, I've met Captain Harakh." The guardsman joined them.

"I do not know what account the king has given you," Choula said. "I am afraid he tends to put the best face on things."

"He told me he'd behaved like an idiot," Hael said bluntly.

"Not really," Harakh said. "He is just an aging man who wants to think he is still the dashing officer he was thirty years ago. And, even after the first battle, he could not believe that he could be bested by a mere raiding pirate."

"Tell me what has happened," said Hael.

The two Nevans told him of the preparations for the voyage, of the voyage itself and of its disastrous end. Hael interrupted frequently with questions and often wanted to hear accounts of the same events by both men, to get two different viewpoints.

"This is even worse than I had thought," Hael said when they were done. "The king did not mention that Shazad was captured because she came to rescue him, nor that she had all his officers killed."

"I cannot say for certain," Harakh said. "But when I went up to the aftercastle they were all dead, her women's weapons were bloody, and there were no Islanders around yet. I will say that no pack of incompetents ever deserved it more."

"Choula," Hael said, "I will need your best maps of northern Neva, with all the parts now occupied by Omia marked."

The scribe lifted a leather-covered case from the floor and put it on the table. "Here they are."

"Have the Omians moved recently?" he wanted to know. "Have they seized more territory?"

"This morning's messengers say that they have stayed north of the River of Lizards."

"How do they fight?" he asked.

"My specialty has been sea combat," Harakh said, "but at the military school we were told that the Omians use mainly light infantry: slingers, bowmen, javelin-throwers and the like. They do not depend much on heavy infantry, and such as they have is armed with long spears and small shields. It is a light, mobile force."

"Do they use mounted troops?" Hael asked.

"They have some light lancers," Choula said. "These vary in number, but they have never had more than two or three thousand. Indeed, the kings of Omia have traditionally had only a tiny standing army, and the rest of their troops are supplied by semi-independent satraps. Thus it is extremely difficult to predict how many men they may have under their control at any given time. King Oland must have won the support of many of his lords to mount such an attack."

"Word of the defeat last year must have given them the nerve," Harakh said. "Now that they know of the harbor battle, they will probably try even bolder moves."

"The king fears an alliance of convenience between Oland and Gasam. Do you think this is likely?"

"Not only that," Choula said, "I think it all but inevitable. With both forces expanding into Nevan territory, they might well encounter each other. It would do neither of them any good to fight each other before they have destroyed King Pashir. The logical solution is to make common cause, then sort out their mutual differences later. If Pashir falls, Chiwa is almost certain to make a grab for southern Neva, and they might wish to present a united front against Chiwa."

Hael pondered for a while. "Incredible," he said at last. "My foster-brother Gasam, whom the rest of us used to joke about because of his vainglorious posing. Before he is through, he will plunge a whole world into war."

"This is a strange time," Choula said. "History is an uncertain thing. It can coast along for centuries with no great changes. One king after another reigns, none much more capable than the others. One nation will fight another, or a single nation fights in a civil war, but the affairs of men change little.

"Then great figures arise and everything changes. And I have noted that it is seldom a single such figure, but more often two or three at once. You have said that Gasam is remarkable, but what about you, friend Hael?" The scribe gestured at the weapons propped against a wall. "When I first met you, that spear and that sword were your only possessions. Today you came back at the head of six thousand men on cabos. You are lord of a vast kingdom, and you did not take it from someone else. You *created* a kingdom where there was none before. It has been so long since that has happened that it is not even history but legend. So there are two such men making the world an interesting place."

"If Princess Shazad had been born male," Harakh asserted, "she would have been another such."

"It is true," Hael said, "that she sounds very different from the woman I knew when I was here before."

"I do not know," Choula said, "whether it is the doing of the gods, or the stars, or just the current of history, but times like these let exceptional people realize a potential denied them in more commonplace times. For good or ill, the world is about to become a very different place."

In the next days, Hael attended banquets in his honor and war councils that were his reason for being there. He inspected the accommodations his men had been given and saw to it that they stayed out of as much trouble as possible. As soon as he could, he moved them from the city to a campground outside the walls. He was more worried about their health than their character, as a number of them had come down with unfamiliar illnesses. They made little complaint. After the first excitement, with curiosity satisfied, they discovered that they had little liking for city life.

He toured the shipyards, where workmen toiled in double shifts to replace the craft lost in Floria Harbor. The men were another problem. Skilled rowers were at a premium and the merchant seamen's guild protested bitterly that drafting their sailors would destroy Neva as a maritime trading power.

In the camps outside the city, Hael watched the new recruits being put through their paces, drilling under the sharp eyes of grizzled underofficers called out of retirement for this duty.

"We have lost nearly every veteran soldier who served Neva," Harakh complained one day as he rode beside Hael. The marine was more accustomed to a ship's deck and he did not ride well. The two were inspecting a camp where a draft from the countryside was being whipped into shape. "Look at these farm boys! They still hold their spears like rakes!"

"They will learn," Hael said, hoping he spoke the truth. "At least they have never tasted defeat. They have no mistaken preconceptions to overcome, like the former armies." Despite his words, he knew what chances troops like these would have against a formation of Shasinn. Only his mounted archers were the answer to that threat. But if these amateurs could simply hold their formation for a while, that might be enough.

That evening, Hael had to sit through yet another interminable war council. He sat on a throne to Pashir's left while every man had his say, each striving to seem important while accepting little responsibility. In the midst of proceedings, a messenger arrived and all were silent while the king read. Then he addressed them.

"My lords, King Hael, our worst apprehensions are realized: my spies in Floria report that Amus, brother of King Oland, has arrived in Floria with an escort. We may now assume that Omia and the barbarians have formed an alliance against us."

After this, everyone had to speak again. Finally Hael leaned over and whispered: "Dismiss them all. Call in Choula and Guard Captain Harakh."

Wearily the king did as he was asked. Choula and Harakh entered and bowed. Choula carried a case and from it he took rolled maps while Harakh dragged a table into the center of the room. He called for lamps and the two unrolled the maps on the table, weighting down the corners with daggers, goblets, ink jars and other convenient objects.

Hael rose. "King Pashir, I must take the field before half of my men are down with sickness. There has been too much talking going on here, ever since Gasam first appeared. Come, look at these maps."

The king frowned. "Should not my close advisers . . ."

"My friend Pashir," Hael said. "I hope that every one of those men is loyal unto death, but I will make no such assumption. Now let's get to work."

The four men leaned over the table and began making battle plans.

FIFTEEN

It seemed strange to Shazad that for so long she had resented being denied attendance at her father's war councils, but now she was allowed to attend Gasam's. It was true that she was chained to a wall, but she followed the proceedings with great interest. Her hands were now lashed behind her back and she now wore bronze anklets connected by a short chain, because she had tried several times to escape.

She had tried cutting her bonds with a neglected spear leaning against a wall, she had tried jumping through a window and running awkwardly to the stables, only to find that cabos were no longer kept there, and she had tried seducing a guard. Besides her new bonds she was also striped with angry red welts from nape to heels. She had made the mistake of telling Queen Larissa that, while she had endured flagellation for purposes of ritual purification, she truly did not enjoy being flogged. At least, she reflected, in this way she had avoided being branded with hot bronze or having her toes broken, which were the next-favored punishments.

The king and queen were present at the council meetings, along with the king's senior warriors, most of whom were Shasinn like himself. The current meeting was being held in a courtyard of the palace, because most Shasinn were not comfortable under a roof. Seated facing them were Amus, brother of the king of Omia, and a score of his officers. These men wore loose trousers and cloaks of woven quil hair and decorated sandals. Their long, black hair was caught up in topknots and they wore long mustaches flanking their mouths. These last were sources of amusement to the Shasinn who, Shazad had discovered, were not simply clean-shaven, but could not grow hair upon their faces. They considered all facial hair a sign of inferiority.

If the Omians wondered why Gasam kept a slave bound and chained to a courtyard wall, they were too polite to inquire. They were here on serious business and had no attention to spare for slaves. Everyone spoke slowly, for although they spoke dialects of the same basic language, there were many variations and differences of meaning between them. Dunyaz sat behind the queen to interpret in cases where meaning was unclear.

"My brother, illustrious King Oland of Omia," Amus intoned, "outraged by the vile and insolent behavior of the wretched Pashir of

Neva, has undertaken military operations to regain ancient Omian lands, seized from us long ago by Neva's greedy and grasping ruler."

"I see," Gasam said. "Were these lands taken by Pashir?"

"Why, no," said Amus, nonplussed at this interruption. "It was a predecessor."

"Ah. And how long ago was this?"

The Omian flicked his fingers dismissively. "It matters not. The land north of the River of Lizards is the rightful domain of the king of Omia. The bones of our ancestors are buried in that land. The mere passage of time does not negate a sacred claim."

"You may tell King Oland," said Gasam, "that I find his cause just and I will not in any way interfere with his occupation of these lands, so long as he does not interfere in my own campaign."

"Such a thing is far from His Majesty's intentions," Amus proclaimed. "These coastal regions are of no interest to us. We Omians are not seafaring people. We are raisers of livestock like you Shasinn. We graze our herds of kagga and quil upon the hills of our native land, we hunt the wild game from the backs of our cabos. These are the proper activities of a race of noble warriors. The Nevans are scratchers of the earth, they are traders who buy and sell. These are ignoble things, fit only for ill-bred folk."

"Admirable," King Gasam said. "Peoples such as yours and mine should be friends."

"Perhaps more than friends," Amus said, sensing a favorable opportunity. "Perhaps we should be allies, so that we might remain brothers for all time."

"Now that is an intriguing idea," Gasam said, then, feigning chagrin, "but what a poor host I am. You have ridden all this way and must be hungry. We shall have a great banquet this evening, but for now you must take something to sustain you." He clapped his hands and slaves filed in, bearing food and drink. These they distributed among the visitors, who accepted them gratefully. To the king was brought a single, large bowl of beautifully grained flamewood. It held a thick, almost glutinous pink liquid streaked with lurid red. Holding this in both hands, the king raised it and drank, his throat working with each swallow. He passed it to the Shasinn warrior on his right, and that man drank and passed it on. They all drank lustily, with loud smackings of the lips. The queen watched the visitors with amusement.

All of them turned somewhat green and seemed to lose interest in their refreshments. Shazad knew that the bowl contained a mixture of the milk and blood of a kagga. This was a staple of the Shasinn diet, and was practically the only food of the young warriors. She also knew that Gasam rarely consumed the awful stuff any more, having acquired a taste for civilized viands. He was doing this to make the Omians uncomfortable. In this he was succeeding admirably. He had deliberately spread the rumor that the Shasinn drank the blood of their enemies.

"Now," Gasam said when the plates were cleared away, "what manner of alliance has illustrious King Oland in mind?"

Amus cleared his throat. "Ah, well, Your Majesty, my brother the king has planned a campaign that will involve crossing the River of Lizards and . . ."

"Just a moment," Gasam said. "Did you not say that your king claimed land only as far south as the River of Lizards?"

"And so he does," Amus said hastily, "but it is plain that the wretched Pashir, treacherous as ever, plots an invasion, to resteal our rightful lands. In order to forestall any such treachery, we shall march south and smash Pashir's army. . . ."

"You mean what is left of his army, do you not?" Gasam said. "I have already destroyed the bulk of it."

"To the everlasting glory of your name," said Amus through gritted teeth. "If in the progress of this campaign we should capture Kasin, his capital, it would be only what he deserves."

"Kasin is the greatest seaport north of Chiwa," Gasam said. "It would be of little use to noble warrior-herdsmen like King Oland and his subjects."

Amus shrugged. "That is where his capital is. Now, if your ever-victorious army were to join with ours, you might find excellent use for the port of Kasin, with its vast shipyards and skilled workers in the maritime trades. For a seagoing king, the place must hold great attractions."

"So it does," Gasam said, "and I mean to have it. And I need no allies for that."

"It goes without saying," Amus said, "that either of our nations could accomplish the destruction of Pashir and the conquest of Neva without assistance. . . ."

"We speak now of the conquest of Neva, rather than the simple recovery of ancestral lands."

"My king has no territorial ambitions beyond the recovery of lands sanctified by the bones of our ancestors," Amus said. "However, sadly, it is certain that such a conquest will be forced upon us. Pashir, in his cowardly fashion, will ally with Chiwa against both of us. After all, there were Chiwan ships in the fleet Pashir brought hither, and which you so gloriously destroyed in the harbor. That was a battle the bards will sing about forever, but King Diwaz the Ninth must thirst for revenge. To lose a pair of his castle-ships, commanded by a pair of his pestilentially numerous sons, is such shame as he has not endured in his entire, lengthy reign. Should Pashir march north with his army reinforced by the hordes of Chiwa, even such powerful monarchs as my brother and your glorious self might well think upon the advantages of mutual assistance."

"And so we shall," Gasam said. "When you return to King Oland's army, some of my men shall accompany you, to act as my representatives and as liaisons between us." He addressed two hard-faced senior warriors who sat to his right. "Luo, Pendu, you two shall choose some men and go with these honored envoys when they return." Then, to Amus, "These are two of my most trusted and valued officers. We were junior warriors together in the Night-Cat Fraternity. They will assist in coordinating action between your brother's army and mine."

"As our king commands," the two warriors chorused, but not bothering to hide their pained expressions.

Amus excused himself and his delegation to prepare for the evening's banquet. When they were gone, the Shasinn released the laughter they had suppressed through the whole council.

"My king!" protested the warrior named Luo. "Must Pendu and I truly go with these cowardly stripers?" He gestured with distaste. "Death for my king is one thing, but to associate with such creatures. . . ."

Gasam grinned. "It is the fate of my warriors to suffer in my service. Urlik, you saw their army. What did you think?" The man addressed was an Asasa chief. The Asasa were an Island people who resembled the Shasinn except for their dark hair and eyes.

"I took a reconnaissance party eastward ten days ago and we returned this morning," he said for the benefit of those who had not heard his report. "From a hilltop, we watched an Omian army gathering and drilling for most of a day. From what I saw, they have neither the discipline of the land army we fought, nor the warrior spirit of the Chiwans on the big ship. They are contemptible. Only news of our king's victory gave them the courage to attack."

The rest laughed and none bothered to ask about details of arms or of numbers. To the Islanders, only spirit counted. The queen had said nothing through the council, but she looked thoughtful. After a short conference, the warrior chiefs were dismissed. The day was exceptionally fair, so the king and queen did not go back inside.

"What troubles you, my queen?" Gasam asked. "It is not like you to remain silent, especially when fools speak."

"I did not have the opportunity to speak with you, my lord," she said. "Just before the council, I received messages from my spies in Kasin. Hael has arrived, at the head of six thousand mounted men."

The king was silent for a while. Shazad's heart exulted. Perhaps now she, her father and her country could be saved.

"That boy!" the king said. "Is it truly he?"

"It can be no other. All of my spies say that the leader of the riders is Shasinn. His name is Hael. Our little Shazad here says that she met him shortly after his exile, and that he went east and set himself up as a king."

"Why did I not kill him when I had the chance?" Gasam said bitterly.

Larissa placed an arm around his shoulders. "You could not," she said consolingly. "In those days, you were not beyond custom. Now nothing is denied you."

He brightened. "That is true. And six thousand men do not make a great force."

"Still, I have a bad feeling about this," the queen said. "We do not know how they fight. All of them are mounted. We have never seen that before."

"We fought mounted men outside this city," Gasam said. "They were no threat. We know how to handle animals."

"Nevertheless," the queen said, "Hael is Shasinn, and even among our people, no man ever knew animals better. I fear that he has devised some new way of using them, as you did with our Islanders and with boats and ships. Do not underestimate him. My spies report that all of his riders are armed with bows."

"Good shields are all you need against arrows," the king said. He pondered for a minute, then: "But I have not come as far as I have by ignoring your thoughts and your instincts, little queen. I shall use caution. Perhaps this business of the Omians comes at a good time."

"How so?" the queen asked, leaning back, gazing up at him with the worship that Shazad hated herself for understanding all too well.

"The best way to find out what Hael is up to," Gasam said, "is to see how he fights someone else."

Holding both hands before her mouth, the queen laughed. She did this, as she did everything else, beautifully. "Oh, my love! You are a wonder! What better use for these Omians?"

The king smiled happily. "I begin to see a number of advantages here. Consider: Neva is mostly farm country, good for slaves and tribute but little else. Most of Omia seems to be grazing land. In the Islands we have always been constrained to fight one another for the limited pasturage available. This kept our numbers down. With good land for expansion, we can bring more people from the Islands, build large transports to bring whole herds across the water. And we will have the livestock of the Omians, when we have reduced them to slavery. This will be a far quicker process than transforming the Nevan farmland to pasture."

Larissa wound her arms around his lean, hard-muscled waist. "Only you could find such wonderful opportunities in this situation. How

can fools like Oland and Pashir and Diwaz the
Ninth believe themselves to be kings?"

"How indeed?" he agreed. "Soon they must
all own me master. I will have a world that is
properly ordered. There shall be warriors and
there shall be slaves. We Islanders shall grow
numerous and the Shasinn over all. The weak
peoples shall perish, as is right." They kissed
and their hands explored one another.

While the king and queen disported themselves on their couch, Dunyaz came to stand before Shazad. She dropped a cushion to the floor
and sat crosslegged facing her cousin. Behind
her the sounds of passion grew intense.

"You've seen the future, Shazad. Resign
yourself. There will be no rescue for you."

"Then there will be death. Unlike you, I was
not born to be a slave."

Dunyaz smiled lazily. "There are worse things
than being the pet of Queen Larissa."

"Only until you lose your beauty. What then,
Dunyaz? Are you any good for menial labor?
Will you breed slave brats?"

With the long nail of a forefinger, Dunyaz
traced a thin, red line from Shazad's collarbone
to her navel. "As you have said, cousin, you can
choose death over slavery. But I can choose the
manner of that death. It amuses the queen to
indulge me."

Larissa had begun to pant heavily, and Shazad could not block out the sound. "How can
two such monsters love one another so deeply?"
she asked.

Dunyaz sat back, her malice forgotten. "They
are primitives, Shazad. They are barbarians.
They feel *everything* far more intensely than we

do. Don't you envy them? And who else is there for these two? Without each other, they would be utterly alone. He is a conquering king of almost mystical purity. His lordship is total, can't you feel it?"

Slowly, reluctantly, Shazad nodded. "Yes," she whispered.

"And she is his perfect complement. They are like a vase that breaks in two pieces. Alone, each piece is useless. But placed together, no seam is apparent. They were raised together from childhood. He is ambitious and forceful, she is ambitious and cautious. He thinks more quickly and in many directions at once. She thinks more deeply and carefully about each course of action. And they feel no constraints whatever upon their deeds. They know they are not like other people."

Shazad leaned back against the wall, pain in her back and in her bound wrists. "I had thought myself free of the rules by which most people's lives are governed, even the highest. I never saw such freedom from conscience and consequence as those two enjoy. How can it be?" The queen cried out shrilly, again and again.

"You still don't understand them, Shazad. I told you they were primitive. They come of a small, obscure people living on a little island. There was no written law in their world, and no king's will to obey. They had only custom and taboo. To those primitive tribesmen, their customs and taboos are the laws of nature. Once Gasam and Larissa broke with custom and violated taboo, there was nothing else. They placed themselves outside all law and after that absolutely *nothing* was forbidden them! Is it any wonder that their people worship them? We are civilized, Shazad. We have grown jaded with our kings and queens; we know them for people who are lucky or who sometimes scheme better than others. Your own father seized a throne from a man who was old, weak and corrupt. To the tribes, Gasam is a man who came from nowhere to weld them into a nation and then led them to grind other nations beneath their feet. On top of that, they are the two most beautiful people of the world's handsomest tribe."

She leaned close. "Shazad, they are *joking* when they call themselves king and queen. They are god and goddess and they know it."

The king had left. The queen called for a basin and towels and Dunyaz rose to do her bidding. Shazad could almost feel the alien emotion of pity. Dunyaz, in her insupportable combination of arrogance and submissiveness, had found the only people in the world to whom she could give herself as slave without reservation. Gasam and Larissa were two great, predatory monsters tearing at the carcass of the world, and Dunyaz was grateful for any scraps they left for her. Then she remembered the floggings and the pity disappeared.

Instead she wondered about Hael.

SIXTEEN

When they were two days' ride from the capital, Hael allowed the army to begin their archery practice. There had been no chance on the march, and once they were in Nevan territory and had leisure for practice he would not allow it for fear of spies. At this stage, he was no longer worried about spies racing ahead of his army. Such tactics as he had developed on the plains could be a surprise only once, and he did not wish to give Gasam time to prepare.

King Pashir's field army was behind them, and farther behind yet was the siege train. Seeing the train, spies would report that the army marched forth to besiege Floria. If so, then so much the better. The siege might come, but he intended to leave it to the Nevans. He would not subject his men to a filthy, disease-ridden camp while they waited for starvation or plague to reduce the city.

Hael had insisted that Harakh take personal charge of the field army. The man was not experienced in such warfare, but, thus far, experience had proven to be of little use against Gasam. Hael was more interested in loyalty and he was fairly certain that Harakh was loyal. After much argument and cajoling, he had convinced Pashir to stay at home and let someone else be in charge. The deciding argument had been that, should Pashir leave the capital one more time, there was almost certain to be a coup. Leaving Pashir with a heavy guard to keep control of the capital, Hael had taken the army north.

He had also convinced the king to lend him Choula. The scribe had, for the sake of form, protested that he was getting too old to go forth on yet another land campaign. Hael knew that nothing could have prevented his old friend from coming on this expedition.

The scouts rode far ahead. Much to their indignation, Hael had ordered the scouts to wear Nevan clothes, bear Nevan weapons and use Nevan cabo-trappings. He wanted his presence unheralded until the last possible moment.

Hael's confidence was great, but it was not total. He was aware that he led his army into their first true test of battle. He had used his warriors as a unified force in past years, first to rid the plains of the many outlaw bands that infested it, later in skirmishes with the minor powers along the southern and southeastern borders. But never had they been committed to battle with an army of one of the major civilized states. He had more fear of his men's over-confidence than that they might be outfought. And he was apprehensive of what Gasam might try. The man's mind did not work like that of an ordinary man, nor even like that of an extraordinary man. Gasam was mad, but in a fashion that did not incapacitate him for leadership, planning or action. On the contrary, everything he did was so original that it looked divinely inspired to his followers. It meant that even a man like Hael, who possessed insight far beyond the scope of most men, could not second-guess Gasam.

He had other concerns. He did not intend just to fight Gasam. He wanted to prosecute his part of this war to a successful conclusion, and return to his nation with his army intact. Some casualties were inevitable. His own men would consider it a poor sort of war if some of them were not killed. But he had no intention of winning a victory that would cost him so dearly that it might as well have been a defeat.

Gasam could be prodigal of his men's lives. They meant nothing to him. Men were the instruments of his ambition. At that, Hael thought, everything he had heard indicated that Gasam was miserly with the lives of his Shasinn, sacrificing lesser peoples first. Whether he did this because the Shasinn were the people of his birth, or whether it was simply that they were his most valuable fighters was a mystery. It could be either, or both, or something else entirely.

Larissa was something else. Hael tried not to think about her, but it was futile. He had loved her, and she had betrayed him for Gasam. And now she was here. She had accompanied her husband from the Islands and reigned as queen in Floria. Pashir had shown him letters sent by Larissa to Shazad, although they had actually been written by a niece of Pashir's who was a captive at Larissa's court, a young noblewoman Pashir was suspiciously reluctant to discuss. In the letters, Hael had been unable to detect any trace of the Larissa he had known. That woman—no, girl—had been a strange child, almost as strange as Hael himself. They had been close as children because they had both been different; he because he was an orphan and had always possessed an affinity for spirits and animals that was not fitting in Shasinn society; she because, as a child, her looks had been odd and out of the Shasinn norm. But there was a difference. He had been of low birth by Shasinn standards and had remained that way. She had been the daughter of a chief and the tribal midwife, and in young womanhood she had blossomed into great beauty.

He knew that such thoughts were stupid. Had he remained a Shasinn, Larissa could never have been his. And he had broken with that society. He now had his own kingdom, and a wife and children he loved. Still he could not think of Larissa without feeling pain. Pain for his former love, pain for her betrayal. Had Gasam corrupted her, or had she been evil all along? Or had evil nothing to do with it? Hael had cast loose from the moral moorings of his youth, and he was no longer certain of what genuine evil was. He knew that it wasn't simply violation of taboo.

He had thought Shazad was evil. Once he had

thought that she had hired a man to kill him. Hael had killed the man instead, and had never found out. Now he thought that she was simply a young woman who had spent her high-born, privileged life in a state of bored dissipation until, incredibly, Gasam had appeared on the scene and forced her to become the unofficial queen of Neva. She had acted ruthlessly, and even the jaded Nevans had spoken with awe of the crosses, the torturings and executions that she had ordered. But in none of this could Hael detect that she had ever acted for her own pleasure. Everything she had done had strengthened Neva and supported her father. In the final stages of the battle in Floria Harbor, she had sacrificed her own freedom, possibly her life, to save her failing father. Besides, he thought suddenly, it was as likely that Pashir had hired that long-ago killer. Whatever the truth, all that was long past and what remained were the realities of statecraft. Foremost among which was the problem of Gasam.

Gasam, Hael remained convinced, was wholly evil.

The scouts were certain. "It is the Omian army, my king. Many, many of them. They stand in lines, not as pretty as the Nevans. We saw spears and shields, maybe some swords. But very many men, my king, perhaps two or three times our own number."

"Lots to kill," said another scout helpfully.

"Did you see any that looked like Gasam's army? Any men with hair like mine, or spears like this?" He held up his famous weapon.

"We could not get close enough to be sure,"

said one. "They are in an open field. We got as close as we could, but the only good forest cover was full of their woodcutting parties."

"I'll have to go see for myself," he said. He gave orders to his officers. "Make camp here. When the rest of the army catches up, they are to stay here too. Post sentries as usual. If we are to fight, it won't be earlier than tomorrow, so care for the animals and keep them rested."

With one of the scouts, Hael rode toward the enemy army. They were still well south of the River of Lizards, but he had expected the Omians to cross. The important question was: had they linked up with Gasam yet? If they had, the fighting would be more intense, but he would have a chance of catching the combined force by surprise and destroying both armies in a single battle. If they were not yet united, he would have a longer war, but it would not be a bad thing to engage in a number of smaller battles in which he was more certain of victory. His green army needed blooding and even a small victory would do wonders for Nevan morale. They would march to their next battle with far more confidence.

An hour's ride brought them to a wooded hill. Here they stopped. The road continued to a saddle between two peaks. "From the top of the hill you can see them," the scout said. Hael dismounted and handed the man his reins. From his saddlebag he took a fine telescope.

"Get out of sight and wait here. I will go on alone on foot." To the Amsi, going anywhere on foot seemed an extreme measure.

Hael left the road and entered the treeline. He had left his longsword on his saddle. It would be an encumbrance on his mission. He tucked the collapsed telescope beneath his belt and from his pouch he took a long, rolled sheath of gut. This he slipped over his spear to hide its gleam. Every Shasinn warrior carried one of these sheaths to protect his spear from the weather.

He began to climb the hill. There was no need for haste and he climbed slowly, letting his senses stretch out before him and to all sides. Everywhere he could feel the life of the forest. Aroused from the somnolence of the season of storms, the animals and birds were in a frenzy of mating, nest-building and territorial squabbling. They had no interest in men, who were about to engage in a similar, larger-scale dispute over territory and dominance.

According to his maps, beyond this hill was a wide floodplain that wound between the hills and the River of Lizards. With the stormy season runoff from the mountains, the river was usually swollen at this date. There were not many good crossings, but the road led to a spot where the river could be forded at low water and was a convenient site for a ferry when the water was high. If, as he suspected, the Omians had built ferry rafts, the crossing must have taken several days. With the river at their backs, they could not retreat northward. It would also make it difficult to surround them completely.

At the crest of the hill he gazed down upon the encamped Omian army. They were midway between his position and the river. He estimated their numbers at about fifteen thousand. His scouts had not exaggerated greatly. Of course, they had counted only his own mounted force. They did not consider the Nevan footmen to be worth consideration. When the two armies confronted one another on the field, their numbers would be nearly equal, with only a small numerical advantage to the Omians.

This would not be apparent at first. If all had gone as planned, the Omians would not be expecting Hael's mounted archers. They would see before them only an army of Nevan infantry they outnumbered almost two to one. Hael planned to exploit that mistake to the fullest.

Cautiously, he worked his way down the hill. He would know of Omian scouts or wood-gathering parties long before they could see him. He could feel the disturbance of the forest creatures when men were near. He moved through the woods like a ghost and when he reached the edge of the heavy growth, he sat crosslegged, his spear on the ground by his side, and opened his telescope.

The detail provided by the telescope was an improvement, but the distance was still too great for him to make out many features. Men were tiny figures and details of dress and feature were not discernible. He saw tents of every size, shape and decorative design, indicating that a great many tribes had assembled here. The Shasinn did not use tents in their homeland, so he had no way of telling if they were present from the shelters here. The Omians were not drilling and most of the men seemed to be lounging around their fires, with their arms stacked nearby. It was a sloppy camp and he could smell it from his position. They had posted sentries only around its periphery, a near-useless precaution. Hael would have posted sentries on foot along the crest of the hills and sent mounted pickets several miles down the road. They would not know the Nevan force was in the region until it was directly in front of them. That was all to the good as far as Hael was concerned, but it infuriated him to see men wasted by such careless soldiering. It also meant it was unlikely that Gasam was among them.

Near the center of the camp was a great tent, probably that of King Oland or whatever general he had sent with the army. Hael trained the telescope on its entrance. Two men with long spears flanked its entrance. Before the entrance, Hael saw a number of long, bronze-colored streaks. These, he thought, might be Shasinn spears thrust in the earth by their butt-spikes. He twisted the telescope in a futile effort to bring them into focus, but it was no use.

A prisoner would help, but he could not wait until some forager should stray toward him. He collapsed the telescope and stuck it under his belt, picked up his spear and stood. He had learned all he was going to here.

When he returned to the campsite, the foot army had caught up. Tents had been erected and he went to the command tent: a three-sided canopy large enough to accommodate Hael and his senior officers. There he found Choula and Harakh seated at a folding table. The scribe looked up crossly.

"Energetic as ever, I see. It is the privilege of the young. I rejoice that my backside has been numb since noon. Otherwise it would be aflame with pain. What did you find?"

"They are at the crossing," Hael said.

Choula looked at Harakh triumphantly. "Didn't I say that was where we would find them?" Then, to Hael: "And are they still coming across?"

"I could see rafts being hauled across the river by ropes. It looks like they are still ferrying supplies. That means they will still be in place in the morning. That is where we will fight them." He turned to a guard who leaned on his spear outside the tent. "Summon all officers." The guard called to a trumpeter, and that man blew the officer's call, turned ninety degrees and blew it again, repeating until he had sounded the call to the four quarters of the camp. Within a few minutes all the officers, mounted and foot, were in or around the tent. Hael ordered the sides to be rolled up so that he could address them all.

"We fight in the morning," he announced. There was an excited murmur, looks of eagerness and of apprehension.

"We march two hours before dawn," he went on. "I want us to be forming up on that plain before they know we are there." He described to them the road ahead and the nature of the battlefield. "I will personally place every unit leader and his men will then fall in behind him.

"I want fires out as soon as the men have had their evening meal. I want no one stepping into hot coals when we leave camp in the morning. The men are to carry nothing but arms on the march. Orders will be relayed by voice only, and quiet voices at that. There will be no torches, no matter how dark it is in the morning. The last mile will be marched in as near perfect silence as we can achieve. Now listen carefully as I give you your order of march. I will form our battle line from left flank to right, so the first unit named will hold the left flank, the next will be to their right and so on. There will be no reserve. I must have the maximum frontage when we fight tomorrow." He began to call out the names of units and officers scratched notes in wax tablets.

Later, when the others had gone, he sat once more in the tent with Choula and Harakh. There was nothing more to be done and he was enjoying his brief respite from the cares of command.

"No reserve," Choula said. "Is that wise? Every military account I have read agrees that a wise commander always keeps a substantial reserve against the unforeseen circumstance, the need to quickly reinforce a hard-pressed part of the line."

"My archers are the reserve," Hael said. "They are ten times more mobile than any infantry reserve. Besides, with these soldiers, I have to keep my tactics and formation as simple as possible. There can be no complicated maneuvering on the field. I will put them in place, and they must stand there and fight. If they can hold against the first attack, the battle is won."

"I envy your assurance," Choula said. Harakh said nothing, but he looked grim.

Hael saw no reason to tell them of his own doubts. There was nothing to be gained by that.

The ghostly light of the black-scarred Moon dimly illuminated the scene. The men were shuffling sleepily amid a subdued rattle of arms as each unit was quietly called out. As soon as it was formed up, each group set off up the road and the next was summoned. The men, stumbling at first, quickly grew alert with the realization that, at last, they were truly marching into battle. Like all soldiers, whether veterans or green recruits, they marched with the knowledge that some of them would not live to see the sun set. Unlike true veterans, these did not think of how many would live and wish they had died quickly.

They were strangely confident of victory. They were not likely to meet the terrifying pirate king today, just contemptible Omians, renowned for cowardice and stupidity, unaware that they enjoyed the same reputation among the Omians. Most of all, they believed in the outlandish king from nowhere who led them. He had arrived like a whirlwind from the desert at the head of an army such as no civilized land had ever seen. Cavalry had always been aristocratic warriors who fought with sword and lance. This band of well-ordered savages, fiercely loyal to their king, had no precedent. For that reason they seemed invincible. And King Hael was the sort of leader who inspired confidence. He was as unlike the effete courtiers who had led Neva to disaster as it was possible to be.

Hael was satisfied as the last units left the campsite. There had been surprisingly few desertions reported during the march and there had been none at all the night before, a matter of some amazement. A small guard of lamed or unwell men was left to keep the local peasants from plundering the camp and Hael trotted his cabo to the front of the long column, passing first his mounted warriors, then the files of Nevan infantry. The riders grumbled at having to follow the foot soldiers, but this order was essential to Hael's battle plan. At the head of his army, he rode on through the last hours of darkness.

A strip of gray lightened the eastern horizon when they came over the crest of the hill and descended to the plain below. Between them and the river they could see the glow of many low-burning campfires. They encountered no one and the enemy camp remained quiet.

Hael began placing his commanders. From left to right he stood them at the intervals he wished. On the extreme right, the traditional place of honor, he placed Harakh with his re-inforced company, containing most of the army's few veteran troops. They would be most at risk should the army be flanked, because the enemy would then come around against their unshielded side.

Abruptly the enemy camp came alive with the sound of trumpets, drums and flutes. Men were shouting in alarm. At last the Nevans had been spotted. Omians began boiling from the camp, screaming battle-cries as they formed into several ragged lines. Hael's own lines were much better formed, and now the first rays of the morning glanced from the bronze points of their long spears. The officers held shortswords or longswords of bronze edged with steel. Hael thought of the great cache of steel he had dis-covered in the desert, and he wondered what it would be like to have an army like this, only far

larger, all armed with weapons of steel. Such
an army would be invincible, providing that it
was properly led. Nothing could stand before
it.

The Omians were over their momentary
fright. Once their numbers were fully assembled, they saw how few their enemies were.
They began to crow and jeer at the Nevans.
Some sang battle-chants. A fat man on a decorated cabo rode in front of the Omians and began to harangue them. At every pause in his
words they cheered fiercely. They shook weapons.

The Nevan ranks remained silent. Each man
stood with his shield propped on the ground before him, one hand resting on it, the other gripping his spearshaft. The men of the front three
ranks wore armor of bamboo splints, stitched
over with tough hide and lacquered against
moisture. Splinted greaves protected their shins
and helmets of hardened leather studded with
bronze protected their heads. The next ranks
wore no leg armor. The rear ranks were armed
with javelins and they had only light shields and
hide helmets for protection. There were no foot
archers.

The Omians sent no one out to parley. They
were not interested in terms when victory
looked so easy and certain. With a rattle of
drums, the Omians began to move forward. The
officers walked a few steps ahead, turning to
walk backward from time to time, waving their
swords and shouting in an attempt to keep the
lines in some sort of order.

"Up shields!" shouted the Nevan officers. The
men thrust their arms through the shield straps

and raised the long, oval defenses to just below eye level. Arrows began to arch from the Omian lines. Hael saw that most of the fire came from the flanks where archers, all of them unarmored, walked well behind the soldiers in ranks, pausing now and again to fire. The Nevans raised their shields overhead for protection and the arrows inflicted few casualties.

Hael sat in his saddle on a rise of ground just behind his army. He scanned the enemy, but nowhere could he see any sign of Gasam's troops. Then he noticed something on the far side of the river. He took out his telescope and trained it on the crude ferry landing. A tall, rickety structure had been erected there, and men, made tiny by distance, were gathering upon it. Then the Omians charged and he had no attention to spare for the far bank of the river.

With savage cries, the Omians broke into a run, hurling javelins as they came. The Nevans replied with javelins of their own and the sides collided. Lowered spears pushed against shields, swords licked out, axes chopped. The Omians had little armor and were more vulnerable, but their spears were longer, making them hard to reach. Grimly, the Nevans dug in their heels and held their ground. A mass of Omians began to swing around like a great door against the Nevan right flank, where the right-hand files had turned to bring their shields between themselves and the enemy.

Hael raised his spear and pumped it up and down. Behind him, he heard the thunder of cabos' hoofs coming down the hillside. The first squadron to come off the hill sped to the right.

They massed just behind the infantry and to their right, less than fifty yards from the stunned Omians. There they halted as Hael had ordered. The first volley of arrows stopped the flanking Omians in their tracks. The slender shafts passed through shields and men and lodged feather-deep in their bodies.

The rest of the riders massed behind Hael. The Nevans were still holding their ground stubbornly and, except for their left flankers, the Omians were still unaware that the riders had arrived. Amid the noise, dust and excitement of battle, few fighters ever saw anything that was not directly in front of them. When the bulk of his plainsmen were behind him, Hael thrust his spear into its saddle-socket and took out his great bow. Fitting arrow to string, he led his archers in a wide loop around the Nevan army's left flank.

As they rode, the horsemen spread out, to give themselves plenty of room to traverse their weapons. At this point there was no need for orders. The warriors knew exactly what to do. The arrows sleeted into the Omian ranks in a terrifying storm. Each rider loosed one or two shafts as he rode past, then wheeled to the left, making a circle to come into a good fighting position again. They could easily have ridden behind the Omians in a complete encirclement, firing into their unprotected backs, but Hael had given strict orders against this. There was too much likelihood that arrows would fall into the Nevan ranks. In any case, he did not want to drive the Omians against the Nevan line. On the far side of the battle line, the other band of riders, having cleared out the flankers, began the same maneuver. Soon the arrows were pouring into the Omian army from both sides and still the Nevans were holding their position.

The strain on the Omians became insupportable. The middle and rear ranks began to panic. They had no one to fight and no way to defend themselves from these terrible arrows that went through shields as through so much smoke. The rear rankers saw that they had a clear field behind them. By ones and twos, then in great mobs, they broke away from the battle line and fled. Officers tried to flog them back into ranks, but arrows soon silenced these. The Omian army began to disintegrate. As the pressure lightened, the Nevan lines began to advance. Slowly, one slogging foot after another, they began to push the Omians back. The ground behind the front lines was now so littered with bodies that the Omians were stumbling and falling into heaps. Amid a screaming panic, the Omian army collapsed and began mass flight.

Archers and footmen kept up the pressure, giving the panicked enemy no chance to rally. Back the Omians fled, tearing through their camp, pursued at every step by the terrible arrows that seemed to come from the bows of demons. They tripped over tent ropes and fell into fires. A horde of camp followers saw the rout and went into their own frenzy.

There was no place to run except to the river. As if the water guaranteed safety, soldiers and camp followers tore off their garments and leaped in, many of them forgetting that they could not swim. The riders pursued them re-

could not swim. The riders pursued them relentlessly, pouring shaft after shaft into the struggling mass.

"Stop shooting!" Hael shouted. He rode among his men, flailing with his spear. His officers saw and began to shout at their men. This army was shattered, and it would not come back. Hael had no taste for pointless slaughter. All over the field, his men were dismounting and retrieving their arrows from the bodies of the fallen. These arrows were of Hael's own design. Instead of the broad, barbed heads used for hunting, these had small, compact heads triangular in cross section. These saved on valuable bronze and punched through armor and shields more efficiently than the old type. Another advantage came after the battle: they were far easier to withdraw. Such arrows could be reused many times.

"Look, my king!" said a warrior who had pulled up next to him. The man pointed to a small group of men who stood by the riverbank. "There are some that look just like you!"

Astonished, Hael looked where the man was pointing. He saw tall, black shields and behind them men who seemed to be made of bronze. Hael called some of his chiefs to him and walked his cabo to the little group who stood staring defiantly. There were no more than twelve of them, some wearing the plaited hair of junior warriors. He had not seen them at the battle. Probably they had been in the camp.

He reined in before them and studied faces. He found two that he thought he recognized. "Luo? Pendu? Is that truly you?" Their expressions were stony. Could these two brutal-faced

known? But he knew he must look much changed to them as well. No one stays a boy forever.

"Hael!" said Pendu, not sounding pleased. "So it is true. You have become a leader of cowardly archers and cabo-riders." It was strange to hear his native Island dialect again, after so many years.

"These men rode across half a world to be here today," Hael said. "Show some respect. This is a poor greeting to receive from two old brothers of the Fraternity of Night-Cats."

Luo snorted through his nose. "The old fraternities are no more, Hael. There is no room for them in our new world. You did well to run away when you did. A fool like you would not have lasted long when our king began to lead us."

"I did not run away," he reminded them. "I was exiled. Gasam and Larissa arranged that. Tell me, has Gasam ever managed to kill a longneck single-handed? No man before me ever did and I am sure that he never has. He always used others to do the things he feared to do himself."

"You talk like the boy you were, Hael," Pendu said. "Gasam is our king and he has made us great. What are you?"

"A good question. Where is Danats, my old *chabas-fastan*?"

"Dead," Luo said, "in the fight to take over the Islands."

Hael lowered his head. He and Danats had been like brothers. "And Raba?"

"Raba leads a contingent of the Squall Island Shasinn," Luo said. "He is a loyal warrior of the king and has no more use for you than we have. Come, Hael, we are warriors, not white-haired elders to sit about talking of old times. Are you going to kill us? You are no longer Shasinn and have probably forgotten how to use your spear, but I am sure that your half men can stand off at a safe distance and fill us with arrows."

As if he had not heard, Hael asked: "What of Tata Mal?"

"The king had him killed," Pendu said, "at the same time he had all the spirit-speakers killed. They were his enemies, and his enemies must die."

"He has destroyed the Shasinn, then," Hael said with true grief. "We were a people of custom and ritual. We were regulated by the spirits who spoke through our spirit-speakers. Now Gasam has killed all that. No more warrior fraternities, you say? No more headmen, just Gasam. No more spirit-speakers. You have become merely the instruments of a single man, a man you once despised."

"That is not true!" Pendu said, but there was an uneasy edge in his voice. "We are a race of conquerors! Our king has revealed this to us and has proven it by his actions. The spirit-speakers kept us fearful. We could do nothing truly worthy for fear of breaking one of their stupid taboos! Now we are unfettered, free to yoke lesser peoples and crush them beneath our heels."

"Where is this man of destiny?" Hael asked. "I notice he is not with you."

Pendu grinned without mirth. "He was here, but he has gone back to the City of Victory."

"Here?" Hael said, surprised. "Where was he?"

"There," Luo said, pointing across the river. The water was full of bodies, some struggling, some swimming, some unmoving. On the bank, some of his warriors were using poles, trying to drag in the bodies that had arrows in them. On the other side stood the rickety structure Hael had remarked earlier.

"That's where the King of Omia's fat brother pretended to supervise the ferrying of the army across the river. Our king arrived last night and when you came onto the field this morning, he watched from up there. He brought a few hundred men as a show of support, but he never intended to aid these worthless Omians. He was here to see what you would bring. He knew you would show up soon."

Hael cursed inwardly. Gasam had not chanced being caught by surprise. He had come, personally, to observe. "What were you doing on this side of the river?" Hael asked.

"We have been with the Omians for a number of days," Luo said, "supposedly to maintain contact between our armies, but truly to report on them to the king."

Hael thought for a while. "I am not going to kill you," he said. Their expression did not change. "You will go back to your king, bearing a message from me. I will put it in writing, so that I will know that he will receive my true words. Wait here. If you try to go before I bid you, you will be killed."

He wheeled his mount and rode toward the Omian camp, where he might find writing instruments and paper. He was saddened, forced,

finally, to admit that the past was irretrievably
lost. He had cherished a vain hope that it was
only Gasam, that if he could eliminate him,
things would return to their old order. But that
was not possible.

In the camp, Jochim came to him. "My king,
we have a fat man here who claims to be the
brother of the King of Omia."

They went into a huge tent and found the fat
man sitting on a folding chair looking sullen,
displeased and very stupid. He did not look at
all fearful, apparently confident that his royal
status protected him.

"I am King Hael. Were you in command
here?"

"*You* are a king?" Apparently, Hael's appearance, sweaty, dusty and dressed in worn riding
clothes did not meet with his standards for royalty.

"I do not wear a crown, but I am a king. Ask
any of my men."

"Well, I am Prince Amus, younger brother of
King Oland. I suppose you have terms to discuss?"

"No terms," Hael said. "Demands. Your king
has ten days to remove all his troops from
Nevan territory. If he does not comply, we will
slaughter them all. You have seen my forces and
you know I can carry this out. King Pashir will
dispatch diplomats to deliver terms for repa-
rations to be paid for the damage your brother
caused by this foolish invasion."

"Oh, very well." Then, peevishly: "You had
no call to interfere, King Hael. Relations between Omia and your grassy kingdom have been

amicable. We have enjoyed trade of mutual benefit. Why do you do this?"

"I came here to help King Pashir against Gasam, who is the enemy of the whole world. It was your king who foolishly allied with him. Now go and deliver my words. Oh, by the way, can you swim?"

"Can I *what*?" Amus demanded indignantly.

Hael jerked his head toward the entrance and two grinning warriors hauled the protesting Omian to his feet. Still squawking, he was hustled out of the tent. Hael began to search the tent for writing materials.

SEVENTEEN

" 'From King Hael of the Plains to King Gasam, Lord of the Islands,' " Dunyaz read, " 'Greetings.' "

"He does not acknowledge my mainland holdings, you'll notice," Gasam said. He sipped *ghul*, a fermented drink of the Islands. With him were the queen and the warriors Luo and Pendu, who had come to deliver the letter. "Continue, girl."

" 'I have defeated the army of your ally, the King of Omia. This you have seen with your own eyes. As the ally of my friend King Pashir of Neva, I now come to eject you from the mainland. I suggest you use your limited time to evacuate your noncombatants. You must also release the Princess Shazad, whom you hold captive.' " At this, Dunyaz glanced at Shazad, who was chained to a wall of the room.

"Still the same old Hael," Gasam said. "Foolishly sentimental as always."

" 'Now I shall speak as Hael, who was once a Shasinn warrior. Gasam, my treacherous foster-brother, I have been told that you have murdered my old friend Tata Mal, along with the other spirit-speakers. You have ravaged the customs and practices of the Shasinn. In doing this, you have murdered the Shasinn people. For this I intend to kill you personally. You may flee with your army, or you may flee alone, but I will find you and kill you. I would rather do this without waging a war, but I will do it, however it must be accomplished. I will not live under the same sky with you.' " Dunyaz paled a little, trembling to read such words to the king. Gasam, however, laughed delightedly.

"His single-mindedness belongs to the Hael I knew, but not this arrogance. He was always such a modest boy, eager to please his elders and be on good terms with the spirits. Is there anything else, girl?"

"Just a short addition, my king. It is written below, as if it was an afterthought. 'Please tell your queen that I no longer hold her responsible for my betrayal. If you can corrupt a whole nation, the suborning of one lonely girl must have been as nothing to you.' After this, he signs it." She was shocked by the frozen look on the queen's face.

"That insolent wretch!" the queen cried, uncharacteristically furious. "Turn him over to me when you take him, my king. He must learn what suffering is really about!"

"In time, my queen, in time," Gasam said soothingly. "Luo, Pendu, I could not pick him out among that mass of riders, even with a telescope. You knew him in the old days. What is he like now?" The warriors sat on the floor, drinking *ghul* from tall beakers. Gasam was rarely formal with his Shasinn, and even less so with these two, whom he had commanded when they were junior warriors in the Night-Cat Fraternity.

"Like the rest of us," said Luo. "Older, harder. He always had a lot of that spirit-presence about him, and he still has it, but without the dreamy look."

"I remember," Gasam said. "He always went around looking like someone had rapped him between the eyes with a spear-butt. That was what came of believing in spirit-speakers."

"I would not compare him to you, my king," said Pendu, "but he has something of the same quality of command. I could see how men would jump to obey his commands as if they came from one of these mainland gods. I was impressed."

"Living with me as a child, some must have rubbed off on him," Gasam said, but the good humor did not reach his eyes. "How did his riders impress you?"

"Much better than any we have seen since coming here," Luo said with the enthusiasm Shasinn reserved for warrior matters. "One of them would make ten of the Nevans and twenty of the Omians. They move with their cabos like a single creature with four legs and two arms. We spoke insultingly of them to Hael, of course, but they are as impressive as the women warriors from the Chiwan ship."

"I saw at least two separate breeds among them," Pendu added. "There were some tall, lean men with very long, black hair; they had skins darker than ours. The others were stockier, with lighter hair. All were armed the same, but the dark-haired men wore mostly leather and the lighter ones wore more cloth."

"Is this what you saw also?" Gasam asked Luo.

The warrior nodded. "I think I saw a few of other breeds as well, but the bulk of them were of those two types. Their bows are strange-looking, not just curved sticks but with a sharp outward curve at the ends." He took a flower from a pot, snapped off the stem and bent it into the curve he wanted to describe. "Like so. And they are thick. I wish I could have handled one. They look like they are made of horn, or of horn and wood together."

A Nevan slave came in and prostrated himself at the king's feet. "The chiefs have assembled, my king. You asked to be notified."

"Let us not keep them waiting," Gasam said. The group filed into the courtyard. Last of all came Dunyaz with Shazad on a chain leash.

The king sat on the end of a couch and Larissa lay on her side behind him. Hael's letter had reawakened sensations of guilt she had thought long forgotten.

"My chiefs," the king began. "I think most of you have heard some account of how our brave Omian allies"—he paused and was rewarded by rich laughter—"came to grief. I witnessed their defeat and it came about thus." The king described what he had seen from the swaying observation tower. When he had finished, he had other warriors who had been there speak of details they had observed at the battle. Last of all, Luo and Pendu spoke of the riders they had observed at close hand. The king had cautioned them to say nothing of Hael's words.

"Let there be no foolish talk of heroism and cowardice," the king said when they had heard all. "These riders fight in a way we have never encountered. I will not meet that army in the field until I have devised a way to meet this threat which negates the advantages they have.

"The mounted soldiers we have defeated were lancers. They had to come to close grips to use their weapons, and we know how to deal with beasts. These plainsmen use their animals as mobile platforms from which to shoot. And they use a type of bow we have not encountered before. In our islands, bows were used only by hunters, and they had to use poisoned arrows to be sure of a kill. Here on the mainland we found bows to be used in war, but they are poor weapons, and shields will stop their arrows. The bows these riders use are different. They are far more powerful. They will pierce shields and the sort of armor worn by the mainlanders. In the open, I do not think we could beat them. We could not get close enough to use our spears. They could stay at a distance and pierce us with their arrows." He watched them closely and was pleased to see that they did not look downcast. They wanted to hear what he had to say.

"This is no more than a temporary setback, no more," he went on. "We have had these before, and they have been no permanent stop to us. When I had united my home island, I had to conquer the others. In order to do that, we Shasinn and the other warrior peoples of that island had to conquer our fear of the sea, and to learn to use boats to travel from one island to another. When we came here, we had to learn to fight at sea, a new thing for us. But we learned it well, did we not?" This was answered with a ferocious agreement.

"So now we must learn another way to fight. Only the foolish and weak peoples think they can learn nothing new. They are conquered when they refuse to change their way of fighting to meet a new threat, and rightly so. A superior people, a true warrior people, learn from what they see and take for their own anything valuable, including skill and knowledge. I will study upon this problem, and I will find the solution. These are an excellent people led by the renegade Shasinn Hael, and they will test us well. We shall be the worthier for our eventual victory."

His chiefs raised a victory chant, which he quieted with a gesture of his hand.

"Do not proclaim victory so soon. That we must earn. For now, we must make preparations. Chief Kousla!"

"My king!" said a shaven-headed man from one of the southern isles.

"I gave you the task of learning this city's defenses against siege. Are you prepared?"

"My king, I did not expect to have to put them into use, but I have the workmen and I know where the equipment is stored."

"Excellent. Hael's army will be here soon.

Prepare the walls and gates for a landward siege."

"As my king commands," said Kousla. "My king, I know that you are using all suitable timber for your new shipbuilding project, but I think we shall need stout timber shields atop the walls. The men manning the walls will need protection from those arrows you spoke of."

"That is a good thought," said the king. "Draft whatever workmen you need and demolish houses and temples for timber. If that proves insufficient, then you may go to the shipyards."

"My king," said a bold-faced warrior. "Surely you cannot intend that we sit huddled in a city while conscripted soldiers sit outside and make our lives miserable?"

This time the king laughed with honest humor. "No, I have no such intention. One thing is plain from what I saw at that battle: This way of using mounted archers is of no use against a fortified position. We will man the walls with the Nevans who have come over to us. They are used to this sort of warfare. Sealing the city merely provides me with necessary time."

The king sat back on his couch, taking Larissa's hand in his. She had overcome her earlier mood and smiled at him. "My chiefs, when we came here, we were ignorant. We had no idea how immense the mainland is, how rich in peoples and kingdoms, all ours for conquest. This little city has been pleasant, but there is much, much more. We are not like the kings of this land, to dwell in one place, to give a land a name and declare its borders our limits. *All* of the land is ours, and it is our right to go as we please, and to take what pleases us: goods and buildings, slaves and livestock!" This was received with applause, the warriors as always roused by the power of his words, if somewhat unclear on his meaning.

"Go now," the king said. "Prepare for this siege, although it will not be the sort of fighting warriors should have to trouble with. I am your king, and I will lead you to the conquest of the world."

After they left, the king sat for a while in deep thought. Larissa stroked his back and Shazad thought of the siege to come. She regretted now her earlier, futile escape attempts. With the army of Neva outside the walls she would have had a much better chance, but now she was heavily bound. How would she manage an escape this time?

"What shall you do, my lord?" the queen asked.

"We are going to need to learn more about these animals." He spoke to Dunyaz. "Girl, have you had experience riding cabos?"

"Every person of noble birth learns to ride. In Neva, only the nobility breed and ride cabos."

"That does not seem to be the case in Hael's kingdom," the king said. "Where are great numbers of these animals to be found?"

"I have always heard," Dunyaz told him, "that the king of Chiwa has vast herds of them."

Gasam smiled again. "Very good. I must pay a call upon my brother king, Diwaz the Ninth of Chiwa."

King Pashir himself came north to take personal charge of the siege. The victory on the banks of the River of Lizards had restored his prestige and public confidence. He could now leave the city without fear of a coup being plotted behind his back. Hael, for his part, was perfectly willing to turn these operations over to the king. Hael had neither the experience nor the taste for siege work.

King Pashir, on the contrary, delighted in the task. "This is why, in the end, we are always successful against barbarians. Should we fail in the field, we can always retire to our fortresses and our walled cities. Barbarians thrive on excitement. They have no liking for the arduous and artful tasks of siegecraft. After a while, they grow bored and go away."

The work, indeed, was awesome. Hael's army had marched from the River of Lizards to the city and encamped outside its walls, just out of range of the throwing engines atop the battlements. They could not attack the place, but they prevented anyone else from entering or leaving. A few days later, the siege train arrived. They had set up their own engines and commenced battering the walls and the single landward gate with stones. They had constructed covered galleries and pushed these beneath the walls so that men with tools could work away at the hard stone of the walls. Other galleries had treetrunk rams slung from their roofbeams and these began to slam into the walls day and night. Drafts of sappers arrived and these began tunneling operations, seeking to undermine the walls or to drive a tunnel into the city.

Hael's plainsmen watched these proceedings with great interest. They marvelled that human beings could behave so much like insects. They also amused themselves by shooting at the men upon the walls. At first they scored many hits because the defenders thought themselves safe at such ranges, but they learned quickly. Soon large timber awnings appeared atop the walls, making it far more difficult to get an accurate shot. The warriors took this as a challenge and tried to get close by stealth in order to shoot between the top of the battlements and the lower edge of the wooden shield, a narrow space that called for delicate judgment of trajectory. Hael had to order a halt to this practice, to stop the taking of unnecessary risk and the attrition of arrows.

The defenders, for their part, were not passive. Their own hurling machines, although not as heavy as those outside the walls, had far lighter targets. From time to time there would come a creaking of ropes working in pulleys, a section of the wooden shield would swing aside and a heavy stone would hurtle from the wall. Men would scatter from its probable path. If it struck one of the covered galleries or wooden engines, there was terrible destruction. They dropped stones and poured boiling pitch from the wall. They kept up a steady rain of javelins and arrows.

"My king," said Jochim one morning, "this is an incredibly stupid way to fight."

"I can only agree," Hael assured him. They sat around a campfire, the king and his higher officers. There had been little for them to do since the siege began.

"Then let us return home," said Bamain. "We have had one fine battle, and now we are feared from the plains all the way to the sea. But this is not real fighting that goes on here."

"That is true," Hael said. "This is a sort of mass labor that involves killing. But I came here to help Pashir against the man in that city. If we leave now, they will come out of there and massacre this army. All that keeps them inside is fear of us. And I have a score to settle with Gasam. Be patient. It cannot be long now, and there is plenty of time to reach the mountains before the passes are blocked with snow. I want to collect our pay from King Pashir."

"He had better pay well," Jochim said.

"He shall. And you can tell the men that the journey back will be far more pleasant than the one hither. We will not go back through the desert, but through Omia. I will exact payment from King Oland for the trouble he put us through. We can always use more cabos and other livestock, and our path will take us through many of his estates."

At this his officers regained their good humor. Their only true grievance through this whole campaign had been the lack of opportunity for raiding. The prospect of pillage in Omia was a pleasant one. It was more the honor of it than the plunder that attracted them. They all counted themselves rich since Hael had become their king. Their herds had grown phenomenally and dominating their huge domain in organized armies was even more enjoyable than the old small-scale raiding against neighbors.

There were those who missed the days of war between tribes, and a few plainsmen sometimes lamented that they could no longer go into the hills on slave raids, but these complaints were few. When Hael pondered it, it occurred to him that he had done for the people of his domain much the same thing Gasam had done for the Islanders. But he had done it without the wholesale destruction and enslavement that Gasam seemed to delight in. Hael believed he had made his subjects happier and more secure. But did Gasam believe the same thing? Could Hael himself be just as destructive without knowing it? These were questions that could torment him on sleepless nights, but all his life he had felt a destiny that he had to fulfill, later on knowing that he was one of the rare men who had the power to move nations and races into new paths, to change everything. He could no more avoid that destiny than change places with Gasam.

A day came when Harakh asked Hael to accompany him to the command tent. When the two arrived, the tent was occupied only by Pashir and Choula. The king looked up and smiled.

"Welcome, Hael. You will be pleased to learn that, tomorrow, we take back Floria."

"That is good news indeed," Hael said. "But, how do you know that tomorrow is the day?"

It was Choula who explained. "We have had an unexpected success in tunneling beneath the wall. This low-lying coastal area is made up mostly of loose soil, sand and soft stone. Our chief of mining operations reported that this morning his miners broke through to the basement of a disused house in the city. It seems that the city wall at that point is built on a foundation of the soft stone. The miners cut through it and passed beneath the wall without even knowing it."

"We have kept this a strict secret," Pashir said. "The tunnel is now being widened. Tomorrow we shall mount a heavy attack against the walls. But while Gasam concentrates his defenses on the battlements, we will be infiltrating the city by way of the tunnel. A picked force will enter and secure the gate, opening it for the army outside. Once we are in, the city will be ours. No skillful maneuver or warrior spirit will save Gasam then. In taking a city street by street, nothing counts except weight of numbers and good, heavy infantry."

"This sounds promising," Hael said. "My army could only tarry here a certain time before we must return home." He looked down at the table, where a map of the city lay. The place where the tunnel broke into the city was marked. "I will go in tonight," he said.

The others were aghast. "What?" said the king. "Why should you do such a thing?"

"Two reasons. One, I have sworn to kill Gasam and I intend to do it. The other is to find Shazad and bring her out, if she is still alive. Once the city is breached, Gasam might kill her out of spite."

"I fear terribly for my daughter, my friend," Pashir said. "But I would not have you put yourself at risk when her plight is none of your doing."

"This I must do," Hael insisted. "With Gasam slain, his army will collapse. They think he is a god and they will not recover from his loss."

"You will be seen and recognized," Harakh protested.

"Once inside the city I will be just another Shasinn warrior," Hael said. "It will be dark, and there can be very few who would know me instantly by sight."

Choula did not try to dissuade him. "Gasam and his queen, we are told, have established themselves in the finest house in the city, here on this hill." He pointed to a spot on the map. "It was the royal governor's house. As you can see from the elevations on this map, all the ground in the city slopes upward to this place. Even in the dark, you can find it by simply going uphill." Choula looked at him very seriously, as if he expected it to be for the last time. "Of course, we have no way of knowing if that is where the princess is being held."

"If I find Gasam," Hael promised, "then I shall find Shazad."

In his tent, Hael removed his jacket and trousers and boots. He donned a plain loincloth and chose a selection of the sort of ornaments favored by the Shasinn. He gathered his long hair at his nape with a silver ring, one of several styles used by senior warriors. He decided against taking his longsword. He had won it in his very first battle and had worn it during his last days among the Shasinn, but it was too large and distinctive, and it might attract notice. He retained his dagger. Then he waited until nightfall.

With the onset of night, he left his tent and took his spear from its place by the doorway of his tent. He walked silently through the camp. The men were mostly gathered around campfires and none took notice of him. He came to a place where men were toiling by torchlight. A man-made tunnel slanted into the ground and from this came a steady line of men bearing baskets of earth on their shoulders. Others entered with empty baskets. This earth was taken to places where it would not be seen from the walls lest the enemy suspect the extent of the undermining.

The officer in charge of the operation saluted Hael. "We were told to expect you, sir. If you will come with me."

Hael followed him into the tunnel. It was narrow and they had to walk sideways to let the basket-carriers pass. There was a reek of torches and sweaty men that made the air close, almost masking the pleasant scent of newly disturbed earth. As they progressed, the air grew chill and dank. The soil was muddy beneath their feet.

"It's wet digging this near the sea," the officer explained.

The men worked in silence as they neared the city. The last few paces of the tunnel were as yet unwidened and the officer pointed to the narrow opening.

"That's the basement, sir," he whispered. "There's a stair up to the ground level. Good luck."

With that, Hael inched himself through the gash in the brick wall and into the basement. The darkness was total, but he needed only a few seconds to find the stair and he climbed to a wooden door at its top. He pushed the door open, wincing at its squeal of unwaxed wooden hinges. It opened into a room full of toppled furniture. It had probably not been disturbed since the first day of the invasion, when the inhabitants had fled in haste and the raiders had combed it for loot. The street door stood par-

tially open. Hael opened it fully and leaned out.
The street was narrow and empty, partially
blocked with trash and furniture thrown from
upper floors in the first frenzy of looting. He
stepped out. Wasting no time, he began walking
uphill.

This quarter of the city seemed to be near-
deserted. Not a sound came from the nearby
buildings but, being near the wall, there was a
constant racket of men shouting, catapults
creaking, wooden shields being shifted and the
occasional clatter of a catapult missile striking
the wall or a mantling.

He came to an open square fronted by three
temples and here he encountered people. There
were torches in brackets to provide a modicum
of illumination. Unhesitatingly he crossed the
open space. He had fallen unconsciously into
the arrogant Shasinn stroll, spear on shoulder,
not deigning to glance at lesser people. Townspeople scurried to get out of his way. Island
warriors made way for him as well, although
not as hurriedly. As he neared the high ground,
he saw more Shasinn. Junior warriors nodded
deferentially as he passed them.

Soon he was at the top of the hill. Much of
the high ground was covered by a sprawling
building which bore several new wings, some
of them as yet unpainted. There was much activity considering the hour, with processions of
slaves carrying burdens from the palace. Small
groups of Shasinn stood about on the broad
steps, talking and laughing. None seemed in any
way concerned about the progress of the siege.

His spear slanted over a shoulder, Hael
walked up the steps. As he had expected, he was

not challenged. The Shasinn were too new to civilization to have acquired the formalities or protocols of the courts. To them, this city was only a large village, and the king's palace was no different from a chief's hut, where tribesmen came and went at will. There were no guards, no courtiers, no passwords or letters of introduction.

He crossed a broad terrace and entered the palace. Inside, overseers were directing work parties by lamplight. There could be no doubt of it. The palace was being stripped. Hael shouldered past the workers and found a man who had the look of a steward.

"I have a message for King Gasam," Hael said. "Direct me to their quarters." The man pointed down a long corridor and Hael went in that direction. After a few more questions he found himself in a small courtyard where a fountain made music. The sound of voices came from a suite of rooms across the courtyard. He could not make out the words, but the sound of Island dialect was unmistakable. He took a deep breath and began to walk to the suite's entrance. Halfway there, he stopped when a woman came into the courtyard. She was small, with black hair and honey-colored skin. She wore a brief, filmy tunic and had a metal collar encircling her slender neck.

"Shazad?" he said, not expecting to find her so easily. The woman's eyes widened and then she frowned in puzzlement, and Hael realized his mistake. The resemblance was close, but this was not Shazad.

"I do not think I know you, warrior," she said. "What do you know of Shazad? Who are you?"

She began to back away but, quick as a serpent's tongue, his hand shot out and grasped her collar. Pulling her close, he placed the point of his spear beneath her chin.

"Excuse me," he said. "I haven't seen Shazad in years, and you look much like her. Would your name be Dunyaz?" Eyes wide with terror, she tried to nod without impaling herself on the spear. "I have business with your master and your mistress. Are they in there?" Again the nod of assent. "Excellent. Now, where is the Princess Shazad? You can speak, just do it quietly."

"She is in there."

"That is convenient. Let us go pay them a visit." He released her collar and whirled her around. Holding both wrists behind her back, he nudged her toward the door.

His eyes took in the room at a glance. A fair woman reclined on a couch. A darker one sat chained to a wall, black hair tumbled over her face. The fair one looked up, frowning. "Dunyaz, what do ... who is ..." Then her face turned deathly pale. Her jaw dropped, lower lip trembling. At this the chained woman looked up and her dull eyes brightened. "Hael!" said both women at once. In spite of the occasion, he could not help grinning at Shazad.

"Still in your favorite attire, I see, Princess," he said.

"Hael," Shazad said, smiling wildly, "get me out of here! Now!"

"In good time," he said. "I have some business to take care of first." He looked at Larissa. It seemed impossible, but she was even more beautiful than when he had last seen her. "No greeting for an old lover, Larissa? Well, we didn't part on the best of terms, did we? After I condemned myself to exile by saving your life."

"Fool!" she said, her voice trembling. "Why did you come here?"

"Can't you guess? I came here to kill your husband. Where is he?"

She was recovering quickly. "You are madder than ever, Hael. You really think that you can kill Gasam?"

"Only if I can find him." He shook Dunyaz. "I thought you said he was in here."

"How could I say anything with that spear at my neck?"

He turned her loose. "Release Shazad. Do it quickly."

"Go now, Hael, if you want to live," Larissa said.

"Where is he, Larissa?" Hael demanded. "Where is Gasam?" He leveled the spear at her throat. She glared at him without fear.

"You could never do it, Hael. You loved me once, and that is sufficient to keep me safe from you. You were never one tenth part the man that Gasam is."

Hael lowered his spear. "A man is what I am and Gasam is not."

"Oh, Hael," Shazad said impatiently, "give me this." She was loose now, although her ankles were still connected by the short chain. She snatched Hael's dagger with one hand and with the other grasped a handful of Dunyaz's hair and forced her to her knees. With the keen edge against the other woman's throat she snarled: "Where is he, you little slut? You know I don't share Hael's compunctions! I'll carve you a bit at a time until you tell."

"And if I don't know?" Dunyaz said.

"Then I shall have had an enjoyable experience. I'll start with this ear." She nicked the lobe and Dunyaz collapsed.

"He is at the docks! They are loading the ships!" She tried to say more but she could choke out no words through her sobs.

Hael turned on Larissa. "Is that true? Is he abandoning the city? Has he had enough of this insane invasion?"

"What do you mean, *abandoning*?" the queen said. "We Shasinn do not live in cities, how can we abandon one? This was a convenient place to tarry awhile, and now we go to fight somewhere else, as Shasinn always have."

"Then we go to the docks." He handed his spear to Shazad. Surprised, she took it. He knelt and grasped the chain connecting her anklets. With two swift twists of his powerful hands, the soft bronze links snapped off at each anklet. He straightened and took the spear back. "You had better get some clothes on, Princess," he said. "Someone might mistake you for a prisoner."

"The way this woman dresses there may be no real women's garments in the palace." Shazad pulled a fine coverlet from a couch and wrapped it around her body so that she was covered from armpits to knees. "This will have to do."

"Then let us take a walk," Hael said. "Is there a way out of this place without going through the whole palace?"

"There is a terrace out through that door,"

Shazad said. "Stairs go from it down to the stables. I tried to escape that way once. We can go from there to one of the streets leading down to the harbor. It is only a few minutes' walk from here."

"Then let us be off," said Hael. "What could be more natural than the queen going down to see what progress is being made at the docks, accompanied by her slaves and her stalwart Shasinn bodyguard?" He hauled Dunyaz to her feet and prodded Larissa. "Get up."

She rose. "If I must. I have some fond memories of you, Hael, but if you insist, I shall come and watch my husband kill you."

Shazad, still holding Hael's dagger, stepped behind the queen and touched its point to the skin over her left kidney. "King Hael may not be able to kill you, but I certainly can. No cries for help, now. That means you, too, Dunyaz."

"Why should I?" sniffed her cousin, recovering some of her composure. "The king will kill this upstart without my help."

They left the chambers and descended the steps. Beyond the empty steps they found a descending street. There was a constant mutter of crowd noise as people descended the broader thoroughfares toward the harbor. On the upper floors of the buildings they could see the flickering shift of torchlight. The few people they encountered looked at them curiously, but none interfered.

They did not reach a major street until they were near the harbor. There the street they had been following debouched upon a small plaza where several streets reached the harbor gate of the seaward wall. Here the crowd grew dense, made up mainly of warriors filing through the gate. They joined the throng. When the warriors recognized the queen they drew back quickly. The four passed beneath the gate and into the dockside area.

"Where is the king?" Hael demanded of a Shasinn who supervised the loading of a ship. The man swung a long arm and with his spear pointed toward a raised wooden platform whereon stood a group of warriors. With colored lanterns they were directing the maneuvers of the dozens of ships and canoes in the harbor.

The harbor itself was a spectacle. The quays and the dockside plaza had been lined with torches and fire-baskets. The ships in the water were brilliant with torches and lanterns, and huge bonfires had been built on the mole. It was a massive fleet of cargo ships, captured Nevan galleys and new-built ships still smelling of fresh paint. A trumpet sounded from the platform and the fat merchant ships began to make their way out of the harbor under oar power.

On the wharfs, line after line of warriors and slaves crossed gangways onto ships or descended ladders into canoes. Even fishing boats had been pressed into service. It looked as if Gasam intended to take his whole kingdom with him on this armada.

Hael, the queen, the princess and the slave made their way toward the platform. Hael got his first close look at Gasam in many years. The man was clearly in his element. There was nothing he loved so much as to see thousands of people together, all of them doing his bidding.

Hael turned to Shazad and said, quietly: "Lose yourself in this mob. Find an empty building and hide. Your father's army will be in control of the city shortly after first light. Go!" Wordlessly she backed away into the milling throng.

A stair rose to the platform and Hael nudged his two remaining charges up the wooden treads. Behind them, the last of the crowd pushed through the gate and the huge wooden door began to close. Gasam caught a glimpse of movement and turned.

"Ah, my queen, I was wondering when you would get here. Is this not ..." He began a sweeping gesture toward the scene in the harbor, then stopped abruptly, frowning. "No. It cannot be." Now the others on the platform were turning. All were Shasinn.

"But it is, Gasam," Hael said. "Have you no greeting for your foster-brother?" He stood from behind the two women, his spear held loosely by his side in deceptively casual fashion. He was as alert as the island night-cat.

"I have," Gasam said. "And it has been delayed for far too long." He turned to the nearest warriors. "Kill that fool for me." Before they could move, Hael raised his spear aloft.

"Gasam!" he cried in a voice that cut through the bustle of the harbor, "as a senior warrior of the Shasinn, I challenge you to the thorn circle!" Silence spread through the crowd like ripples through a pond as all became aware that an extraordinary drama was being played out upon the platform.

Gasam laughed, loudly, for maximum effect. "Hael, you are sadly out of date! There are no more spirit-speakers to hallow such rituals. I have overthrown all custom and only my word is law now."

"Then the people you lead are no longer worthy to call themselves Shasinn. In all our history no Shasinn warrior ever refused the challenge of the thorn circle. Do you wish to acknowledge yourself a coward? This is a warrior custom, not a spirit matter."

Gasam looked around him and saw stony looks from his Shasinn. "But, Hael," he said, "the thornbush does not grow here on the mainland." If he expected to divert his followers, he failed.

"What counts is the warrior's heart, Gasam," Hael said. "You were always afraid to face me, and why should you not be? It was I who slew the longneck single-handed, and saved the woman who is now your queen, not you. When did you ever have the stomach to do your own killing, Gasam? A warrior stands before you. Fight like a warrior, if you know how." From far back in the city, they could hear a great commotion.

"Listen!" Gasam shouted. "You hear? They have broken into the city! That is what this renegade wants! He wants to delay us here while his wretched mainlanders trap us!"

The Shasinn warriors looked to the east, where the first gray of dawn began to spread. The sounds grew louder, but seemed to be no closer. One of the warriors went to Gasam, and Hael recognized Luo.

"There is time, my king. They are attacking the gate. It will take them a while to get into the city, even after they find there is no one left on the walls. Fight him, Gasam. Even a king may not refuse a warrior challenge."

Gasam glared in hatred and frustration. Larissa came to him and laid a hand on his arm. Quietly she spoke. "This is stupid, my love, but you must do it. You must above all have the respect of your Shasinn. Do this, and you will never be challenged as long as you live. Kill him, Gasam, for me if for no other reason."

There was no help for it. Knowing he was neatly trapped, Gasam tried to put a good face on it. "Very well," he said loudly. "I generously declined to kill this fool when we were boys, so now I must exert myself to make up for my mistake." He glared around him. "I want nobody standing around gawking! Keep loading the ships, you can watch from there. A king should not have to stoop to such foolishness, but if my people wish it, I shall not fail them."

The other warriors left the platform. Larissa and Dunyaz remained, and the two kings stood in the center. Each gripped his spear with his left hand holding the short wooden grip, his right on the long metal shaft of the butt-spike. They held the long, swordlike blades slanting upward before them, each with his point leveled at his opponent's throat. Gasam wore a shortsword as well. Hael had not recovered his dagger from Shazad. He hoped she had hidden herself well. Beyond Gasam, he saw more ships cruising out through the harbor entrance. The stars were quickly fading, and the noise from the city was growing loud. The two men circled warily, eyes locked.

Gasam stepped in, his spear engaged on Hael's right. He dipped his point and came up to the left of Hael's spear, lunging for the broad chest. Hael sidestepped easily, bringing his spear across to the left and batting the other blade aside, replying with a short jab to Gasam's face, turning that blow to a swift cut with the blade's edge, directed toward Gasam's leading wrist. This Gasam avoided with an adroit sweep of his spear in a wide circle, catching Hael's, swirling it around, down and away from his body. Both men leaped back a step and continued circling. The exchange had lasted only seconds, the sound of the ringling blades loud in the harbor, where the only other sounds now were the creakings from the ships.

Hael had learned much from the brief exchange. Gasam was not quite as strong as he, nor as swift. But the steel spear was lighter than the bronze, and that made up for the other man's deficiencies. Steel was also harder than bronze. He could see the nicks made by the other weapon. And it occurred to him that a truly forceful blow of the steel blade might cut through his own. He pressed Gasam with a quick series of jabs, some of them feints, some in earnest, driving him back against the railing of the platform. Hael tried to end it quickly with a full-body lunge, but Gasam dived past him in a roll and Hael had to whirl desperately as Gasam sprang to his feet and aimed a thrust at his back. Gasam made the move too quickly, before his balance was perfect, and Hael was able to avoid it by a finger's breadth. He was not so lucky with the backstroke, which opened a slash along his ribs on the left.

They circled again and Gasam grinned. After a few seconds a ragged cheer came from the watchers as they saw the blood begin to stream down Hael's side. "First blood to me, foster-brother!" Gasam crowed.

"Only last blood counts," Hael reminded him. It was high summer and the dawn came quickly at this time of year. The sounds of the Nevan army were very close now.

"Finish him, my lord!" Larissa cried. "We can wait no longer!"

With a wild cry, Gasam charged, swinging his blade straight down like a longsword. Hael knew that the instinctive move, a block with his own blade, might be fatal: the steel blade could cut through his bronze one. Diving to one side, he swept the butt-spike of his own spear across, catching Gasam behind the ankles and taking his feet out from under him. Gasam dropped heavily to his back, his arms flying wide and the spear clattering away on the platform. Hael jumped to his feet, his right arm rocking back, spear-blade aimed down and he saw Gasam's eyes go wide in fear. Behind him the gates opened and the Nevans began to pour into the harbor. His muscles tensed as he began the cast that would put an end to Gasam.

"No!" The scream startled him and something leaped onto him. So total had been his concentration on killing Gasam that he could not understand what had happened. His nose filled with the smell of perfume and he thought it was Larissa, and then a heavy lock of black hair blew before his eyes. It was Dunyaz. He struggled with her hysterical strength to get a clear cast at Gasam.

Recovering from his momentary shock, Gasam snatched forth his shortsword and he pushed away from the platform, lunging with his whole body. Hael swung around, blinded by the woman's hair, trying to clear his vision and bring his spear down, to kill Gasam. She clung tight, her arms gripping Hael's, her legs scrambling to lock around his, to immobilize him. With a wrench of his body, she swung before him.

Gasam's shortsword went into her lower back, just beside the spine. The point came out just beneath her sternum. Her screaming halted abruptly, her mouth agape. Her eyes rolled up until only the white showed and she fell.

Hael, shocked, watched her fall away. He saw Gasam standing before him, but the man was looking down at the woman he had killed. Then he looked up and Hael saw something in his face he had never thought to see there: remorse.

"Go!" Larissa grabbed at Gasam and whirled him around, pushing him toward the forward rail of the platform. He stumbled away and Hael broke from his trance, raising his spear for the final cast.

Larissa caught the movement and put herself between Gasam and the spear, pushing her husband, urging him. He sprang to the rail and jumped, clearing the dockside and cleaving the water cleanly. With a look of triumph, Larissa followed. Hael rushed to the rail but he could not see them at first. Then he saw two figures swimming strongly for a nearby galley. He laid his own spear down and snatched up Gasam's all-steel weapon. The lighter spear would be better for a long cast. The targets in the water were difficult. With their hair darkened by dampness, it was difficult to tell which was which. Hands reached down from the galley rail and the swimmers grasped oars to pull themselves toward the side.

"Isn't it incredible?" Hael looked down and saw that Shazad stood beside him. "What women will do for him, I mean."

"What has been going on here?" It was Harakh. He saw Shazad and performed a quick bow.

"Where are my archers?" Hael said, not taking his eyes from the two figures who now scrambled over the rail of the galley. Immediately the oars began to stroke.

"Far behind us," Harakh said. "They'll never make their way through those streets in time to help us here. Are those rogues going to get away after all this?" At the dockside, men were hurling javelins toward the galley, but the range had grown too great and they fell into the water or clattered among the oars.

"Not if I can help it," Hael said. Gasam now stood in the waist of the ship, Larissa near him, both looking back toward the platform. Hael braced his whole body and his arm rocked back. then it shot forward. Hael had been the greatest javelin-thrower among the Shasinn, and he made this the cast of his life. The steel spear made a silver streak in the dawn sky, midway in its arc catching a blood-red gleam from the rising sun, then descending.

Everyone watched, hypnotized, as the spear made its impossibly long traverse. Soldiers watched gape-mouthed, unable to believe a mortal man could make such a cast.

To Gasam, the spear could have been only a

silver dot, seen point-on in its flight, its speed and trajectory difficult to judge. Yet he did not try to dodge and stood with his arm over Larissa's shoulders, unmoving. When the terrible blade was within an instant of impaling him, Gasam leaned aside, almost lazily, Larissa swaying slightly with him. His hand flashed sideways, missing the razor-edged blade by a fraction of an inch, grasping the small wooden grip, rocking slightly with the momentum of the weapon and twirling it in a brilliant silver pinwheel of reflected dawn light and holding the unique steel weapon high amid the deafening cheers of his men. On the shore, a few of the Nevan soldiers cheered as well, until glared down by their officers.

"Gods!" Harakh breathed. "What style!"

Hael knew it was true. Whatever prestige Gasam had forfeited by losing the fight atop the platform, he had won much of it back with the bravura gesture of catching the spear. A Nevan trooper picked up Hael's own spear and handed it to him. Slowly, reluctantly, Hael raised his weapon in salute. Gasam's galley nosed out through the harbor entrance.

Hael turned and saw something he did not expect. Shazad knelt with Dunyaz's body cradled in her lap, stroking gently the thick, black hair so like her own. She looked up as Hael came to stand by her.

"Poor Dunyaz," she said. "She came of the noblest house in Neva, yet she was a born slave. Well, she wasn't much, but she was my cousin. I will give her a fine funeral. Her rank deserves it, and it will help to reconcile her father and mine. I must reassemble this shattered kingdom." She looked out toward the harbor entrance. Through it a few ships were still visible. "Where will he go, Hael?"

"I don't know," he said wearily. "We'll know all too soon."

The kings sat on a broad terrace of the mansion that had been a governor's house and then, briefly, a royal palace. The essential matters had been settled. Gold, silver and other metal had been packed away for Hael's army's return march. Each warrior had been given something far more valuable by plains standards: one or more fine, blooded cabos from Pashir's own herds, according to his rank.

"I wish I could accept all of your invitations, my friend," Hael said, "but I must go. Winter will not wait, and I have promised my men some raiding among King Oland's estates. You are certain that this can be done without incurring lasting bitterness?"

Pashir made a dismissive gesture of the hand. "He needs the chastening for his stupidity. We know how I have suffered for mine. For a few months we shall make ferocious noises with one another, and then things will settle down. I know him. Do not worry, by next trading season, he will be calling you brother-king again and will cause no trouble. With you on one side and me on the other, he had better not. Besides, he is my brother-in-law."

Hael was surprised. "He is Shazad's uncle?"

Pashir shook his head. "No. It was an earlier wife. But now that we speak of wives, and of Shazad. . . ." Hael had been expecting this. "Hael, I think of you as a son. As you know, I have no true son to follow me on the throne of Neva."

"You have a daughter worth ten sons," Hael told him.

"As I acknowledge now," Pashir said. "But the Nevans have never allowed a woman to reign over them."

"Pashir, my friend, if Shazad wants to reign in Neva, nothing the people of this land think will stop her. I have a queen. She is the woman I love and the mother of my children. I miss her terribly and I want to go home to her."

"Well, yes, to be sure. But what of that? Among us, it is not necessary for a man to limit himself to a single wife. Certainly a king should not be so constrained. A linked kingdom is not a bad idea."

"Pashir, there are some things I am not willing to do even to extend my realm. One wife is plenty for me. Now if you are looking for a consort for Shazad, that man Harakh might not be a bad choice."

Pashir pondered. "Well, the lad is of good family. And he gave sterling service. If I may use a terribly outdated word, he is a patriot."

"And he is in love with Shazad," Hael prodded.

"What of that? Half the men in Neva are. Still, I will take your words to heart, since you seem intent upon spurning my daughter. Well, go with my blessing. Have a fine summer raiding Oland. I fear you and I shall be worrying over Gasam all too soon."

Shazad found him as he was leaving the palace.

"I see the royal match-making did not go so well."

"Shazad, were I not already married . . ." He tried to look gallant.

The effect was wasted. She laughed. "Hael, you are a poor liar. Go back to your queen, the lucky woman. You and I would never have suited one another as Gasam and Larissa do. And, though it shames me to say it, I am almost glad that you didn't kill him. You are the better man and the greater king, but there is something about him that women like."

"I shall try to take solace in that," Hael said.

She wound her arms around his neck and kissed him. Breaking the kiss, she looked up at him. "Get out of here, Hael. I might change my mind."

In the fields outside of the town, Hael found his men mounted and ready to go. Jochim rode up to him, leading Hael's favorite riding animal. The king mounted.

"Let's ride home," the Matwa chief said. "This has been enjoyable, but we want to return to the homes we know."

Hael sat for a moment, thinking of Gasam and Larissa, thinking of the great cache of steel in the desert, thinking of the strange fire-weapons coming in from the east. "There will never be such homes as we knew, ever again," he said quietly. He thought of his queen, Deena, whom he had found half dead, a runaway slave, when he had been a penniless wanderer. As a spirit-driven visionary he had forged a kingdom from warring tribes, but as a man the home he had made with her was more precious. He thought of their children, how they had anticipated the arrival of each new infant and the joy with which they had watched the little ones grow.

Since leaving her side he felt less than half a man. This journey had reunited him with Larissa and Shazad, the women of his past, and the meeting had made him value Deena all the more fervently. He had thought that their home was secure, that he had created something good and enduring, which would support and protect his family forever. Now he felt that all he had created was built upon ground that shook like the plains surrounding the smoking mountains.

Then he thought of the pool in the hills, the place where he and Deena had first made love and had pledged themselves to one another. The pool was still there. The pool endured as the spirits of the land endured. When he returned, he would take her to the pool again. They would renew their vows to strengthen themselves against the trying times ahead. He knew that there were some things meant to last forever.

"What did you say, my king?"

Hael shook himself. "Nothing. Let's go home." With that, they spurred their mounts homeward.

BESTSELLING BOOKS FROM TOR

THE BEST IN FANTASY

☐ 53954-0 SPIRAL OF FIRE by Deborah Turner Harris $3.95
   53955-9   Canada $4.95

☐ 53401-8 NEMESIS by Louise Cooper (U.S. only) $3.95

☐ 53382-8 SHADOW GAMES by Glen Cook $3.95
   53381-X   Canada $4.95

☐ 53815-5 CASTING FORTUNE by John M. Ford $3.95
   53826-1   Canada $4.95

☐ 53351-8 HART'S HOPE by Orson Scott Card $3.95
   53352-6   Canada $4.95

☐ 53397-6 MIRAGE by Louise Cooper (U.S. only) $3.95

☐ 53671-1 THE DOOR INTO FIRE by Diane Duane $2.95
   53672-X   Canada $3.50

☐ 54902-3 A GATHERING OF GARGOYLES by Meredith Ann Pierce $2.95
   54903-1   Canada $3.50

☐ 55614-3 JINIAN STAR-EYE by Sheri S. Tepper $2.95
   55615-1   Canada $3.75

Buy them at your local bookstore or use this handy coupon:
Clip and mail this page with your order.

Publishers Book and Audio Mailing Service
P.O. Box 120159, Staten Island, NY 10312-0004

Please send me the book(s) I have checked above. I am enclosing $_____
(please add $1.25 for the first book, and $.25 for each additional book to
cover postage and handling. Send check or money order only — no CODs.)

Name _____

Address _____

City _____ State/Zip _____

Please allow six weeks for delivery. Prices subject to change without notice.

JACK L. CHALKER